W9-BWU-733

THE BROKEN PLACES

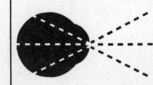

This Large Print Book carries the
Seal of Approval of N.A.V.H.

THE BROKEN PLACES

ACE ATKINS

THORNDIKE PRESS
A part of Gale, Cengage Learning

GALE
CENGAGE Learning·

Detroit • New York • San Francisco • New Haven, Conn • Waterville, Maine • London

Copyright © 2013 by Ace Atkins.
A Quinn Colson Novel Series.
Thorndike Press, a part of Gale, Cengage Learning.

Thorndike Press® Large Print Basic.
The text of this Large Print edition is unabridged.
Other aspects of the book may vary from the original edition.
Set in 16 pt. Plantin.

LIBRARY OF CONGRESS CATALOGING-IN-PUBLICATION DATA

Atkins, Ace.
　　The broken places / by Ace Atkins.
　　　　pages ; cm. — (A Quinn Colson novel series) (Thorndike Press large print basic)
　　ISBN-13: 978-1-4104-6174-2 (hardcover)
　　ISBN-10: 1-4104-6174-2 (hardcover)
　　1. United States. Army—Commando troops—Fiction. 2. Murder—Investigation—Fiction. 3. Mississippi—Fiction. 4. Domestic fiction. 5. Large type books. I. Title.
　　PS3551.T49B76 2013b
　　813'.54—dc23   2013016626

Published in 2013 by arrangement with G. P. Putnam's Sons, a member of Penguin Group (USA) Inc.

Printed in the United States of America
1 2 3 4 5 6 7 17 16 15 14 13

In memory of David Thompson

The world breaks everyone and afterward many are strong in the broken places.

But those that will not break it kills. It kills the very good and the very gentle and the very brave impartially. If you are none of these you can be sure it will kill you too but there will be no special hurry.

— ERNEST HEMINGWAY,
A Farewell to Arms, 1929

Don't ever take a chance you don't have to.

— ROGERS' RANGERS
STANDING ORDER NO. 5

1

"This ain't no joke," Esau Davis said. "We go home, you go home. But a few more years on our sentence don't mean jack shit to us. We'll kill you if we need to."

The prison guard, face flat to the concrete of the ag shed, made a short grunt in agreement as Esau removed a knee from the man's spine and a good two inches of baling wire from his ear. Just to make sure the guard was listening, Esau slammed the man's forehead into a trailer hitch before looking to a skinny black man with a misshapen head and crooked teeth. The black man, Bones Magee, set about binding the guard's hands and feet. This was the third guard he and Esau had snatched up in the last ten minutes. Bones wore black-and-white pants, while Esau wore green-and-white stripes, Esau being the one who'd earned minimal confinement on Parchman Farm.

"What do you think?" Bones asked.

"We got twelve minutes till second watch," Esau said. "We better get gone or we gonna be tasting buckshot."

Esau gripped the bound guard by the collar of his jacket, which read MISSISSIPPI DEPARTMENT OF CORRECTIONS, and dragged his ass into a storage room where they kept the seed, fertilizer, and sprays. The large bay doors on the equipment barn were open, a big sprawling picture of the Mississippi Delta stretching out table-flat over the Mississippi River and a thousand miles beyond. The sun burned up half gone and diminished, hazed and fuzzy with the storm clouds blowing in from Texas. Another convict — officially, "offenders" these days — ambled up and watched the black clouds smudging up the last of the sun, thunder signaling a shitstorm on the way. The convict, short, white, and bald, with a homemade swastika scrawled on his naked chest, scratched his belly and said, "Let's go."

"Not yet," Esau said.

"You want me to set us out a picnic with Vienna sausages and Little Debbie cakes to watch the storm?" Dickie Green said. "We could sing some songs."

"I just got your stupid ass out a lifetime of

10

shoveling shit and dead birds from the chicken house," Esau said. "Only reason you're part of this is 'cause of me."

"I'm here 'cause you need me," Dickie said. "I'm a part of this thing. I am the driver of the rig. I don't drive the rig and you don't get to the stables. You don't get to the stables and you ain't got the horses. You don't get the horses and you're floating down Shit Creek."

Dickie counted each of his efforts on his stubby, dirty fingers.

"I'm pretty sure of the progression of our situation," Esau said. "Since it's my fucking plan."

Esau stood a little over six feet, broad and muscular, with copper-colored hair and a brushy, copper-colored beard. The same wiry orange hair sprouted across his thick arms and along the nape of his neck and down his back. He had a pale white complexion burnt up red and pink from working a tractor for the last eight years. He didn't care for Dickie Green one goddamn bit, but the son of a bitch was right. Dickie had to be the one to return the horses to the stables. They'd done it and done it well a thousand times before. All they needed was a good storm to make the tracking all the more difficult in the night and they were good to go. Out of the stables. Out of Unit 29. Out of Parchman Farm.

"And the sheet shows we're checked out?" Esau said.

"I tole you my woman took care of us," Bones said. "We got some extra duty tonight on account of the storm. More tractors and shit to bring in from outside. All set up. You know, I do believe that woman loves me."

"Is she blind or just stupid?"

"I tell her I'm running off to Mexico and send her some money to meet me," Bones said. "Just like in that movie with Morgan Freeman. She think we gonna get married and that all her five fucking kids comin' down, too, and we gonna drink margaritas and eat fish tacos on the beach."

"I don't want to kill no one," Esau said. "But I don't promise nothing. Once we leave this shed, ain't no turning back. We do what needs to be done."

"I just helped you gag and tie up four guards," Bones said. "Right about now, I'm stripping the motherfucker and about to put on his clothes. I would say I'm already in this, white man."

Esau rubbed his coppery beard and nodded. Dickie Green checked the false bottom of the horse trailer, the two horses nickering and lightly kicking up their feet as the

12

lightning snapped out across the mud and flat-ass land. Esau knew it was a plan but not much of one, twenty-six miles to freedom, with not a tree or any cover between. The plan had been in place for six years now, Esau working his way through every smiling detail, from landscaping the superintendent's house to welding Dumpsters and barbecue pits to finally getting to drive that big Steiger 9170, planting cotton, beans, and corn.

Esau pulled himself out of the striped convict pants and white convict shirt that no matter the washing still smelled like dead fish and ammonia. He kicked off his work boots and got down to his skivvies before zipping himself into a blue coverall. Bones fitted himself nicely into a guard's uniform, with the ID still clinging to the official jacket. Dickie waited by the trailer, opening up the gate, pulling away the false bottom and having them lie down flat. Esau thought they were taking a hell of a risk with Dickie Green's dumb ass at the wheel, but he also knew everyone wanted this to work. Bones lay next to him, as snug and tight as cheap corpses buried two for one, as Dickie slid a thick metal sheet over them and left them in darkness. There was the sound of hay spread on top of the sheet and then the affixture of a ramp. Two of the guards' quarter horses hefted up and heavily *clop-clopped* on into the trailer, standing with all their weight on the thick sheet and over Bones and Esau. "Damn, damn, damn," Bones said. "Just don't let one fall through onto my balls."

Esau laughed a little as the big diesel started and pulled on out of the equipment shed and into the wind and the coming rain, rambling and breaking and bumping up over the long road back from the ag buildings and far away from the housing units. Dickie stopped the truck twice, Esau and Bones listening to muffled talk with the guards, and then Dickie moved on. He was taking them east toward the stables and the dog kennels, where Dickie would snatch the woman guard and get the horses out. Dickie wouldn't ride with them on account of him having a bad case of hemorrhoids and not caring all that much for horses. He told Esau he wanted to drive the trailer out of the front gates bigger than shit, because he said he'd set things in motion with another female guard who must be so fat and ugly and generally stupid that she would fall for a guy like Dickie Green. Fine by Bones and Esau, because the guards would be on Dickie in two seconds and not watching

14

them hauling ass across open land.

"You good?" Esau asked.

"Don't care for tight places."

"Just breathe, man," he said. "Don't think of it."

"Can't see, can't move," Bones said. "Don't like this. Shit, get me out. I can't breathe."

"Close your eyes," Esau said. "Dark is dark. You want to spend the rest of your life in Unit 29, jacking off to *General Hospital* and Victoria's Secret?"

"Just paid thirty dollars for a *Playboy.*"

"Ain't no way to live."

"No way."

"With another man spending our money."

"How do you know he hadn't already?"

"We don't," Esau said. "But if he has, be nice to confront him on it."

"Our money," Bones said. "Our money. Our job."

"Breathe, brother, breathe," Esau said.

"Don't trust that motherfucker," Bones said.

"Says he found God."

"Found him a way out, leaving us behind."

The diesel slowed and rambled to a stop. There was the chugging motor and the rancid, uneasy breath of Bones Magee. Some talk and then a long, long wait before

15

the gate creaked open and those big-ass animals got helped out as the metal buckled and popped overhead. Esau heard the nearby wild, wailing cry of the bloodhounds that had been raised at Parchman for the last hundred years.

Dickie Green pulled the metal sheet back and grinned with his grimy brown teeth and shithole breath. "Hello, gentlemen."

"What'd you do with her?" Esau said.

"Hit her in the head with an ax handle," Dickie said. "Ain't no nice way to do it."

Esau pushed his way from the hole and helped Bones out. They walked into the stables built of thick slats of wood and corrugated tin. The tack room smelled of rich leather and tannins and big open buckets of molasses. He handed Bones a blanket, saddle, and bridle. "Yippee-ki-yay," Bones said. "Never rode no horse before. Black people don't care to play cowboy."

Esau reached for the tack he needed and hustled back to the center of the stables, where Dickie held both horses. He slipped the bridle over one's head but had to coax and cool the second one, the horse smelling and sensing the convict hands on him. The one with the more gentle nature, a painted gelding, was given over to Bones. Esau took the reins of the nervous horse, canting back

16

one to three steps, and lifted his big frame onto his back. Dickie tilted his head and looked up at them in the soft-bulbed light. "You boys are on your own."

He offered his stubby hand out to Esau. But Esau just kept his hands on the leather reins, making for the mouth of the barn, rain pinging the tin roof real good, hoping the second horse would just follow on along and not dump Bones Magee into a ditch. They weren't even out of the barn when Dickie started the truck and pulled out and away from the stables and onto Guard Road, toward the main gate of Parchman. Esau kicked the horse's ribs to head north, away from the howling hounds that'd be on them soon, and keeping close to the edge of the cemetery, where they buried men whose families had written them off long ago, their flat headstones just slick places in the dirt. Ain't no way Esau would be buried there. Ain't no way he'd let another man take his rightful reward away from him. He'd written nearly five dozen letters and tried calling every chance he got. No response. And his lawyer, that rotten piece of shit, hadn't gotten a dime of all that money been promised to work some kind of miracle on Esau's release. Escape was the only way.

Lightning flashed, spiderwebbing and

cracking out far and wide across Parchman. Twenty-six miles of road and sixty miles of ditches. The hounds howled and yipped, sensing what was going on before the guards even leashed them up. Esau turned back to Bones, who was dog-cussing his horse, his ass riding everywhere but the saddle. But hell if he weren't staying on. The wind, the rain beat down hard on their faces; hard-packed dirt became mud and mud became a river. There wasn't much light, only the twinkling jeweled lights of Rome, Mississippi, and Tutwiler miles and miles beyond. But a few miles into the ride, the storm and darkness became all, and all Esau could do was try his best to find due north. North was gone and away. Away from Parchman and onto Jericho, where they'd left the loot at the bottom of a bass pond with those two dead men. The lightning struck once so close he could feel the strike pitch from the ground and into the horse's back. You could smell that coppery-coffee topsoil like the earth was just created new.

Esau whipped the flank of his horse now, blinded by the wind and the rain but tasting his freedom all the same.

2

Ophelia Bundren slid into the booth across from Sheriff Quinn Colson and passed along another file thick with reports on her sister's killing from a decade ago. "This town might believe Jamey Dixon's bullshit, but I know who he is and what he's capable of. Did you know he was on the Square yesterday, passing out flyers about some revival at a barn?"

Quinn nodded.

"He wouldn't even look at me as I passed. He knew I was there but kept on smiling and shaking hands. Dixon has no shame or sense of honor. A revival in a barn? I guess that sounds about right for him."

"So what's in the file?" Quinn said. It was early, daylight just coming on in Jericho, Mississippi. He'd been on patrol from 1800 to 0600 and was looking forward to a hot bath, a shot of whiskey, and some sleep. Out the plate-glass window of the diner, he spot-

19

ted his cattle dog Hondo sniffing the air from the tailgate of his truck. Hondo looked beat, too.

"A psychological profile of his time in prison," Ophelia said. "He's a sociopath."

"Is that what the report says?" Quinn drank some coffee from a heavy mug that read FILLIN' STATION.

"He convinced his shrink he's a new man," Ophelia said. "He said he doesn't recall two years of his life before he killed my sister. You believe that?"

"No, ma'am," Quinn said. "Not at all."

"How do you think he got on the pardon list?"

"Ophelia," Quinn said. "We've been through this maybe a hundred times. And I agree with you that Dixon hasn't changed. But it doesn't sound like what's in that file is going to move things along."

Ophelia looked down at her hands, nails cut boy-short but still painted a bright red. She was dark-complected, with high cheekbones, Indian doll eyes, and a tight red mouth. Quinn had known her his whole life, and even before her sister's murder had never known her to smile. Still, she was pretty and looked good that morning in a short navy dress with cowboy boots and a gray cardigan. Unless you were from Jer-

20

icho, she'd be the last one you'd figure for a funeral home director. And now that Luke Stevens had taken a job in Memphis, she was also the coroner of Tibbehah County.

"Why?" she asked.

"He was on the governor's pardon list."

"But who put him there?"

"And the other two hundred and fifty shitbirds?" Quinn said. "Most of them were friends of political cronies. Others worked in the governor's mansion. We don't have any choice but to live with it."

"Jamey Dixon didn't have powerful friends," she said. "His mother cleaned rooms at the Traveler's Rest."

Quinn nodded. "He knew somebody."

Ophelia nodded. She took a deep breath and steadied herself. Quinn drank some black coffee and let the silence settle over them. He touched the file and slid it closer to him.

"You would have to be a damn moron to believe him."

"Never a shortage," Quinn said.

"Can I look at the police file again?"

"I'd rather you not."

"I am entitled," Ophelia said. "It is public record."

"You are entitled, but you're making yourself sick," Quinn said. "I don't like to

21

look at those pictures. I don't want you to, either."

"They had to scrape her off the highway with a goddamn shovel," she said. "My parents still found little parts of her that the county men had left."

"Ophelia."

"Son of a bitch."

"Yep."

"Well," she said, straightening a bright red scarf around her neck. "I appreciate you meeting me so early. What time do you get up?"

"Actually, I'm headed to bed."

"I'm sorry, Quinn."

"Don't be," Quinn said. "Just my shift." He drummed his fingers on the file and smiled over at Ophelia. She was easy to smile at, although she'd worked her mouth into a tight questioning knot. About the same age as his little sister, twenty-seven or twenty-eight, but somehow seemed years older. "Can I buy you breakfast?"

"No, thank you," she said. "I have clients."

"Dead or alive?"

"Eleanor Taylor," Ophelia said. "I have to color her hair."

"She would have liked that," he said.

Ophelia nodded. She studied Quinn as he drank his coffee. Quinn leaned back into his seat and waited for what he knew she really wanted to talk about. The Bundrens had always been closemouthed people, always some kind of contagious strangeness you wanted to avoid unless you needed someone buried. Kids used to call Ophelia Wednesday Addams behind her back. She'd often get a new boyfriend and then lose him just as fast once she got to talking about embalming.

"Aren't you concerned?" Ophelia asked.

Quinn drank some coffee. Outside, Hondo was barking at a red truck racing by with rumbling dual mufflers. His coat was a mottled gray and black.

He waited.

"How long has Caddy been with him?"

Quinn took a deep breath. "Few months."

"And you're not worried about your sister being with a man who's done such horrible things?"

"She says his sins have been washed clean by the blood of the Lamb," Quinn said. "She believes Dixon is a new man."

"What's the big brother say?"

"I say it's hell being sheriff in the same town as your family."

"What about your momma?"

"Verdict is out with Jean."

"But you don't like it?"

23

"No, ma'am."

"Then we're together on this."

"Yes, ma'am," Quinn said, eyes shifting off hers. "Always have been."

Ophelia straightened up and gave just the flickering of a smile. "Quit acting like we're old, Quinn," she said. "The U.S. Army has aged you a hundred years."

Quinn started to say something but stayed quiet while he stood and Ophelia slid from the booth. He shook her lean hand and the smile was gone. As she passed, she whispered into his ear, "If Caddy was my sister, I'd lock her up far away and not let her get within a mile of that monster. The devil wears many disguises."

"And plays a guitar and sings old hymns."

"He can't contain who he is forever," Ophelia said.

Quinn thought on that as the bell over the Fillin' Station door jingled and she was gone.

Caddy Colson was pretty sure that Jamey Dixon loved her. He had not said it in so many words, but it was more in the way he introduced her to people in the church, held the door for her when they had dinner in Tupelo, or the surprise and joy on his face when she took off her bra and panties and

24

crawled in bed with him. Jamey said he knew what they were doing was wrong but he'd soon be making it right. And Caddy believed him. If she didn't believe Jamey Dixon, then the whole idea of faith was horseshit.

The winter was behind them, and green leaves had started to appear on skeletal trees, patches of grass showed in the mud of logged-out land, and wisteria, azaleas, and dogwoods had returned even though most of the farmhouses were long gone, the parcels all divided up against feuding families. The air felt lighter and warmer and breathed soft and easy through the wood slats. The hard rains from last night made everything smell rich and fertile, and of flowers and spring planting.

Jamey's church had moved into the old barn only a few weeks ago, but they'd already painted the outside a bright proper barn red, laid out a number of flower beds in creosote-soaked railroad ties, and had a local welder named Fred Black craft them a handmade sign that read THE RIVER, set off the county road for the short drive down the gravel road. She stood back, the wide doors of the church full open on what felt like the first day of spring, and admired Jamey, who was hanging a string of white

25

lights across the big, empty space of the church. He had crisscrossed several different strands, plugging the lights into an orange power cord while he worked, the church coming into a soft white glow, making everything pleasant down and around the grouping of wooden folding chairs and hay bales, and on up to a pulpit fashioned of barn wood, copper nails, and barbed wire. It had been Caddy's idea to use the barbed wire to give a solid reminder of a crown of thorns. It had also been her idea to keep the barn looking like a barn and to embrace the message rather than tear it down and build some kind of facility made of prefab metal like an airplane hangar.

"Give me a hand, baby?" Jamey said from the ladder. He wore Birkenstock sandals, a pair of tattered Wranglers, and a faded black Johnny Cash T-shirt. She stood below him and helped thread the string of lights up into his hands. He smiled down at her, all rugged and handsome, with long, blondish hair and a solid manly jaw and blue eyes. A tattoo of Christ on the cross ran the length of his muscular left forearm, crudely inked during his time inside, a reminder of a bad stretch of road.

He moved the ladder one more time, set the end of the lights on a crossbeam, down from the ladder. Jamey stood and admired his handiwork.

"What do you think?"

"I love it."

"Yeah?" Jamey said. "Well, that's the idea. Just like you said. We don't need a pretense to get people to worship. This isn't social. At The River, we won't ask what you do for a living. We don't ask where you've been."

He rested his arm around her shoulders, and Caddy smiled so big, she felt like she might lose her breath. Her son Jason, now almost five, wandered into the barn with his head tilted upward, amazed by the bright light in the old place. The PA system lightly played George Jones singing "Peace in the Valley," a song that had been a favorite of Jamey's grandmother's. Jason walked over to them and Caddy snatched him up, twirling him around the empty space, feeling so happy she could explode.

"You get that compost dumped?" Jamey asked.

"Yes, sir," Jason said with a thick country accent. The accent sometimes threw them because of his curly hair and light brown complexion with African features. Jason was Caddy's reminder and the only blessing to come from some dark days. And not once had Jamey spoken to her about that time.

It's all ahead; the past is nothing but jur in our rearview mirror.

"Can you make dinner at Momma's?" Caddy asked.

"I'll try," Jamey said. "But Randy is coming by with his Ditch Witch. We're gonna try to put in that water line. Can't have a church called The River without water."

Caddy nodded and smiled, trying not to show the disappointment on her face. Jamey pulled her in close and kissed her on top of her head. "Just let me get this church going and I'll make your momma's Wednesday nights."

"I just figured you didn't want to come."

"Why's that?"

"On account of Quinn."

"Your big brother doesn't scare me," he said, grinning. "After ten years, I've grown accustomed to law enforcement watching me eat. Kind of makes me feel comfortable, in a way."

"He shouldn't have spoken like that to you," Caddy said. "I'm sorry. Sometimes I think Quinn got his brain scrambled in Afghanistan."

Jason had lifted himself up into the low loft, where bales of hay had been artfully placed. He jumped from small bale to bale, playing and laughing. George Jones was now singing about what a friend we have in Jesus.

"Just words."

"He doesn't know you," she said. "He will after time. Quinn has always been hard on my boyfriends. He thinks he's doing the right thing."

Jamey looked down at his empty arm and the long tattoo of Jesus on the cross. He leaned into Caddy some more and said, "Has your brother been saved?"

"He goes to church."

"But has he really thought of the reason?"

"Whatever you do, please don't ask him that question."

"Why's that?" Jamey said. "That is *the* question."

"Because Quinn is bound to answer you in some profane way," she said. "He may have left the Army, but he'll always think like a sergeant."

"There will be a time," Jamey said. "I know him seeing what he's seen in the last ten years must have been a profound thing."

"Same as you," Caddy said. "Only he loved what he did and wasn't forced to do it. Of course, he won't talk about it."

"With no one?"

"Nobody but Boom."

"Why?"

" 'Cause Boom lived the same thing but

came out worse," Caddy said. "Quinn and him have always been like brothers, and now even more so."

"Boom doesn't care for me much, either," Jamey said. "Looks at me like I'm something scraped from the bottom of his shoe."

"You said yourself that people would doubt your mission," Caddy said. "Isn't that why you came home to Jericho? To face your persecutors? To build something that will outlast all of us and our problems?"

Jamey smiled down at her and kissed her nose. She felt his strong arm around her neck, hardworking sweat and heat against her. Jason followed them outside to the gravel lot where she'd parked their car, finding a mud puddle to toss sticks and rocks into to make the muddy water ripple. He looked up at his mother with a big grin at what he'd done.

3

Esau and Bones came onto the Parchman fence line at daybreak, sliding off the stolen horses and whipping them back toward the twenty-six miles they'd just crossed. The horses' mouths foamed with exhaustion, and they turned for a slow moment before dropping their heads to the nearest ditch of muddy water. Esau had pocketed a pair of wire cutters, and in less than thirty seconds, they crawled out and under the fence and into the real world, still and gray in the false dawn. They stood well back from Highway 49 at the edge of a creek bed, Esau consulting the map he'd hand-drawn. Bones unwrapped some Hershey bars and peanut butter crackers he'd bought from the canteen and a couple bottles of water they'd filled up back at the ag shed. Both of them wet and sore and hungry as hell. Esau's heart raced just hearing the sound of cars speeding past on the highway, going about business the way normal people do.

"First thing I want is a bottle of Aristocrat vodka and a goddamn cigarette."

"They gonna have helicopters out," said Esau. "You hear that?"

"I only hear the fucking mosquitoes," Bones said. "Can you try her again?"

"Can't get a signal," Esau said. "That's what you get for buying a cell that's been stuck up someone's ass."

Bones nodded as if he hadn't been the one who'd gotten the cell smuggled in for him. Esau had tried to get through to Becky for the last ten days. He couldn't speak to her directly, with every word said on a Parchman phone going right into the superintendent's ear. He thought about leaving a coded message where she worked at the Dollar General but then thought better of it. Becky had planned to drive down from Coldwater and pick them up, bring them fresh clothes, guns, and cash. But he hadn't been able to tip her off.

He tried the cell again. Nothing.

"We could steal a car," Bones said.

"Got to find one first," Esau said. "Let's keep off the road and head straight. We got maybe two miles to Tutwiler."

"Home of the blues."

"Every fucking town in the Delta says

they're the home of the blues."

"Yeah, but in Tutwiler they got a sign and shit."

They walked a good two miles not seeing a thing but plowed fields and road signs telling drivers DO NOT STOP OR SLOW DOWN for the next ten miles. They finally came upon a half-dozen rusted-out trailers off Highway 49. Just as they were about to cross the road, a couple highway patrol cars sped past, their sirens and lights on. Esau waited until they were long gone, crossed and walked into the group of trailers, testing the knob on the first one they found. Inside, a fat woman holding a Chihuahua looked up from a flat-screen television, a half-eaten Toaster Strudel in hand.

Bones coolly walked up to the woman, snatched the remote, and turned it from a sitcom with a lot of canned laughter over to the morning news out of Memphis. The Chihuahua on her lap wouldn't stop yapping at the men, finally not being able to stand it and going right for Bones, jumping up and biting him on the pecker. He knocked the dog away, the dog whimpering and crawling under the couch. The big woman hadn't said anything, just looked at them both with her piggy eyes and slack jaw.

"You got a car?" Esau asked.

The woman kept on staring.

Bones slapped her on the back of the head. "Listen up."

She shook her head. Her mouth was still filled with Toaster Strudel.

"Who does?"

"My boyfriend."

"Where's he at?" Esau said.

"Gas station," she said. "Went to get us some breakfast."

"What the fuck you eatin'?"

"Just a snack."

"Well, sweet Jesus." Bones grinned. "You done look like you had too much breakfast."

He ripped the plate of Toaster Strudel from her lap and grabbed a couple. He broke his in two and tossed half to Esau. Esau didn't think he'd tasted anything so good in a long while. He asked Bones for another, and they both found a spot on the woman's sagging flowered couch, listening to the news like they were all part of the same family. The woman didn't say anything, just held the Chihuahua tight to her fat bosom, eyes shifting from the men to the shabby door hanging half open. The dog started yipping again, and Bones growled back, as the woman held the little dog's mouth closed and tugged him closer.

"Bad storm last night," Esau said.

34

The woman didn't answer, only held the dog so close that it disappeared under her heavy breasts.

"Another bad front tomorrow," Esau said.

"Shh," Bones said. "Trying to hear this shit."

The anchor was blond and had a nice thick body and talked with a big grin about the storms that had passed through the mid-South and a double homicide in West Memphis. They waited until she started talking with the goofy weather guy, who seemed to be getting a hard-on about another front moving in from Texas. Bones looked up from the television, just hearing a car drive up and the motor quit.

He turned off the television and nodded in the silence to Esau, who stood up and found a place on the wall beside the door. He picked up a ceramic cat statue on a little bookshelf and waited for the door to open wider. A little redneck strutted into the room with a big white sack, grinning like he'd done something special until he spotted the black man on the couch with the woman.

"Who the hell are you?" he said.

"Guy who's gonna take your car out for a ride."

"Shit," said the little man. He reached for

something in his red Windbreaker.

Esau came down hard and quick on the back of the man's head with the statue, the cat's head breaking off and the skinny little redneck dropping to the floor. The big woman screamed and the dog jumped from her lap, trying to attack Esau this time, yipping and tearing at the leg of his coveralls, and finally getting distracted by the smell of whatever was in the paper bag. Esau opened it, snatched out a big greasy sausage biscuit, and handed it to Bones. Three more inside.

"You got some coffee?" Bones asked the woman.

She shook her head.

"Well, damn, get off your thick ass and make some."

The woman was nervous, and she had trouble standing, her hefty legs a little woozy and weak, but she made her way back to the kitchen and started to fill the pot with water.

Esau reached into the man's heavy work coat and found a .357 fully loaded in a side pocket. "Well, hello there."

Bones had already stuffed the whole sausage biscuit into his mouth and was chewing as he pulled aside a sad yellowed curtain and looked outside the trailer. "Sweet Jesus."

The man on the floor was coming to and rolling onto his hands as Esau walked past and kicked him hard in the head, sending him flying against the wall. He joined Bones at the window and looked out in the trailer court to see a Chevy Chevelle with dual chrome pipes and a slick blue paint job with a narrow white stripe down the hood.

"Bad taste in women," Bones said, swallowing, looking to the big woman measuring out coffee into the machine. "But great taste in an automobile."

Quinn got five hours' sleep, waking up at 1200, and spent the next couple hours on his tractor, delivering hay to his cows, with Hondo riding shotgun. After his chores were done, he showered and shaved, dressing in a crisp khaki shirt with patches for Tibbehah County Sheriff, a pair of laundered blue jeans with a sharp crease, and a pair of cowboy boots. By the time he finished his second cup of coffee and first La Gloria Cubana of the day, he had pulled his truck into the sheriff's office lot. He walked through the front door, saying hello to Mary Alice, who was the office administrator and answered the phone, did the filing, and also ran dispatch for the seven-man and one-woman office.

Quinn had the usual conversation with her, talking about it being too wet to till the garden yet and what Mary Alice planned to plant this year: some kind of German heirloom tomatoes. He finally made his way back to his office, where he hung up his coat and ball cap. The same Beretta 9mm he'd worn in numerous tours of Iraq and Afghanistan with the 3rd Batt of the 75th Regiment perched on his leather belt.

After a few new reports, he made his way back to the reception area and refilled his coffee, walking back to his office to find his chief deputy Lillie Virgil sitting in his lone visitor's chair, tilted back, boots on his desk, and taking a puff of his cigar.

"How the hell do you smoke these things every day?" Lillie said, letting out a long stream of smoke and passing it back to Quinn. "Tastes like a dog turd to me."

"You ever smoke a dog turd, Lillie?" Quinn said.

"How'd your meeting with Ophelia Bundren go this morning?"

Quinn sat down behind his desk and propped up his boots as well on the desk that had been his late Uncle Hamp's when Hamp had been sheriff for nearly thirty years. The desk was beaten to hell and badly in need of repair, but Quinn liked the common history of it.

"Who told you?" Quinn said.

"I saw your truck and I saw her car."

"Meeting went the same as it always does."

"I feel for her," Lillie said. "I really do, but she's driving herself batshit insane with this. She needs to see a shrink or it's going to drive her to a room in Whitfield."

"I don't know if I'd be much different," Quinn said.

"How long had you been gone when Adelaide was killed?"

"I was just at Fort Benning for Ranger school," Quinn said. "My mom sent me the newspaper clips. I liked Adelaide."

"I would have never imagined them as twins," Lillie said. "Adelaide had fair skin and blond hair; Ophelia still looks like that girl from *The Addams Family* to me."

"Wednesday," Quinn said. "Yeah, I've heard that a few times."

"That's her," Lillie said. "When I first saw you two together, I was thinking that maybe you were getting a piece. But I never could see Wednesday Addams out at the Colson farm, picking tomatoes and eating deer meat you shot. Relieved to know it was all professional."

"I happen to find her very attractive."

Lillie leaned forward and picked up

Quinn's cigar from the ashtray, took another puff, and set it back. "Yep," she said. "You would."

"I read back through the original files," Quinn said. "And it looks like there wasn't enough of Adelaide to make more than manslaughter. How'd they prosecute for murder?"

"The Bundrens said Dixon had been beating the shit out of her for more than a year," Lillie said. "Adelaide and Dixon had shared an old house over in Dogtown. The family said he ran her over in a rage and then sat on the bed of his truck while what was left of her got run over by passing cars. Family said they had witnesses who said Dixon sat there drinking Busch from the case and smiling while their daughter got hit again and again."

Quinn shook his head.

"Most evidence was circumstantial," Lillie said. "Your uncle found where Dixon had blocked in Adelaide's car with his truck. Her car had been rammed into their carport, knocking the crap out of a support beam. There wasn't much left of her, but they found her in her pajamas without any shoes. Your uncle worked with the prosecutors in Oxford to say she was running for her life, presenting two witnesses to show prior abuse. After a few weeks, Hamp found this fella who drove a logging truck who saw Dixon standing on the road, unfazed by the mess that had been his girlfriend. The truck driver thought someone had hit a deer."

"Ophelia believes there is more to the pardon than our outgoing governor believing in the power of redemption."

"You think?" Lillie said, dropping her boots to the floor. "But shit, what the hell could a shitbag like Jamey Dixon have to offer the governor? He's got no money, no sense, and has reentered society as a two-bit preacher."

"You know Caddy is one of his flock?"

"And she's fucking him, too," Lillie said. "Damn, Quinn. You need to plug in a little bit more to what's going on in the county."

"Trust me, I'm well aware of Caddy's love of Jamey Dixon and Jesus Christ."

"Was Ophelia trying to warn you?"

"Yep."

"She's an authentic weirdo, but smart."

"Yep."

"What are you going to do?"

"You know Caddy," Quinn said. "There isn't shit I can do. I think she's planning on bringing him to dinner tonight at Momma's house."

41

Lillie laughed.

"I'd pay to see that, Quinn," Lillie said. "Can I please come? I want to hear you say, 'Pass the peas, dickhead.' "

"I'll be civil."

"Yeah, that was the motto of all the Rangers I've read about," she said. "Jump out of airplanes, pull your gun, and be civil."

"I'll be polite." Quinn tapped the ash of his cigar.

"Can I come?" Lillie asked. "What's Jean making tonight?"

"Fried chicken. And no."

"What a shame," Lillie said. "I do love me some of Miss Jean's fried chicken."

4

Esau and Bones made it all the way to Olive Branch and a Pilot truck stop off Highway 78. They could blend in with the truckers and travelers, who did not give the two scruffy, stinky men a sideways glance. But just to make sure, Bones had parked the slick Chevelle on the far side of the truck stop, by the diesel pumps. Besides the loaded .357, the muscle car, and four sausage biscuits, Esau had taken the little redneck's wallet, two hundred dollars and some change, and a Visa card. The truck stop was one of those places they call a travel plaza, with a restaurant, a convenience store, a Western-wear shop, and a dozen showers by a trucker rest area. They bought some fresh T-shirts, stiff flannel shirts, a couple pairs of Wranglers and work boots. They paid cash, saving the card for where nobody would be watching.

They bought soap and shaving cream and

razors, too. Esau decided to leave the red beard growth, knowing his prison mug showed him with a clean face. Bones shaved off everything but a thin, smart-ass mustache. And thirty minutes later they met back at the trucker room, where a bunch of fat guys drank coffee and farted, watching a flickering television playing the Maury Povich show.

"Leave the car," Esau said.

"I love that car."

"But they got to know."

Bones looked up at the wall clock, which showed it was two hours since they'd hightailed it from the trailer. He shrugged and thought on it. "Couple more hours."

"Couple more hours get us kilt."

"This ain't the place."

Esau looked through the glass window into the truck stop store and bustling restaurant. If they were going to steal another car, they sure as hell needed a spot with fewer witnesses. Of course, he could do it all cool and easy, pointing a .357 in someone's ribs, have him ride down the road with them, and then keep him in the trunk until they were done with the car.

"Two more hours," Bones said. "I want to see what that bitch can do."

"Until we find something else."

Bones nodded. "Yeah, sure," he said. "How long till Jericho?"

"About a hundred miles, I figure."

Bones nodded. "Damn, been a long time. Think we can still find it?"

"Only thing I think about lying on my back at night is Becky's nekkid body and that little bass pond. I think I'll find both."

"You call her?"

"When we slow things," Esau said. "When we ready to get our shit together."

"Nice shirt," Bones said.

Esau looked down at his chest, not even sure what was on the T-shirt besides it being yellow. It was a cartoon of a hunter chasing a woman in a bikini and something about WHITE TAIL FEVER.

"Should have given that to me."

"That would get you noticed."

"And I got stuck with a fucking shirt that says WELCOME TO THE MAGNOLIA STATE," Bones said. "Now, how's that any fun?"

"You get to drive that car."

"I'll fill her up and then let's roll to Jericho," Bones said. "You thinking on what we gonna do when we get that money?"

Esau nodded. "I think we divvy it up and then we split up. I think us traveling separate is the way to go. Me and Becky get you settled and straight before we do."

45

"She must be some woman," Bones said. "Stay with you while you in Parchman for seven years. 'Least you got some conjugation visits."

"Sure," Esau said, smirking. "We did a lot of that conjugating."

"Hell, you know what I meant."

Esau nodded, the trucker sitting next to him snoring so loud it sounded like a freight train. A teenage girl on the television was talking about how she had been impregnated by one of her eight cousins. Esau shook his head at how the world was just as sorry as he'd left it.

They saved a chair for Jamey Dixon even though he didn't show at Jean Colson's Wednesday dinner. Quinn was relieved that he could actually sit down and enjoy the meal his mother cooked. Fried chicken, collard greens, and cornbread. Had Dixon been there, he would have taken his meal to go and eaten back at the sheriff's office. If Caddy wanted to involve a convicted murderer in her life, that was up to her. But Quinn didn't have to break bread with him.

Tonight it was just Caddy and Jason, his mom, and Boom. Boom, Quinn's oldest friend, had known him all his life, running rabbits and deer, fishing every creek, pond,

46

and lake in Tibbehah County. Boom was a large black man and missing his right arm from an injury in Iraq when his convoy hit an IED outside Fallujah. But some time back when Quinn needed help rousting some methhead white supremacists from town, he learned Boom could still shoot just fine.

"Still can't get used to that thing," Boom said, removing his prosthetic arm and setting it on the floor. "Works decent for tools. I need it. But hell, I don't need it to eat a piece of chicken."

"Can I see it?" Jason said.

"Not now," Caddy said.

"Kid can see it," Boom said, picking it up off the floor and carrying it around to Jason. To a child almost five years old, a high-tech prosthetic hand was pretty cool.

"You be careful," Jean said. "Hear me?"

"He can't break it, Mrs. Colson," Boom said, taking a seat back at the end of the table. "Thing is tough as hell. I can hold a wrench or a screwdriver on an engine block. For once, the VA actually came through. A near miracle they didn't screw this up."

Caddy seemed too busy to sit down, shuffling from the kitchen to the table to refill glasses and plates. This was the new Caddy, the attentive Caddy, who wanted to show

47

off her responsibility. Before she sat down, she cleared the empty plate and silverware from where Dixon would have sat.

Quinn looked to Boom. Boom raised his eyebrows. Caddy sat with a great whoosh of breath. "You know Jamey said he's almost got the water line finished," Caddy said. "He's really sorry he couldn't make it."

Quinn stayed silent, reached for another chicken breast, and started eating. Jason kept on playing with Boom's arm and hand, separating out the fingers and then shaking the mechanical hand in his with a giggle.

"You know about this band Jamey has coming in from Nashville?" Caddy said. "We put out a bunch of posters."

At the end of the table, Boom continued to eat. Jean poured some more wine, this being Jean's third glass from the refrigerated box of chardonnay.

"You know, Momma, the band's guitar player once sat in with Elvis," Caddy said.

"What's his name?" Jean said.

"I don't recall," Caddy said. "Jamey will know. I think he only played on Elvis's final album. That one he was recording at Graceland because he hated to leave the house."

"Sad times," Jean said. "So sad. All those backstabbers mooching off him. He bought them Cadillacs and they broke his heart."

Jean had grown a little heavier since Quinn had left for the Army, but she still had the red hair and the smoky voice and was popular among widowers and divorced men in Jericho. Quinn ran criminal checks on several when they started to call. The newest owned the Ford dealership in town and had hair plugs and halitosis.

Quinn kept eating and let the conversation move over him and on across the table. Boom would eye him every so often, knowing his buddy was itching to say something about Dixon but was somehow keeping his cool. Quinn nodded back at Boom, the sleeve of Boom's flannel shirt pinned up to the elbow, as he switched from fork to tea glass with great speed.

"This band, they call themselves Manna, became interested in Jamey's story," Caddy said. "You know, about him being wrongly accused?"

Boom stopped chewing. Quinn took a deep breath and wiped his mouth. "Is that a fact?" he said. "I thought he was just pardoned."

Jean kicked Quinn under the table. Quinn only shrugged. Jean couldn't kick that hard.

"They didn't even want gas money for their drive," Caddy said. "It was important for all of them to play the first service at

49

The River."

"Hmm," Quinn said.

"So you'll be there?"

"Nope," Quinn said.

"Why?" Caddy said.

"I have my own church," Quinn said. "You remember Calvary Methodist where we grew up? Our pastor, Miss Rebecca?"

"I never left our church," she said. "I'm still a member. I'm also a member of Jamey's church, too, because I believe in what he's trying to do. He's one of the few folks who actually cares about the future of this screwed-up place and actually seeks out the misfits and the forgotten."

"I can't recall anyone being excluded at Calvary," Quinn said.

Again, Jean kicked him under the table, this time a little harder, tipping the rim of her wineglass at him. Jason had put down Boom's arm and was now eating a very large piece of cornbread. Caddy smiled and reached her arm around her son. Quinn had to admit Caddy looked happier and healthier than he had seen her in some time. Her pale skin had the healthy flush of working outdoors, and she was dressed in a simple flannel cowboy shirt and blue jeans. No jewelry. Very little makeup. She pretty much looked like his kid sister.

And hell, Jason was happy to have her home. No matter what Jean and Quinn did, there was no substitute for his mother.

"I want all y'all to get to know the real Jamey, not just the rumors and gossip," Caddy said.

"Being sent to Parchman prison isn't rumor and gossip," Quinn said. "He was convicted by a jury and sentenced by a judge."

"Would anyone like some pepper sauce?" Jean asked.

Boom raised his fork and nodded. Boom kept his head down as he ate, knowing where this was going, and probably enjoying the waiting before the fireworks. Jean disappeared into the kitchen. Jason asked to be excused to go watch cartoons; these days he was into something called *Beyblade*, a Japanese show.

"You weren't here when it happened," Caddy said as soon as Jason was out of earshot. "You never knew how our uncle railroaded him because of his friendship with Judge Blanton. I feel for their whole family. But Judge Blanton could never believe that his granddaughter was an absolute mess and addicted to crack."

Quinn put down his chicken bones and pushed back the china plate. The plate came

51

from Jean's good china with the blue flowers that had belonged to their grandmother. "I read Dixon's whole file, and to be honest, I'm worried about you and Jason being in his company."

"Uncle Hamp wrote that mess to give the family an excuse," she said. "He thought Jamey was a troublemaker and didn't like him. He wanted him gone."

Jean emerged from the kitchen holding a chocolate pie with the whipped cream piled about three inches high. She set the pie closer to Boom and began to serve him a generous slice.

"This is why we friends, Quinn," Boom said. "Ain't nobody makes pie like this. You whip that cream, too?"

Jean smiled and set a fresh fork beside Boom's plate.

She served Caddy, then Quinn, and dished out a final piece for Jason. She brought it to him in the living room, where there were sounds of rockets and exploding spaceships. Quinn dug into the pie and was thankful for the change in conversation. After he helped with the dishes, he'd have to roll back into duty and stay on until dawn. He'd have his mother fill up his thermos with coffee before he left.

"Can I ask you something, Quinn?"

Caddy said.

"Sure."

"Are you seeing Ophelia Bundren?" Caddy said.

Quinn kept chewing but raised his eyebrows. He took another bite of pie, not answering and not wanting to.

"There's nothing wrong with it, Quinn," Caddy said. "She's beautiful and smart. Beautiful eyes. I've always liked her a lot. Maybe even better than Anna Lee."

Boom glanced up at Quinn and then quickly away. Quinn kept eating.

"Have you been by to see Anna Lee since she had the baby?"

"I see her at church," Quinn said. "Sometimes downtown. Why?"

"She wasn't right for you, Quinn," Caddy said. "Be glad she married Luke before you came home. I never wanted to tell you this, but I didn't like you with her. Now, Ophelia is different. I can see how you two would fit."

"It doesn't bother you that she doesn't care at all for Jamey Dixon?"

Caddy shook her head, the ponytail swatting back and forth. "People have said the same or worse about me," she said. "I had to deal with a lot when I decided to move back from Memphis. The only thing that was different is that what they were saying was pretty much true. I was all those things. Jamey just has to live with the blame. Even if he drove Adelaide to what happened, he's paid for seven years. Can you imagine living seven years in some kind of hell?"

Boom just shook his head. Quinn thought he noticed a trace of a smile.

"Yeah, Caddy," Quinn said. "I think all of us here have visited hell once or twice."

Caddy held her breath, but then after a moment smiled at her brother. She'd come a long way from that neon club in south Memphis where Quinn had found her not even two years ago. "But we're back."

Quinn smiled back and nodded his head.

5

Quinn met up with Lillie at the Hilltop, a gas station on the other side of the Big Black River, not far from Yellow Leaf, a little hamlet north of Jericho but south of the Natchez Trace. Lillie was leaning against her official vehicle, a Jeep Cherokee freshly painted Army green with a new light bar on top, all courtesy of Boom at the County Barn. Lillie was drinking coffee from a foam cup and wearing a satin sheriff's office jacket. She looked bemused as Quinn pulled his truck in facing the opposite direction.

A couple men sat inside the gas station, eating barbecue plates and staring out a steamed-up plate-glass window. Bad weather coming in from the west, showing in pockets of blooming yellow light and far-off thunder. She handed Quinn a cup of coffee.

"OK," Lillie said. "I admit it. I want to know. How'd dinner go with the convict?"

"Dixon didn't show."

"Well, now," she said. "That at least was classy of him."

"I don't think it was out of respect," Quinn said. "Caddy said he was busy working on his church barn. And by the way, Caddy is absolutely positive that our uncle railroaded Jamey Dixon into Parchman because he and Judge Blanton were friends."

"God rest his soul," Lillie said.

"Sure," Quinn said. "God rest both of 'em."

There was more thunder across the bottomland, where they were planting soybeans and later cotton. Rain started to patter, moving up in a fast sheet, hitting the pavement until it started to fall on the Hilltop lot.

"You got to love a shitstorm in the night," Lillie said. "Just as you're coming on."

"Is it possible?"

"What?"

"That Uncle Hamp fixed the case?"

"Hell no."

"You've always been a little blind when it came to my uncle."

"I know what he did," Lillie said. "I know how hard he fell. But at the time that happened, he wouldn't have fixed a case. Judge Blanton or not."

"Funny world without the Judge or Uncle Hamp," Quinn said, standing in a soft rain. "Who the hell put us in charge?"

"The voters of Tibbehah County."

Quinn grinned.

"I appreciate you taking on nights," Lillie said. "I know that's not easy."

Quinn shrugged. It had been the only thing to do since Lillie had adopted an infant Mexican child from a nasty human trafficking case last year. A woman and her husband had been selling third-world babies on the Internet. Lillie and Quinn had found the children, but the couple had vanished.

Quinn drank some coffee. The rain pinged a little harder on the bill of his ball cap. The police radio crackled with the voice of Mary Alice's night replacement and another deputy, Kenny, answering back.

"How's Rose?"

"Beautiful," Lillie said. "I don't know who her parents were or how she got into the hands of those shitbirds. But her folks must have been good people. I know it. If they are alive, I wish they could know how much their daughter is loved."

"How come all the shitbirds seem to set up in Tibbehah County?"

"Plain lucky." Lillie grinned. "And we're too close to Memphis."

57

Quinn nodded. He started back to the truck.

"So, you and Ophelia Bundren?"

Quinn didn't answer, placing his hand on the truck's door handle.

"Hey," Lillie said. "Besides this storm, Mary Alice got a call from Mrs. King on County Road 381. Some peckerhead has gone and stolen all of her turnips."

"You're making that up."

"Nope."

"That sounds like a prank call," Quinn said. "Someone stole all her turnips."

"Small county," Lillie said. "Big crimes."

"I'll swing by," Quinn said. "And maybe notify the Feds. You think she might also be keeping Prince Albert in a can?"

"So?" Lillie said.

"Yeah?"

"Ophelia Bundren?"

Quinn shook his head, crawled into his Ford F-250, and started the diesel engine. His headlights lit up Lillie's wicked smile as she got into her Jeep and made her way home for the night.

Bones parked the sweet Chevelle out back of some mom-and-pop restaurant in Eupora and killed the engine. It was past ten o'clock now, and Esau figured the place must be closed. The lights were off in the windows facing the two-lane blacktop, and this was as good a place as any to ditch the ride and look for another. Next door was a roadside motel with plenty of pickings.

"What color do you want?" Esau said.

"Don't matter a shit now."

"You really pissed about the car?"

"I love this car."

"We ain't got time to hide it," Esau said. "We get what we need and you buy ten of 'em just like this one."

"Yeah," Bones said, taking the keys from the ignition. "But I like this one. I swear this car loves me, way it reacts to my touch. Reminds me of this girl I used to do up in Corinth."

"Her panties like Armor All?"

"No," Bone said. "But I get my hands on her parts and she purr just like this Big-Block 632."

"Just don't stick your dick in the tailpipe."

They were out of the car now, standing over its warm hood, smoking cigarettes and drinking some Wild Turkey straight from the bottle. Esau hadn't had a drop of liquor since he got to jail, never tasting that crap convicts make in their toilets out of fermented peaches and apple parts. The cigarette tasted new and exotic, too, although he did get a pack from time to time at the Farm, smuggled in for fifty bucks.

"When we get to Jericho," Bones said, "where we gonna stay? I don't think Jamey gonna let us sleep on his couch."

"Preacher Man do what we tell 'im."

"So we just go up to where he live," Bones said, "knock on the door and say, 'Hello, motherfucker, how you been?' "

"Yeah," Esau said, cigarette burning down in his fingers. "Something like that."

"Hello, motherfucker," Bones said, laughing. "He gonna shit his drawers."

"He'll know," Esau said. "He'll be waiting."

"But it won't make no difference."

"Nope," Esau said. "No, it won't."

Without warning, the back door to the little clapboard restaurant opened and a white man in a greasy white T-shirt walked out carrying a fat trash bag in each hand. He looked at Esau and Bones by the car. His face was lean and weaselly, with a thick black mustache and black hair pulled into a net. He tried to seem unaware of the two men as he moved past and swung the trash bags up over his shoulder and into a Dumpster. He wiped his hands against each other, passing the car, and then rubbed his hands on his filthy T-shirt, suddenly seeming pissed off.

"Help you fellas?" he said.

Esau shook his head. Esau gave him a look like helping was none of his damn business.

"Restaurant is closed."

Bones smoked down the cigarette and tossed it on the asphalt. He ground it out with his new pair of truck stop boots. "Don't say."

"Move on, then," the man said. "This is private property, and y'all trespassing."

Esau glanced up behind the man and to each corner of the restaurant. He didn't see a surveillance camera. Hell, they couldn't even afford to fix the roof.

"You boys speak fucking English?" the man said. "We keep this clear so we ain't robbed every fucking night."

Bones stood up straighter and tucked in his stiff, cheap T-shirt. He lit another cigarette and passed the pack to Esau. He drew on the cigarette in contemplation, the ash glowing red-hot and lighting up his face. He looked up, cigarette clamped in his teeth, still wearing a pair of cheap sunglasses. "You know, we wasn't plannin' on it," Bones said. "But shit, now you mention it."

The cook reached up under his T-shirt for a little gun, maybe a junk .32, and made it almost level when Esau shot him once, just once, in the center of his forehead. The jolt of the man, jerking back and then shaking and crumpling like a tumbling leaf, made Bones laugh like hell. There was something so comical about people dying to Bones's crazy ass. Esau remembered the way Bones laughed and laughed the time that white-boy credit card thief from Pascagoula got shanked on the basketball court. The thought of the boy's jerking spasms and crazy redneck cussing and prayers always brought a smile to Bones's face. And this man, the mustached man in the white shirt, was just perfectly dead. Bones got down on one knee and reached for the gun the man had dropped.

"What a piece of shit," Bones said. "Ain't worth five bucks."

"But what's in the till?"

"Hell," Bones said. "Let's find out."

They pulled the dead man by his belt into a hollow space behind the Dumpster and then moved into the part darkness of the catfish and steak joint, finding the man had just cooked himself a T-bone and a baked potato. The steak was still warm and bloody, his cigarette smoldering next to it. Esau grabbed the knife and fork and cut off a thick piece of the steak.

"You want some?"

"Ain't gonna eat no dead man's steak."

"Why?"

"Bad luck is why."

"Says who?"

"Common fucking sense," Bones said, finding the little key already turned in the cash drawer. "Three hunnard and twenty."

"Add to what we got."

"You gonna finish that whole steak?"

"Yep."

Bones turned off the kitchen light and walked to the front door to look out the glass, at 18-wheelers, pickups, and sedans blowing by. "I think the man here owns that Caprice Classic," he said. "Seems like a real shame to leave my baby for that piece of shit. But hell. I'll drive it for a few miles down the road and we can ditch it."

"Highway Patrol will know it's us."

"Not if they can't find his car," Bones said. "Or his body."

"You want to toss him in the Dumpster?" Esau said. "They still gonna find him."

"Go get the keys out his pocket," Bones said. "I pull around his ride and we stick him in the trunk of my sweet Chevelle. We drive east from here, like we headed to Alabama, and leave the Chevelle and his ass in the trunk. By the time they find it, they think we outta Mississippi."

"Bones," Esau said, shaking his head and chewing on some gristle. "Don't ever let me say you stupid as shit."

"And don't ever let me say you look like your momma was raped by an orangutan."

"Yeah, you probably shouldn't say that," Esau said, finishing off the steak. He picked up the T-bone to get off every bit of gristle and meat. His hands and orange beard felt shiny and slick. "Or I might have to kill you, too."

"Cool," Bones said. "Now we know where we stand; go grab that dead motherfucker and pack him up to go."

6

Caddy could hear the tapping rain on the tin roof of the home she shared with Jamey Dixon. Dixon didn't officially live there, he had a little trailer he kept out back of the church, but most nights he would knock on her side door about eleven after Jason had gone to bed. He'd help her clean up, finish putting up the dishes, maybe bring some of his own laundry. Mostly they would sit on her old back porch and talk, sometimes having a little red wine while he would discuss what excited him most about being a Christian. The excitement is what got her, talk of country music and ministry and ways of doing things different from before. Jamey never preached to her, never really preached to anyone. He just believed in everything he read from the Bible or learned from Johnny Cash. He believed in redemption and forgiveness and helping the poor and sick. He believed that worldly possessions were junk that weighed you down. He knew that love was beyond all other things, the most important thing in this world, and the most powerful. Everything was simple, with no judgment or hang-ups.

When they were together, naked and kissing and feeling hands and mouths and bodies hot across each other, she never once believed he was thinking about where she had been, the men she'd been with, or whether she would fuck it all up again. Jamey believed in who Caddy had become.

She nuzzled into him, his strong arm around her. Both of them stared up at the ceiling, hearing the wind and storm outside, rain on the roof. She knew Jason was safe asleep in his bedroom, although she always locked the door to make sure he didn't surprise them, and the lights were off and the dishes done. Part of her felt domestic, and the scariest part was that it didn't scare her at all. She wanted Jamey here all the time, a husband to her, a father to Jason.

"I'm sorry I couldn't make dinner," Jamey said.

"Were you really working?"

Jamey was quiet. His arms held her close and she could smell the nicotine and Lava soap on his fingertips. "No."

"My family will come around."

"At least your mother now says two words to me."

"She likes you."

"But Jason still doesn't feel comfortable unless you're there."

"Not true."

"He sees how Quinn reacts to me, and he follows his lead."

"Quinn has been lied to," Caddy said. "There is still a part of him that can't accept that our uncle was corrupt as hell, no matter that he found the proof. And if Uncle Hamp helped out some drug dealers, he sure would set up a man like you."

"He'd been wanting to for a long while."

The rain on the roof was so comforting. The gentle shift of oak leaves, winds through the blood-red azaleas by her bedroom window. "I'm so sorry," Caddy said. "Did I ever tell you that? You don't ever seem to take notice of the way people act around you, good or bad. You just remain yourself. How in the world do you do that?"

"I may have talked a few times about this guy Jesus."

"I'm so sorry," Caddy said. "I'm so very sorry that happened to you."

Jamey maneuvered off his back, propped himself on his elbow, and ran his middle finger between her breasts and down along her ribs. Her skin contracted with goose bumps. "I don't care what people say," he said. "I'm where I want to be. This is the place."

The wind rattled the tin roof and the rain fell harder against the glass. Caddy pulled him in closer. "Where do we go from here?" Caddy said. The words fell from her mouth, escaping thoughts she had held close.

"We start over."

"For how long?" she asked.

Jamey sang a few lines from "When My Last Song Is Sung." His voice was deep and weathered and earnest. Caddy laughed. "Just like Haggard."

Quinn got the call from dispatch to meet Kenny out on County Road 381. He'd barely climbed from his truck when Mrs. King came out into the dark, garden hoe in hand, held like a royal staff. Kenny nodded in agreement as she explained she'd heard one of her dogs barking and came out to find a fella tossing turnips into the bed of his pickup truck. When she yelled for him to stop, he jumped in the truck and nearly took out one of her pecan trees.

"How many you think he stole, ma'am?" Quinn asked.

"You the sheriff?" asked the old woman.

She was still in her nightgown, hair in a pink shower cap.

"I am."

"I knew your uncle real well," she said. "Me and him went to school together before they built the new high school. We just had one big school for everyone in Jericho. That would've been back in 1953. Everybody loved Hamp. Respected him. Went off to Korea."

"Yep."

"And now you've taken over?"

"Yes, ma'am."

"How is Hamp doing?"

"Not good."

The old woman studied Quinn's face.

"He died." Quinn decided not to explain that his uncle had shot himself with a .44 out of self-pity and shame and for throwing in with the worst man in the state of Mississippi. If the woman didn't know that already, or had forgotten, then what was the use explaining?

"Sorry for your loss."

"And yours," Quinn said.

"Nobody died."

"You lost your turnips."

"Yes, sir," the old woman said. "That son of a bitch."

Kenny shook his head, sure-footed and

69

Barney Fife–serious about the whole thing. If he asked Quinn to dust for prints, Quinn decided right then and there to go straight home and pour himself a double Jack Daniel's.

"You recognize the vehicle, ma'am?" Kenny asked. He was a portly guy with a thick stomach and a mustache and goatee to hide a weak chin.

"I didn't. It was a white truck," she said. To Quinn, "You know, you sure favor your uncle."

"Yes, ma'am," he said. "I get that a lot."

"You used to hunt out here," she said. "With that black boy."

"Boom Kimbrough," Quinn said. "Yes, ma'am."

She nodded and chopped the ground with her hoe.

"Well, that fella took the whole patch," she said. "We were gonna pick them on Saturday. I had a whole lot of people who asked for greens at church. Now I'm going to have to tell them that they're gone. I've been living here for fifty years and never had any trouble. We don't even lock our doors."

"Probably should."

"You know what your uncle used to say?"

70

Quinn smiled. "I recall a lot that he used to say."

"He used to tip his hat at me on the Square and say if folks started locking their doors, then he wasn't doing his job."

"My uncle and I have a different viewpoint on that." Quinn nodded. "I prefer to plan for the worst."

"If a man plans for the worst, then won't he get the worst?" Mrs. King said.

Kenny turned to Quinn and waited for his answer, hands folded over his large stomach.

"That's not exactly my point of view," Quinn said. "I just never have been big on surprises."

They dumped the sweet Chevelle and the dead man in Aberdeen before heading back northwest toward Tibbehah County in the old Caprice Classic. They took the Natchez Trace part of the way, finding a public bathroom set back from some Indian mounds to use the toilet and clean up. Bones wanted to head over to Tupelo to buy some weed, but Esau convinced him to stay focused, and Bones said he was so goddamned focused that some weed would mellow him out. He settled for another pint of Turkey, and by one a.m., they'd hit the Tibbehah County line, dumped the Caprice

Classic at a highway truck stop, and stole a Toyota Tundra. They decided to cruise a bit west, checking out spots around a hamlet called Dogtown for a solid place to hole up. Esau had smoked two packs of cigarettes already and was onto the third, Bones passing the whiskey over to him as they roamed the dirt roads up and over the hills, seeing signs for a national forest but staying on county roads, and riding through a cemetery until they found a nice stretch of woods with no houses and thick with trees. They drove with the windows partway down, the rain making the windshield fog.

For a good mile, Esau kept seeing signs for the Vardaman Hunt Club and how there was NO TRESPASSING. Esau, getting curious about the club, slowed when he got to a locked cattle gate that shut off the private road on into the place. The gate was more of a message to people who wanted to drive up and have a look-see, but whoever had built the gates should have known there was plenty of space on each side of the posts for a 4×4 to get across. Esau hit the gas on the Toyota and dipped down into a little gully and then popped quickly out, spinning dirt and gravel as they raced past the gates and onto the hunting club land. Bones was so excited as he slumped in the passenger seat

72

that Esau figured he might just fall asleep.

Esau followed the dark road for maybe a mile through some old land with tall, old-growth pines. There were more and more NO TRESPASSING signs, Esau taking this to be a good omen because something was so damn good on top of the hill that someone wanted to make damn sure that the shit-birds weren't invited. And sure enough as they crested the hill, a small gravel road broke to the right and they followed it straight up high and fast onto a thick, shadowed shape of a log house overlooking the forest and valley below. Esau got as close as he could and killed the engine. Bones stirred awake and stumbled from the car to the tree line, where he took a leak. The rain fell weak but steady, thunder sounding off far into the forest. The air smelled electric and piney.

Esau grabbed the keys, his cigarettes, and a bottle of Wild Turkey with a fresh seal. He mounted the steps and made his way to the side door of the cabin, really more than just a cabin, a big-ass log house, and tried the door. And of course the door was locked, but it wasn't much for his elbow to break the glass and for him to feel inside for the deadbolt. They were in the kitchen, which hummed with electricity and big silver appliances. Bones was coming on in behind him, yawning, and rubbing his eyes. He pulled open the refrigerator and whistled. "Holy hell."

"What they got?" Esau said.

"What they don't got?"

Bones opened a beer on the side of a counter and passed it to Esau. He cracked another one open, helping himself to a block of good cheese, and the men walked side by side into a great room fashioned of big pine logs running high and wide, maybe thirty feet into a ceiling. Someone had tacked ducks and deer heads and a stuffed wildcat or two on the wall. There was the biggest television Esau had ever seen, as flat and wide as one in a movie show, and when Bones punched it to life, he quickly recognized an old film he used to watch with his stepfather, *7 Men from Now,* with old Randolph Scott. Esau finished the beer in three sips and cracked the seal on the Wild Turkey. The room was filled with a lot of thick leather furniture and lamps fashioned from antlers, a bar stocked with Scotch and bourbon so good that Esau handed the rest of the Turkey to Bones. He made himself a Glenfiddich neat and walked toward the far wall, finding a ten-foot section of glass set into the pine beams. He counted out twenty-two shotguns and rifles shining as bright and beautiful as the day they came from the smith's hands.

"Ain't bad," Bones said. "Ain't bad at all. Yeah, this'll work."

Esau nodded. "Tomorrow, we find Dixon."

7

It was nearing 0100 and the next wave of storms was blowing across Tibbehah County. Quinn had stopped at the sheriff's office to refill his thermos and to check the storm online. It looked like they might have some flooding, but on a night like this, you could always bet on the accidents. Quinn drove his F-250 north of his farm onto the road that ran from Fate to Providence, beyond the hills and the National Forest. He got maybe a mile and a half down Horse Barn Road when he saw the lights on Kenny's cruiser. Kenny's yellow slicker worn over his thick and squat body flashed on the roadside, next to a couple flares lit on the road. Quinn slowed softly directly behind Kenny's cruiser, since there were no shoulders on the rural roads.

He stepped out into the wind and rain, wearing a tobacco-colored rancher and his official cap. He had an unlit cigar in his teeth, the nicotine keeping him sharp as he ran the roads.

"I thought he was dead," Kenny said. "Gave me a jump when he snorted."

A small white pickup truck had run into a tree, not hard enough to dent the hood but just enough to stop at a crazy angle off the hill. Quinn walked up with Kenny and opened the passenger door. The smell of urine and alcohol overwhelmed them. A man lay passed out across the bench seat.

"Damn."

"I told you, Quinn," Kenny said. "You know this son of a bitch?"

Quinn looked at the young man's gaunt, unshaven features. "Nope."

Quinn shook the man's shoulder. His mouth was wide open, eyes rolled up into his head. In the full light of the cab, the man had at some point pulled his blue jeans down and exposed himself.

"Don't you wish Lillie had this call?" Kenny said.

"Why's that?" Quinn said.

"Funny is all," Kenny said. "Man flashing his junk to the world. Didn't want to reach for his wallet. I'll go get a stick or something."

"Got some rubber gloves in my truck."

"Guess he wanted to take a piss but

couldn't stand up."

On the driver's-side floorboard was a pint of flavored vodka, the kind that tasted like cough syrup mixed with rubbing alcohol.

"You look around for anyone might've been with him?"

"Yes, sir."

Quinn nodded and rubbed the comatose man hard on his breastbone. The man stirred for a moment and then turned back to sleep. He left the passenger door open and met Kenny at the edge of the truck, where Kenny was putting on some rubber gloves. "Call dispatch," Quinn said. "Get an ambulance. They get him up, do a DUI test."

"Yes, sir."

"And then let's get this thing towed," Quinn said. "You can call Boom, but I wouldn't advise it this late. Who's working?"

"Someone at the Rebel."

"Wake up Johnny Stagg himself if you have to, or even if you don't."

Kenny wandered up the hill to get a better signal on the cell. The rain was falling at full slant now, the flares still burning bright on the dark curve. Quinn walked around the truck, canted at an angle, and looked inside the tailgate. The entire space had been loaded down with piles and piles of

78

turnip greens. A whole garden's worth of them, muddy and unwilted, fresh from the ground.

"Kenny?" Quinn said, yelling. "Bring your camera. I think we found our thief."

Kenny nodded, pocketed his phone, and made his way back to the truck. He took a dozen or so pictures in the dark and rain, inside and out of the cab. When he'd finished, Quinn rolled the young guy over to his side and reached for his wallet. Thankfully, the back of his jeans was dry and he took the wallet to his truck to run the plate inside his cab. The man had twenty-three dollars, an EBT card, a worn self-posed photo of a nude woman looking in a mirror, an expired Mississippi driver's license, and a U.S. Army ID. Quinn studied the military ID in the small overhead light and read that the turnip thief had been assigned to 82nd Airborne in Fort Bragg. He learned the man had reached the rank of E-3, was twenty-four, and lived about two miles down the road.

Quinn got out of the truck. Kenny was back on his phone, busy explaining his location to dispatch. He said they needed a wrecker from the Rebel Truck Stop.

Quinn held up his hand.

Kenny squinted his eyes into the rain and

headlights of his cruiser.

"We got it," Quinn said. "Call off the wrecker."

"Call you back," Kenny said to dispatch and pulled the phone from his ear. "What's that?"

"I'll pull my truck down to the next road," Quinn said. "You pick me up and take me back here. I'll be driving this man's vehicle home."

"You know him?"

"Yeah, I guess."

"Sorry, Sheriff," Kenny said. He tilted his head in the light rain. "I don't understand."

"Let's get him out of the road and back home," Quinn said. "I don't think either of us wants to spend the rest of the night doing paperwork."

Kenny shook his head in confusion as Quinn turned and headed back to his truck. He cracked a window and relit his cigar, staring out into the dark and rain buffeting his truck.

"You just let him go with nothin'?" Boom said. "That's mighty white of you, Quinn."

"Yeah, I always let white people go," Quinn said, working on the second half of the cigar. "Got to look out for my own."

"He ever come to?"

"I used some smelling salts," Quinn said, enjoying the last bit of the La Gloria Cubana. "Helped walk him inside to his house. He lives with his parents in Carthage. Now, that was a scene."

"I hope you washed your hands."

"He was embarrassed he pissed himself," Quinn said. "His mother was yelling, praying, and crying, and not helping the situation."

"Not like you not to lean on a drunk driver."

"He wasn't driving when we found him."

"And what about the stolen turnips?"

"I told him he needed to address that with Mrs. King," Quinn said. "And if it's not to her liking, she's welcome to press charges. I'm betting he'll try and work it off through her church."

"You never that easy on me," Boom said.

"How would you have responded if I'd gone soft?"

"Better to never know."

It was five a.m. at the County Barn, the shed where Boom maintained the police cruisers for the SO and the heavy equipment for the road crews. An early gray light fell through the open doors, and the shed smelled of fresh grease and of Quinn's cigar. There were several long metal benches and

81

Peg-Boards lined pin-neat with Boom's tools. Each piece had its slot; a current *Playboy* lingerie calendar hung on the wall alongside an 8 × 10 of Boom's Guard Unit taken before he'd lost his arm. Boom had on his prosthetic that morning, fixing a screwdriver into place and dipping back under the hood of an ancient Crown Vic.

"Did the man thank you?" Boom said.

"In his way."

"And what did Kenny say?"

Quinn looked at the end of his cigar, smoldering down to the nub. "You know Kenny," Quinn said. "He doesn't question much. I think he was relieved he didn't have to write more reports and show in court."

"And if you catch the guy driving shit-house drunk again?" Boom said.

"That's another deal."

"Mmmhmm," Boom said from under the old car's hood.

Quinn tossed the cigar butt and walked over to a small coffeepot set atop a tool bench. A small radio played the *Drake & Zeke* morning show out of Memphis, the hosts talking about overnight damage across the mid-South and the endless bad weather. But the morning smelled fresh and new to him, and there was a terrific gray-gold light breaking from the east.

"Notice las' night you didn't even flinch when Caddy said that about Ophelia Bundren."

Quinn nodded.

"So, you hittin' that?"

"That's a pretty crude question," Quinn said. "You been talking to Lillie?"

"Are you not the sheriff of this county?"

"Yep."

"And well known?"

"Yep."

"So it stands to reason that if you are in frequent company of an eligible young lady, people start to talk. I don't give a shit if the woman sometimes acts strange and embalms folks. She's got a fine little body."

"Thanks, Boom."

"So, are you?"

"If I were," Quinn said, "wouldn't I tell you?"

Boom lifted his large self from under the hood. He removed the screwdriver from his hand and fit in a socket wrench. He nodded and smiled as he replaced the tools. "Damn if I ain't become Inspector Gadget," Boom said, screwing in the wrench. "You know, you hadn't had a date since you were seeing that agent from Oxford. And everybody knows that didn't work out too great."

"She tried to get me fired," Quinn said.

"Did you know that? I just found out she wanted the local special agent in charge to make a case I'd helped with that gunrunning down to Mexico."

"Mean, mean woman," Boom said. "Just stay away from redheads and women who pack heat."

"Solid advice," Quinn said.

"Just looking out for you, man."

Quinn smiled. Boom offered his prosthetic hand, and Quinn lightly bumped it with his fist.

Quinn had been home for an hour, and to get comfortable, he'd removed his Beretta's leather rig and khaki sheriff's office shirt. He wore a simple white T-shirt and his jeans, feeling almost weightless and naked, with boots set by the back door, as he fried up some bacon and made some coffee. He stared out the big window over his kitchen sink, watching the cows and many new calves playing in the half-sunlight shooting from the broken slots in the clouds. The window was open, and the air smelled strong and earthy, of tilled soil and cow manure. He never grew tired of the color back in Mississippi. Even in the winter, things were brighter and more vibrant than any inch of Afghanistan. The landscape there was a colorless void of purgatory, where it seemed a sensible day when a man or woman or child would strap on a bomb and decide today was it. Quinn still had a six-inch scar across his forearm where a suicide bomber had shot him square in the chest, the bullet whizzing off his breastplate and into his arm. He'd fought for six hours in that Takhar Province compound before they sealed him back up with needles and staples. After thirteen tours, that became the new normal.

The grease popped and Quinn wiped up some splatterings with a hand towel, forking the bacon from the skillet. He cracked open three eggs and set aside a loaf of Texas bread and some butter. It was after eight now and he was tired. But being on the night shift made early morning his only personal time when he could read and feed the animals, watch the day start up from the long porch of his old farmhouse.

Just as he lifted the eggs from the skillet, he heard the familiar-sounding car drive up into his driveway and shut off the engine. Quinn could almost count the seconds from door slam to front screen door creak and boot thumps down his hallway.

Quinn didn't even turn as he set the bread in the skillet to brown and felt the familiar arms around his stomach and soft head against his neck. His stereo playing the new CD from Bryan Ledford, country and bluegrass, love, heartache, and revenge. She smelled of fresh powder and a light perfume, her hand pressing down onto his scarred forearm, turning him around and kissing him full hard on the mouth.

Quinn turned off the flame and reached his arms around her waist, hands across her lower back, mouth on hers and then down on her neck and feeling under the light silk of her top, bra strap snapping off, over her smallish breasts and then lifting off her shirt and bra, now with her only in dark blue jeans and dirty cowboy boots. He lifted her up and onto a cabinet as she kissed his face and chest while he pulled off his T-shirt and started working on his belt, barely getting it unbuckled as her legs wrapped around his waist and he carried her through the kitchen and the hallway, the door wide open, the screen door showing deep across the road and into the pasture, sun beating on the hay bales, steam rising in the morning cool. He laid her down roughly on the bed and slipped her from her jeans and boots and pulled out of his, both of them not even fooling with the covers in Quinn's bedroom. The room was dark, with a thin spindle of daylight cutting through the lace curtains and over the solitary, almost monastic iron bed in the center. The only other furniture was an armoire and an Army footlocker where he kept several of his guns at the end of his bed. She reached out strong and confident below him, gripping the thick iron headboard and holding on as he kissed her harder across her neck and over her body, hating every minute they couldn't be together, loving her but resenting it all the same. He held her up off the bed as she arched her back and held on, white-knuckled, to the bed as it shook and shuddered with so much intensity that the feet skipped and scraped hard against the wood floor.

When it was over, Quinn moved to the edge of the bed, feet touching the floor. He tried to catch his breath, the sunlight shifting from the floor to across the bed and keeping his face in a half-light. He breathed slow and tried to steady his heart the same way he did when shooting a pistol or rifle, but everything felt uneasy and off-kilter. She was behind him now, her body pressed behind him, chin on his shoulder, her skin moist on his back and breath hot in his ear. The old house was calm and easy except for the country music playing muffled from the kitchen.

"Can you stay for breakfast?" he said. "I cooked it before you came so you couldn't make an excuse."

"No," she said.

"Five minutes won't matter."

"No one can see me here."

Quinn did not turn around, staring into the curtain as it fluttered and settled in the spring wind. "I don't much care anymore."

"You don't have as much to lose."

"You know what I want to say," Quinn said.

Her hand reached up over his shoulder, and she put two fingers to his mouth. "Hush."

"I want to say it."

"That just makes this all harder," she said, getting off the bed, the mattress creaking and releasing as she stood small-breasted and wide-hipped, with her strawberry blond hair cut in blunt bangs that shielded her eyes. She laughed as she searched on the floor for her panties and her jeans and walked from the dark room into the kitchen, where she returned clothed and holding her boots. She sat on Quinn's locker and slid her stocking feet into them and then stood and walked to the half-closed door. "At least this is something," she said.

88

"Who's at your house?"

"My mother."

"Does she know where you are?"

"Sure," she said. "Grocery shopping."

"You do know," Quinn said, standing and dressing.

"I do," she said. "But if you ever say it out loud, I swear to Christ that this will all end. I don't know what this is. But it's something and works for now."

Quinn rubbed his temples, listening to the heavy steps of her boots and the door slamming behind her. Anna Lee Amsden was back in his life.

8

Caddy liked having a purpose. Most mornings, she would drop Jason at preschool, and, if she didn't have to go to work, she'd head right for The River, knowing there was plenty of work to be done. Jamey left her in charge of the gardening and the gathering of used clothing. They planned to open a thrift shop in an outbuilding, and the cleaning and organizing took most of her day. But it was spring now, and she had to continue to plant, scatter the compost, and cultivate rows for the small tomato plants she put in the ground last week. If everything worked the way Jamey saw it, they could feed and clothe most of the congregation. And those who joined the church would work and earn, giving their life some purpose, too. Jamey said that was the only way he'd survived the Farm, getting away from lying in his bunk and watching television and getting out in the fields. And from the fields, finding the course work through that seminary in New Orleans. He walked away from prison not only a free man but a full and complete human being and an ordained minister.

She was on her hands and knees that morning, the sun breaking through the clouds, dirt up under her nails, and feeling good spreading the mulch around the little plants. Caddy stood up to wipe the sweat from her face when she saw the silver truck running down the dirt road toward the barn. She'd never seen the truck before, but that wasn't that peculiar. Jamey invited everyone he met to come out and join them, and even if he got turned down, he'd ask them to think on it and come out and just see what The River was all about. He didn't care if they became members, only that they witnessed what they were doing. If Jamey and Caddy could serve as examples to those they met, then they had done something.

Two men got out of the truck, one white and one black. The black man was tall and skinny, and the white man had hair the color of copper wire. They were a far bit off, and as she was deciding whether to meet them, she saw Jamey emerge from the barn and walk toward them, suddenly stopping where he stood. They were exchanging words and

Jamey was pointing for them to turn around and head back down the road they'd come.

The copper-haired man kept walking, and Jamey threw down the paintbrush in his hand. He was repeatedly shaking his head until the man, looking thick and muscular, got within a foot of Jamey and punched him square in the stomach. Caddy wasn't even aware she was running until she was ten feet away, tripping and crushing the new plantings and heading from the garden. She ran to Jamey, who was on his knees. The man yelled at Jamey, telling him he was a coward and a piece of shit, and Caddy didn't know much about the situation but found herself in front of the man with the red hair and beard, spitting right into his face.

"Leave us alone," Caddy said. "Get the hell out of here."

Jamey was back on his feet, taking in big gulps of air and pulling her back. He told her to run away, this wasn't her business.

"Get out of here."

The black man joined his friend. He looked Caddy up and down like the men used to appraise her in Memphis. And she thought back on the time when she'd work for forty dollars a dance, two for sixty, in a uniform of bra and panties, dancing full of

92

vodka and pills and being numb to the lights and dance music and not being a participant in her own existence. She wanted to spit on him, too, but her mouth was too dry.

"Glad to see you back with women, Dixon," the black man said. "You come a long way from Louis Scott cornholing you in that tool shed."

She looked to Jamey, feeling like she wanted to cry but instead setting her jaw. Jamey pushed her behind him and looked right at the man with red hair. "Don't make me call the police," he said. "Get gone from here."

"Is your brain fried?" the red-haired man said. "You got something belongs to me."

"I got nothing but what I wear."

"Motherfucker," the black man said.

"Don't make me call the police."

"Call 'em," the red-haired man said. "But I swear I'll kill you before they get here. I am not going back before I get what's mine or before you're dead."

"I don't know what you're talking about." The man struck Jamey again hard in the mouth, reeling him backward, stumbling on his feet. But he stood his ground, telling the man to leave. "Not here, not in this place."

"What is this?" the black man said. "Some kind of dope-smokin' hippie commune? I

93

thought you'd be up to your eyeballs in pussy and Cadillacs about now. Although this one sure is something sweet. I can smell her from here."

"You nasty piece of shit," Caddy said. She reached for her cell phone, dialing for 911, and Jamey pulled the phone from her hands.

"Not here," he said. "We'll talk. But I don't have what you want. I need you to understand that. Anything we talked about at the Farm is gone. That's not my life now."

"Well," the red-haired man said. "It's my life. It's all I got."

"We have volunteers coming," Jamey said. "Where can we meet?"

"You tryin' to set us up?" the black man said.

Jamey looked to Caddy and then back to the men. "I set you up, and I kind of do the same to myself."

The men studied Jamey, thinking on what he said. The daylight white and slatted, running for acres and acres through the tilled land and the half-painted barn. Caddy held on to Jamey's arm, holding him back, holding herself on her feet. Without a word, the men were back in the truck, cranking the engine and turning away in a spray of dirt and gravel.

"OK," she said, steadying herself. "Just

what the hell is going on?"

"Why'd we leave?" Bones said, driving the Tundra down the long gravel road. "Ain't no reason to leave."

"You want to talk to the locals?"

"Hell, naw."

"Dixon is right," Esau said. "He fucks us, he fucks himself."

"That really true what you said about Scott cornholing that motherfucker in the shed?"

"Don't know," Esau said. "That's what I heard. I know they took the hide off his ass before we started looking out for him. Wasn't for us, Dixon knows he'd be dead."

"We take care of him," Bones said. "Protect him. And then he supposed to take care of us. Only when he get out, he can't even remember our fucking names."

Esau gritted his teeth, nodding.

"Where do we go?" Bones said, hitting the main county highway and driving north, up toward Jericho and the Town Square. A handmade sign on the side of the road read: HELL IS REAL. ARE YOU READY?

"Back to the hunt club," Esau said. "Let's eat and wait for Dixon to call."

"What if the man who owns the place shows up?" Bones said.

95

"Son of a bitch probably owns ten places just like that one," Esau said. "Rich men don't value what they got. That's what makes them have soft bellies and little dicks. Reason their women don't have respect for them."

"You give me a bunch of money and I don't care if I get fat and my pecker shrinks," Bones said. "How about you?"

"Guess not."

"So how come Dixon pretending like he don't know what the fuck we're talking about?"

"He was putting on a show for his woman," Esau said. Lots of rolling farmland and open barns with heavy equipment zoomed past. Along the county road stood cattle, some donkeys, and a large, hilly pasture dotted with goats. "You know Dixon is starting to believe his own bullshit now? He can't be connected with men like us."

"And who the fuck are men like us?" Bones said.

Esau scratched and smoothed his beard. "Men with the road map to hell who quit caring about fifty miles back."

Bones grinned and turned west on another county road right before the Jericho Square, passing an old gas station that had been turned into a diner and a cinder-block

building with a big picture window advertising extensions and weaves. Men worked on the loading platform of a county co-op, heavy sacks of feed on their shoulders. A VFW sign told about a fish fry and country band on Friday night.

"I'll meet with Dixon alone," Esau said. "If he turns me in, make sure you kill him."

"Done."

"You know, he may never have touched that armored car," Esau said. "Maybe he's trying to keep clean and wants to sidestep things he used to do. Maybe that car's still buried deep with them dead men."

"*Bull*shit."

"Yeah," Esau said. "You're right."

"Why don't we just go down to that bass pond tonight and see if it's still down there? We might can't get the money, but we sure as hell can see if he's pulled it out the car."

Esau stared out at the greening countryside and dark clouds on the horizon, more fucking rain over the big forest, a dense fog clouding the top of the hills. He leaned forward in the passenger seat, staring down the road as they got close to the hunting lodge.

"What's eatin' on you?"

"Up there," Esau said. "Whose car is that?"

Bones kept driving up into the forest and the wooded hills, toward the big lodge tucked into the old-growth trees. A tired old Honda Accord, red paint worn thin on top, sat parked crooked by the front path. Esau was out of the car before Bones had fully stopped.

"Hey, man," Bones said. "Hey! Let's just keep going. No need for this shit. Let's just keep going."

"Don't you want some steak and eggs?"

"Hell yeah," Bones said, falling in beside him. "But I don't want to have to kill a motherfucker to eat 'em. Let's keep it cool till we get our money and drive out of Shitsville."

"You know I grew up in a county just like this," Esau said. "Back in Alabama."

"Ain't that nice."

The hunting lodge's side door was cracked open, and Esau and Bones walked right through the big kitchen, the appliances humming softly, a couple more lights on in the great room, making the dead animals' glassy eyes stare numbly at them. Doors lined the walls downstairs and up along a squared balcony that overlooked the space. Somewhere up there, Esau heard a shower going.

He reached for the .357 at his waist and

walked the steps above.

"God damn," Bones said to his back. "Sure hate to fu k up such a good thing."

Quinn had come into Mr. Jim's barbershop fifteen minutes earlier to get his weekly high-and-tight. Keeping his hair blade-short was just something he couldn't shake after leaving the 75th. He woke up every day, checked his weapon, shaved his face, and ran a hand over his head to see if he was getting sloppy. As he waited for the old man ahead of him, he thumbed through a new copy of *Field & Stream,* a story on "16 Early-Season Wall-Hangers and the Tactics That Took Them." He was also interested in a consumer story about the "Best Hunter's Hatchets," Quinn always feeling that a man and a hatchet could survive a good long while out in the woods.

Mr. Jim stared at the television atop the Coke machine showing *The Price Is Right* and sadly shook his head. "Sure miss Bob Barker. I don't care for this goofy son of a bitch in glasses. He ain't funny atall."

"What else do you all watch?" Quinn said.

"I have to admit I got hooked on *General Hospital* about fifteen years ago," he said. "Don't think I've missed a show since."

Quinn read a little more about a hatchet

99

with a carbon blade and a handmade handle. He felt like he'd been sitting on that same mustard-yellow Naugahyde sofa most of his life. His father, Jason Colson, had first taken him to Mr. Jim for haircuts. And then when Jason left Jericho for good, everyone knowing that Jason had made it big as a stuntman in L.A., Uncle Hamp had tried to make Quinn keep his hair short and his attitude straight. When that failed, he pointed the way to the local Army recruiter.

Luther Varner, smoking down an extralong cigarette, sat in a chair by the gumball machines. He wore a mesh baseball cap with the words DA NANG printed above the bill, forearm showing a faded *Semper Fi* tattoo. Luther glanced up at the television set and agreed with Mr. Jim. "Since when do they got men showing off the prizes?" Luther said. "What happened to the women in bikinis?"

Mr. Jim spun around another old man in the barber chair, showing the man the mirror. He pointed out the work he had done and made sure it was to his liking. The customer, a bald man with a thin strip of hair over his ears, nodded with satisfaction.

"Quinn," Mr. Jim said, motioning that it was his time.

Quinn closed the magazine and stood. He

waited till the man had paid his ten bucks and then took a seat. Last year's football schedule for the Tibbehah High Wildcats hung on the walls among the stuffed ducks and deer and an old electric clock advertising Dr Pepper. Outside the glass door, there was a spinning barber pole and a flag that Mr. Jim, a veteran of Patton's 3rd Army, brought in and folded every night when he closed up shop.

"My road's a mess," Mr. Jim said. "I was gonna plant corn this weekend, but ground's too wet."

"Why waste your time?" Luther said, lighting up another lengthy cigarette. "I gave up farming when they opened up the Piggly Wiggly."

"Who's minding your store?" Mr. Jim asked.

"Peaches," he said. "She's working the Quick Mart regular since Donnie's been gone."

"Any word on his sentence?" Quinn asked.

"His lawyer wants him to make a deal," Luther said, a long ash on the end of his cigarette. "He has to say he stole those Army guns and they take off charges he helped the illegals smuggle them out."

"Sounds like a solid deal," Quinn said.

"When have you ever known my son to

do the sensible thing?" Luther said.

Quinn shrugged. Mr. Jim fluttered a cutting cape over Quinn's chest and lap and tied it at the neck. He reached for the clippers, setting them on the lowest level possible, a notch up from a straight razor.

"Ever think of trying out a different style, Quinn?" Mr. Jim said.

"Nope."

"You know you could do this yourself and save ten bucks?"

"Yes, sir."

"Then why don't you do it?"

"I appreciate y'all's entertainment value."

In the mirror, Quinn watched Mr. Jim and Luther Varner exchange looks. Luther ashed the cigarette into the palm of his hand and walked to the trash can. On TV, *The Price Is Right* stopped for a moment and the news station cut in with an update on the storms. There was a lot of footage of downed trees and power lines up in Memphis, roof damage and flooded roads in north Mississippi. The weatherman said they could expect more of the same for the next few days, a front headed in from Oklahoma, listing flash flood and thunderstorm warnings for most of the mid-South.

"Maybe I should prep my johnboat," Luther said.

"You hear about those boys who escaped Parchman day before yesterday?" Mr. Jim said. "They stole a couple horses and rode about twenty miles up to Tutwiler, where they stole a car. Law hadn't caught them yet."

"We got an alert yesterday from the highway patrol," Quinn said. "They think they may already be in Alabama. One of the convicts is from there. And a third son of a bitch got through the front gate. All of Parchman is on lockdown."

"Hell, maybe they'll all drown," Luther said.

"Rats always find higher ground," Mr. Jim said, lathering up Quinn's neck and pulling out his straight razor. "The way of the world."

9

Bones asked Esau to shag ass one final time before he said fuck it and walked back to the lodge kitchen, leaving Esau to walk up the steps to the second-floor balcony. That's where Esau had heard the shower and could see the steam coming out from the cracked door. He inched along the upstairs railing, looking down into the big square opening of the room, silent and still with all those dead animals and cold guns. He used the .357's barrel to crack open the door and stepped inside a small bath just in time to see the flash of a woman's naked leg emerge from the tub. Esau slipped the gun into his belt and reached for a monogrammed beige towel and walked toward the woman with a grin.

She let out a shriek, covering her mouth, her titties jiggling a bit, as she'd gotten a start from seeing Esau. She reached for the towel, laughing, covering her mouth with the back of her hand and then wrapping the towel around her body. Damn if Becky didn't look better and better to him. Trusted and true, going through all them years at Parchman for nothing but a throw every few weeks at the visit house and eight bucks a year. Man, it was good to see her when they didn't have a guard waiting with a stopwatch and fifty horny stinking men waiting in line to use the same damn room. Never was much time for cuddling in that trailer.

"Door was open," Becky said. "Just helped myself. You say this is your buddy's place?"

"That's right," Esau said. "He wanted me and you to have somewhere special to go when I got out."

"I never saw a refrigerator like that in a house before," she said. "Hell, I could live in there."

Esau put his rough, stubby fingers on her and pulled her close, reaching up under the towel and feeling her large and firm butt. "Damn, I love how you smell."

"You still smell like prison," Becky said, pulling away, twisting her wet blond hair in her hands, wringing out the water. She walked to the bathroom counter, where she'd stowed a zebra-print overnight case, and pulled out a fresh pair of panties and some cutoff jeans. First thing Esau had noticed about Becky at that Tupelo Waffle House where she waited tables was her legs. And she hadn't lost any of it. She slipped into the panties and shorts, and then fit a red bikini top over her head and asked Esau to tie the back.

"What you putting that on for?" he said.

"Duh," she said. "Hadn't you even seen the pool? That's the best part of this log cabin. I turned on the heater and set out some chairs. Let us make some margaritas and play around. I don't care if it rains on us or not. I'll put on some Kenny Chesney and we'll pretend we're in Florida."

"How about we just go back to one of them bedrooms and I'll fuck you?"

"Which one?" she said. "They got about forty of 'em."

Esau pulled her pale body in close to his chest. He nibbled at her ear a bit, saying some dirty ideas that had come to him in prison. Esau marveled at the sight of them together in the mirror till he spotted something move down the hall and come toward them. Sure as hell wasn't Bones. He pushed Becky away, pulled the .357, and aimed it hard and fast at the white man sneaking up on them.

The little guy flinched, dropped to one knee, and covered his head. At first Esau thought he was shaking from fear but then realized he was giggling.

"Little jumpy, ain't you, Red?" Dickie Green said.

He slowly got up, hands raised. And Esau set the pistol back on his belt.

"What the hell?"

"Went to Miss Becky's house in Coldwater and she tole me she was comin' to you," Dickie said. "Figured we just ride together. Ain't this something?"

Esau looked down over the railing onto the first floor. Bones stood in the center of the big room, shaking his head. "Dickie," Bones said up to the balcony. "Good to see you."

"See?" Dickie said. He wore a flannel shirt without sleeves and a pair of Wranglers. Bald head shining in the lamplight. "Y'all still need me."

"How's that?" Esau said to Dickie, but more looking down at Bones.

"Dickie?" Bones said. "Didn't I hear you can swim real good?"

Quinn stood at the edge of the Rebel Truck Stop parking lot, watching the 18-wheelers come and go, a large grouping of trucks, maybe fifty or so, hooking into free cable and Wi-Fi, until their next leg or word from the dispatcher. The Rebel's sign along Highway 45 was a girl's silhouette often seen on mud flaps against a neon blue-and-red Confederate flag.

Lillie pulled up her Cherokee two feet from Quinn and got out.

"You must have a good reason for calling me over here," Quinn said. "I haven't had much sleep."

"Maybe I just wanted some of the Rebel Truck Stop's fine chicken-fried steak."

"Their chicken-fried steak tastes like shit."

"Or maybe today is the day that we finally break down the door to Johnny Stagg's strip club and raid them for prostitution?"

"And they'll open an hour later."

"Or maybe we got a vehicle here possibly connected to a robbery in Webster County." Lillie motioned Quinn to a Chevy Caprice Classic parked over toward the neat rows of 18-wheelers. "Car belongs to a cook over in Eupora who was working the late shift. Man never stopped by the owner's house last night, as was custom, to deliver the earnings."

"Any sign of the cook?" Quinn said.

"Nope."

"How did we know about the car?"

"Would you believe Johnny Stagg himself called it in?" Lillie said. "It was blocking an exit lane for his truckers. He told Mary Alice it was time we did something on the job, other than just cruise around the county and drink coffee."

"Ole Johnny," Quinn said. "Concerned citizen."

Lillie grinned. A large Kenworth loaded down with pine logs blew past them, kicking up some grit and drowning out any words.

"So you ran the tag and got in touch with the sheriff in Webster?" Quinn said after the truck passed.

"Yep."

"This guy have a record?" Quinn said.

"Nothing to worry over," Lillie said. "Name is Highsmith. Been arrested a few times for possessing dope and petty theft. Sounds like a burnout."

"Who got some ambition late last night."

"So much ambition, he stole a whole three hundred dollars and fucked up his life."

Quinn turned to the Rebel's main building, the Western-wear shop and restaurant's long bank of picture windows with truckers downing coffee and loading up for breakfast. A sign advertised a Denver omelet for four bucks and ninety-nine cents.

"I'll talk to Stagg," Quinn said.

"You always take the fun parts of the job."

"He may know more than he's saying," Quinn said. "I can always tell when the son of a bitch is lying."

"Hell," Lillie said. "That's easy. Hard part is knowing when he's telling the truth."

"Who were those men?" Caddy asked Jamey Dixon. They had parked outside the Sonic drive-in, waiting for some burgers, fries, and Cokes. She didn't have much time before picking up Jason from school. She and Jamey had spent the rest of the day in the garden, not speaking, since the men peeled away from the church.

"Just a couple fellas I knew."

"Men from Parchman?"

Jamey nodded.

"What did they want?"

"Like I said, they think I have something that belongs to them."

"But you don't."

"I don't, Caddy," Jamey said. "I'm done with all that. They're the kind of people looking for a free ride and always have excuses about what they've become."

"They looked pretty rough."

"Not a lot of the clean-cut types in the Farm."

"That one man, the black man, I didn't care for the way he looked at me."

110

" 'Cause he was black?"

"Because there was something wrong with his brain," she said. "He thought it was OK to look at a person like an animal. He looked like he was in ecstasy."

"Maybe he had to go to the bathroom."

"I'm not joking with you about this."

"One thing I know for sure," Jamey said, smiling. "We aren't that far different from animals. It just depends on how you decide to evolve."

A teenage girl on roller skates and in a pair of shorts and a tight Alan Jackson T-shirt appeared and handed them a couple Cokes and a big sack of burgers. She smiled big at Jamey, and Jamey tipped her two dollars, sending her off on skates.

"Caddy, I appreciate all you done," Jamey said. "The garden is going to be beautiful and help a lot of folks in need."

"I about made a mess of it, tromping through when those men came up."

"Caddy?"

She looked at Jamey behind the wheel, wearing sunglasses, not touching the food between them. "I want you to forget about those men and what they said," he said. "More than anything, I don't want you to talk to Quinn about it."

"I don't tell Quinn anything."

"Good," he said. "It will just get messy for me. He's looking for an excuse to get me in trouble with the parole board. He hates that we're together."

"But those men," Caddy said. "They'll come back for you. What about then? What if they try to hurt you or the church? Or what if Jason is around?"

Jamey reached into the sack for a cheeseburger and a couple fries. He thought as he ate, nodding to himself with what he seemed to believe was a solid answer. "When they get what's happened through their thick heads, they'll leave us all alone."

"But if they don't," Caddy said. "I still don't know what happened. What the hell do they want from you? More money?"

"I don't want to discuss it," Jamey said. "But I swear to you that they'll never get close to you again."

Jamey set his jaw and ate in silence, studying on a part of his life he'd never share with her. It didn't make her mad as much as it made her face flush with jealousy.

10

"Sheriff," Johnny Stagg said. "Good to see you. Come on in."

"Thanks, Johnny."

Stagg smiled his satyr grin, his face an elongated mask of self-confidence, and pointed to an empty wooden chair before a big old desk. Behind him there were dozens of 8×10 photographs of the famous, nearly famous, and almost famous who'd come through his truck stop over the last three decades. The only two Quinn could really place were Goober from *The Andy Griffith Show* and B.B. King. Several of the pictures showed Johnny with his arm around the athlete or ballplayer or state politician. Johnny seemed to collect meeting people the way some kids do bubble-gum cards.

Quinn stood behind the chair, resting his hands on the back.

"You come to talk about that stolen car?" Johnny said, still smiling, all bemused in

Quinn's presence.

"Yep."

"I didn't even see it," Johnny said. "It was Leonard come in this afternoon and tole me that some truckers were complaining that it was blocking a turn."

"Probably where the girls can hop up in their cabs," Quinn said.

Johnny grinned some more, looking downright civil in a red Ole Miss sweater, a checked shirt with spread collar, and stiff khaki pants. He was in his late fifties or early sixties, with the purplish reddened skin of a hill person and the pompadoured hair of a 1950s rockabilly star. He sucked on a tooth, took a seat at his desk, and looked up at Quinn, hating the disproportion. Johnny Stagg was the head of the Tibbehah County Board of Supervisors and often incorrectly assumed he was Quinn's boss.

"The girls don't work in a parking lot, Sheriff," Johnny said. "We keep to the county ordinance and don't let them step off the property unless their shift is over and they have to tend to something personal."

"I heard you were thinking of renaming the bar?"

"Can't think of a better name than the Booby Trap," Johnny said, grinning wide

114

with his picket of veneers. "Says it all."

"So you never saw the car or anything strange," Quinn said. "More than usual."

"No, sir," Johnny said. "Just reported it."

"Ever hear of this man Highsmith?"

"No, sir," Johnny said, grinning.

"Why didn't Leonard report it?"

"You and Leonard had never seen eye to eye," Stagg said. "I'm sure you realize he didn't feel comfortable, thinking you might harass him."

"That why you put him up to be new police chief in Jericho?"

"That's between Leonard and the Board of Aldermen," he said. "I got nothing to do with that."

Quinn nodded. He scratched his neck, taking a bit of paper off that Mr. Jim had left after nicking him.

"I'll need to pull video from your security cameras," Quinn said.

Stagg leaned back in his chair, wood creaking, and crossed his arms over his little potbelly. He reached back to a molar, trying to work some of his lunch away. He didn't react at all, just watched Quinn.

"Maybe we can see what time he parked that car," Quinn said. "I'm not interested in anything else around here."

"Easy to say."

115

"Have I tried to roust you yet, Johnny?" Quinn said. "I've been sheriff now for a year and haven't once tried to shut down your place. If truckers want to get their gear shifter worked, that's up to them. I only care when some of your business spills out into the county."

"On their own time," Stagg said. "You see a girl with a trucker, that's on her own time."

"Of course it is," Quinn said, letting go of the back of the chair and standing straight. He stayed silent, waiting for Johnny to keep talking.

"I'll get those videos," Stagg said. "Although they ain't videos now; they put them on a computer drive. Y'all have the capability of working with something like that?"

"You'd be surprised," Quinn said. "We got some capable folks."

Johnny Stagg leaned forward, moving his arms off his belly, and reached his elbows onto his desk. He looked up and said, "I can bet Lillie Virgil will get a kick out of watching those girls in them little skirts."

Quinn said nothing.

"Oh, come on now, Sheriff," Johnny said, laughing. "Everybody knows that Lillie doesn't care too much for the fellas."

Quinn nodded. "I'll make sure I tell her

that, Johnny. I'm sure she'd like a chance to respond."

"Come on," Stagg said, his face turning the deep shade of a ripe tomato. "Hell. Don't stir up that wildcat."

"See you at the supervisors' meeting."

Stagg swallowed and reached for a trashcan, spitting out whatever little morsel had been giving him trouble. Quinn turned and walked back into the truck stop without a word.

Esau picked a good bottle of Scotch from the rich man's stash and sat down at the kitchen table with Bones and Dickie. Becky was too busy going through the lodge room by room, Esau not caring less. He'd seen the kitchen, the bar, the bedroom, and toilet. Who cared about anything else? But Becky was impressed he knew folks of such good taste, even asking Esau if she might write them a thank-you letter at a better time.

"So you said you know how to dive?" Bones said.

"Hell yes," Dickie said. "I grew up in Panama City, Florida. My dad was in the Navy. We used to go out and look for sunken treasure."

"In Panama City?" Esau said.

"Good a place as any."

Esau looked to Bones and shook his head, sadly.

"Becky got a couple tanks filled for me in Memphis and some gear and flares," Esau said. "You can dive with me."

"Where?"

"Down in a pond, to look for a big-ass car."

"Sure," Dickie said. "Ain't like I got anything better to do."

"Who told you to go see Becky?" Bones asked, still working on the last bit of steak and eggs. He dotted the last egg with some Tabasco and took a bite.

"I knew all about Becky after Esau talking so much about her," he said. "I seen her once or twice when she come for a poke in the trailer. All the men loved looking at her in those hooch clothes. Exactly what is that tattoo she got on the back of her neck?"

"It says NONE OF YOUR FUCKING BUSINESS," Esau said. "I didn't tell you to go see her, and I sure as hell didn't tell you where she lived."

"I knew she worked at the Dollar General over at Coldwater."

"Son of a bitch," Esau said. He cracked the seal on the Scotch.

With a mouthful of food, Bones said,

"Don't matter none now. All we got to worry about is hauling that car out of the pond. We ain't got no equipment and no big winch. We could try using two 4×4s, but I still don't think that'll work. We gonna need some tractors."

"First we got to make sure that we ain't wasting our time," Esau said. He poured out three heavy measures of Glenfiddich into some lowball glasses. He shoved the glasses before the two men. He sat back and waited.

"I told you I can dive," Dickie said. "Hell yes. I knew I could help y'all out. But I only got one question."

"What's that, Dickie?" Bones asked.

"What's my cut?" he said. He smiled, showing off the top and bottom rows of some real bad teeth.

"I'll tell you right now," Esau said, holding the Scotch up to the light, watching the brown stuff roll around in the thick glass. "We ain't partners in this. You think we partners at any point and your ass is gone. You are hired help only."

"Like I said," Dickie said, sniffing the booze and making a face. "How fucking much?"

"Five grand."

He scratched his face, a jailhouse spider

tattoo high on his Adam's apple. "See here, I don't know if that's a fair price, or y'all jacking my dick."

"Five grand is more than you got right now," Bones said. "Or you want to apply for a job scraping shit stains outta toilets at the Walmart?"

"Y'all are funny," Dickie said. "OK. I'll take the five grand. When do I get it?"

"You don't get dick till we get what we come for, and to get what we come for, tonight we got to dive that pond."

"At fucking night."

Esau nodded. "We got flares," he said. "Be the same as day, only we won't have the farmer and everyone else in this shithole coming back, craning their neck, and trying to get into our business."

"Gonna storm tonight," Dickie said.

"What's it matter underwater?" Bones said.

Dickie nodded. Bones held up his glass, and Esau did the same. The two men drank down the twenty-year-old Scotch. Dickie got only a half-swallow before he turned his head and spit the liquor all over the floor. "Damn, don't y'all got some Jäger around here? This stuff tastes like ass."

Becky strolled into the kitchen, holding up a pair of silver earrings that resembled

Indian dream catchers with feathers. In her other hand, she had a matching silver necklace with crimson stones. "Can you believe someone just left this here? It was sitting right out on the dresser. I figured I could wear it till we leave. Does it match my bikini top?"

Esau kept on staring at Dickie where he'd spit whiskey all over the wood floor. He turned back to Becky in her red top and Daisy Dukes and said, "Sure thing, baby. Grab what you want. Keep it if you like."

"I couldn't do that, Esau," Becky said, reaching up high, giving the men a good gander at her best features as she clasped on the necklace and earrings. "That would be very tacky."

"Ain't nothin' tacky 'bout you, Becky," Bones said.

Dickie just rubbed the stubble on his head and sniffed at his glass again. He screwed up his face at the smell of the whiskey and shuddered.

11

Caddy met her mother out by the boat ramp on Choctaw Lake. Jason was playing on a jungle gym set in a thinned oak forest, while Jean sat on a park bench reading a book by June Juanico about the summer of '56. Jean thumbed her place in the book and stuck it back inside her purse. She shook her head. "She says she never had sex with Elvis, you believe that?"

"No."

"I think she would have stayed with him, too, if it hadn't been for Natalie Wood," Jean said. "Natalie just wouldn't leave Elvis alone. Not that I blame her, but she was so open about it. Right under June's nose."

"Momma?"

"Yes, baby."

"How come you've never asked me much about Jamey?"

"I didn't think you wanted my opinion."

"But you being quiet always means you

don't like it."

"I like Jamey just fine."

"But you don't like me being with him?"

"Is that what you are now?" Jean said, somehow still managing to smile and wave to Jason as he made his way up a rope ladder. "With him?"

"Don't you know it?" Caddy took a breath. "I love him."

Jean nodded. Her eyelids fluttered a bit, and she bit her lip. Being subtle had never been part of her momma's skill set.

"Nobody in my entire family wanted me to be with your father," Jean said. "Jason Colson was ten years older, Hollywood trash, and wild as hell. He chased me endlessly, flying me out to California. Can you see me back then, in Hollywood? I about gave your grandmother a heart attack. Come to think of it, may be what killed her."

"That's not true," Caddy said.

"Who's to say?"

"She had cancer."

"They never did like your father," Jean said. "But you know that. You remember how awful the holidays were? Remember how she used to hide your daddy's Jack Daniel's and cigarettes and turn her nose at all his stories about being on the set with Burt and making those racing movies?"

"I remember you talking about *Cannonball Run.*"

Jean nodded. "I once smoked a joint with Jack Elam and Adrienne Barbeau."

"Mom."

"Well, I did."

Caddy rolled her eyes. "I think Jamey is in trouble."

"This have something to do with the Bundren girl?"

"No, ma'am."

"Oh, Lord. What did he do now?"

"Nothing," Caddy said. She placed her head into her hands. "Why would you say it like that?"

"Is it another woman?"

"No," Caddy said, knowing she'd said it too harshly. Jean was silent. When Caddy looked up from her hands, Jason was balancing himself on top of the swing set. Caddy raced over to him, telling him to get his butt down this instant, pointing to the ground. Jason smiled and leapt down into her arms. Not for a moment did Jason think she wouldn't be waiting to catch him.

Caddy walked back and took a seat by her mother on the bench. The lake was still and smooth, oaks and old pines reflected off the surface. A couple old men were way out in a johnboat, fishing for crappie.

"Some men came to see him today," Caddy said.

"About what?"

"I don't know," Caddy said. "But they scared the hell out of me. One of them punched Jamey in the stomach."

"What did Jamey say?"

"He said not to ask and not to tell Quinn."

"Oh, hell."

"Momma, please," she said.

"Well, it sounds to me like he's gone and gotten himself into some more trouble."

"More trouble?" Caddy asked. "How could he get in *more*? What happened before was a lie."

Jean bit her lip some more. She nodded, holding back whatever it was she wanted to say.

"Go on," Caddy said. "Say it."

Jean shook her head, pulling the paperback and a pack of cigarettes from her purse.

"I'm worried," Caddy said.

"Talk to Quinn."

"I told you, I can't."

"You can't stop some men from being stupid," she said. "A particular kind of man will run just about the time he's feeling settled. They're all like that."

"Oh, Momma," Caddy said, standing, whistling for Jason to come on. "Just who are we talking about again?"

One year on the job and Quinn had finally gotten things settled in his office. He'd finally had the painted letters for SHERIFF HAMP BECKETT scraped from the door and replaced with his name. On his wall, he'd hung a photo of his platoon after they'd hoisted the flag at Haditha Dam. There was also a framed flag that his friend Colonel George Reynolds had presented him from Camp Spann in AFG, and old photos of Quinn fishing with his uncle and a couple more of Quinn with Jason. Lillie had once asked if he had any pictures of his father. Quinn had just shook his head and said, "Not anymore."

Quinn opened his door and walked out to the gun rack. He unlocked the safety bar and pulled a Remington 12-gauge from the wall. He was locking up the rack when Ophelia Bundren walked in from the front desk, Mary Alice not even giving him a warning.

"You got a minute?"

"Just about to take a ride," Quinn said.

"Expecting trouble?"

Quinn shook his head. "Nope, just checking it out," he said. "Got a couple new guns in last week. Most of these guns were a lot older than me."

"Fresh guns?"

"Something like that."

Quinn walked to his office and held his door wide. Ophelia, looking awkward in a black skirt and blazer with nametag attached, took a seat. She nodded to the open door, and Quinn closed it.

"That will really get people talking," she said.

"Are you hearing that, too?"

"I guess Jericho doesn't have a hell of a lot else to do."

"Heard we may be getting a new pizza place, too."

"Big-time," she said. She smiled at Quinn, and Quinn smiled back. He sat at the edge of his desk, shotgun lying crossways behind him, Beretta attached to his belt.

"How'd it feel?" Ophelia said, looking at the neatly hung pictures.

"Combat?"

"No," Ophelia said. "Being so far away from home."

"You get used to it," Quinn said. "After the second or third time, it's all the same."

"You get to know many locals out on patrols?" she said. "Sheepherders and kids. Winning hearts and minds."

"Not really our job," Quinn said, moving

the gun slightly.

"What did you do?"

"I guess it was sort of like housecleaning," he said. "Making it safe for someone to move in and do their jobs."

"Winning hearts and minds."

Quinn nodded. "Of a kind."

Ophelia took a quick breath, her knees together, black department-store shoes set close together. "I found someone who can help us," she said. "There's a man who saw what happened that night. With Jamey. He saw him arguing with my sister. He says he saw Jamey chasing her down the highway."

"Ophelia?"

She nodded, hands in lap.

"Dixon was convicted and spent time in prison for killing your sister," he said. "He can't be tried again. He was pardoned. That's it. It's over."

"I'm not bringing this stuff up to get Dixon. I'm doing this for Caddy. You do realize how much time she and Jason are spending at that phony church? You do realize that Dixon is living with them?"

Quinn set his jaw. He nodded.

"I want you to meet with this man," Ophelia said. "You get him to talk to Caddy and tell her what he saw."

"Doesn't matter. She won't listen."

"My insides were ripped away when my sister died," Ophelia said. "Dixon in jail was the only thing that let me sleep and breathe, and now the son of a bitch is out and is the town hero. Jesus, Quinn."

Quinn set his boots on the floor and walked to Ophelia and put his hand on her shoulder. She was sitting just as still and proper but was now crying. Not much, just a little bit, more shaking than anything.

"OK."

"You'll meet with him?"

"If that's what you want."

Ophelia wiped her eyes. "Sure," she said. "Please."

"But I already know," Quinn said. "Caddy believes what she wants."

"You can't bury what's inside of you forever," she said. "That rage will come out. He still has it in him. I see the way he looks at me."

"Has he threatened you?"

"It's more in the way he stares."

"He does that again, and you let me know."

Ophelia nodded. "Just what we need, you beating the hell out of Dixon for me," she said, sort of laughing. "That will really get people talking about us. Half the town is already planning on our wedding."

"Rather hear about you planning a wedding for me than something else."

"I always figured to see you the other way," she said. "I have helped bury eight boys from here. I kept on waiting for you."

"Sorry to disappoint you."

Ophelia Bundren gave Quinn a very serious look, pulling her dark hair from her face. Her eyes were very large and brown; they didn't speak for a few moments. "You could never do that, Quinn Colson."

She left the door open and walked away. Ten seconds later, Lillie poked her head in the office and said, "Y'all have a quickie?"

Quinn stared at her. He nodded. "Yep."

"I knew it."

Quinn waited for whatever it was that Lillie wanted.

"Just got a call from the sheriff in Monroe," Lillie said. "They found that cook from Eupora."

"And the money?"

"Didn't find much on him," Lillie said. "Someone had shot the bastard in the center of the head and dumped his ass in the back of a '68 Chevelle."

"OK."

"Aren't you gonna ask about that Chevelle?"

"Sure."

130

"Stolen maybe a mile from Parchman Farm," Lillie said. "Owner of it was knocked in the head and tied up by some convict named Esau Davis. Ever heard of him?"

12

Quinn drove with Lillie out to the Monroe County line, where they met the sheriff at a defunct gas station right off the highway. He was an old man named Cecil Locke, who had been in law enforcement longer than Quinn had been alive. He wore a uniform not unlike the one Andy Griffith used to wear on the television show, stiff and khaki, completed with a fresh shave and pomaded hair. He greeted them both with a handshake, asking Lillie about her daughter and what could be expected in the next football season for Ole Miss. Most people knew Lillie had been a star shooter for the Ole Miss rifle team.

"So we got a couple convicts loose?" Lillie said.

"Three," Locke said. "Third one is named Richard Green." He slipped some reading glasses from his pocket and read a printout. "He had four years into a twenty-year stretch for manslaughter. This was his second visit to Parchman. Once for statutory rape and for armed robbery."

"And the other two?" Quinn asked.

A couple trucks blew past on the highway. Dirt and gravel scattered.

"Esau Davis would be the leader of the three," Locke said. "Or should be. Six-four, weighs two-fifty, and has bright red hair. Y'all should have gotten his picture. He looks like that fella selling Bounty paper towels. He was in for ninety years for two armed robberies and killing a security guard at a Best Buy outside Jackson. Don't know much about the black man, Joseph Magee, other than folks call him Bones. Uglier than dog shit, and good at stealing cars. Of course, this only what they got caught doing. Sure they done a lot worse."

"They killed Mr. Highsmith in Eupora," Lillie said.

"Looks that way," Locke said. "Real pretty car. Man who owned it drove right over from Tutwiler, got down on his knees and started talking to it like it were a baby. Mad as hell when he saw all that blood in the trunk. Didn't matter, sat and waited for the state folks to process it out and took it home. Y'all have any other car thefts around the truck stop?"

"No, sir," Quinn said. "If they stole a car in Tibbehah County, it hasn't been reported."

"Can't think of another reason for them doubling back if they were headed east and out of state."

"You see anything that ties them to this area?" Quinn said.

Locke shook his head. "Nope," he said. "First thing I checked. Just got off the phone to the superintendent at Parchman. He was madder than hell. He's shut down the whole prison. Everybody inside is on lockdown; all privileges are being withheld. I can tell you if those boys get turned back to prison, they won't find no welcoming committee."

The windows were broken out in the garage; an old Sinclair Oil sign hung crooked from a pole. A logging truck with an empty trailer rattled past.

"Anything else?" Lillie said.

"Superintendent said Davis and Magee were buds," he said. "Doesn't show up on the records anywhere, but it seemed to him they'd known each other before. He said some federal man had come to talk to both of them maybe two years back about a few bank jobs. But he didn't get nowhere."

"Did he know much about the jobs?" Lillie said.

"I got a call into a Fed in Oxford," Locke said. "I hear something of interest and I'll shout."

"I bet they got some family in this area," Quinn said. "Only reason I can think of them sticking around."

"Or maybe they left something special?" Lillie said.

"Good to know about those bank jobs," Quinn said.

Locke nodded. They all shook hands. The old man hobbled back to his car, hung on his door, and shouted to Lillie, "Can you really hit a half-dozen clay pigeons before they hit the ground?"

"Want to see?" Lillie said.

"Next time I'm in Jericho," Locke said, tipping his hat. "It would be a pleasure."

"Why don't we just go out to that bass pond now," Dickie Green said. "Get it over with. I like this place, it's sweet as hell, but I'd just as soon head on before someone finds us."

"The hunting lodge belongs to Esau's friend," Becky said. "Hadn't you been listening?"

"Sure," Dickie said. "But sounds like you

is coming into this conversation kind of late."

Esau left them talking to each other like that by the swimming pool while he and Bones drove out into Jericho. It was nearing four o'clock. They got stuck behind a school bus heading into town from the high school and nearly tried to pass when Bones pointed out a state trooper hidden up in some brush. Esau kept it on forty all the way into town, hugging the Square, the Laundromat, and the offices to a newspaper. There was an old movie theater all boarded up and a check delay business. All shithole towns had a check delay run by the greedy bastards. Before he got sent back to prison, Esau lived off that shit, getting nearly twenty percent stolen for an advance on his pay. About the best days he'd known before robbing banks was when he had his truck running and didn't have to walk up the road to buy beer and a Little Debbie snack cake for supper.

"Well, hell," Bones said.

"What?"

"Ain't that her?"

"Who?"

"Dixon's woman?"

"Yes, sir," Esau said. "Ain't you the eagle eye."

"I never forget a tight ass," Bones said.

Esau slowed the Tundra as they took a third lap on the Town Square, watching the woman they'd seen at Dixon's church. She was holding the hand of a little black boy and some shopping bags, and walking into a flower shop. Esau found a parking spot and killed the engine but left on the radio. The truck's owner had kept some good old David Allan Coe in the CD player, "If That Ain't Country."

"Pass me a beer," Esau said.

Bones stuck one in his palm from a foam cooler they'd bought at a bait shop. The gun they'd stolen sat in the folds of the seat between them. They both lay back in their seats, sipping beer until Dixon's woman and the black boy came back out. The boy balanced a big display of flowers, and they walked clockwise on the Square to an old Honda and drove off. Esau kicked the truck into gear and followed, keeping the Busch between his legs. He punched up the lighter and set a cigarette in his lips, damn well feeling like a human being again.

The woman drove north of the town on Main Street, passing by a good amount of big old pretty houses with big old pretty porches, many of them with those historic markers out front saying they hadn't been burned during the War. Esau figured there must have been a mess of rich folks in this old town before it all turned to shit.

The Honda turned left down a road called Ithaca and stopped in front of a smaller house, a brick ranch with flat boxwoods and holly. He kept driving, window open, hand with cigarette hanging out the window. The little boy ran out of the car with the flowers, the blond woman following slower, closing the car door and turning her head just in time to see Esau and catch his eye.

Esau just gave her a simple nod. She looked like she'd just swallowed some glass.

"Back to the hunt club?" Bones said.

"Yep," Esau said. "I'm out of beer."

"What if that truck's not there?"

"I've been thinking on that," Esau said. "Figure nobody likes to leave empty-handed."

"Dixon doesn't look like he's got shit."

"He owes us," Esau said.

"I think Dixon always figured it was the other way around."

Esau felt his face fill with blood. "That was five years ago," he said. "He done what he thought was right."

"Still figure he might think this is calling it square."

"He does that," Esau said, "and I'll choke every inch of life out his ass."

Bones was quiet. He sipped some beer as the hills raised up out of the flat farming land and curved up to where rich men could afford to drink whiskey and raise hell for the fun of it. He turned up the stereo, more David Allan Coe to fuel his thoughts.

13

Quinn drove back to the farm and lay down on the made-up iron bed. The front door was open, screen door letting in a cool breeze, the evening smelling of new flowers and damp earth. Hondo knew how to let himself out and use his nose to let himself in, the door thwacking upon his return. Quinn hadn't even taken off his boots, lying back in the big, cool room and tipping the brim of his baseball hat over his eyes to shield the light. He had two hours before he'd be back on duty. In the Army, he'd learned to sleep whenever possible. He could stick a rucksack under his head and sleep at the edge of an airfield or nearly to the minute he'd rappel from a Black Hawk. He was nearly asleep when he heard a car pull into the drive.

Hondo was on his feet and back out the screen door. He didn't bark. If it was someone he didn't know, there'd be much barking. Hondo was good that way.

The door opened and feet in the hall and a knock on the door.

Quinn lifted up the brim of his ball cap to see Anna Lee standing in the light of the door. A bright light shined from behind her and through her long strawberry hair, blurring her face a bit.

"Don't you have to be up in an hour?" she said.

"Yep."

"At least you got to sleep all day."

"Yep," Quinn said. He did not move.

Anna Lee took a seat on the edge of the bed, springs creaking. She ran a hand over his chest and sighed. "I brought you some supper," she said. "You can take it with you."

"What'd you make?"

"Lasagna," she said. "I made a little salad, too. And some garlic rolls."

"Appreciate it."

Anna Lee wore tight Levi's and a long white T-shirt under a thin yellow cardigan. The cardigan had holes on one elbow. Quinn remembered it from back in high school. He couldn't recall all the times he'd found it in the back of his truck. Why she didn't give that thing away, he had no idea.

"Did you sleep in your clothes?" she said.

"We got some escaped convicts headed this way," Quinn said. "Not to mention I was up late tracking down a dangerous turnip thief."

She rubbed the flat of her hand on his chest some more. He caught her at her wrist and pulled her close, his arm slipping behind her back.

"Come here."

She held firm and stayed quiet.

"I'm awake."

"Luke's coming back," she said, sort of just blurting it out. "Tonight. He'll be here until Monday."

Quinn nodded and thought for a moment. "Well. You are his wife."

"You don't have to be nasty."

"I'm just stating the truth."

Quinn closed his eyes. A cool breeze shot through the center of the old house, the chain on Hondo's neck jingling. He held on to her hand for several moments. She finally squeezed back, leaning down and kissing him on his chin.

"When can I see you?" he said.

"I think we need to slow things down."

"I was waiting for that," he said. "Maybe tomorrow we both can get a really good sermon and help us all figure it out."

"It's the way it is," she said. "It's what we got."

"This isn't usual," he said.

"You ever think maybe we're just telling ourselves that?"

Quinn held her hand. "Nope."

In Caddy's living room, Jamey sang and played his Martin, with her Uncle Van on second guitar and J.T., the local master of auto body repair, on a fat acoustic bass. All three men wore baseball caps and T-shirts and jeans, kitchen chairs huddled together, cords strung from two of the guitars into amplifiers. Even Jean had come along and was harmonizing on "The Model Church," tapping her white tennis shoes and sipping that rancid white wine.

Jason lay on his little belly by the amplifiers, head in hand, legs kicking back and forth to the music, as he worked on a coloring book.

Music filled the wood-paneled room that hadn't changed much since it had belonged to her grandmother. Same two couches Caddy had gotten out of storage, a leather recliner, and an antique standup piano. There were old-lady doilies on headrests, a glass case in the corner with figurines of cats and ladies with parasols, and lots of old frames of family members she'd never even met. The entire house made her feel like she lived in a museum.

"Again," Jamey said.

"Hadn't y'all practiced enough?" Caddy said, smiling.

Jamey grinned. "Again."

And he sang on, foot thumping, about walking through that crowded old church, finding that pew to hear the trumpet voice of the preacher and that angel choir. She knew he'd worked up a whole sermon around the song, and would say how a model church was made up of real people, not just a physical space of grandeur or stiff traditions put upon us. He'd talk about Jesus walking and preaching in sandals and robes, bringing his good news to whoever would listen, not caring where you lived, who your people were, or where you'd been. Jamey talked about giving away all you owned and following the real path.

As Jamey strummed and harmonized with Uncle Van, he winked at her. Van Colson, fat and compact, with a mustache and goatee, had his eyes closed all corny as he played and hummed. To Caddy, he looked just like a redneck Buddha wrapped in an XL Mossy Oak tee.

"Jamey?" Caddy said. "Can I talk to you a

minute?"

Jamey lifted his eyes from where he played with a capo on the guitar's neck and nodded. Caddy went on into the kitchen to unload the Piggly Wiggly sacks, stocking their shelves. She thought about frying up some thin pork chops tonight, wishing it didn't take so damn long to make mashed potatoes. Hell, the peas she could microwave.

Jamey walked into the little kitchen, kissed her on the cheek, and helped himself to a cold beer, reaching his arm around her and hugging her tight. "You never told me your Uncle Van could sing."

"Maybe 'cause I never heard him."

"Never?"

"Does doing karaoke to the Marshall Tucker Band count?"

"Sure," Jamey said. "I caught him humming while we were doing some painting. When I complimented him, he said he could play some guitar, too."

"Go figure," Caddy said. "I never thought Uncle Van did much but watch wrestling and smoke grass."

"We all have our talents."

"His karaoke wasn't too bad," she said. "He really tore up 'Can't You See' at the Southern Star."

The wind had started to lift a little outside, the small trees in her backyard twisting left and right. A sudden darkness covered the sun, and rain started to hit the roof and fall in sheets off her back porch.

"Jamey, I saw those men again."

Jamey looked at her as if he was saying "What men?" without giving the words. He just waited for Caddy to speak again.

"They followed me and Jason back home to my momma's house."

"You sure it was them?"

Caddy nodded. "That one with red hair looks like he should be swinging from a vine."

"They were looking for me."

"You were at the church," Caddy said. "Your truck was there. Those sonsabitches wanted to know where I lived."

"They follow you back here?"

"I drove around to make sure they didn't. But they know where Momma's house is. I think we should warn her or something. Jamey, who are they? Quit tryin' to bullshit me."

"No bullshit," he said. "They're just men wanting a handout."

"What's that mean?"

"Just what I said."

"Son of a bitch," Caddy said. It looked

like night outside now, although it wasn't more than five o'clock. She turned back, hearing the good-time laughter of J.T., Uncle Van, and Momma out in the salon. Real knee-slappin' stuff.

"Come on, baby," Jamey said.

"I trust you," she said. "Always have. But don't bring my son into whatever kind of deal this is."

"Ain't no deal," Jamey said, sliding into his playful country twang he could put on or take off.

He wrapped his arms around her waist and nuzzled his chin over her shoulder as she turned. "Those boys were just trying to scare you," he said. "I find them, I'll give them a talking-to."

"I don't want Jason to ever be scared. I don't want them nowhere around us."

"Like I said, those men were with me in Parchman," he said. "They heard about my church and see I'm doing well and they want a piece of it. It's that simple. I offered them a place to stay, a way to work for food. But that's not how they see the world. They believe that I and everybody else owes them something."

Caddy studied the reflection of the two of them together at the sink in the little picture window. She smiled despite herself. "Don't get hurt."

"I won't."

"Or go all redneck on me."

"I can be persuasive."

"I can call Quinn," she said.

"And him learn about a couple convicts hanging out by The River?" Jamey said. "I'd rather for that not to happen."

She turned and faced him, both his hands wrapping her. "I do love that hymn y'all were singing," Caddy said.

"Uncle Van did say he can do a killer 'Heard It in a Love Song.' "

"How would that sound in church?" she said.

"Not too bad," he said. "Hell, why not? Who made up all these traditions, anyway? It sure didn't happen in Jesus' time. My Jesus would dig Marshall Tucker more than some slick contemporary."

"And Uncle Van, too?"

"Especially Uncle Van."

The house shuddered a bit from the wind and rain, bringing a strange safe comfort to her. She placed the pork chops in a bowl to thaw and heated the skillet, while the songs in the parlor started again. Everything would be just fine. She was almost sure of it.

14

"What the hell I don't understand is how this son of a bitch knew about this dang armored car if he wadn't in on the job," Dickie Green said.

Esau eyed him, tossed his cigarette butt, and took a breath. "I told him."

The men stood down in a valley about four miles from the hunt lodge. Dickie had found an outbuilding for a construction company with a big-ass back bulldozer and a trailer that would hitch up fine on the Toyota. He wasn't sure if the Toyota could haul it, but Dickie said it'd be plenty of power either way. Power enough in the Tundra and power enough in the CAT to pull out the damned Wells Fargo car. Bones and Becky were going to meet them at the pond with some chains.

"That doesn't make a fucking bit of sense to me," Dickie said, swilling a Coors, stifling a belch. "I mean, shit. You and Bones were the ones who robbed this thing."

"Yep."

"And y'all executed a perfect fucking job," Dickie said. "Y'all didn't get caught for it and for them other jobs, but got nailed for what?"

"Robbing a Best Buy."

"How'd you get caught for it?" Dickie said, tossing the bottle over his shoulder in a big mess of pea gravel. The bottle shattered. Didn't matter, there wasn't jack around this place for miles.

"I forgot to get Becky's little sister an iPod and ran back in."

"You shitting me?"

"Nope," Esau said. "She liked listening to that Britney Spears."

"Man, that pussy will trip you up."

"I'd appreciate you not talking about my woman like that in my presence."

"I apologize," Dickie said. "But you got to admit it's kind of funny."

The outbuilding and the gravel pits were situated at the dead center of the small valley. Up and around the bowl dotted with big oaks and old-growth pine, lightning flashes zipped up and around, only the tops of the trees bucking kind of nervous. The thunder was sparse but powerful.

"So, why'd you do it?" Dickie said. He'd

150

taken to wearing clothes he'd found inside the lodge. He had on camo pants and a black-and-red flannel worn open with the sleeves cut off, his small, tattooed belly hanging out the front.

"Do what?"

"Tell Dixon about where to find the money?"

"He was supposed to get it when he got out," Esau said. "He was from here. Knew people. And he got to keep a third of it and use the rest to get me and Bones a good lawyer."

"What'd he say about that?" Dickie said. "When y'all found him and probably made him shit his drawers."

"He said he didn't want to have nothing to do with it," Esau said. "He said that plan was over when he got pardoned. Said our plan only meant something if he'd gotten out five years from now like we'd talked about."

"Were y'all like queer lovers or something?"

Esau knocked Dickie to the ground with the back of his hand. Dickie cackling, laughing, and bleeding just the same on the ground. "Well, good goddamn. I was just funnin' with you. Hell."

"Me and him had a deal."

"I seen one boy in my pod who'd take it in any hole for a dollar," Dickie said. "He wasn't queer. He just was addicted to eating candy bars and sweet things. He'd sure do anything for one of them Butterfingers."

Dickie laughed and wiped the blood off his lip.

The thunder came again, the tops of the trees moving. The sun had set, but the sky was even more of a full black now, almost like smoke blocking out the sun. It was like nothing else existed outside that little valley, making the world hell if he was stuck with Dickie Green for the rest of eternity.

"What on God's green earth could someone like Jamey Dixon do for you?" Dickie said. "I don't recall him doing shit but talking to us a few times about Jesus and the apostles. He always looked like one of them Nashville fags to me. Like Keith Urban or another one of them boys who don't know shit about being country but got to tell you all about how they is."

"What if I said he saved my life?"

"I'd say that sounds like bullshit."

"He gave me work."

"How?"

"He had pull with the guards."

"Shit," Dickie said. "Hey, can I have a smoke?"

Esau gave him one fresh from the pack. Dickie fired it up.

"Gave my life some purpose," Esau said. "I was wasting away on that bunk. I walk from bed to chow to sitting there watching that fifteen-inch television set, trying to know whether to be a Gangster Disciple or Crip. Time is hell. I hate the smell. I washed in vinegar last night, and Becky says it's still on me."

"Funny, before I got to jail, I thought those gangs were just for the blacks."

"There was one guard, dull-eyed and dumber than a fucking stick," Esau said. "He'd work me out in those fields. Didn't matter if it was legal or not, he did it for sport. Cotton. Corn. He'd run and run me. Keep me in close at Unit 37 before they closed it. One night I figure it got up to a hundred and forty degrees."

"And so John the Baptist got you another ticket?" Dickie said.

"Something like that."

"That how you come to work at the canteen and in the restaurant for families?"

"Yep."

"So you got all the bubble gum and Fritos you could stand?"

"He gave me purpose," Esau said. "You know anything about that? That guard

153

wanted to kill me for sport. I just wouldn't die."

"So why not leave it all for the preacher?" Dickie said. "He did that much."

" 'Cause we had a deal," Esau said. "Plain as anything. We even shook on it."

"You know what they call a handshake in prison?"

Esau watched the dark clouds cross the rim of the valley to the west. A splattering of a fast rain on leaves, even harder, maybe hail.

"Second base."

Dickie laughed at that, showing his bad blackened teeth, flannel shirt blowing about him like a damn cape. "Ah, hell. Get a sense of humor."

"You get that dozer up on that trailer," he said. "We ain't got much time till that shit-storm gets here. And I'd just as soon not work in the mud."

"Where we live, brother," Dickie said and hopped up in the cabin of the CAT with a screwdriver and a set of needle-nose pliers.

Quinn was awake at 1630 and pulled on some PT gear and hit the fire roads and deer trails on the ridge by his farm. The trails zigzagged for nearly five miles up through scrub pines and an old dead pond where he used to play as a kid. Hondo jogged at his side, Hondo being the lucky one not carrying a rucksack loaded down with fifty pounds of sand on his back. Quinn had done his best to keep his body sharp since leaving the Regiment; softness of body led to softness of mind. And as an old sergeant had said to him, it's easier to maintain than get it back. He didn't use weights, mainly sticking to what he knew. Push-ups, pull-ups, and flutter kicks. He had hung a heavy bag from an old oak tree in his side yard to practice some Muay Thai he'd learned from a Bangkok-born RI.

He finished up the run on the heavy bag, took a shower, and within fifteen minutes was back at the sheriff's office, a pot of coffee brewing at Mary Alice's desk.

"You must bleed Colombian," Lillie said.

"Probably."

"Regret taking the night?"

"Nope."

"Didn't want to call you out to the Rebel," Lillie said. "But you said any business with Johnny Stagg was worth a call."

"And now it's a homicide."

"Lovely."

"I'm supposed to meet with Ophelia Bundren in twenty minutes over at the funeral home," Quinn said. "Want to join me?"

"Wow. You really mean it?"

"I'd feel better if you came along," Quinn said.

"Look less like a date?"

"Being that funeral homes are such romantic places," Quinn said.

"Maybe they are to Ophelia Bundren," Lillie said, reaching for the pot and pouring a cup. Lillie smiled and handed the cup to Quinn, who walked back to his office. "OK. OK. What's she got now?"

"Says she's got a witness to her sister's killing," Quinn said, turning at the door. "May be worth it to get on record."

"How many ways can you explain it doesn't matter anymore?"

"Just in case we need it."

"You worried about Caddy?"

"Are you coming or not?"

Lillie stood there and stared.

"Sometimes I think you're confused who is in charge here," Quinn said, with a slight grin.

Lillie saluted and headed back to her office. "Roger that, Sergeant."

15

They sat together in a room reserved for grieving families, with plenty of Biblical verses in gold frames, fake flowers, and neat folded tracts on grief. Ophelia, her mother, and brother tight-knit in folding chairs with Quinn and Lillie. A young skinny man in one of those Ed Hardy shirts — this one with a skull with flaming eyes wearing a top hat — joined them. He had scruffy facial hair and wore his ball cap cocked at an angle. Quinn used restraint to not remove the hat from his head or at least straighten it in the proper direction.

The man's name was Dustin. He was twenty-eight, with three kids, and unemployed. Within two seconds, he blamed his problems on the president of the United States.

Lillie took a deep breath.

"So you saw Miss Adelaide that night?" Quinn said.

"Uh-huh."

No *yes, sir.* No *yes.* Just kind of a grunt.

Dustin scratched his chin. Ophelia and her brother and mother waited. Her mother was portly and dressed in black, lots of thick makeup and dyed black hair. Ophelia's brother was just a kid, still in high school, wearing his Tibbehah Wildcats letterman's jacket. Quinn had heard he was set to play quarterback in the fall. He must've been about nine or ten when his sister died.

"What did you see?" Lillie said.

"I saw Jamey Dixon," Dustin said, eyes flicking to the face of Ophelia and her mother and then back down at his hands. "I saw him run out after her. They were cussing at each other. She was running from him. Screaming."

"And what else?"

"That was it," Dustin said. "I was trying to get to work. People had jobs back then."

"Where'd you work?" Quinn said.

"Ammunition factory, before it moved to China."

Quinn nodded. "You tell anyone?"

"I didn't know who it was," he said. "She had blood on her face. Screaming and shit."

"And you didn't stop?" Quinn asked.

"Ain't none of my business."

"And you didn't see it in the newspaper?"

158

Lillie asked. "Later?"

"I don't read no paper."

"Or hear it in church?" Quinn said.

He shook his head. "I saw this thing on Facebook about it," he said. "Miss Bundren trying to collect names of people who want to see Jamey Dixon get what he deserves."

"You know Dixon?" Quinn said. "Is that it?"

"Hell no," he said. "I wouldn't piss on the son of a bitch."

Mrs. Bundren dropped her eyes into her hands. Ophelia's brother just nodded, agreeing with the sentiment.

"So after seeing this thing on Facebook, you decided to be bold and come forward?" Lillie said.

"I just wrote that I seen him chasing a woman," Dustin said. "Hell, I didn't know it was her. But I knew it was him. I knew she was scared. It's the same man; don't tell me it ain't."

Quinn shook his head and held up his right hand.

"He knew it was my sister after we showed him some pictures," Ophelia said.

"You two getting in touch through the Facebook page?"

Ophelia nodded, not wearing work clothes today but a black-and-white flowered dress

159

with black leggings and high-heeled dress boots. Her hair was pulled back into a dark ponytail.

"You said this was the day she died?" Quinn said.

"Ah-huh. Yeah."

"How do you know?" Quinn said.

"I recalled I was late for work that day 'cause I'd been over to Tupelo for the Elvis Fest," Dustin said. "I got real tore up drinking and dancing."

"Can't figure out why you wouldn't be a model witness," Lillie said.

" 'Cause they didn't know about me," Dustin said. "Shit. Ain't you listenin'?"

"Yes, sir," Lillie said. "I am."

"So what can you do, Sheriff?" Mrs. Bundren asked. She was wide-eyed and attentive, a pair of reading glasses hung around her powdered neck.

Quinn looked to Lillie. He leaned in, back bent, hands clasped in front of him. "Dixon has been pardoned."

"We want everyone to know what he's done," Mrs. Bundren said. "Our Facebook page has nearly two thousand members. It's an education."

"Yes, ma'am."

"He'll do it again."

Quinn nodded.

160

"And we wanted you to know most of all," Ophelia said. "You said you wanted to keep up with Dixon's moves since he got out. Every time I hear him explain he's innocent, I want to throw up."

"I don't blame you," Lillie said.

"But wouldn't what Dustin here says make a difference if Dixon starts to be a nuisance?" Mrs. Bundren said. "Wouldn't it mean something to the parole board? He still has to report to them."

"More of a technicality," Lillie said. "He is legally pardoned."

The Bundrens were not pleased. Dustin looked fidgety and confused.

"Something will happen," Ophelia's brother said. "He's gonna get pushed, and when that happens he's gonna go batshit crazy."

Quinn stayed silent.

"Only way he'll get caught," the brother said.

Dustin looked at Lillie with narrow-set eyes and said, "Can I go? I got to meet some folks at the bar."

Quinn nodded. The group didn't speak until he walked away.

"That stupid church of his is opening tomorrow," Ophelia said. "Can you believe that? He'll be talking innocence the whole time there, too."

"Probably."

"You have to do something," Ophelia said. "I don't want y'all to be sitting in this room until it's y'all's time."

"And when's our time?" Lillie said.

Hell, the woman just couldn't help herself.

"I only know it's not for Dixon to decide," Ophelia said.

"Sure as shit," said the brother.

Becky should've at least put on a decent pair of pants. But hell no. She stood there in Daisy Dukes and cowboy boots, a man's white dress shirt knotted up over her red bikini top. The idea was to do this thing at night and not to get noticed. Esau just hoped it would keep on raining. More rain and less moon.

"Can't you dress right?" Esau said.

"I thought we were going to a swimming hole," she said.

"We ain't swimming," Esau said. "Dickie's swimming."

"But it's raining; ain't no reason in changing out of my suit."

"Whatever you say, darling," Esau said. "Hook up them chains, Bones."

Bones nodded at Esau and dragged a hundred-foot section of thick chains up to the trailer and the bulldozer. Dickie was already monkeying on the back of the trailer, stoop-backed and telling him to wait a good goddamn second for him to get the machine off. "And then you hook it up," Dickie said. "Shit, you don't do it while it's still parked."

"I wish everybody was as smart as you, Dickie," Bones said. "The world would be a better place."

Dickie pulled off his shirt and pants, standing there in the rain in a white pair of Fruit of the Looms, and said, "You bet your black ass."

He hopped into the CAT, scruffy, wiry, and tattooed, cigarette hanging out of his mouth, and turned the engine over. Dickie drove it off, let down the stabilizers, left the dozer idling, and said, "Now you hook them up, geniuses."

Bones dragged the chain to the edge of the pond, the two chains having a decent-sized hook on the end. Becky walked up to Esau and handed him a diving mask. "All they had at the Walmart," she said. "Got a dolphin and starfish painted on the glass. Real cute."

Bones had gotten the flares, twisting the cap and igniting one. He handed one to Dickie at the edge of the pond. The pond

163

was only maybe a couple acres, too deep for catfish; probably just some blue-gills and bass. Esau watched Dickie wade on into the muddy water, placing the kids' mask over his face, holding a flare and taking a breath. "I'll come back for the chains once I find what we're looking for."

"You sure you don't want to put on a pair of pants?" Bones said.

Dickie turned back to him. Rain falling harder now.

"Why's that?"

"In case you got some piranhas or some shit down there," Bones said, grinning a crooked smile. "One of them might think your pecker is a worm."

Dickie grabbed himself between the legs and told Bones that ain't no one complained yet.

He took a deep breath and disappeared under the water.

Bones popped a cigarette in the corner of his mouth, leaning against the truck. "Knew that boy never been with a woman."

Becky had untied the man's shirt and was using it to cover her head, hands holding it out like a canopy. There was wind and it was as warm and salty as the Gulf. "Y'all sure this is the place?"

Bones nodded. Esau was quiet. Damn if

Dickie hadn't come up yet. Be a shame if he'd gone and drowned himself.

"How do you know?" she said.

Esau pointed to the spot where the old county highway, named Horse Barn Road on the map, intersected Highway 9. "Right at that T is where Bones sat waiting in that Dodge diesel with a cattle guard. How far back did you make a run?"

"Hundred yards."

Esau nodded.

"I was running the John Deere with a Bush Hog, making the car slow down, keep him running about twenty, thirty miles per hour. We had timed the sonsabitches down when they took a piss."

"Why didn't they just pass you?" Becky said.

" 'Cause I had a Bush Hog on the back, making sure I was taking up the whole road. I mean, hell, we didn't pick this spot by accident."

"And y'all kept him slow and easy till Bones comes at him full tilt and knocks that armored car on its ass?" Becky said.

Esau nodded. "That's about the size of it."

"Y'all didn't think it would skid all the way into that pond?"

"Didn't really skid," Bones said. "It more

165

kind of tumbled over and over and then finally rolled twice before it settled at the bottom of the pond. I hit that car right in the sweet spot. T-boned it just right."

"OK," Becky said, chewing gum and talking under her man's-shirt canopy, arms stretched wide. "Then how come they didn't find it? That's what I don't understand. You know they got one of them satellite things on it."

"Not ten years ago," Esau said.

They'd nearly forgotten about Dickie Green as his dumb bald head popped up from the far edge of the pond, the reddish glow of the glare ringing where he was treading water. He gave a thumbs-up. "Found it," he said, yelling. "Found it."

Esau winked at Becky, walked to the muddy edge of the pond, and started pulling the chains into the water, walking onto the slick, silty bottom, nearly up to his neck, Bones feeding him the chains, till he met Dickie out there, still treading water.

"You get that bumper?" Esau said.

"Naw," Dickie said. "I figure I'd just pull it out myself. What the fuck you think?"

Esau handed over a length of chain so heavy that it nearly took Dickie full to the bottom. Esau turned and marched back out of the water, trudging out onto the shore

166

with his boots heavy and thick with mud.

"Watch your pecker," Bones said. He chomped his big teeth together.

"Shut your black ass and toss me another flare," Dickie said.

Bones knocked the cap off another and fired it up. He laughed as he walked back to the Tundra and leaned against it. Esau reached into the Tundra for a half-pint of Jack Daniel's and took a good swallow. He passed the bottle to Bones and then from Bones to Becky. He trudged over to the backhoe and used its stabilizer to scrape his boots, and then checked the chains. A length of chain rattled and stretched down deep into the water. That son of a bitch must of have been underwater for nearly a goddamn minute.

"Must really be part fish," Bones said.

"We know most of him ain't human."

"He told me today that it was lucky he came around because black people always sink," Bones said. "Kind of wanted to shoot him."

"People been wanting to shoot Dickie his whole life," Esau said. "Reason he's the way he is."

"Maybe there's a time for that," Bones said.

Esau nodded.

"Y'all are just rotten," Becky said. "You're kidding, right?"

Dickie's head popped up, no flare but treading water and coming back to shore. "Burnt my fucking hand," he said. "Son of a bitch."

His hand was bleeding and bright red. Dickie clutched it to his body.

"You get it?" Esau said. "We ready or not?"

Dickie shook his head. "Hell no. I was right there. Nearly got the axle."

"Go back," Esau said.

"I can't," he said. "Ain't you listenin'?"

Esau pulled out the .357 and told Dickie if he didn't, he'd shoot him where he stood.

16

"I appreciate you coming," Ophelia said. "Even though it won't make a bit of difference to Dixon."

Quinn nodded. Lillie had left. And it was just him and Ophelia in the funeral home parking lot. The big Bundren sign — SERV-ING JERICHO SINCE 1958 — burned bright on the wet asphalt. There was a long black hearse parked inside a big portico to the left of the entrance. The air kind of swelled with rain and warm heat.

"I guess you think our family is going crazy," she said. "Wanting you to meet all these people."

"I know what you're trying to do," Quinn said. "And I appreciate it."

"You going to his church service tomorrow?" she asked.

"Nope."

"Are you going to talk more with Caddy?" she said. "Tell her what you heard?"

"I stopped a long time ago trying to tell my sister what to do."

"You know Caddy and I used to be real close," Ophelia said. "After you went in the Army. We had a lot of good times. Trips to Memphis and over to Ole Miss. We partied hard, Quinn. Stupid shit. Boys. A lot of stupid boys."

Quinn didn't say anything. Ophelia was doing that tight, nervous thing with her mouth, catching Quinn's eye really hard and then looking away.

"I want you to know I tried to help her," Ophelia said. "Your momma knows. I think what happened to Caddy should have happened to me."

"Caddy is a grown woman," Quinn said. "She made some bad choices."

"Your momma and I went up to Memphis about three years ago and found her living in an apartment off Mount Moriah. Nasty place. Must have been six girls living in one room. Knee-deep in trash and beer bottles. There were drugs just out in the open. Men coming in and out."

"I know you tried to bring her back."

Ophelia nodded.

"And she fought it," Quinn said.

Ophelia turned over her wrist and showed him a pair of diagonal scars. "Looks a lot

170

better now. It was a hell of a fight. Your sister has some real claws."

"But you tried," Quinn said. "That's more than me."

"You were on the other side of the world," she said. "What do they say about fighting that war? We could play it at home or on the road."

Quinn nodded.

"I don't want her back in that messed-up place in her head," Ophelia said. "When Dixon turns on her, I want her to know what he does to women. You think anything will help?"

"Nope."

"Can I ask you a very personal family question?"

Quinn nodded.

"Did she ever tell you about Jason?"

Quinn waited.

"About how she got pregnant?"

Quinn looked down and smiled. "I'm pretty sure I know how that stuff works."

"I mean, did she ever tell you about Jason's father?"

Quinn felt his blood run a little cold. He watched the long, broken highway stretching out from the funeral home and east over the Big Black River bridge. A semi rambled past them and disappeared over the river.

171

The old bridge had always looked like a rusted erector set to him. It should have been replaced twenty years ago.

"I asked her once," Ophelia said. "When she came back the first time. After Jason was born. And she wouldn't tell me."

"It doesn't matter."

"I got the feeling that she didn't know."

"I think that's pretty much the case," Quinn said. "What does it matter? Jason is part of us."

"But with Dixon," Ophelia said. "And that crazy church? Money and power? Caddy breaks too damn easy, Quinn."

He took a deep breath. Cars coming and going off the old bridge, bright lights shining up on the slick blacktop. Ophelia walked up close to him. She placed her palm flat over his chest, leaned in, and pressed her head close to him. Quinn stood still for a moment, hand coming up behind her and pulling her in, cupping her shoulder. The soft cotton dress felt comfortable and familiar.

"I think of Adelaide every day," Ophelia said. "It hurts less. But you never stop thinking of it."

Caddy dressed in front of a long oval mirror, slipping into a pair of weathered jeans and a slim-cut cowboy shirt. She brushed her hair to the left, the style easy to wash. Just about right for who she'd become. Two months ago, she'd walked right into the Mane Attraction, sat down in April's chair, and said take all this shit off. April, cocked hip and cigarette in hand, asked if she wanted it like that 'do Carrie Underwood had been sporting. *Take it all down as short as a boy's.* Caddy had smiled the whole time as her old self had been lopped off, ten-inch bleached strands falling onto the ground, April cutting up over the ears, nice long bangs and cut up on the neck.

Best part of the hair was that people looked at you differently, taking a moment to decide on if you were who they thought. And that long pause was sometimes all it took to be reconsidered.

She walked out of the bedroom and found Jason watching cartoons, already thirty minutes late for bed. Full dark and rainy outside. She turned off the television to groans and pushed him on into his bedroom. Jamey had gone back to The River, installing some amps and more strands of lights for tomorrow's service and laying out the bulletins in the makeshift pews and on hay bales. They'd be up at five a.m. to make sure that first service was a special one.

173

They planned to watch the sun rise.

She helped Jason change into his pajamas and turned on a lamp by his bedside table. The wind rattled the shutters of the old bungalow, and rain tapped at the glass. She picked up a copy of *King Arthur's Very Great Grandson* and lay next to him, reading about a boy who'd just turned six going out to fight dragons and Cyclops and a great manner of mythological beasts.

A car drove past, headlights sweeping through the house at the turn. The car idled for a long minute. Caddy got out from the bed and pulled back the curtains. The car idled for a moment longer and pulled away. She replaced the curtain.

Jamey would be home soon.

By the second book, Jason was asleep.

She turned out the table lamp and closed the door with a tight click. She tried Jamey, but he didn't answer, and when he didn't answer, she checked the window again.

The rain was steady as she walked back to her bedroom and reached for the 12-gauge she kept at the top of her closet. She checked the load — as her Uncle Hamp had taught her when they went hunting — and jacked in a round.

There was cold coffee, but she heated it up. Caddy sat on the couch in silence with the gun and the rain, waiting for Jamey to get home soon.

Esau wrapped Dickie Green's hand with some torn cloth from Becky's shirt. Becky was almost glad she got to contribute something as they sent Dickie back in the water with the chain and the hook. He came back a minute later, and Bones handed him the second chain and the second hook. This time it took only twenty seconds and Dickie walked back to the edge of the pond in the spotlight of the cars and said, "Done. You know how many people used to watch me clean them tanks at the pirate caves? I mean, I wasn't even the star; the star was the gator we kept in there, Captain Crunch. But folks couldn't believe a kid like me could hold his breath so long. They called me fish boy."

"Ain't that somethin'," Bones said. "Never heard this before."

"I ain't lyin'," Dickie said. "Made the papers and everything."

"Hmm," Esau said. "Mr. Fish, you want to go ahead and get that dozer going so we can get the hell out of here?"

Dickie shook his head, still in nothing but the tighty-whiteys and the blue swim mask he'd pushed up to the top of his head. He looked kind of like one of those little monkeys who dance for a quarter as he scrambled up that big CAT and cranked it up. He pushed a button and the dozer started to move, heading up and over some little bumps, rolling on its track, pulling that chain behind it until it yanked hard and tight. The dozer stopped cold, Dickie working it into another gear, belching that diesel until the track started to spin in place in the muck. The thing finally caught and moved slowly away from the light and toward the big open field.

Esau was smoking another cigarette. Bones stood by him, with Becky opposite. All three of them were backlit in the Tundra's headlights, watching the pebbled surface of that fishing pond and the spot where the tight chain reached and disappeared, link by link coming on out of the water. Esau flicked some ash and squinted into the darkness. The dozer was straining in a high gear, whining and belching, and the surface bubbled a bit, chain coming out slow and hard. "Come on, motherfucker," Bones said. "Come on."

"How y'all gonna open it up?" Becky said. "Figure it's gonna be locked."

"Cut that fucker open with a blow torch," Bones said softly.

"You got one?" Becky said.

"Yes, ma'am," Esau said. "We've had some time to think this thing through."

First the top of the armored car appeared and then the whole rear end, coming out brown and mucky and slick but still reading clear as hell WELLS FARGO. He and Bones were grinning, Becky doing a little dance like she had to pee, until they noticed that the back doors were loose, water sloshing from them, as most of the car was above the surface now, rolling backward up out of the pond and onto the banks. Esau walked to the thing almost like he was in a trance, not hearing whatever Becky was yelling to him, just seeing that big slick metal car from his dreams. The car hit the stiff bank and found solid footing, Dickie somewhere out in the dark still driving like hell, two of the driver's-side wheels lifting up, the back of the car turning, ready to topple over. Bones ran for Dickie to shut the damn thing off.

Esau glanced up at the windshield slick with green, knowing there were two men locked inside and not giving a good goddamn. Two men who'd gotten blamed for maybe pulling the robbery themselves. There was a time when he first got to Parchman that he could recall their names and took some kind of pleasure in knowing they'd become famous as thieves, not as two unfortunate bastards who might've spent eternity at the bottom of a bass pond. He circled the side door and walked to the half-open back, Becky not needing a bit of instruction about looking for money. She jumped in front of them and threw open both doors and walked on into the back of the armored car.

The headlight bled on in just a bit, but enough to show them all the car was empty.

"Y'all robbed a fucking empty truck?" Becky said.

Esau clamped down on his jaw, both hands resting on the edge of the rear of the car. He shook his head, feeling that old familiar rage, vision narrowing as he walked to the driver's door and tried the handle. Through the glass he saw the pickled white shape of something that might've been human at one time. Everything was still locked.

Dickie was with them now, big shit-eating grin on his face, slapping Esau's back and talking more about being a kid fish.

"It's empty," Becky said. "They robbed an empty fucking truck."

Esau shook his head. Bones slammed one of the two doors and kicked at the dirt.

"I thought y'all saw the money?" Dickie said.

"We watched the guards load it," Esau

said. "We followed them from their last stop."

"Maybe the fish took it," Dickie said. He started to laugh, grabbing his belly, thick smears of mud down his arms and legs. "I think I seen a few down there driving little fish Cadillacs and sporting some little fish jewelry. Real little gold chains."

Esau shook his head, pulled the .357 from his belt, and shot Dickie in the chest.

Becky screamed and ran for where Dickie lay on the ground, open-eyed and open-mouthed and real dead.

"What the hell?" Becky said. "He didn't do nothing. What the hell, Esau?"

"He fucked us," Esau said. "That mother-fucker."

"Dickie?"

"Jamey Dixon," Bones said. "Esau shot Dickie just 'cause."

"Y'all are both crazy," Becky said. "Fuck-ing crazy. Let's get the hell out of this county."

"I ain't doin' jack shit till the preacher gets me my due," Esau said, trudging up to the car. Rain coming full tilt, washing mud off the little hill and down into the pond. Becky held Dickie's head in her lap and cried. Bones just stood looking into the

empty truck, shaking his head. God better
help that son of a bitch.

17

They came. Hundreds of them from all over Tibbehah and as far as Tishomingo and Lowndes County. Caddy knew it might not last, but they were curious about the convict-turned-preacher and his message of redemption and the transformative power of God's grace. They parked the cars end to end up on the rolling pastures of knee-high grass where cattle had grazed just a season before. The music started early, coming out of the open barn doors and filling the bright day with old hymns and Johnny Cash songs and even one Jamey had picked from The Band. Uncle Van and J.T. and a mandolin player from Jackson made the old barn shake and become alive. This was more of a church than some sad old place where people sat stock-still, checking out their watches, or raised their hands in praise to a high-definition projection screen. All of 'em mostly worried about what their neighbors thought about them. Not here. She could feel His presence. She felt it every time Jamey took to telling his testimony.

Caddy couldn't really say if there was a certain kind of person who came to The River that morning. Some folks looked like they maybe came for the free meal after the service. Other people looked like they had plenty of money, nice shoes and haircuts, but wanted to experience something real. *Real* being the word she kept on hearing that morning. People were thirsty to hear a story that wasn't unlike those two men flanking Jesus on the cross. Two thieves being bled of life, only one coming to understand He still loved them.

"He's a fine man," Uncle Van had told her.

"Proud to be a part of this," said Fred Black, a local welder whose ex-wife and daughter had been mixed up in a shit-ton of trouble lately.

She'd picked out a simple dress for the occasion. Light cotton dotted with tiny flowers with her nice pair of boots. She was glad she'd worn the boots. The field around the barn was a true muddy mess.

Jamey had on jeans and a neatly pressed black shirt. Before the service, Caddy had cut his hair into a neat straight line above the shoulders and made sure his boots were free of mud before he started to preach. The sermon on the Model Church brought on more amens than she could count, people wanting something authentic and real and beyond all the judgments and forced expectations and silly traditions. Jamey just resonated peace, and everyone could feel that he walked with God.

At the altar call, just seconds after delivering his sermon, more than forty people came forward to dedicate or rededicate their lives to God. Caddy lost count. Jamey placed his hands on each one of them, praying over them as the band played "Ain't No Grave." *When I hear that trumpet sound, / I'm gonna rise right out of the ground / There ain't no grave can hold my body down.* People cried, almost shy and unwilling to come before the altar but somehow being pulled up to Jamey. She joined them all below the homemade cross with some of the men and women who'd be the church elders, almost all of them no more than thirty. They fell to their knees and hid their faces until Jamey touched them, prayed over them, and then they'd throw their heads back, looking up to the cross, tears flowing, and say everything they felt right in front of Jamey and the church and God and the band, even if sometimes it didn't make sense. One teenage girl really broke her heart, coming there and standing alone without a parent or her friend, not seventy pounds in a Walmart dress and tennis shoes, crying and praying and wanting redemption at fifteen. Caddy whispered to her that everything was going to be just fine.

She had never felt such a part of something.

After the final song, Caddy stood at Jamey's side as he shook hands and met the congregation as they left the old barn. Long picnic tables had been set up outside and covered in red-and-white checked cloths lightly blowing in the wind. Everyone remarked that this was the first time they'd seen the sun in days, it looking like a true miracle, shooting through the scattered clouds as plates of barbecue and beans and coleslaw and soft white rolls were laid out. "Ain't it pretty?" Caddy said to Jason.

She wished her mother and Quinn could have come. *Why won't they open their eyes?*

She and Jason sat at the table with Jamey and Uncle Van and Bobby Pickens, one of the county supervisors, and a waitress from the Fillin' Station who'd been seeing her uncle at the time he'd decided to kill himself. Black families and white families ate side by side, which wasn't unusual at all for Jericho except at church time. Reaching out to the black community, many of them coming from the hardscrabble Sugar Ditch, was key for Jamey.

"Y'all have such a beautiful family," said an old woman who had paused by the table, complimenting Jamey on the sermon. Caddy turned for a moment, not sure who she was talking about, and then her face colored when she realized the old woman was talking about the three of them. The woman with fuzzed cataract eyes placed her hands on Caddy and Jason's shoulders, saying family was everything in this world.

Jamey looked up from his plate and thanked the old woman.

"Yes," he said, winking at Caddy. "I do have a wonderful family."

Caddy swallowed and looked back at her plate, holding tight to Jason's knee under the table.

Lillie called Quinn at the sheriff's office.

She was headed on duty. Quinn was headed off.

"Can it wait?" Quinn said. "I heard about this thing called sleep and I'd love to try it out."

"Not really," she said. "Better tell Jean you won't be making church, either. We got

185

ourselves a first-class clusterfuck this morning."

"I'll make sure to use those exact words."

Quinn was rolling onto Highway 9 five minutes later. He'd brought Hondo with him that morning, the dog's head hanging out the window as Quinn crested a long, flat hill right where the road made a T with Horse Barn Road. Lillie's Cherokee and the cruisers of Kenny and Ike McCaslin were parked up into a pasture set back from a large bass pond. Quinn turned onto a narrow dirt road leading up to the pond. As he drove closer he saw the large, mud-slimed truck and a yellow bulldozer at the pond's edge.

Hondo jumped out the window as he slowed. A light warm wind blew over the water and deep into the rolling fields. Yellow light shot from the clouds and down onto the armored car with back doors wide open.

Lillie led him around the side of the truck to where a little skinny man with a bald head and tattoos lay dead on the ground. Hondo sniffed at him, and Quinn told him to back up. The man's eyes and mouth were wide open, as if he were about to scream but was caught in the act. "You already call the techs in Batesville?"

"Yes, sir," she said. "Got a couple more

186

tracks running from here. Be careful, this road is a mess. Supposed to stay dry enough to make some molds. Maybe this sun will dry it out a bit. And we got some clear tracks closer to that CAT, look like some mud tires."

Quinn twisted his head and studied the dead man's face. He was as ugly in death as he'd probably been in life.

"Our boy from Parchman?" he said.

"Richard Green," Lillie said. "Friends call him Dickie."

"What's that tat say?" Quinn said. "On his chest."

"CELTIC PRIDE beside the swastika and another one that reads PISS ON IT."

Quinn stepped back. "How long you think that Wells Fargo truck's been down there?"

"Tennessee tag. I'm sure the bank noticed it missing. But I don't recall a truck going missing here. Looks like a couple years before my time."

Kenny and Ike McCaslin were unspooling some crime scene tape around the truck tracks and footprints on the muddy banks right by tracks for raccoons and deer. The breeze felt warm and sluggish. Overnight there had been a chill. A push and pull of currents that left you hot and cold within the same hour.

187

The bright light was gone for a moment and then back on them, shining in a long slanted curtain across the greening hills.

"I didn't open the door," Lillie said, "but I'm pretty sure we got the two guards still up front. The condition of the bodies doesn't look pleasant. I'd just as soon have the state techs deal with that mess."

"I'll call the Marshals in Oxford," Quinn said. "I'm sure they'd like to hear about the convicts."

"You know they've got to be long gone now," Lillie said. "Looks like they got what they came for."

"Doesn't mean they're still not close," Quinn said. "Anyone see or hear anything? Hell, that dozer must've made some noise. I wonder who owns it."

"The land belongs to the Hardins," Lillie said. "You call Mrs. Hardin. I'd just as soon not deal with her, too. She is batshit crazy. You remember when she thought some young man was looking into her windows? I still say it wasn't worry, more of wishful thinking."

"Go ahead and get as many photos as you can," Quinn said. "Just in case we get more rain. I'll head back and check in with the Marshals' service and Wells Fargo. And I'll tell Mrs. Hardin to call you at home if she has any questions."

"Appreciate that," Lillie said.

Quinn stood on a little hill as McCaslin and Kenny tied off the scene with some wooden stakes Kenny pulled out from the trunk of his cruiser. He whistled for Hondo, and the dog headed straight for Quinn's truck. Lillie walked at Quinn's side. "You leaving me here?"

"You're in charge," Quinn said. "Why? You think I could do better?"

"Nope."

"That's what I figured," Quinn said. He opened the passenger door for Hondo and walked around to the driver's. He wondered just when he might get some sleep, federal people coming to the town, state people coming to run the crime scene. He'd need to call Parchman, too, and update their superintendent.

He scratched Hondo's head as the front of his truck bucked up and over a little hill, turning out from the Hardin property and heading back into Jericho.

Nothing like three bodies to really screw up a Sabbath.

18

Caddy ran into her house, wanting to change out of her new dress before she met up with Jason and Jean at the El Dorado for lunch. It never failed for her to spill some salsa or queso onto herself, and no matter the dry cleaning, it would never come out. She grabbed a pair of jeans and a fitted Dixie Chicks T-shirt, reaching under the bed for her buckskin boots. She'd been working so hard on making sure that first service had launched that her little house had become a mess. The living room still had open beer bottles and pizza boxes from Jamey's rehearsal. The kitchen sink was overflowing with dishes. Even Jason's room was nothing but a rat's nest of tangled sheets and toys. As soon as they got back from the El Dorado, they'd get down to work. She'd get Jason to put away his toys while she got into the wash, thinking Jamey would probably want to cook out tonight, drink a beer and reflect on the big day.

She pulled her dress overhead and hung it up onto the oval mirror by the closet. She turned this way and that, examining her body, the embarrassment of a blue tattoo of an angel at the small of her back. She huffed and turned to grab her jeans when a man came from the closet at damn near full tilt and placed a big hand over her mouth and face and rushed her down onto the bed. She screamed and tore at him, but the man was large and heavy, red-bearded and muscle-bound, telling her to shut the hell up, that he had more important things on his mind than her nekkid bony ass.

She tried to fight more. He just held her there, as easy as he would a kitten or a puppy. His breath smelled of cigarettes and onions.

"I'll stay here all day," he said.

She bit at his hands.

He knocked her hard against the face. She could taste blood in her mouth, the one window of her bedroom half cracked, lace curtains flowing over the writing desk where Jamey wrote sermons.

Three steps, maybe four, was the closet. At the top of the closet was the gun.

"Listen," he said. "Where's your boy?"

She shook her head. Her mouth was

awash with the blood.

The breeze rushed on into the window and cooled off the room. The smell of his breath and testosterone all over her. He had narrow eyes nearly yellow.

She shook her head some more.

"Where's Dixon?" he said.

She lay still, body slowly starting to relax, knowing and feeling he hadn't come for her but Jamey. The man was too calm, not even looking once at her in her bra and panties, not putting a hand on her except to pin her down and shut her mouth. The curtain fluttered over the writing desk and one of Jamey's old Bibles.

"This ain't no complicated deal," the redheaded man said. "I want you to explain to Dixon that I want to see him. I gone to that church after it let out and he was gone. 'Least I got something to eat. Me and my buddy were pretty hungry."

The man sat at the edge of the bed just as calm as you please, almost like they'd been lovers or friends, talking over old times. Just Caddy Colson in her underthings, not worried about nothing. He slowly removed his hand from her mouth. She tried to move upright, but he placed a rough hand onto her throat and eased her down against a pillow. "You sure are a wildcat," he said. "How in the hell did you fall for a piece of shit like Jamey Dixon? You can do lots better."

"Get your hands off me, or I'll goddamn kill you."

"Come on, baby," Esau said. "Come on."

And with those hot breathed words in her ear, she was eight years old again in another old barn in another part of the county. She was flat on her back, pinned down, unable to move, a heavy whiskered man pressing her against the rotted hay, telling her how pretty she was as he unbuckled his trousers and did his business. You press it hard from your mind and try to fill it with other things, but he and that man from all those years ago were made of the same stuff. "I'll goddamn kill you."

"That's fine," Esau said. "That's fine. But before you do, I want you to tell Jamey Dixon that Esau is coming for him. He wants what's rightly his and what he's had stoled from him. You tell him that?"

"He didn't take nothing from you."

"Ask Dixon," Esau said, grinning. "We want what's ours, and we coming for it tonight. If he runs, we will follow him to goddamn China. He calls the law, and they get us, we give up all his rotten shit and that pardon'll be worth as much as yesterday's toilet paper."

"Get your hands off my neck."

The man called Esau did. He stood up from the bed; a large pistol hung in his leather belt. He looked her over as she reached for a T-shirt and pulled it on, eyeing him walking back, trying to find a way to get around him and get that gun. She could end it right here. She'd kill him just the same as Quinn had killed that diseased man all those years ago. She and Quinn were the same. They could kill if things came down to that sort of situation.

Caddy spit on the floor. "You mind if I get my pants?"

"Right there on the bed, doll."

"I need a pair in the closet."

Esau looked her up and down, thinking on it, and then finally nodded and stepped back. Caddy walked to the sliding door, calmly went through some hanging clothes as if deciding, and then ever-so-gently slid her hand up to the top shelf, knowing she'd loaded at least three shells in the chamber. She knew she had it set and ready and all she'd have to do is point, pull, and be done with it. The hell of it would be cleaning up after.

The big hand was on her wrist, yanking her backward, back-handing her down to the bed.

194

He pulled the 12-gauge, checked the breech, and then slammed it shut.

"Been needing one of these for what we about to do," he said. "Tell your boy he got till nightfall. We'll come to the church. He'll bring our cut of the money. He does what we say and he'll never see us again. Y'all be drinking fruit punch and singing hymns until Judgment Day. You tell him."

She nodded.

"What's your name, girl?" Esau said.

She shook her head.

"Afraid to say it."

"Caddy."

"Beautiful," he said. "OK, Miss Caddy. Let's be friends. You sure as hell don't want me to have to come back and truly make a real fucking mess of your world. Let's make this nice and clean."

Caddy nodded. The room felt hollow and silent and cold. His boots were heavy on the old pine floor as he took the shotgun and moved under the fluttering curtains, fleeing the room like a teenage boy at midnight.

She walked to the mirror. Her face was a goddamn mess. *How would she explain that to Jean? Or Quinn?*

The U.S. Marshals were sitting in Quinn's

office in less than two hours. Two men sent over from Oxford, but said they'd been just over in Lee County when they got the call. Apparently they'd had a pretty good sighting of Dickie Green at the Barnes Crossing Mall eating at the food court. Quinn told them he was pretty sure it hadn't been Dickie Green, explaining details from what he'd seen out by the pond.

The Marshals' names were Buster Wilson and Toby Sisk. Sisk was short and stocky and kept a neatly trimmed black mustache that influenced the way he spoke. Wilson was larger and kind of doughy, clean-shaven, with saggy skin and windblown hair. Sisk took the lead, spitting some snuff into a foam cup as they discussed Esau Davis and the man named Joseph "Bones" Magee.

"I guess you got the whole rundown on who they are and how they escaped?" Sisk said. He seemed to kind of fancy himself as a slow-talking gunslinger, with slow-eyed careful movements and the mustache. He looked to Quinn like a thousand shitkickers he'd known over the years. Couple of them had turned out to be decent people.

"They rode out of Parchman on horses and out of the Delta in a Chevelle," Quinn said.

Sisk spit in the cup and nodded.

"But Dickie Green drove straight out the front gates," Wilson said, shifting in his chair. "Still figuring out how that whole deal worked. Somebody got paid."

"Doesn't matter much to Mr. Green now," Quinn said.

"He got used," Sisk said. "He wasn't buddies with either of these two, but they needed his horse trailer. Dumb shit should have seen that coming. Did you say he got shot down in his underwear?"

"All he took out of this world was a pair of dirty white Hanes."

Wilson glanced around the little office at Quinn's photos and the framed flag that had hung in AFG. "You military?" he said.

Wilson didn't seem much of an investigator. Quinn just nodded.

"So, has anyone seen these shitbirds around your county?" Sisk said.

Quinn shook his head.

"We know they got a woman probably traveling with them," Sisk said. "Woman named Becky, who used to come visit Davis at Parchman."

"I think they're long gone," Quinn said. "They raised that armored car and got what they'd come for. I'm still trying to find out how that truck stayed down there for so long."

"Either it didn't have a GPS or whatever they used to call it," Wilson said. "Or the pond shorted it out. Hell, these days we could have tracked both those guards with their cell phones. You said you saw two bodies in the truck?"

"I saw one," Quinn said. "My deputy was pretty sure both men are inside."

"Body count may be old, but sure as hell is adding up," Sisk said.

"We've been tracking Davis and Magee since the breakout," Wilson said.

Sisk spit into the cup. He smoothed his mustache. Wilson crossed his legs and took a deep breath.

"We're pretty sure they got some more friends here," Wilson said. "We tried to figure out why they'd come to Jericho. I don't mean anything by that. But it's not exactly the kind of place people light out for."

"Now we know it was all for the money."

"Maybe," Sisk said. He had carried a leather satchel into Quinn's office and reached into it for a file. He pulled out a couple printed sheets with mug shot scans attached.

Quinn took the file and flipped through the pages. He set the file down and leaned back in his chair. He shook his head and cleared his throat.

"We got it on good word from the warden in Unit 33 that this fella and Magee and Davis were great pals," Sisk said. "And now we got them escaped and coming for some hidden loot to this man's hometown. Did I tell you this man was just pardoned by the governor?"

"I know him," Quinn said.

"We figured you'd been notified of the release," Wilson said. "Has he been causing any trouble?"

"Nope."

"I voted on the governor, but pardoning all these shitbags doesn't make a lick of sense to me," Sisk said. He rubbed his mustache. He spit. "You know where we can find Jamey Dixon?"

"Well," Quinn said. "Let me call my sister; she's been dating him."

The two U.S. Marshals laughed like it had been a joke. Quinn told them about The River and the ministry Jamey had set up outside city limits.

"A church in a barn," Sisk said. "Hallelujah."

Both men stood up and headed for the door.

"What makes you think Dixon has anything to do with these turds?" Quinn said.

"Dixon did these men personal favors at Parchman," Wilson said. "He apparently got them some plum assignments, made sure they got the right detail. Dixon was a regular prison rock star. He was real close with the former superintendent, too. People really believe he's the real thing."

Sisk nodded. He spit one more time and dropped the cup in Quinn's wastebasket. Standing tall still had him staring at Quinn's chest. "Even if it's not connected," the Marshal said. "Seems like they'd go to their old buddy for some help."

Quinn nodded.

Wilson patted Quinn's back as they left. "Dating your sister," he said. "That's the funniest thing I heard in a long time."

Quinn held the door for them both.

19

Caddy called Jean and told her and Jason to go on and eat Mexican without her. She hadn't had a bite of the food at The River, making sure everyone else got what they needed, and now she'd spent the last hour trying to find Jamey. After the chairs and PA equipment had been broken down, Uncle Van said Jamey had run back into Jericho for supplies. On Sunday most everything closed up, and that pretty much meant he'd gone to the Dollar Store or the Piggly Wiggly. Ten minutes later, she spotted his truck parked in the nearly empty lot of the Pig and wheeled in, finding him in the frozen food section, reaching for a couple pizzas. His cart was already loaded down with Mountain Dew and Pepsi, Jamey saying how much he'd missed that stuff when he was inside. Pepsi, cigarettes, bacon, and sex pretty much topped his list.

"We still cooking out?" Jamey said. "I hear

it might storm."

"Why didn't you call me?"

"You said you're having lunch at the El Dorado," he said. "Aren't you full yet?"

"I didn't get to eat all day."

Jamey placed the pizzas in the cart and rolled toward the back of the store and the meat section, marked by that antique scrawl across fake red brick that hadn't changed her whole life. Buckled linoleum and weak fluorescent light. Jamey spoke to a few folks, a couple asking how the service went. Jamey smiled and made a comment about how they should see for themselves. When they got to the breakfast meats, she leaned in and said, "That man Esau is looking for you."

"Don't worry about him," Jamey said. "I got it."

"Hell, you do," Caddy said. "The son of a bitch popped out of my closet. He wrestled me down to the bed."

Jamey's face blanched. He shook his head and said, "When?"

"He didn't do nothin'," Caddy said. "He said he didn't give a shit about anything but the money. What the hell is he talking about? I could have had Jason with me. He just breaks into my house and steals my shotgun. He looked mad enough to explode."

"When was this?"

"Just an hour ago," Caddy said. "Aren't you listening? I'm worried he's going to try and kill you."

"He won't do that."

"How's that?"

" 'Cause he needs me to tell him about what happened to all his dirty money."

A very fat woman on a Rascal motor scooter parked herself right in front of the country ham. She had black bouffant hair and oversized glasses with rose lenses. "Would one of y'all reach up for the Jimmy Dean?"

Caddy reached up and tossed the sausage hard enough into her cart that the woman's neck snapped. She shook her head and motored off.

"Fuck Jimmy Dean," Caddy said.

"I got it." Jamey leaned into the grocery cart and pushed it forward, moving the back way from the way a person is supposed to shop. He'd started in the damn middle of the grocery, and now he was headed back to the produce and milk. Any sane person knew that you started with the damn produce and hit the bread aisle last. Just common sense.

"Jason could have been with me."

Jamey nodded. They were alone by the cereal, rows and rows of Frosted Flakes and Lucky Charms and Cocoa Puffs and assorted shit that could rot your teeth. She'd always told Jason that kind of stuff would leave you toothless and crazy.

"He won't come back."

"What are you gonna do?" Caddy said. "Shoot him? Did you forget the part about he took my daddy's shotgun?"

"Those men shouldn't be here," he said. "You hear about the breakout at Parchman?"

Caddy nodded.

"That's them."

"I want to know what they're looking for," Caddy said. "If some redheaded ape popped out of your closet while you were changing your panties, I think you'd like to know, too."

Jamey shook his head.

"What did you steal?"

"Nothing," he said. "They stole it. Esau just told me where to find it."

"How much?"

"A ton."

"Where'd you put it?"

Jamey shook his head.

"Damn you," Caddy said, grabbing onto

his arm and looking up into his face. He was smiling at her getting so mad, rubbing his hand on her back.

"Calm down. I called the Marshals. They'll find them. We don't have to worry about that mess. We got bigger things. They're not in the plan."

"Talk to Quinn."

"No way."

"You won't talk to him," she said, "then I will. Where is that money they stole?"

"I gave it away."

"You gave it away?" Caddy said, confused as hell. "You mean to start the church?"

"Not exactly."

"Damn you, Jamey." Caddy gripped his arm tighter.

He swallowed and started rolling that old cart again in the exact opposite direction he should be traveling. "Don't you know how to shop?" she said.

He placed a hand over hers. He smiled, and she steadied her breath. "Don't tell Quinn," he said. "Let me handle it."

"Where'd you put those men's money?" she said. " 'Cause if it comes down to me and Jason being safe, I promise you I'll tell."

"Tell 'em," he said. "I'm free of it. You can tell them the same thing I will. All their money is with Johnny Stagg."

Caddy took a breath. She started to speak. She looked at Jamey and gripped him tighter, turning the cart in the proper way toward the bread.

"Stagg has their money," Jamey said.

She let go of his arm. "Now, that's a twist."

"Isn't that how the world goes round in Jericho?" he asked. "Or have you forgotten?"

"How about we start at the beginning of this story?"

They got fucked up in the rain.

Bones had got into the beer and Becky got into the tequila. And Esau hadn't been back fifteen minutes before he said what the hell and joined them at the hunting lodge pool. He was lying flat on his back on a float, Becky resting her head and arms by his side. He was sipping a cold one, watching with interest an endless stretch of flat-ass black clouds rolling in from the west. He sipped some Coors, trying to rest until the show started, thinking on how things had not at all gone the way they had intended.

"I still don't know why you had to go and shoot Dickie," Becky said, kind of dreamily, studying more on it than cussing him.

"Did you like Dickie?" Esau said.

"Not especially."

"Then why the hell do you care if I shot him?" he said. "I never intended for him to come here with us. You're the one who brought him here."

"You didn't have to kill him," she said, kicking a little bit with her feet in the water.

There was thunder. Esau didn't see no lightning. He sipped his beer and thought some more about Florida.

"You think he would have gone nice?" Esau said. "Without making so much noise that we got caught?"

"People know we're here," she said. "You left a waterlogged Wells Fargo truck out by a pond with some dead men inside."

Esau took a sip of beer. Hell, she had him on that.

Bones was blowing through the beer, taking all the hunt lodge's owner's guns from the rack and playing with them a bit on an umbrella-topped table. Bones was always thinking about making money. Didn't matter they'd need to get gone within a few hours, Bones was thinking on what he could take with him.

"Nice house," Becky said. She kicked her feet a little bit.

Sometime in the morning she'd traded out the red bikini for a camo one.

"We can't stay," Esau said.

"Maybe we could come back?"

"I'm never coming back to Mississippi for the rest of my life," Esau said.

"Don't say things like that."

"You want to stay in Coldwater?" Esau said, crushing the beer can and launching it into the deep end. "You go right ahead. I'll call you from the beach sometime."

"I still say Mexico or Jamaica."

"Jamaica ain't nothin' but blacks," Esau said.

"Bones is black."

"Bones ain't just some black," he said. "Bones and me got a history."

"So, where is this place?" she said. "What's it called again?"

"Indian Rocks Beach," Esau said. "I got a buddy of mine runs a trailer park down there. He said he can get us some jobs tending bar or renting out boats. We live down there making some money, not drawing too much interest but the whole time having money for whatever we need. I want some sand. Florida is sand. Mississippi ain't nothing but mud."

"What about Bones?"

"He's coming, too."

"What if we can't get the money?"

"That's not an option."

"Shit," Becky said, sliding up onto the raft, nearly toppling them both. Esau grabbed her and pulled her up by his side. "Didn't you just say we got a place to live and jobs? Why don't we just take that? Longer we stay here, the easier it's going to be to find you boys."

Now there was lightning. That forever black cloud blocking out the sun, pine trees shaking in that warning wind. There was electricity in the warm air.

"Let's go on inside," Esau said.

"We're already wet."

"I don't care for lightning," he said. "We can take a shower and get all soapy."

"Together?"

He swatted her butt with his hand, looking back under that umbrella, Bones burning down a cigarette and toying with a collector's-model Winchester. Maybe she was right. But if he left without getting his due, what kind of man was he? He'd just go on and let Jamey Dixon steal what was rightly his?

"Does Dixon know you're coming for him?"

"Yes, ma'am."

"Was his girlfriend pretty?"

"If you like skin and bones."

"What do you like?" Becky said.

"I like a big-ass country girl who knows how to handle a shotgun," he said. "That girl was scared to death."

"Money or not, we got to leave tonight."

"Yep."

"I don't want to see you and Bones go back," Becky said. "I can't handle the smell of the visit house on me. It makes me feel like some kind of whore."

"Indian Rocks is nothing but sunshine and margaritas."

"Forever?"

"Ain't no other way."

20

Quinn parked his truck at the east side of the Big Black River next to Lillie's Cherokee and walked out to the middle of the rusted bridge. He stood right beside Lillie, who was wearing a green canvas coat and rubber boots pulled up to the knees of her jeans. Quinn watched what she watched, the big muddy churn of the river, the sandbars hidden from view, sticks and big broken limbs twirling and being carried on south. The rain was a good steady pour now. Quinn now in his poncho and sheriff's ball cap, light traffic rolling over the old bridge.

"How high's the water, Momma?" Quinn said.

"Five feet high and risin'," Lillie said.

They leaned over the rail. Lillie had yet to meet his eye.

"Looks lots deeper than that."

"If it doesn't stop raining," Lillie said, "half the county is gonna wash away."

"Sugar Ditch always floods," Quinn said. "How close?"

"Another day of rain and we'll have to evacuate."

Quinn studied the strong pull of the river, the water the color of coffee and cream, rolling and tumbling under them. He used to fish the river a lot from the very same spot. He and Boom and sometimes Caddy. There used to be a bait store down the road, but that had burned down long ago. There was a dress shop there now.

"I met up with the Marshals," Quinn said.

"How'd it go?"

"Not well," Quinn said. "They tell me that these guys Davis and Magee were good friends with Jamey Dixon at Parchman."

"Shit."

"Yep."

Under the brim of her ball cap, Lillie raised her eyebrows. "C'mon," she said. "Let's go get the son of a bitch."

"Hold up," he said. "They don't believe he was part of the armored car deal. They think that came before, and now they've reached out to him for help. He got them both on special detail at Parchman, helping out on some of his services. The Marshals said they were all good buddies."

"Half the county is about to wash away

while we deal with this shitbag reunion. We better go and find Caddy."

Quinn nodded. "Marshals said they'll call us if they find them. They were firm that they may, or may not, need some help."

"They will," Lillie said. "Always do."

"What do you have in the trunk of your Cherokee?"

"Bolt-action Remington M24."

"Nice to have a good sniper with us."

"You don't have snipers in law enforcement, Sergeant," Lillie said. "I've been over this. We conduct surgical shooting. In our world, snipers are the bad guys."

"OK," Quinn said. "I'll let those men know we have somebody good at surgery."

Lillie nodded. They watched the river for a while, Lillie saying she'd go ahead down south to check on the situation in Sugar Ditch. The Ditch being an all-black community where traditionally calling on the law or help from Jericho had been a joke. The whole place looked strung together from clapboard and tin, like something out of a WPA photograph, not well into the twenty-first century.

"You think Caddy will tip off Dixon?" Lillie said.

"Probably."

"But you're going to reach out anyway."

Quinn nodded. They walked back together on the narrow walkway on the bridge to the sloping muddy banks where they'd parked. "Be sure and keep that Remington handy," he said. "And your cell phone on."

Lillie nodded.

"Never met a woman who loved guns so much," Quinn said.

"I don't love them," Lillie said. "Men like guns. I like to shoot and prove myself. I'd rather not turn that on someone."

"You know, if I explain to Caddy the situation, she'll dig in," Quinn said. "I'd just as soon get her away from Dixon for a couple days without her knowing why."

"Ordinarily I'd say that's a horseshit plan," Lillie said.

"But with Caddy?"

Lillie slowly nodded, unlocking her Jeep doors. "Right about perfect."

Caddy drove. Jamey had left his truck at the Pig.

"I won't sugarcoat it," Jamey said. "I used to be an absolute piece of shit. I don't think I've ever lied about that to you. Have I?"

Caddy shook her head. She knocked the windshield wipers on high.

"I drank whiskey like water and tried every drug ever invented," Jamey said. "I

214

was completely absent in my own life. I had nothing to hold me. What do they say, a natural man? Like an ape or another animal? I had no center. No existence. If I hadn't gone to prison, I'd be dead or on the street."

"I don't care," Caddy said, turning off Main Street and heading down Cotton Road, down toward the farm co-op. The wipers on fill tilt.

"You know the Bundrens still believe you killed Adelaide? They've gone insane with it and want everyone to know you should be rotting in hell."

"You blame them?"

"Guess not."

"Neither do I. Adelaide was with me during the worst of it," Jamey said. "We were together in high school and out of high school. I worked at the ammunition factory, boxing. She worked when she could with her family. But she hated it. She didn't like the funeral business. She wasn't like her sister, who saw death as a natural act. I think it messed with her head, growing up with those dead bodies."

"I don't care what they think."

Caddy cut up on Highway 9W as if they were headed to Uncle Hamp's farm, still having a hard time thinking of it as Quinn's place. The rain was coming down so hard now that she could barely see, running down to thirty and catching the light coming up from the Dixie Gas Station.

"I know you don't care," Jamey said. "I appreciate that. But I got to tell you something, Caddy. I swear to God I don't know what happened. There are whole pockets of time that go like that. At Parchman, I had plenty of time to go inward and think of things and try to make some sense of it all. But all that happened with Adelaide just kind of runs together. We fed each other, made each other sick. We did what felt good to us at the moment, but those things were all just a sickness. Just sex and getting high. I'm real sorry. I thought you wanted to hear."

"I knew Adelaide," Caddy said. "She was a true mess."

"I guess we were in love," Jamey said. "But it was the kind of love that didn't fill you up. It was the kind of love that drove you running and screaming nekkid with your hair on fire. You know?"

"I've had that."

"That's not love."

"You were going to tell me about Johnny Stagg," Caddy said. They were now passing Mr. Varner's store and then down past the gun range that Mr. Varner's son had used to run guns last year. Quinn nearly got himself killed down that road.

"Mr. Stagg and I worked out a deal," Jamey said.

"When?"

"I wrote him letters at Parchman," Jamey said. "This was when I was taking correspondence classes with the seminary in New Orleans. I knew I was ready to get out. And I was pretty sure that wasn't going to happen. So I just decided to reach out to Mr. Stagg."

"You really call him Mr. Stagg?"

"What do you call him?"

"A rotten piece of shit."

"Mr. Stagg done me a solid," Jamey said. "He came to see me at Parchman with this sheriff's deputy. Hell, I can't remember his name."

"Leonard," Caddy said. "He's the police chief now."

"Yep," Jamey said. "Leonard. After I wrote him, he came out to Parchman to see me, and we talked about working out a deal. I told him where to find the money those two convicts stole."

Caddy nodded. The rain was coming down so damn hard that it shook the car, pounding the roof and hood. She slowed down to twenty, coming up close to Quinn's farm, but then taking a U-turn at the three-way and heading back down south to Jericho. She wasn't sure whether to talk to Quinn or not. And this goddamn day had started out so perfect.

"I need a cigarette," Caddy said. "I need a fucking cigarette."

" 'Cause I worked with Stagg?"

" 'Cause I don't know who the fuck you are."

"What would you do?" Jamey said. "I done my time for something I didn't do."

"You said you didn't know whether you did it or not. That doesn't make you an innocent man."

"I'm not that man," Jamey said. "I don't deny my life was worthless. But I got out for a reason. There is a purpose to my life. God would not have opened the doors had there not been something for me to do."

"God?" Caddy said. "God? Or Johnny Stagg. Sounds to me like you sold out your buddies in exchange for your freedom."

"OK."

"You sold out your friends?"

"I have purpose."

Caddy was crying and used the back of her hand to clear her eyes. They were back in Jericho, rounding the Square and that half-boarded-up, half-wonderful, half-awful town that she could never escape. Every day, round and round, over and over, there was the fucking Square.

"Johnny Stagg?" she said. "He bought your freedom."

"Mr. Stagg has a lot of friends down in Jackson."

"Johnny Stagg is a cancer on this town and this entire county," she said. "You made a deal with the devil."

"You're talking to a man who lived in sin and no purpose," Jamey said. "I have a chance to be in society again and tell people the good news of Christ. You think that's a lie? You think I'm just a two-bit con man, trying to hustle and get by? Because if that were the case, Caddy, I'd just as soon find another line of work than saving souls."

Caddy turned off the Square, back down Cotton Road, and the new stores to Jericho. Hollywood Video and the Dollar Store and Subway. Shit to buy. Shit to live. She reached into her purse and reached for a pack of cigarettes she'd taken from her mother and punched up the lighter on her car.

"You better be the real deal, Jamey Dixon," she said. " 'Cause if you are lying to me? Lying to everyone? I may be the biggest goddamn fool that ever walked this earth."

Jamey placed a hand on Caddy's knee. She drove east toward Highway 45. The rain kept on pounding the hood of their car as if there would be no end. The windows were fogged, light was dim, tough to see.

"I love you," Jamey said.

"Sure."

"I want you to be my wife."

Caddy searched the blacktop for that middle white line. She kept on driving. No direction. Nowhere to go.

21

"About time you got here," Jean Colson said.

"Been a little busy, Mom," Quinn said.

"Anything good?"

Quinn slid in next to Jason in a booth toward the back of the El Dorado. He wrapped his arm around Jason and pulled him close for a hug. "Nope," Quinn said. "Where's Caddy?"

"Running late," Jean said. "She told us to go ahead and eat. You know we waited on you thirty minutes?"

The table was littered with a half-empty basket of chips and a couple platters of picked-over Mexican food. Jean already had another damn cigarette out, Quinn hating it when she smoked around Jason. But if he brought up cigarettes, she'd bring up cigars. And when he tried to explain they weren't as hazardous as bullets, the conversation was already derailed.

"So, what was going on?" Jean asked.

He winked at her. "How about we talk about it later."

"You have to shoot someone?" Jason said.

"Nope."

"I like it when you shoot those bad guys," Jason said. "Them bastards."

Jean's face colored a bit and she stubbed out her cigarette in what was left of her chimichanga. She reached for Jason's hand and politely excused them as they both walked outside to talk.

Quinn went ahead and ordered a couple steak tacos and a Coke, wanting that beer that would never be served in Jericho on a Sunday. From where he sat, he could see Jean getting down on one knee, a bit awkward with her added weight, speaking to Jason in those careful, plaintive tones about making the right decisions. As soon as he turned twelve, Quinn would have to give him a talk about how he'd been right. That some bastards really did need shooting down.

He ate some chips and checked his phone. He'd eat quick and then head back out to find Caddy. Even if she didn't respond to him, Jean would know where to find her. Quinn stood and hung his damp coat on a hook, setting his ball cap on top.

When he sat back down, Anna Lee and Luke Stevens walked through the front door and said hello to Javier, who took them to a table not five feet from Quinn. She was holding their daughter, all of them dressed for the First Baptist Church, which was a bit more formal than Calvary Methodist or The River. Quinn stood and spoke to them. Anna Lee met his eye but turned away, Luke gripped his hand and patted him on the back. He told Quinn how good it was to see him and wondered what was new in Tibbehah.

"You missed a triple homicide this morning," Quinn said. "Could've used you."

"Can't say I miss coroner work," Luke said, still smiling, hand still on Quinn's back. "How's Ophelia working out for y'all?"

"Just fine," Quinn said.

Luke loosened his tie and grinned some more. "Not bad lookin', either."

Anna Lee glanced up from where she'd settled the baby into a high chair, eyes flashing on Quinn's and then back on Luke's. Everything kind of paused there for a moment, and Luke's hand left Quinn's shoulder and he walked back to his table. He said he hoped he and Quinn might get to do some turkey hunting next weekend.

"Or we can just sit around and drink some whiskey," Luke said.

Quinn nodded. Anna Lee studied the menu.

Jean and Jason were back through the front door, Jason looking a little sullen until Quinn pretended to reach for the rest of Jason's food. Jason giggled and pretended he might stab Quinn's hand with a fork, pulling away his quesadilla and biting into it just to show his uncle. Jean said her hellos to the Stevenses, walked to their table, and made over the baby.

"How was church?" Quinn asked Jason.

Jason shrugged. He was quiet and a little fidgety.

"You have fun?"

"They sing a lot."

"Did you sing?"

"No, sir," he said. "Lots of people prayed and cried."

"Yep, that's what they do."

"Why do they do that, Uncle Quinn?"

"It makes some people feel a lot better."

"Would it make me feel better to pray and cry?" Jason asked.

"Not especially."

"Or to sing?"

"You feel like singing?" Quinn said.

"No, sir."

"Did your mother have a good time?"

"Yes, sir."

"Did she sing?"

"Yes, sir."

"Did she cry?"

"No, sir."

"You know where your momma is right now?"

Jason squinted in thought and then shook his head. Jean came back to the table, pushed away her food and leaned into the table, saying how any day was a good day with her boys. "That baby is just darlin'."

"Has Mr. Jamey or your momma had any company lately?" Quinn said. "At the house?"

Jason shook his head.

"What are y'all talking about?" Jean said.

"Just wondering if Jason has seen any mean men," Quinn said.

"I'm not supposed to talk about mean men," Jason said.

"You can tell me."

"Grandmomma says I can't."

"Grandmomma just doesn't want you to call them rotten bastards."

"Quinn," Jean said.

"So have you seen any mean men around Mr. Jamey's church or your momma's house?"

"No, sir," Jason said. Quinn smiled at him and stole some chips off his plate.

Jean, settled in beside Quinn, leaned in and whispered in his ear, "What the hell is going on? Is Caddy OK?"

"Fine," Quinn said, keeping a smile. "Everything is just fine. But would you mind calling my sister and tell her I want to see her? We can talk later."

Jean shook her head in confusion and reached into a large red purse for her half-glasses and cell phone. Quinn looked up from the table and watched Anna Lee and her family. Quinn thought about all those evenings when Anna Lee's folks would be out late and he'd come over to watch television only to end up in her canopy bed, trying like hell to get her out of her Levi's. Both of them wandering and experimenting, and her trying like hell to keep his hands from where they shouldn't go until neither of them could stand it and she finally shed her jeans. Quinn pulled her into her lacy bed, knocking off pillows and stuffed animals to be with her again and again and again.

Luke had his arm around Anna Lee, staring at their daughter, talking with the baby. He pulled Anna Lee tight and kissed her on the cheek, and something in Quinn's chest

226

felt a little ragged and open.

Luke looked up from the table and met Quinn's eye with a wink, asking him again about getting together next weekend for a hunt. "We'll tear it up, buddy."

"Can't wait," Quinn said.

"OK," Jean said, placing her phone back into her purse. "Caddy says she'll meet you at home."

Esau and Bones dumped the Tundra and picked up a nearly new Dodge Charger, basic black, at the Cook Bros. dealership at the city limits. The lot was closed for the weekend and the Charger wouldn't be noticed till Monday, and by then they'd be long gone. The Charger had an all-black interior and a fine stereo system. Bones listened to a black church service as they rode around town, trying to find Jamey Dixon. They stopped off at a Sonic and ate a couple burgers and tots, and then decided just to head out to Dixon's church and sit there for a while. Bones tucked the car off to the side, where Dixon couldn't see them when he drove up that long stretch of gravel road. They sat in the car for a long while, resting, rain pelting the car, turning the radio to a station out of Tupelo doing a double shot of Alan Jackson.

227

Bones said he liked Jackson a lot better than most country. "But ain't nobody Charley Pride," he said. "My momma's favorite."

"You got that right," Esau said.

After a couple hours, they got tired and decided to stretch their legs, running through the rain to the back door of the church. It didn't take nothing to bust the back door, nothing but a clasp and a Master Lock, Esau and Bones wondering why Dixon even went to the trouble. They walked on into the barn or sanctuary or whatever Dixon was calling it. Being back around Dixon made Esau think on all those services at the place called the Spiritual Life Center, being too wrong to call anything in prison a damn church. Dixon used to put on shows where he'd play guitar and witness, closing out every service with "Knockin' on Heaven's Door" to all the murderers, thieves, and rapists wanting to hear that message. Esau figured he'd been part of that group, following Jamey Dixon and seeing him as the real deal walking among the prisoners. Many long hours they would pray together and have debates on the Bible and theology, and all that shit rang pretty true until Dixon got himself released and never looked back. That left a man with

228

a real burn in his heart. Esau promised Dixon a partnership, a share of the spoils of another life in order to make them better. He listened, never committing, and Esau wondered now if he hadn't just gone stupid and returned the money. But hell, a convict was a convict, and all this equipment and guitars and lights and just the damn barn and the land cost money. This was where some of it was going, the rest of it probably stashed with his girlfriend.

They walked the dirt floor, chairs neatly stacked and hung from hooks on the wall, until they heard a truck's motor grow close. He and Bones just stood there as they heard the clatter of chains and the big bay door slid back on the headlights of an old GMC truck shining straight on them. Esau squinted into the light, knowing it was Dixon behind that wheel. He crossed his thick arms over his chest and just waited.

Dixon killed the engine and then the lights.

Esau moved his hand to the .357, touching the butt of the gun.

22

Dixon got out from behind the wheel, left the truck door open, and walked through the rain and oozing mud on into the barn. His hands were empty, and he kept them loose by his sides for Esau and Bones to see. Esau nodded at him, all of them knowing this could end only with the three of them. If not, they'd all head on back to Parchman, where a man's worth was measured in cigarettes, tattoos, and candy bars.

"Where's Dickie?" Dixon said.

"He shot the motherfucker," Bones said. "Man was getting on our last nerve."

"I don't have the money," Dixon said. "Y'all need to just head on."

Esau walked out to Dixon's truck, checked inside for anyone hiding, and slammed the door shut. He ran back into the barn.

"Why'd you go see my girlfriend?" Dixon said. "She ain't a part of this."

"Yeah?" Bones nodded, rubbing his nappy

chin. "I'd say she's neck-deep in shit now."

"I didn't raise that truck."

"You think someone else just happened to find it and took it for themselves?" Esau said. "Maybe they were fishing and just kind of hooked a Wells Fargo truck and thought it was a big bass?"

Jamey shook his head. "You're missing my meaning."

"How about you explain it?" Bones said.

The rain fell in long sweeping sheets outside. The wind blew in hard from outside, knocking a tablecloth off a picnic table and sending the homemade cross over the altar to swing back and forth off chains. Dixon looked over his shoulder at the cross. He raised his hand and said, "I told someone," he said. "I guess they took it. You can blame me or kill me or whatever you want. But I didn't see one penny from what y'all stole. I didn't want to touch it. Two men died because of that robbery."

"You say you just told somebody?" Bones said. "Like, 'Hey, motherfucker, you want to know where to find a big ole armored car loaded down with loot?' What the hell you do that for?"

"To cornhole us," Esau said. "Right, Dixon? Jesus Christ. You think we believe that? These Peavey amps and guitars and

231

light rigging and all that shit cost money."

"It was donated," Jamey said.

"*Bull*shit," Bones said.

"Maybe we should believe him," Esau said. "He's riding high on the path to redemption; to hell with his old buddies."

"I helped you inside," Dixon said. "You wouldn't have made it through. Let's call it even."

"Nobody's ever even," Bones said.

Dixon lowered his head and studied the ground.

"Who's got our money?" Esau said. He figured he'd been calm on the whole matter up to a point.

Dixon shook his head some more. Esau lifted his eyes at Bones, Bones nodding back.

Ain't no way to remedy the situation without a good old-fashioned ass-whippin'.

Quinn met Caddy outside Jean's house, the same house where they'd both been raised. Jean's car wasn't there, only Caddy's Honda parked outside, windshield wipers going, engine idling as she waited for Quinn. She hit the locks and he slid inside, the interior fogging up. Her eyes were swollen as if she'd been crying for a while, and she looked mad and confused, not saying a word for a long while as they sat.

"I need you to listen," she said.

"Where is he?"

"Let me talk."

"You know about these men broke out of Parchman? His friends?"

"I need you to listen, Quinn," Caddy said. "Can you just do that for me for one second?"

"Nope."

"Then get out," she said. "I didn't have to meet you here. This is my business."

"Caddy, this stopped being personal after we found three dead men this morning," he said.

"We don't know anything about that," Caddy said.

Quinn reached over and pulled the keys from the ignition. "We're going to go inside, sit down at the table, and talk this thing out. I had two U.S. Marshals in my office this morning, looking for Jamey's pals."

"I don't care what those men did or why they're here."

"Marshals said inside they were buds with Jamey," he said. "They believe they'll go to him for help."

She held the wheel very tight, staring straight ahead, and said, "Why is everyone here trying to pull him down?" she said.

"This is the most rotten, backstabbing town. Everyone dressed up today to sing hymns and pretend to know Jesus."

"Jamey ever talk to you about having money hidden?"

Caddy shook her head.

"Have they come to see him?"

Caddy shook her head but said, "Yes."

"When?"

"Yesterday," Caddy said. "He told them to leave and never come back."

"That ought to work."

Caddy shook her head some more and rubbed her face. All the windows of her car had fogged, closing them into the small space, the air sluggish and warm. Around the edge of the house, back behind the driveway, stood their old tree fort. Quinn had spent a few days in the summer repairing the rotten boards for Jason. He found a couple of Caddy's Barbies buried in the muck along with his toy soldiers. Jean was too sentimental to tear it down when it had been time.

"How'd y'all buy that land out there?" Quinn asked.

"He didn't buy it," she said. "Mr. Bishop is letting him use it till we can build a place."

"Mr. Bishop's never been that generous."

"Give me back my fucking keys."

234

"You can sit out here or do what you like," Quinn said. "You try and walk off and I'll arrest you."

"For what?"

"I can make up a lot of shit, Caddy."

"You don't know anything about him."

"I learned a lot from the Bundrens."

"Ophelia Bundren is batshit crazy," Caddy said. "She gets off on telling people how to embalm the dead, how she'll see everybody naked one time or another. She's a sadist. Sick and disgusting. Her sister was a fucking whore."

"Easy."

Caddy's face flushed, gripping the wheel. "Give me back my keys."

"Where's Dixon?"

"His name is Jamey," Caddy said.

"I'll call him what I like."

"Well, you do that," Caddy said. "And then you can explain to Jason why you won't call his new father by his first name or treat him with respect."

Quinn stayed silent. He watched a pair of old bamboo wind chimes flail in the wind from under the old tree fort. Sometimes at night, he would awake thinking he could hear them from a million miles away.

"It means we're getting married, Quinn," Caddy said. "Jamey is going to be your brother-in-law."

Quinn nodded. He took a very deep breath.

"Sure must be nice being that high up," Caddy said. "Have you forgotten who we all used to be?"

Esau rushed Dixon and punched him hard in the mouth. He stumbled, keeping his feet while Bones reached up on the wall for an ax handle without a blade and took to Jamey Dixon like he was a Tijuana piñata. He whipped him hard across the back and then took out his knees, really going to work on his ass as he was on the ground, tearing into him like chopping logs. Esau decided to circle about and took turns kicking him in the stomach and head whenever he saw a clear shot. After a few minutes, Bones was breathing hard, worn out from using the ax handle, and stepped back and slung the wood down onto the dirt floor. Dixon looked like shit. His face and arms were bruised and bloody.

"Who got our fucking money?" Esau said.

Dixon leaned over and spit out some blood. He got to his knees, and then fell over on his side in pain. He probably had several cracked ribs, maybe one of the bones poking him in the lungs. Man should have had more common sense.

Bones picked up the ax handle again, and Esau repeated, "Who?"

Dixon did not answer.

Esau nodded to Bones, and the man went back to work for a while. Esau kicked him hard in the stomach, stomping his ass good with his truck stop cowboy boots. They took him to the edge of passing out and backed off as he seemed to lose consciousness. Esau could care less about hurting the son of a bitch, only getting to the point of the matter.

"Mr. Stagg," Dixon said.

"Who the fuck is Mr. Stagg?" Esau said.

"Man who paid for my freedom," Dixon said.

"Where's he at?" Bones said.

Esau reached for Dixon's hand and pulled him to his feet. Dixon shuffled and nearly fell into some stacked hay, barely holding himself upright while he took a breath, bloody bubbles coming out of his mouth and nose. He turned to Esau and said, "Satan comes in many guises."

Esau laughed. "So who the hell is Johnny Stagg?"

Dixon nodded. "Y'all need to get gone. I prayed long and hard about what I've done. But that money was wicked from the get-go and something that never belonged to any of this. I am asking you to go as a friend."

Bones looked to Esau. Esau nodded in thought.

"Appreciate that," Esau said. "But you're coming with us to see this Mr. Stagg."

"He controls this county and most of Memphis," Dixon said. "He'll have us all killed if y'all go knock on his door."

"Ain't no y'all," Bones said. "More like we. You're full-tilt in this, preacher."

Esau snatched up Dixon by the arm, Dixon yelling in pain as they dragged him to the Dodge Charger. "So, just where does Satan set up shop in Jericho, Mississippi?" Esau asked.

"He's a good man, Quinn," Caddy said. "I think that's what bothers you the most."

"Nope," Quinn said. "I think your brain is clouded. And I believe Dixon's ties to his jailhouse buds are tighter than anything he has with you."

"He told them to leave."

"You want to risk you and Jason getting hurt on what you suppose?" Quinn said. "A sensible person always plans for what could happen. The worst of it."

"You're the one who seeks out violence and killing," Caddy said. "Jamey has come home to make Jericho a better place and help people."

"I don't seek out killing," Quinn said.

"But you always find it," she said. "You ever think about that?"

Quinn looked up the hill, water coming down a narrow ravine from the playhouse up in the scraggly old pines. He used his hand to clear off the fogged windows, trying to think out what he wanted to say and help Caddy not speed off half-cocked.

"Evil people live among us," Quinn said. "You and I've known that our whole lives. Uncle Hamp knew it, too. He looked out for all the children."

"And look what it did to him."

Quinn nodded. He leaned back in the seat, windows fogging again.

"I love Jamey," Caddy said.

"If those men are gone, then they're gone. But I want to have a real heart-to-heart with Dixon and see exactly where he stands."

"His name is Jamey," Caddy said. "He wants to marry me."

"I love you, Caddy," Quinn said. "It's just the four of us. But you need to trust me. Dixon is bad news."

Caddy placed her fingers to her mouth, thinking and trying to quiet herself. She turned to Quinn and nodded.

"Call me about the when and where," Quinn said, and gripped the door handle and opened the door out into the rain.

"OK. But I'll need my goddamn keys first."

"Caddy, if you're gonna be a preacher's wife, you might want to think of better ways to communicate."

23

"You think she'll call you?" Boom said.

"Yep," Quinn said. "And I think Dixon will come and see me."

"But you don't think he'll have much to say?"

Quinn shook his head. Boom had closed the big bay doors to the County Barn once Quinn had driven his F-250 inside and killed the engine. The electricity had been knocked out in the last hour or so, and a diesel generator chugged in a far corner. Three orange extension cords pulled from the generator across the concrete floor to the benches where Boom worked.

"I remember something about that armored car being stolen," Boom said. "Some Feds were down here interviewing people if they saw anything. The truck serviced the Jericho bank but never made it. You think Dixon was in on the job?"

"Robbery was a year after he was sen-

241

tenced," Quinn said. "Newspaper stories I found said that truck was carrying almost a million dollars."

Boom gave a low whistle and told Quinn to get back into his truck and try that winch again. Quinn hit the button, and he heard the motor whiz and engage. Boom gave him a thumbs-up and Quinn got back out. That winch had been sticking since Christmas.

The metal barn was as dark as a cave, wind and rain shaking the structure. Opposite his truck, a single bulb hung over an engine of one of their Crown Vics. Since he'd been elected, Quinn had asked the county supervisors to buy new vehicles. Every meeting, they came up with more road projects and more ways to deny Quinn's request. One supervisor said he couldn't rightly spend taxpayers' dollars all willy-nilly. In the same meeting, he agreed to a five-thousand-dollar pay raise and the construction of a barn on his own property.

"A crew just left out of here with sandbags for Sugar Ditch," Boom said. "Mount Zion Church taking on some water."

"I got Kenny and Dave Cullison down there," Quinn said. "Highway by the three-way is submerged. You need a johnboat to cross it."

"When you think this shitstorm is gonna let up?"

"Never." Quinn shrugged. "You mind if I catch some sleep?"

"Here?"

"Faster to roll from here than back at the farm."

"How you gonna sleep?" Boom said. "All I got is that old truck's bench seat in the office."

"That works fine," Quinn said. "I got a radio and a cell. If this thing rolling in looks as bad as they say, I won't be sleeping for a few days. They got tornado watches for every county north of I-20."

Boom nodded. He had a screwdriver fitted into his hand, a long cigarette hanging out of his mouth. "Got a horse blanket back there somewhere. A pillow, too."

"Appreciate it."

"Caddy will come around," Boom said. "Anybody who's been bad fucked up and then gets some perspective will do what it takes to not get back to that place."

"She's not backsliding," Quinn said. "She just has some misplaced faith."

"You mind me asking you something?" Boom said. He pulled the cigarette from his mouth and ashed it.

"Have I ever?"

Quinn pulled the handheld from his truck and his jacket. He walked back into the dim patch of light where Boom worked from his spotless rows of tool benches. There was the comfortable smell there of tobacco and grease, reminding him of his grandfather's work shed. Tools gleamed brightly and clean fitted into their proper slots.

"You ever think that maybe Dixon is the real deal?" Boom said, tossing the cigarette into an empty coffee can, leaning back under the hood of the Crown Vic. "I known a few people who come out of prison straightened out and clean. Just 'cause those men broke out doesn't mean he's a part of it."

"You do know exactly what happened to Adelaide Bundren?"

"Everyone knows," Boom said. He turned back around, walked to the tool bench, and fit a ratchet into his hand and added a socket. "But let's say he did that when he was under the influence. Maybe he really don't remember what happened. Ain't nobody ever said that he pushed her."

"He was convicted of killing her."

"They said he chased her out into the street," Boom said. "But is it possible he didn't? That she just ran? Both of them were a real mess back then. They were part of that crew that hung out at Mr. Horace's place. That juke joint in that old single-wide."

"Doesn't much matter. Our esteemed governor left this flaming pile of dog shit on our doorstep as he left office."

"But if he did chase her," Boom said. He popped a cigarette into his fresh mouth and picked up a lighter. "And he was all fucked up back then. Do you believe we should forgive him?"

"As sheriff?"

"As a Christian," Boom said.

"Hell, I don't know," Quinn said. "I got to get some sleep, Boom." The police scanner squawked in Quinn's hand, water rising down in Sugar Ditch. Two tornadoes touching down in Cohoama County. "We can debate this shit later."

"But what if something had happened to someone who'd been with me when I was drunk and high?" Boom said. "You know how many times I was driving drunk before I got myself clean?"

"Don't want to know."

"You would have forgiven me."

"That's different," Quinn said. "You're my friend. And you never killed anyone."

"Me and you both killed a lot of folks," Boom said. "But me and you both figured what we were doing was right."

"Line of duty isn't in the line of being fucked up."

Boom nodded. He blew smoke from his nose. "Hell of a point."

"Dixon beat up a lot of women before he got to Adelaide Bundren," Quinn said. "Even if he hadn't killed her, would you want him to marry your sister?"

"They're getting married?"

"That's what Caddy says."

"Oh, shit," Boom said, laughing. "What's Miss Jean say about that?"

"I don't think Jean knows."

"How about Jason?"

"I want Caddy to think on this before she talks to him."

"So maybe in that time, you can connect Dixon with those two shitbirds out of Parchman."

"If that's the case, I'd like to make things clearer for her."

"Be real clear if the preacher goes back to prison."

"I thought you were the devil's advocate," Quinn said.

"Caddy sees something in him."

"But would you trust Caddy?"

"Your sister has made so many bad decisions I just figure she's due for a good one,"

Boom said. He thought on that as he ashed his cigarette again and set back to work on the old Crown Vic.

Quinn found the pillow and the horse blanket in Boom's office and was asleep in two minutes.

Jamey Dixon was beat to shit. But it was an amazing thing to witness the power of a .357 against his spine. He limped like a hurt dog as they walked toward the Booby Trap lounge, its big neon sign facing Highway 45 coloring oil-slick puddles. He'd said that's where Johnny Stagg kept his real office, the other one in the truck stop just for show. Dixon said this was the place where they could talk out the entire situation. With the gun pressed hard into his ear, Esau made Dixon call Stagg and make sure he was waiting for him.

If anyone gave them any shit, he and Bones would shoot them down. They didn't have a lot of time to converse.

The titty bar wasn't nothing special, like a hundred places Esau had been in over the years, from Shreveport to Gulfport. Spinning colored lights and loud music and broke-ass girls working the pole. Most of the girls here looked young and underfed. Most of them had little tits and no asses and wore too much makeup and perfume. The whole place smelled of smoke and cherries and coconut oil. A bunch of old truckers wandered in and out of a back room, the place where they could get their pistons greased.

Dixon nodded toward another door and another room beside the bar. They wandered on over, Dixon looking like walking roadkill, face bloody and bruised, and asked a pretty girl pouring drinks if she might inform Mr. Stagg they had arrived.

"Don't get nervous," Bones said. "You won't be the last preacher seen inside a whorehouse."

"And then y'all let me go?" Jamey said.

"Ain't for you to decide," Bones said.

"He ain't gonna give up nothing," Jamey said.

The bartender had disappeared into the back room. Esau kept the gun on Jamey, holding it real close as a skinny thing in a pink bra and panties did the splits and then turned around and smacked her ass to a Skynyrd song. She didn't even have enough meat to make it shake. Bones shook his head in shame.

The door opened and a fat guy in a cop uniform emerged. Esau started to pull the gun fast, but the guy just motioned for them to come on in. He wore a buzz cut and had one wandering eye. His badge said he was the chief of police of Jericho and his name was Leonard.

They moved down a long hall and into a curve and then the fat cop stopped them cold. "Give me that gun."

Esau shook his head.

The fat cop, Leonard, reached for his hand like he had some kind of power, and Esau whipped him hard across the mouth, knocking his fat ass against the wall. Bones was on him, pulling a gun from the man's waist and checking down his body and legs for more. He found a little .22 on his ankle, pocketed it, and walked on into the office.

Inside, a weathered old hillbilly in a bright red sweater had his feet kicked up on a desk. He was talking on a phone, not a cell but a real-deal old push-button phone held to his ear. When the three of them walked on in, his hooded eyes wandered over them and he said into the mouthpiece, "Let me call you back."

Esau gripped Jamey Dixon by the neck and threw him onto the man's carpet. The fat cop stumbled on in after them, shaking his head like there was something stuck in his ear.

No one spoke for a while.

Dixon tried to get up. Esau knocked him back down.

"You Johnny Stagg?" Esau said.

The old hillbilly nodded. His room filled with all kind of photos and certificates and six flat-screen monitors, about the size of what he used to keep at his bunk at Parchman, tuned to different spots in the truck stop and the girls dancing on poles.

"You got something that belongs to us," Bones said.

"I got men coming in here in about thirty seconds," Stagg said. "Y'all better talk fast or shoot faster."

Stagg had yet to drop his feet off the desk, wearing oxblood loafers buffed to a high shine and fancy socks that didn't suit a hillbilly at all. His eyes flicked over the television monitors and then back to Esau and Bones and Jamey Dixon bleeding on his carpet.

"Leonard, get Reverend Dixon a towel," Stagg said. "He's making a real mess in here."

Stagg had a slight facial tic, not speaking, waiting all cool, feet still, hands still. The man didn't look a bit concerned that he was holding court with a couple armed escaped convicts.

"This man made a trade to you with

something wasn't his," Esau said. "Just when did you pull up that armored truck?"

Stagg smiled in a curious way.

"You mind me asking you first how you did it?" Stagg said. "Y'all managed to sink that son of a bitch before anyone in this county saw a thing. That old road is pretty highly traveled. I have to commend you on your incredible stealth."

"My buddy T-boned the son of a bitch with a diesel fitted with a steel grille guard," Esau said. "Didn't mean to knock it into the pond. It just kind of worked out that way."

Stagg smiled and nodded, just sort of amused to be in their company.

"So why don't you just open up your safe and hand over what you got," Esau said. "It needs to be close, but we won't count you to the penny."

"Appreciate that, boys," Stagg said.

His eyes roamed over the monitor, smile growing bigger, looking just like a Halloween jack-o'-lantern. Bones glanced over to the monitor and back to Stagg. "Those your boys with the shotguns?"

Esau saw the bright images from a security camera of two men in dark rain jackets holding pump shotguns heading toward the front door.

"No, sir," Stagg said, grinning a set of teeth as big and flat as a row of tombstones. "I guess y'all geniuses didn't notice you were being followed by a couple U.S. Marshals. See what it spells on their jackets right there? Did I mention these TVs are high-def? You can count the freckles inside a woman's thigh."

Esau looked to Bones. The men were coming through the door now. Another monitor showed them inside the club, yelling something. That pounding bass you could hear through the walls suddenly stopped. Now there was only the rain on the windows. Johnny Stagg recrossed his feet at the ankles and grinned at them.

He lifted up his hands in surrender and said, "Y'all boys got me now. What was it you came for again?"

24

Lillie Virgil lived in a little white house by the old train depot just north of Jericho. Caddy had always loved Lillie's little house, the white clapboards covered with pink climbing roses and yellow jessamine and blood-red canna lilies that grew to huge heights in the hot summers. She had a nice wide screened porch on the side of the house and a potting shed she'd pulled together from barn wood and scrap tin. There was a composter and a big stack of antique bricks she figured Lillie was using to expand a little backyard gazebo, and white Christmas lights strewn overhead, clicking in the strong wind and rain. Caddy knocked on Lillie's side door, her hand firmly holding Jason's, and waited. Her car was still running. It had been two hours since she'd seen Quinn, and she still couldn't find Jamey.

Lillie came to the back door, drying her

hands. Inside the kitchen, Caddy spotted Lillie's adopted daughter Rose sitting in a high chair, face covered in baby food. Lillie was still wearing her sheriff's office uniform.

"Sorry, Lillie," Caddy said. "But I could really use a favor right about now."

"Come on," Lillie said. "Feeding Rose some supper. Y'all want something to eat? I was heating up some peas and making some cornbread."

"I need you to watch Jason," Caddy said, almost in a blurt.

"Y'all come on in."

"I can't."

She had pulled Jason up under her jacket, but his face and hair had gotten very wet. Lillie nodded for him to come on in, her small kitchen with a propane stove smelling warm and inviting. She had one of those antique Hoosier cabinets and a big wooden sideboard, old-fashioned advertisements hung on the wall. "I'll be back in an hour or two," Caddy said.

"Where's Jean?"

"I'd rather we keep this between us."

"You mean don't tell Quinn," Lillie said.

"Please."

Lillie asked her again to please come inside, and Caddy again refused. She did not want Jason to be with her when she found Jamey. And she did not want Jason with her if she had to run into Quinn. She wanted to handle this thing on her own, and the faster she found Jamey, the sooner this could all be over. She did not want Jamey to feel like he was alone in this. She didn't want Quinn to know any more than was necessary.

"Is Jamey coming by the office to talk to Quinn?" Lillie said.

Caddy shook her head. "I don't know," she said. "I can't find him."

"You know what we found today out by the Hardins' pond?"

Caddy nodded. "I just need a little time, Lillie," she said. "A couple hours."

Lillie did not like the situation at all, rag held loose in her hand and baby starting to cry, but she nodded anyway. "If I don't hear from you, you know I'll have to call Quinn."

"I promise, I'll be back," Caddy said. "You have such a beautiful home."

"Please come on out of the rain," Lillie said. "Let's talk."

Jason had already sat down at Lillie's kitchen table. He took off his yellow raincoat and hung it neatly on the back of the chair, where he watched little Rose with a lot of interest. Rose watched him back.

255

"Thank you," Caddy said. "I owe you, Lillie."

"Please don't get me in trouble."

Caddy nodded. "I won't."

"Do you know what you're doing?"

Caddy smiled for the first time since the morning service. "Believe it or not, I actually think I do."

"Where's your back door?" Esau said.

"Figured you'd be asking about it," Stagg said.

"Get your fucking feet off the desk and get your ass up," Esau said. "You're coming with us."

Johnny Stagg shook his head like a man who'd never followed orders in his life. He just folded his hands in his lap and pointed to video screens. "Only one way in and out of the Booby Trap," he said. "We made it that way to keep boys from jumpin' out on their tabs."

Bones wandered up beside Esau and pointed to Stagg's picture frames. "You really get your picture made with Charley Pride? You see that, man? Charley Pride. Where'd you get that taken?"

"Choctaw Casino in next county down," Stagg said, grinning wide. He stood, Esau leveling the .357 at his belly but Stagg seeming to care less. He turned and pointed to the photo like he was giving a grand tour. "He did a beautiful version of 'The Day the World Stood Still.'"

"Charley Fucking Pride," Bones said.

There was more yelling from the big room, and somewhere a girl screamed. Esau reached across the big desk and grabbed Johnny Stagg's bony arm and pulled him clean on over. "Now, march, motherfucker. We're all getting out of here alive and together. And then you're going to be getting us our money."

"Ain't but one way," Stagg said.

They headed back out in the hall. Bones had the shotgun he'd taken off Dixon's woman trained on Dixon and on the fat police chief. They let the three men lead the way out of the back rooms, twisting the corners and coming to the big metal door that was set aside of the bar. On the other side, they could hear a hell of a commotion.

"You really a cop or just a real ugly stripper?" Bones said.

"Mister, you've just gone and kidnapped the chief of police of Jericho, Mississippi," said Leonard the cop.

"Damn shame," Bones said. "Now open the fucking door, Chief. You going out first. And watch out for their shotguns, cut

257

through a man real quick. Don't go fast, and don't try to be a dumbass hero."

The fat man was sweating as he pulled the door inward, Bones and Esau standing back of the three men. The house lights had gone up in the club, and girls were sitting buck-ass nekkid on the edge of the stage. The colored lights still twirled, and the disco ball scattered light on the ceiling. The two U.S. Marshals were waiting on them, standing between them and the door, both of them brandishing pump shotguns. One of them old and white-haired, the other a little quicker, with a drooping mustache and hard eyes. Esau and the law just never could get along. He'd never met a cop that was worth two shits, all of them nothing but grown-up titty babies.

Up above the stage, a teenage white boy with tattoos down his arms raised his hands up, scared shitless.

"How about some music?" Bones said. Esau prodded Johnny Stagg. Bones kicked Jamey Dixon square in the ass to keep him going. The fat cop had his hands up, wandering forward, not needing anyone to tell him how to dance. "I said play some fucking music," Bones said.

Esau aimed his .357 up at the DJ and nodded.

The boy wore a sleeveless black T-shirt showing thin and bony arms. Esau wanted to just shoot him where he stood, but that would bring on those pumps and it would be a hell of a mess. They used the three men as cover and they'd walk from the Booby Trap just as pretty as you please.

"What do you want?" The white DJ's voice sounded high like a woman's. He was nervous as hell. The girls, black and white and Mexican, had started to huddle together and were slipping back into their bras and nighties. The air still smelling of stale smoke and cherries and cheap-ass perfume.

"Play 'All I Have to Offer You Is Me,' " Bones said.

"What's that?"

"Charley Pride, you dumb motherfucker," Bones said.

"Who's Charley Pride?" said the DJ.

"Jesus H.," said Bones.

The Marshals had not moved an inch. Shit, Esau wasn't sure they had even blinked. They just stood there, immobile, breathing, keeping their eyes on Esau and Bones, 12-gauges keeping them from the front door, the cool air outside, and heading on down the road with Mr. Johnny Stagg.

"I should shoot you right now," Bones

said. " 'Who is Charley Pride?' "

"You got it, Brian," Stagg said, grinning like he was still the host of some fish fry. "Look under the country music. We play it up for the Ruritans."

Brian. Fucking Brian went to looking and came up with the CD, smiling like he'd really accomplished something for old Johnny Stagg. "Got it," he said. "Got it. What's that song again?"

The short Marshal with the mustache and Wyatt Earp complex dropped the muzzle a half-inch and raised it up real quick. One of the dumb girls, a black girl with a wide ass, held on to the gold pole as she zipped up a pair of knee-high go-go boots.

" 'All I Have to Offer You Is Me,' " Bones said. "Shit fire."

And then there was lap steel and sad guitar and that steady drumbeat and Charley Pride asking some woman to marry him even though he didn't have a pot to piss in. No crystal chandeliers. No mansion on the hill. No fancy clothes for her to wear. Basically, the woman was fucked. Esau had promised Becky a lot better a long time back.

"Move," Esau said, pushing Stagg forward. The lights danced over them, the strippers huddled together, watching the show. A couple dumb-eyed truckers sat in their easy chairs with shaking hands still raised. Stagg followed Chief Leonard, and Dixon followed Stagg. The shotgun barrels of the Marshals moved with them all slow and easy, almost in time with Charley Pride, as if they were all at a country dance. The girls' mouths open, the Marshals made of wax. Ain't nobody wanted to shoot. That was the shit of the whole situation. Someone was gonna have to fire first, because this thing wasn't gonna end pretty for none of them.

Chief opened up the door to the smell of rain and spring outside, and a sky that was dull and dark. The Marshals pivoting, and then following, .357 screwed down into Stagg's head, Esau ready to pull that trigger any second and send them all on a one-way trip to hell. They backed up, music growing fainter, door slamming behind them, and all coming into the wide truck stop parking lot. Bones tossed a set of keys to Dixon and told him to start up his old GMC. Dixon walked around the battered front grille and got his hand on the handle before getting really stupid and making a run for it.

He got ten feet before Bones shot Dixon in the leg.

Stagg fell flat to the ground and covered

his head. His dumbass buddy got down a little slower. And then those Marshals fired off two, three, four rounds of buckshot right to where he and Bones stood, breaking out Dixon's truck windshield and scattering glass across their faces and onto the wet asphalt. Esau wasn't seeing so good with something very unpleasant in his eye, but he got a good enough view to cut down the short Marshal in the chest. Bones squeezed off that 12-gauge and knocked that old Marshal off his feet and flat on his back. Esau reached for Johnny Stagg, pulling him along with them.

Even with the shot leg, Jamey Dixon had jackrabbited far and away.

"Come on," Esau said, yelling. "Come on. We're taking this son of a bitch with us."

Stagg's easygoing confidence was gone. He looked as if he'd shit his pants.

"I said come on," Esau said. "You ole devil."

25

"You want to take a look?" Ophelia asked.

She and Quinn were again standing in the foyer of the Bundren Funeral Home. A service was going on in the chapel; Tom Cat McCain's wife had finally died after a long and brave fight with something or other. Ophelia had been prepping her when they brought in the dead from the Hardin place. Quinn felt sorry for Ophelia. Even his stomach turned at seeing what was left of the two guards.

"It wasn't so bad," she said when Quinn had asked. "They were kind of half rotten and half pickled. Always interesting to see what happens to a body after time. I don't think I'd ever seen someone had been down there that long. Not much left. I took some photos, looked for anything obvious. But not much to really see. I think I know which is which from measuring them. But they'll have to set the families straight with dental records. Can you believe their uniforms were still intact? That's some fine Chinese craftsmanship. One hundred percent polyester. Shoes, guns, and gunbelt made out fine."

"Anything to note?"

Inside the chapel, a PA system was playing Sandi Patty singing "In Heaven's Eyes." Quinn had never been a real fan of Sandi Patty's. Jean downright hated anything contemporary, citing Elvis's love of old-time hymns as testament.

"One of the men had a bashed-in skull and a broken shoulder," Ophelia said. She was dressed for the job today, not for greeting the bereaved. She wore an old pair of jeans and black T-shirt with sneakers. She had a surgeon's mask hanging from her neck. "Sure you don't want to take a peek?"

"What about the other man?" Quinn said. "The fresh one? Richard Green?"

"I don't like to judge," Ophelia said. "We're all the same in His eyes. But he was one weird-looking human. I've never seen anyone with teeth in such decay. And I've never worked on a body with a tattoo on their penis. Why would someone do that?"

"I guess it can get boring in prison," Quinn said.

The Sandi Patty stopped. Thank God.

264

And some prerecorded organ began. Or at least Quinn thought it was prerecorded. As many times as he'd been in the Bundren's wood-paneled little chapel, he'd never seen an organ.

"Did I wake you?" Ophelia asked.

"Nope."

"You just sounded tired when I called," she said. "Like you'd been asleep."

"Always call for something like this," Quinn said. "I'd like to get these reports written and moving down the line. The bank is notifying the families of the guards, but I'm sure the Feds will be down here sooner than later."

The chapel doors opened, and people in uncomfortable suits and dresses came filtering out. Ophelia motioned for Quinn to follow her back into her father's office and turned on a light on his desk. The room looked as if it had been unchanged since 1976. More wood paneling and one of those glass cubes for family photos. The cube and several photos on the wall were of the twins, Ophelia and Adelaide.

"I'm sorry about cornering you," Ophelia said, noticing Quinn staring at the family photos. "I guess you know it all now. And it's up to you to talk to Caddy."

Quinn had yet to take a seat and looked

Ophelia right in the eye. "Caddy says Dixon has asked her to marry him."

"Holy shit."

"Yep."

"What did she say?"

"What do you think?"

"Holy shit."

"Yep."

"I know a half-dozen girls in Jericho who went out with that piece of shit, before Adelaide and during. You know Connie Fisher? The one who owns the tanning parlor? She says Dixon knocked her unconscious one night. He'd been drinking Jäger and taking pills, and said he didn't like the way she was looking at some boys at a field party."

"Can you get me those results tonight?"

"How about the morning?" Ophelia said.

Quinn nodded. Ophelia sat down on the edge of her father's desk and pulled the mask off her neck and tossed it in the trashcan. "I got to get those bodies tagged and bagged and then I'm locking up. You want to head down to Pap's for some catfish? My treat."

"I'd love it, but I'm just coming on."

"I thought you were just headed off?"

"Nights," Quinn said. "I'm on nights for the time being."

"That hadn't stopped you from getting

called during the day."

"Perks of the job."

The only light in the room came from the green-shaded banker lamp, sounds from the murmurs of well-wishers talking out in the hall. You could hear most of what they were saying very clearly. Most of them wondering if they'd get Miss McCain in the ground tomorrow with the weather being so bad and all. Quinn and Ophelia sat in the half-dark, listening for a while. She looked down at her slim hands, red mouth in a knot, having something to say but holding it back a bit.

"My mom and I appreciate the warning," Quinn said.

Ophelia nodded. "Some other time for dinner?"

"You bet," Quinn said.

"There aren't many people in this town that I like, Quinn," she said. "Anyone our age that isn't stupid, crazy, or flat-ass broke has left Jericho. I don't think they are ever coming back."

"Never thought I would."

"Family," she said, large brown eyes lifting on Quinn. "It's a hell of a thing."

"Do you boys have a fucking clue as to what you're doing?" Johnny Stagg said. "I don't

267

have your money. And if I did, I don't go around and carry a million dollars in my wallet."

"You get shot?" Esau said. Bones was driving, heading far out in the county, back to the hunt club. Beyond getting up with Becky, he wasn't too sure about what came next.

"Nah," Stagg said, sitting in the jump seat between them. "I wasn't shot."

"Then how come you're bleeding?" Esau said. "You got blood all over your face."

"Got some buckshot or glass in me," Stagg said. "I don't even know how you can see me with that eye."

"Lookin' rough, Esau," Bones said, turning off Highway 9, driving toward the National Forest, the piney hills rising up out of the misty farmland. "Better get that checked out."

Esau flipped down the visor mirror and studied his eye. His whole right eye was clouded with blood, no white of it left. Down in the deep corner he spotted a gouge where the glass had chipped in. Son of a bitch, live to walk away from two U.S. Marshals only to get a drop of glass in your eye. It hurt like a son of a bitch, and he couldn't see for shit.

"Mr. Stagg," Esau said. "Me and Mr.

Magee don't have much time to waste. And we do appreciate you taking a nice little Sunday ride with us. But we're getting the hell out of this county before midnight and we want to be compensated for what you and Jamey Dixon took from us. So you best quit worrying about my personal health and start studying up on your own dilemma."

Stagg sucked on his tooth and looked at the back of his hand that he'd wrapped with his red sweater. There was some nastiness to the wound but nothing that would kill him anytime soon. Bones was whistling along to that Charley Pride song as they rounded a corner by a grouping of three silos and an old barn, another road twisting and snaking up on into the forest and the hunt club. Esau called Becky, and when she answered, talked fast. He said he just wanted to make sure everything was fine. "And I'm bringing a guest. Who? Just wait, doll. He's a respected member of the community."

The dirt road up to the club was rutted and worn, swinging Johnny Stagg this way and that from Esau and Bones, jerking him up and down till the hunt lodge appeared on the horizon. "Y'all know that there house belongs to a former U.S. senator?" Stagg said. "He's a fine man and won't like it at all if y'all try and get inside."

"No shit?" Bones said. "Guess I shouldn't been wipin' my ass with his silk bedsheets."

"I need all the cash you got on hand," Esau said. "I figure you got it all in a safe at that truck stop whorehouse. What you're gonna do is reach out to your pal the chief and have him wrangle what you can. I don't think I need to explain the situation to you. I think it's pretty clear what we'll do if you don't want to comply and we're not happy with what we get. We've already killed plenty of men, and your sad, old bony ass won't make a difference to us one fucking bit."

"How long you boys been inside?" Stagg said, still bold enough to pretend this was a conversation.

"Ten years," Bones said, as he hit the gravel road up to the final leg of the lodge. "Ten long years."

"Y'all do some business in Memphis?" Stagg asked.

"Plenty," Esau said.

"Ever hear the name Bobby Campo?" Stagg said.

"Sure, we know Bobby Campo," Bones said. "Motherfucker has that town wired."

"He did," Stagg said. "He's serving some time just right now. But you know people who still run some business up there?"

270

"Yeah," Bones said. "Sure."

"I'd recommend you call those boys and see what kind of anthill you just kicked over here in Tibbehah."

"Why?" Esau said, studying his bad eye in the visor. "Are you somebody?"

"Oh, yes, sir," Stagg said. "I think you need to make some calls and figure out exactly what y'all have done."

Bones drove up beside the wood lodge and killed the engine. Rain continued to pelt the windshield and drain down off the high-pitched tin roof. "I don't think it matters a monkey's ass or not, Mr. Stagg. A dead man's still a dead man. I'd say you need to get on the fucking phone and call that fat-ass chief and get us our fucking money before we blow your goddamn head off. That about the size of it, Esau?"

Esau flipped the visor back up. He turned to Stagg's weathered country ass and took in a deep, long breath. "That's about the size of it."

His eye had started to swell all the way shut. He knew if he didn't find a doctor soon, he'd probably lose it. Right now Esau just wanted to throw back some whiskey, have a smoke, and figure out where and when they were gonna be leaving town. He breathed deep and hard again, balled up his fist, and knocked that silly old son of a bitch hard in his throat.

The man gasped and coughed and sputtered.

Bones got out of the truck but leaned back into the cab for a moment. "What'd you go and do that for?"

"Punctuate the fucking thought," Esau said. "His time is ticking."

26

"I know how it looks," Jamey said. "But I swear to you, I'm fine."

"Jesus, God," Caddy said. "Jesus."

"Just a few bruises and cuts," Jamey said. "I guess they didn't hear the sermon."

She'd found him back at The River, lying down on a hay bale and sucking in some ragged breath. He had blood all over his Sunday shirt; one of his eyes had swollen shut. Somewhere along the way he'd lost a boot, and his sock was thick with mud. His jeans were fresh with blood, and a Western belt cinched his thigh.

"Have you been shot?" she said.

"I don't know," Jamey said. "Maybe. It's not so bad."

"We got to get you to the hospital," Caddy said.

Jamey shook his head. He pushed himself off the hay, sitting upright. Caddy was down on one knee, touching his face, tracing over the cuts and bruises. "Are they done with you?"

Jamey shook his head, taking off the other boot.

"Did you give them what they wanted?"

"They forced me to go see Stagg with them," he said. "I got away, but they took Mr. Stagg. A couple lawmen were killed."

"Oh my God."

"Not Quinn," Jamey said, spitting some blood onto the ground. "No one from around here. These were some U.S. Marshals."

"They killed them?"

"Yep," Jamey said. "Esau Davis and Bones Magee. They said they're not leaving Tibbehah County till they get what they came for."

There was much rain on the barn's tin roof, and the church bulletins fluttered in the wind from the big, open doors. Water dripped from above the rough-hewn rafters. "Will they kill Stagg?" Caddy said.

"Probably," Jamey said, trying to stretch the hurt leg. "He can't have that kind of money lying around. Can he?"

"I hope they do."

"Don't talk like that, Caddy," he said. He coughed up some more blood and spit it onto the dirt floor. "Don't you let them infect you. These are some wicked men, and me and you got to stay strong. Think on this. We can figure it all out. Those boys can't run around forever. Every cop in north Mississippi will be heading this way now."

"How'd you get here from the Rebel?"

"A good Samaritan picked me up. I rode in the back of his truck till we got outside Jericho."

"Did he know you?" Caddy said.

Jamey shook his head and tried to stand. Caddy caught him, holding him up under his arms. Jamey took in a lot of air and grunted with pain. She set him down again. "We're going to the hospital. Now."

He shook his head. "Just give me some time," he said. "Get cleaned up. We need to think. I get connected to this mess and everything we got is gone. Did you see those faces this morning? They need this church. I need it. You, too. Let me just rest and let the law handle it."

"If it was anybody else besides Johnny Stagg that was kidnapped," Caddy said, letting the last bit of it hang.

"What?" Jamey said, unbuttoning his shirt and tearing the cloth in wide strips.

"You think my brother is going to be bustin' down doors for Johnny Stagg?" she said. "Especially if he knew he was the cause of all this?"

"I love you, but you don't believe that," Jamey said, having some difficulty tying the strips around his hurt leg. Caddy tied it off and helped him again to stand. This time he was onto his feet and moving slow, asking for some water.

"No shortage of that," she said. "Step outside and open up your mouth."

"You know who caused all this?" Jamey said. "Right?"

"Those two convicts?"

"We got three men dead because of me," he said. "What I did was wrong. I may not be too bright, but I don't lie to myself, Caddy. I love the Lord. But I loved myself plenty to get out of that jail."

"How were you supposed to know this would happen?"

She brought him a cup of water she'd drawn from the well. As he drank, he winced in pain.

"Maybe not a hospital," she said. "But I do know a doctor, and he's home from Memphis."

"Luke Stevens will tell Quinn."

"Don't you believe that," Caddy said. "Luke has always been a better friend to me than he's ever been to Quinn. Their relationship isn't as complicated as some people think. Come on."

"Where's Jason?"

"Safe."

"Let me just lie down."

"Get in the goddamn car, Jamey Dixon," she said. "I can make you hurt even worse."

Jamey nodded, hobbling along. Rain pinging into a puddle by the pulpit. "Yes, ma'am."

Quinn was helping the county road crew when he got the call about the shooting at the Rebel Truck Stop. He'd been filling sandbags and sending them on down the line, water coming up out of the ditch and flooding across the bottomland littered with ragged trailers. A crew of twenty men and women were working to save the old Zion church from being flooded again. They had just finished rebuilding the whole church eight years ago, no one wanting to relocate from where it had been founded by a group of freed slaves. Quinn traded off with Kenny, who'd been getting some rest.

Two other deputies, Cullison and Watts, were still directing traffic in and around the highway crossroads. Quinn called back to Mary Alice and told her to get in touch with Lillie.

Quinn then turned on the light bar on top

277

of his truck's cab and sped up Highway 9 and then over and up Highway 45, exiting for the Rebel. The rain and wind buffeted his truck as he drove. Neon and big parking lamps lit up the crime scene, where two — meaning, all — Jericho Police Department cars were parked. Leonard had his uniform pants hitched up high as he spit some dip into a cup and wildly pointed for Quinn to park a ways back from the scene.

"Didn't know the Rebel was part of your jurisdiction."

"I got here first," Leonard said. "You welcome to it if you want it. But I got a little bit more experience with this kind of thing, Quinn. How long you been sheriff?"

"Can't figure out why I ever let you go, Leonard," Quinn said.

"You can smart off if you want, but we got two lawmen lying facedown in the puddles there," he said. "Them two convicts went and kidnapped Mr. Stagg, too. I called the highway patrol and the sheriff over in Union County. We're gonna need some help with this. Marshals sending their own men."

"Let's get those bodies covered up."

"Patrol said to wait on them."

"Cover them up, Leonard," Quinn said. "We know who shot them."

"I ain't gonna be responsible for contaminating a crime scene," Leonard said, spitting into a cup. Water beaded off and ran down the bill of his baseball cap. "That's basic to what I learned at the academy."

"You work many homicides?" Quinn said.

Leonard spit.

"If you won't cover them," Quinn said, "I will."

Quinn had a 10×10 blue tarp in the tool box in the back of his Ford and got one of two men who worked for Leonard to help him anchor it down over the bodies. He called Lillie himself, no answer, and then dialed up Ophelia Bundren, saying he needed her, explaining the situation.

"Where's Calamity Jane?" Leonard asked.

Quinn stared into Leonard's full moon face, reddened cheeks, and small black eyes. He turned back to the tarp wavering and buckling on the tarmac like a flag. A group of onlookers had made their way over from the truck stop. And some working girls in high boots and six-inch heels stood under umbrellas, whispering and pointing.

Quinn walked up to the first girl he saw. A mousy girl who couldn't have been much taller than five feet. She had brown hair and a thin, delicate face, and wore a black camisole under a pink raincoat. She was taking pictures of the whole scene with her cell phone.

"You see all this?"

The girl nodded.

"Where did it start?"

She motioned back to the Booby Trap. Her raincoat hung wide open, revealing Chinese symbols decorating the tops of both thighs. Quinn fished into his pocket and pulled out two prints of Davis and Magee. He showed them to her.

She nodded.

"Who else?"

"Mr. Stagg and some other man," she said.

"What did the other man look like?"

"He was tall like you and had long hair," she said. "He had blood on him and a black eye. Had a big-ass tat on his forearm."

"Was it of Jesus?"

"Hell, I don't know," she said. "It may have been Willie Nelson, for all I know."

"Could you pick him out if I found a picture?"

"Yes, sir."

"What's your name?"

"Candace Ledbetter," she said.

"Is that the name you use here?"

"They call me Shorty when I dance."

Quinn tilted his chin down at the girl, who barely reached his chest. "Why?"

The girl smiled.

"You from here?" Quinn asked.

"My people are from Paris, Mississippi, over in Lafayette County."

Quinn told her that she needed to stick around till one of his deputies got here to take down her information.

"I don't want to get mixed up with this," she said. "Those men were crazy as hell. Besides, that policeman saw everything that happened. What more can I do?"

She nodded toward Leonard. He didn't see her pointing; he was too busy telling a bunch of people from the Rebel to step back and head the other way. He had one hand on his gun, waddling side to side as he spit.

Quinn nodded.

"Was Mr. Stagg with them or being forced?" Quinn said.

"Forced," Candace said, shaking her head. "He was none too happy about it."

"I expect not," he said. "Did you see these men get shot?"

"No, sir," she said. "They had come in the club and made us stop dancing. They had us all sit on the stage until Mr. Stagg and those men came through. I'd just finished up my set and was collecting the dollars. They wouldn't let me finish."

"Stagg, that policeman over there," Quinn

281

said, again pointing to Leonard, "and those three fellas, two that you saw?"

"Yes, sir."

"Nobody else?"

"No, sir."

Quinn tried Lillie again, and it rang four times before she answered. "I sure hate to bother you, Lil, but we got two dead Marshals at the Rebel."

"Mary Alice called," she said. "Headed that way."

"What took you?"

"I had to get dressed."

"Why weren't you dressed?"

"Had to get someone to watch the kids."

"Kids?"

"We need to talk, Quinn," she said. "They're with your mother now. But Caddy left Jason with me three hours ago and hasn't called. She was headed after Jamey Dixon. I'm gonna take a flying leap and say this has something to do with the preacher."

"Yep."

"You called the Marshals' office and highway patrol?"

"The new Jericho police chief did that for me," Quinn said, turning his back from the crowd and walking back to his truck, boots sloshing in the rain.

"Bless his heart," Lillie said.

"He was with Stagg when those convicts got here," Quinn said. "I'll pull the tape, but I'm pretty sure it was Dixon with them."

"Leonard tell you this?"

"Of course not."

"Why'd they hit Stagg?" Lillie said.

"I don't know."

"Have you spoken to Caddy?"

"Nope."

"I'm sorry, Quinn," Lillie said. "I'm really sorry. I was just trying to help. She promised me she'd be right back. She was scared to death but told me she knew what she was doing. I thought she was going to talk Dixon into coming to you. I am such a fucking idiot to trust her."

"Just come on," Quinn said. "I need you to watch Leonard while I pull that video real quick."

"What about Stagg?"

"I guess we'll wait to see if he's on fire before we decide if we want to piss on him."

"Mary Alice says there's an alert on that car and on the kidnapping."

"Mary Alice has always had initiative."

27

"Do you have to bring your guns to the kitchen table?" Jean asked.

"Right now," Quinn said, "I'd prefer it."

They sat across from each other in the Colson family kitchen. Jean was brewing coffee, Jason and Rose asleep in Jason's bedroom, which had stayed his bedroom even though he lived with Caddy now. It was nearly midnight. Quinn had stayed at the Rebel for three hours with the Feds and then drove around for two more hours with Boom to search for Caddy.

He propped the 12-gauge Remington in the corner by the stove but kept his Beretta 9mm on his hip. His wet coat and ball cap hung by the front door. Sometime in the last few hours the rain had just flat-out stopped. The wind was still wild, blowing broken clouds in from the west, but showing the odd patch of moonlight.

Wind chimes jingled from her back porch.

"You hungry?" Jean asked.

"No, ma'am."

"Can't live on just coffee."

"It works."

"I just wish she would call," Jean said. "I guess she figures Jason is still with Lillie and that we don't know."

"Nope," Quinn said. "If Caddy is with Dixon, she'll have a pretty clear grasp on the situation. One of the girls at the truck stop —"

"One of Stagg's pole dancers?"

"Yes, ma'am," Quinn said. "One of his dancers said a man who looked like Jamey was shot. She may have taken him out of the county for medical attention."

"Why on earth would she do that?" Jean said, sitting down and finding her cigarettes.

"Because Dixon doesn't want to discuss his association with those two shitbirds."

"Quinn," Jean said, cigarette between lips and fanning out a match.

"You really think there is a more true word to describe those convicts?"

"Suppose not."

Quinn stood up, noted the time at 0010, and poured himself a cup of coffee. The front door opened, and his hand shifted for a moment to his hip. Boom walked into the kitchen holding his dad's old J. C. Higgins shotgun and sat down at the table. He laid the gun cross-ways over the red-and-white tablecloth Quinn's mom had owned forever.

"You boys," Jean said, spewing smoke and shaking her head.

"Boom is going to stay with you while I go look for Caddy," Quinn said.

"Why?" Jean said. "Those convicts don't have any reason for coming over here. They don't have any quarrel with you or Caddy, do they?"

Quinn took a sip of coffee and looked to Boom. "It's not those convicts I'm worried about."

"Jamey wouldn't want to harm me or Jason," Jean said.

"I'm not taking any bets on what that man will do," Quinn said. "I don't know much about him. But what I do know, I don't like. Boom, there's plenty coffee."

"Well," Jean said. "Are you at least hungry?"

Boom smiled. "Yes, ma'am. If it's not too much trouble."

"I have some pecan pie and some peach cobbler."

"Peach cobbler would be nice," Boom said. Quinn reached for his keys, and Jean got up for the cobbler, smoke trailing her.

"You want some ice cream on top?" she asked.

"Yes, ma'am," Boom said.

"Then please remove your shotgun from the table, darlin'," Jean said. "How many times do I have to tell you boys?"

Boom grinned, and Quinn went back to his truck. The moonlight, filtered through fast-moving clouds, cast everything in a weird landscape. Quinn placed the 12-gauge in the passenger seat, cranked the engine, and traveled back the way he'd come.

Esau and Bones took Johnny Stagg into the big room and had him take a seat at a stuffed leather chair by the cold stone fireplace. Esau walked to the bar and fashioned a drink, already cleaning the eye as best he could with a hot rag. The skin around his eye and his eye itself didn't look human anymore, more like molded wax without much feeling, only a dull throb. Esau threw back some of the senator's fine Scotch and asked Johnny Stagg if he'd care to join him.

"I don't drink, sir."

"A man who runs the biggest hot pillow joint in north Mississippi has gone and gotten uppity on me," Esau said, smelling and tasting that rich smoke and peat in the

287

crystal glass.

Bones took a seat on a leather couch under all those stuffed ducks, golden show rifle pointed right at Stagg. "You pour me whatever you drinking, Esau."

Esau reached for another crystal glass and filled it half full. He handed it to Bones and stepped back, thinking on how things had gone down. His ears a bit dulled by all that music and gunshots and girls screaming. Stagg hadn't bled much from the punch in the face. But the side of his face had swollen a bit and a small trail of blood fell from one of his nostrils. Stagg kept on wiping it away with a handkerchief he kept in his pocket.

There was a big grandfather clock toward the kitchen, and the clicking and whirring of it filled the room. Stagg looked to Esau and Bones and wiped his nose again. His eyes lifted when he watched Becky wander into the room, wearing tight jeans and a tighter camo T-shirt. She made little noises when she saw Esau's face.

She didn't even seem to take notice of Stagg sitting there until the old man crossed his legs and spoke to the back of her. "Evening, Miss Becky."

She turned from where she'd been crying about Esau's eye. Esau put down his Scotch.

"What in the fuck?" Esau said.

"Uh-oh," Bones said.

"Been a while, Miss Becky," Stagg said, wagging his foot a bit from where he'd crossed it. "You look as pretty as ever."

Becky's face flushed with blood, and she turned back to Esau with her mouth hanging open.

"Go on," Esau said, reaching for the glass. "What the hell?"

"Well," she said. "I did what you said, Esau. Just like you said."

"You never said shit about Johnny Fucking Stagg."

Stagg wiped away more blood and studied the red spots on the bleached cotton. He smiled big as you please, and Esau wanted very much to lift his .357 and shoot him off that couch. He hadn't been there two minutes and was already acting like he owned the fucking place. Talking about how the senator was his friend and telling Esau and Bones how they were going to be handling things. How the fuck did he know how things were gonna be handled, when Esau himself was trying to figure it all out?

"Esau?" Becky said. "Baby? Jamey reached out to me and had me go talk to Mr. Stagg. You said Jamey was helping y'all. You were the one who said Jamey knew what he was doing to get y'all released."

"Did you fuck this ole coot?" Esau said.

Stagg grinned, blood trailing down onto his lip till he dabbed at it.

"Hell no," she said. "I met with Jamey at Parchman. I met with Mr. Stagg in Jericho. How were y'all supposed to explain all this from the inside? You said you couldn't do your business without the guards knowing how many times you wiped your ass."

"Y'all have something back there I could drink?" Stagg said, just kind of piping up from his throne. He didn't seem at all concerned that Esau thought he'd popped a Viagra and screwed his lady. "Maybe a Coca-Cola or Dr Pepper?"

"How about I put a hole right in your head?" Esau said.

"I'd just as soon have a Dr Pepper first," Stagg said and grinned.

"Leave us alone, Becky," Esau said.

Bones's dead eyes hadn't moved, his hunting rifle trained on Stagg. He just watched and breathed, loose and cool, only wondering about what kind of shit would happen next.

"I said leave us alone," Esau said. "We'll talk this shit over later."

"I didn't," Becky said.

"Get the fuck upstairs."

Becky bit her lip and turned and ran shoe-less through the room and up the stairs to the master bedroom, where they'd been screwing since she'd arrived. She slammed the door good and hard. Stagg's face had frozen into a grinning big-toothed mask.

"Women," Stagg said. *"Mmm. Mmm."*

"Did you fuck her?" Bones asked.

"No, sir," Stagg said. "And I find that kind of question completely without honor."

"Now, I'm asking you," Esau said. "Did you fuck my woman?"

Stagg leaned back in his seat, foot tapping up and down as if listening to a real good song on the radio. He stared up at the twenty-foot ceilings and the railings boxing the great room. He sucked on a tooth with thought. "I think you need to concern yourself a little bit more about where you stand in all this," Stagg said. "Y'all been cut out of the show. I need one of you to get up and make some phone calls. Decide exactly what kind of situation you have. Y'all think you're in the armpit of Mississippi, but you need to know who's running things."

"Ain't no man running things that's got two guns on him," Bones said. "Did you miss the part where we just killed two Marshals? We'd shoot you and dump you on some county road for the buzzards."

"OK," Stagg said. "If you don't care who I am or what I do, I understand. But y'all need to think on your time limits. I don't have your money. And if I did still have it, it was money I earned."

"How do you figure?" Esau said, eyes flashing up at the balcony, wondering how long Becky would lock herself up and sulk.

"What did Jamey Dixon tell you?" Stagg said, grinning just like a two-bit preacher licking his lips as the collection plate was being passed around.

"He said he told you about that armored truck, y'all pulled it out and got the money, and that you pulled some strings in Jackson," Esau said. He poured some more booze. Bones shifted the rifle in his hands, getting a steady bead on Stagg just in case the son of a bitch turned to smoke and flew from the room.

"And you think that's where he washed his hands of the situation?" Stagg said.

"Yes," Esau said.

"Get me a Dr Pepper and you boys listen up for the whole story."

Esau looked to Bones, and Bones shrugged. Esau reached for a glass and a warm can of Dr Pepper.

"Can I trouble you for some ice?" Stagg said.

Esau reached into a little icemaker and filled the crystal glass and then topped it off with a can of fizzing Dr Pepper. When he handed it to Stagg, he looked Stagg dead in the eye. "What you say better make a load of fucking sense or you'll be drinking soda pop out your asshole."

Stagg drained the glass, his Adam's apple bobbing up and down as he swallowed. He again took the handkerchief and dabbed his nose and then wiped his mouth. Esau loomed over him from about two feet away, hand on his .357. Bones tilted his head as they waited for Mr. Johnny Stagg to start making some fucking sense.

"So, did you fuck her?" Esau said.

"Let's get beyond that shit," Stagg said. "OK, boys. What this all boils down to is my word against ole Reverend Dixon. Dixon says he gave over that truck no questions asked. I say that's a truck full of bullshit. I did what I did for a percentage. I didn't know a thing about that truck until you boys told me. Dixon got that truck out when he was released. That was our deal. That's what your woman in there made sure of. She may not have screwed me, Mr. Davis, but she sure cornholed you good."

Esau threw his crystal glass hard against the fireplace. Pieces flew everywhere. He breathed hard through his nose, his one good eye getting a bit blurry. The other eye had closed up shop.

"I got me three hundred thousand," Stagg said. "From what I'm hearing now, there was a lot more money left over. That's between y'all and Dixon. I know you both been away a while and don't understand my position in this state. But the former governor and the present governor are on my speed dial. Every lawman in north Mississippi is looking for me. You let me go, and I'll make sure y'all have some time."

"Why the fuck would you do that?" Esau said.

"Give y'all a chance to do business with Dixon," Stagg said. "I think what he did to you both is a disgrace. What he did to me, lying about what he had, was just downright dishonest."

"Honor among thieves?" Bones said, laughing.

"Call it what you like," Stagg said. "But you let me go and you got a better chance to live. How did you both think you could get me to pull out that kind of money? Just get my ATM card and head on over to the machine at the Dixie Gas? Y'all decide on some kind of hostage deal and a SWAT team will be picking you off like gnats."

"Nope," Esau said.

"No way," Bones said.

"First thing I'd do is march on upstairs and apologize to Miss Becky," Stagg said. "Second thing I'd do is let us all figure out an escape plan for y'all. I'm not pleased with my dealings with Reverend Dixon. How long till he has a moment where he wants to witness to the whole state and bring me down?"

Esau looked to Bones. He took his hand from his gun. He shook his head.

"Y'all finish your deal with Dixon and I'll get y'all an airplane out of state," Stagg said.

"You mean if we kill him?" Bones said.

Stagg shrugged and smiled. An offer on the table.

"Maybe you're just lyin' to us so you can crawl on your belly on out of here?" Esau said.

"Son, if I wanted you fellas to get caught, I'd just keep talking," he said. "I liked what I saw back at the Rebel. You men know how to take care of business, and I respect that. Y'all need Dixon's money, and I need Dixon gone. This is what football coaches call a win-win situation."

"And you provide us with a plane?" Esau said.

"You got to prove to me that Dixon is

295

dead," Stagg said, smile settling. "But without my help, I don't see either of y'all getting out of Jericho alive."

"Y'all got an airport round here?"

"Son," Stagg said. "I got one made personal just for me."

28

"You can help him," Caddy said, hands shaking and trying to control herself. "Right?"

Luke Stevens was on a knee, in a plaid robe and slippers, standing outside the open door to her car, checking out Jamey's leg. The open-door bell dinged as dogs barked from the backyard of the Stevenses' restored Victorian a few blocks off the Square. Caddy was relieved as hell it had been Luke who'd come to the door and not Anna Lee. Anna Lee had never been one of Caddy's biggest supporters and was the last woman she'd call if she was in a shitstorm.

"I can't do anything right here," Luke said. "You drive, and I'll follow y'all to the hospital."

"The hospital?" Caddy said.

"What did you think?" Luke said. "You want me to operate on him on my dining room table? He's lost a lot of blood and is in shock. He's a mess, Caddy. He may lose that leg."

"It's just a small hole," Caddy said. "He was just walking on it."

"Caddy," Luke said. "Listen to me. We don't have time for an ambulance. Get in the car and drive."

"He can't," Caddy said.

Luke, tall and reedy in his gold glasses, leaned in, grabbed her shoulders, and said, "Why'd you come to me?"

"Luke," she said. "Please help me. Please. People are trying to kill him." She looked into the car, hugging herself from the wind. Jamey's face was a bright white, and his eyes had started to sag. The white strips from his shirt were a dark red, and his breathing was low and raspy. She felt her own breath catch in her throat and wiped her eyes. "If people know that Jamey Dixon is at our hospital, those sonsabitches will march right in and finish what they started."

"How about we save his life first," he said. "I'll get him checked in under an assumed name."

"You can do that?"

"Caddy."

"OK," she said. "OK."

Caddy got in the car and pulled out, Luke running up the hill to his house for pants or car keys and probably to tell Anna Lee just what kind of shit Caddy Colson had gotten herself into now. "We're gonna be OK," she said in a soft voice. "Jamey? You're gonna be just fine."

She circled the Square, the wind blowing so hard the streetlamps rocked back and forth. The old lamps scattered light across Jamey's white face. She held his hand and prayed quiet all the way.

"Baby," Esau said.

The bedroom was dark besides a small lamp on the bedside table. Becky was under the covers, head turned to the outside window, snuffling and crying a bit.

"I know you didn't fuck Mr. Stagg," Esau said. "I am sorry I implied that you did. His pecker probably don't even work."

"You didn't imply, Esau," Becky said. "You come right out and said I'd gotten nekkid and saddled up to his old ass."

"My mistake."

"Goddamn right."

"What I need to know is why you didn't tell me about working with Dixon?" Esau said. He reached for a pack of cigarettes under the bedside lamp and lit up a smoke. Wind howling like a son of a bitch outside.

"You knew I was meeting with Jamey,"

she said. "You told me to."

"OK," he said. "But what did Dixon tell you to tell Stagg?"

"We could talk at the church at Parchman," she said. "Wadn't nobody listening in. He had written out a letter to Stagg. I wasn't supposed to look at it, but he should have figured I would. It offered Stagg a lot of money if he could get Jamey a pardon."

"Did it tell Stagg where to find that armored car?"

"In the letter?" Becky asked, now turning and facing him.

"Yep."

"He didn't mention it."

"Did you tell Stagg where to find the car?"

"No," Becky said. "Shit. How fucking stupid do you think I am?"

Esau blew out a long stream of smoke, took in a long breath. "All Dixon wanted you to do is go back and forth between him and Stagg to work out a deal?"

"I had to go six, seven times before they came to an agreement."

"You know how much?"

"I don't know final offer," she said. "Stagg came to Parchman, I think for them to settle."

"Maybe he told him then?" Esau said. "Where to find my fucking pond?"

Becky shook her head. "I don't know, Esau. What are you thinking?"

"Stagg says Dixon got that money after he got out," Esau said. "Not before, like he told us. He says he kept some of that money back."

"That rotten motherfucker."

Esau nodded, letting more smoke stream out from his lips. The blinds were closed in the room, and everything felt real closed in. He nodded to himself in thought.

"We ain't getting out of here," she said. "Are we?"

"You can go," he said. "Go on if you want."

"I'm not leaving you."

"I said you'd fucked that old coot."

" 'Cause you love me."

"Guess I do."

"What are you going to do?" Becky said, half raising from the bed, wrapping her arm around Esau's hairy neck. Esau burned down the cigarette and mashed it into a coffee cup beside the bed.

"Plans have changed," Esau said. "But we'll get out by morning. Pack your shit tonight. That old coot is making a lot of sense right about now."

Caddy now had to put her full faith in Luke

301

Stevens and Jesus Christ while she kept praying and walking in a sad little waiting room filled with *People* and *Us Weekly* from three years ago. A fuzzy television sat in the corner of the room, playing some silly sitcom with a lot of canned laughter and people falling down, as all Caddy could do now was think about what life would be like if Jamey Dixon died.

She'd come to God before she'd met him, but there was so much strength in that man. She hadn't cared if she had ever met another, every man she'd ever been with treating her like trash, calling her trash, taking from her and wanting more because she believed she wasn't good enough. Jamey made her feel the way God made her feel. *Loved, valued, and purposed.* She had told him everything about the stupid boys in high school and their big trucks with big cabs and later sneaking off to Memphis and that boyfriend, whose name she would never repeat for all her days, who helped her run up thirty thousand dollars on credit cards. And how all of her Memphis friends told her how sexy and gorgeous she was and how much money she could make just in a couple months putting on big heels and taking off her clothes. Caddy had told Jamey she didn't expect to do it but a couple

302

months. It turned into more than a year.

She told him all about the needy men she knew — Jamey making light of it and calling it her own style of ministry — who came to her with problems about their wives and their girlfriends. Most of them just wanted someone to talk to, even if that meant talking with her naked in their lap. Jamey had asked why she did it. And she told him about what had happened to her when she was eight, something that only Quinn knew about, since her brother and Uncle Hamp had been the ones who took care of the situation. She told him about another boy who forced himself on her at a swimming pool bathroom and that time when she was thirteen and those two boys cornered her that summer. She started to believe these things happened to her because she was worthless and unimportant and trash, and that the only thing God had given her — not really thinking of it as God-given at the time — was sex. And she might as well start using it to her advantage.

The apartment in Memphis became her prison. Three girls and one stupid boy. The boy at one time being a boyfriend to them all, Caddy bringing home her cash every night and him taking it, still getting more credit cards in her name, sending her out to the couch to sleep and watch television while he had sex with another girl. She was worthless. And unimportant. She believed she was fucking trash. The drugs just numbed her, made her a spectator to life.

Jamey Dixon loved her as-is. That's how he put it. "As-is."

And she loved him the same. She started to cry.

He would not die. He'd get on through.

She found an old Gideon's Bible in the waiting room and thumbed to her favorite passage. John 15:5. *I am the vine, you are the branches. If you remain in me and I in you, you will bear much fruit. Apart from me, you can do nothing.*

Nothing.

Caddy could not be nothing again. The room was windowless and airless. A black woman, about her age, walked in with an infant and a five-year-old boy. The woman looked very tired. The kids sleepy. She smiled at Caddy as she hugged her kids close. Caddy wiped her face and closed the Bible, resting it soundly in her lap.

Loved, valued, and purposed.

"Good thing I seen you when I did, Mr. Stagg," said the trucker. "I said to myself, That fella looks just like ole Johnny Stagg, and then I thought, That can't be Mr. Stagg. Mr. Stagg wouldn't be walking by the side of Highway 45. But as I got close and seen your face, damn if it weren't you, Mr. Stagg. Sure am glad I stopped. Real windy out there."

Stagg nodded. The truck kept on rolling north toward the Rebel.

"I can't believe it stopped raining," the trucker said. "Been raining on me since I left OK City. I ran into a hailstorm out there that knocked dents in the pavement. Hail as big as softballs. I had my rig in the shop. If I hadn't, I'd be out of luck without no load. Got to be keeping it moving. Supposed to be down in Meridian in a couple hours. I get a little rest, turn her back around, and get on back up to Kansas City. I got a bunch of TVs and electronics and such for Cowboy Maloney's Electric City. They got stores all around Mississippi. You know them?"

Stagg nodded.

"You OK, Mr. Stagg?" the trucker said. "You weren't in no wreck or nothing. Figured your car just broke down."

Stagg nodded again.

Stagg could see the exit sign coming up for the Rebel Truck Stop, a big billboard for the Booby Trap a half mile from the exit reading SLIPPERY WHEN WET. The sign had been Johnny's idea, knowing that truckers always took heed of road warnings and pictures of a woman's gigantic ta-tas.

"I think y'all have the finest chicken-fried steak in north Mississippi," the trucker said. "I know my stops, and I always stop at the Rebel. I just wish I didn't have such a quick turnaround or I might take a little detour at the Booby Trap. Last time I was there met a fine little ole gal named Brittany. You think them girls use their real names? Something about her didn't seem like a Brittany at all. She was a black girl, and black girls ain't usually a Brittany. I think more about some white girl being named that."

The trucker turned off Highway 45 and crossed the overpass on into Johnny's big, sprawling complex lit up with tall parking lamps and headlights and taillights of dozens of trucks and miles of neon from the Rebel and the Booby Trap. The sign on the Trap talking about Miss Double D Texas, who had been recently voted Dallas's Nude Woman of the Year. Where the hell do they make this shit up?

"I tell you, Mr. Stagg," the trucker said as his brakes hissed on the wet asphalt. "Sure has been an honor having you in my cab. You ever need anything, you let me know. This place sure has meant a lot to me for a long time. That chicken-fried steak is just a-calling."

Johnny thanked the man, jumped out of the cab, and slammed the door, trying to steady his breath as he walked back to the Rebel. He went right through the front doors, past the cash registers, and into the Western-wear shop to the side entrance to the diner and the door to the back offices. A few people waved; others said hello. A big fat Choctaw dishwasher they called Double Down opened the door for him, and he went down the long linoleum hall, fluorescent light scattering on and off, to the back office, where he unlocked the door and turned on the desk light.

The phone numbers were written on the back side of a desk drawer, and he had to yank it on out and dump out all the crap inside. The phone rang and rang, maybe twelve, thirteen times, before the man picked up. Johnny Stagg identified himself as the man from Jericho. The line went silent. The line started to ring again and again. Not as long this time, until a familiar voice answered.

"It's me," Stagg said. "I got two shitbirds on my ass. A couple convicts busted out of Parchman. Some redheaded freak named Esau Davis and his nigger partner, Bones. I got them headed to my property before sundown. I'd like y'all to blast their shit to Kingdom come just as fast as possible. *Mmmhmm.* I sure would appreciate it."

29

Quinn drove back to the farm at 0200 to check on things and leave some chow out for Hondo. He turned on the house lights and set a pot of coffee on his old gas stove to boil. He'd driven nearly every inch of Tibbehah County, looking for Caddy and Jamey Dixon, and was thinking at this point they may have shagged ass until things quieted down. Or at least he hoped they'd made that decision. The highway patrol, the Marshal service, and all his deputies — everyone out and on patrol — couldn't find Esau Davis or Bones Magee, either. Everyone out there, finding some way to make contact in another town and another county, was not the best of scenarios. Until he found Caddy, he'd just keep going, keep on driving, until he made contact and could lock her up in the county jail until this thing shook out.

Hondo had run in from the back field,

where he often slept on hay bales at night or inside one of the old barns. He came in through the dog door to the kitchen and found his chow, wagging his tail and crunching up a mouthful. Quinn was pouring coffee when he heard a car outside, and he wandered out to the porch, lit up from lights he hadn't taken down after Christmas because he liked the way they looked. He watched Anna Lee walk up the front path to meet him on the steps.

"Caddy is safe," she said. "She's at the hospital with Luke."

Quinn nodded her over to the front porch swing, where she took a seat. She was dressed in a navy Ole Miss sweatshirt, khaki shorts, and canvas gym shoes.

"What happened?"

"She's fine," Anna Lee said, pulling her long tan legs up under her. "She came to our house a few hours ago with Jamey Dixon. He'd been shot up and was bleeding. She tried to get Luke to help without having to take Dixon to the hospital."

Quinn shook his head. He leaned against the porch rail and took out a cigar, burning the end with a butane lighter. The coffee mug steamed next to him.

"Luke doesn't know I'm telling you this," Anna Lee said. "He checked in Dixon under a fake name. Caddy said those two convicts were trying to kill him."

Quinn nodded. "That's true," he said. "But Caddy shouldn't run out like that. She left Jason with Lillie, and that put Lillie's ass in a sling. I don't know why Caddy thinks that everyone in town owes her a favor. And I don't know why she keeps on trying to keep away from me. It's not like I don't have some type of professional interest in her matters."

"It's always been that way," Anna Lee said, setting down one leg to rock on the swing.

"Yep."

"Dixon had been shot in the leg, but he's going to be fine," Anna Lee said. "I don't have long. Momma is at the house with Caroline, and Luke will be home soon."

"I appreciate this," Quinn said. He smoked down the cigar, a brisk wind carrying the smoke away. Lightning bloomed and cracked off in the west. Wind would grow strong and then quiet to a lull. The rumbling thunder came in faster and faster spurts. He could feel the reverberation down in his boots.

"What are you going to do?"

"I'm going to finish my coffee and my cigar," Quinn said. "And then I'm going to drive over to the hospital and have a heart-to-heart with Caddy. After that, I'm gonna ask Reverend Dixon to witness to me a bit. I'm sure he's familiar with a come-to-Jesus."

Anna Lee smiled. She had nice cheekbones and wide-set sleepy eyes. Her hair tied up high in a ponytail.

"What about those convicts?" she asked.

"Not my problem," Quinn said. "They killed two Marshals. They just signed off on their own execution. None of the lawmen here will have a hard time punching their ticket."

"Awful," she said. "Just awful. Did you know the men?"

Quinn nodded. "Just met them today."

"After they killed those men, they kidnapped Johnny Stagg?"

"Damn shame."

"Why'd they take Stagg?"

"Don't know," Quinn said. "Don't care. Right now I just want to talk some sense to my baby sister and keep Dixon as far away as possible."

"Are you going to arrest him?"

"Yep," Quinn said. "I just hope he's so doped up at the hospital it won't take much to find his connection to the convicts and that armored car. Or maybe I can just press down on that bad leg."

"You wouldn't."

Quinn shrugged. He blew out some smoke.

"She really loves him, Quinn."

"I don't give a damn."

"You think love always makes sense or has some kind of order?"

Quinn ashed the cigar, watching Anna Lee rocking on his front porch, the muscles in her thighs as she pushed off the swing, the length of her neck as it turned from him to out in the field where a bolt of lightning split the air.

Quinn didn't say anything for a long while. On the way out, Anna Lee kissed him hard on the mouth and then was gone.

"Do you want to know how we met?" Caddy asked.

Quinn sat next to her in the hospital waiting room. Nothing but his sister and a broke-ass TV in the corner showing an infomercial about some kind of magic towel that could clean, polish, and make everything new again.

"I decided to hear him preach when he first came back," Caddy said, Gideon Bible in lap, staring off with a smile. "Remember he was doing those Thursday nights at the Southern Star? I thought it would be just

313

wild to hear a sermon in a Jericho bar. I don't know what I expected. I think I only went because I was bored and needed an excuse to go back to the bar, maybe heading back in that direction. Quinn, I swear to you I felt he was speaking right to me the whole time."

"No kidding."

"He has that ability to talk to everyone at once."

"So does Crazy Chester when he goes on a bender."

"Jamey came up to me after it was all over, I'll never forget it."

"Of course not."

The man on television was saying he would throw in not only an extra towel but an extra can of wax, too. But you had to call within the next hour or the deal was off.

"He said to me, 'Where have you been all my life, Caddy Colson?' " she said.

"Not very original," Quinn said. "Besides, Jamey has known you his whole life."

"You're missing the meaning, Quinn."

Quinn nodded.

"We sat at the Southern Star past closing time," she said. "Only had two beers over four hours. I told him my whole story. And he told me his."

314

"I think he must've left out a few parts."

"He was protecting me."

"Or maybe himself."

"And you bust up in here, wondering why I tried to keep what's going on a secret?"

"You ever think I need to know stuff not as a brother but as a sheriff?"

Caddy rolled her eyes. She clutched the Bible. The television was flashing a montage of all the tricks of that magic cloth along with the 800 number. The man on television was trying to convince everyone this deal was on the sly and that perhaps he'd gone a bit insane.

Quinn stood up.

"Where you going?"

"To talk to Dixon."

"Are you crazy?" she said. "He just came out of surgery."

"For what?" Quinn said. "Someone nicked his damn leg with a .22 bullet."

"He lost a lot of blood and nearly died," she said. "And it wasn't a .22. It was a damn .357."

"Just what did he tell you after he was shot?" Quinn said. "About those men? Why are they after him?"

"Sit down."

"I'd rather stand."

"You sit down and I'll explain it," she said.

"His hands are clean. He didn't want to have a thing to do with them ever again."

"Then why did they break out and come for him?"

"Sit down, Quinn," she said. "I'm going to tell you so you quit harassing Jamey. His hands are clean. Those men just want him dead out of meanness and revenge."

"Revenge usually has a preface."

"They want him dead."

"I got Kenny coming over right about now," Quinn said. "Your boyfriend is going under house arrest. No one coming in or out."

"For what?"

"I got a hell of a grocery list to choose from."

"What about Johnny Stagg?" she said. "You don't think it's strange those boys went straight for that son of a bitch when they knew Jamey was broke? Why aren't you looking at him? You think he's the victim?"

"I'm pretty familiar with Stagg's MO."

"Then sit down and listen," Caddy said. "Jamey couldn't have stopped any of this. Those men protected him while he was at Parchman, and now they've busted out believing he owes them something. They know about The River, probably thinking he's got some money and some kind of pull

316

around here. Jamey can't set them right."

Quinn nodded. He took a seat.

"OK." He rubbed his tired neck and stared down at the worn-out hospital floor. "Tell me what you know."

"I know Jamey has been pardoned," Caddy said. "But everyone wants to see him fail. These men are going to ruin all we've built. Don't join the lynch mob. You're too smart for that, Quinn."

30

There was no wind and no rain, just rolling sand-colored hills and ravines pockmarked and ugly from the diggings of a Chinese mining company. Two Apache helicopters had just strafed a half mile of ground running up to the old mud-packed monastery and the twin headless stone Buddhas covered up by sand and mud before America existed. The Buddhas blocked the entrance to where seventeen Taliban fighters had hidden after a night raid on an Army convoy that killed six soldiers. But the team only found dirt and rocks and soil between that Chinook and the Taliban hidey-hole where they pelted the helicopters and the Rangers as soon as they stepped off the ramp. Forty, fifty meters in the night and open ground to the enemy position. Quinn had five men with him, Quinn with his M-4 and a fire-team leader with his belt-fed MK-46 led the way. The helicopters were gone, although the sound of them remained in his ears, while the second team moved up from the west to east, taking the hell of it. Quinn pushed himself and his men on their bellies over the hard-packed, unforgiving terrain to lay down all they had, suppress the enemy, knowing they were too close to risk another Apache gun run. The enemy returned fire from dual machine guns, Taliban popping up from the copper mine craters, bullets zinging off the walls of the forgotten city. More enemy gunners had come from nowhere, showing themselves in the moonlight, and targeted that second team coming up fast. Quinn and his team could only move forward, crawling toward the enemy guns, their only protection coming from their own bullets, a quick change of a magazine, another belt fed into the MK, forty, thirty, twenty, fifteen meters on their elbows and knees. Quinn could smell those bastards on the wind, all their spice and body odor, dirty clothes and beards. Taliban popped up again from the carved-out earthen maze and fired, Quinn shooting back and catching something that felt like a hot fist launched into his shoulder. The punch knocked him down hard to stone and earth, everything tunneled and raw, radio voices in his ear while his gunner kept shooting and dragged his ass away and backward, heels of his boots catching on rocks, as the second element crossed and moved on into the ravines. The last thing Quinn saw were those headless Buddhas as still and silent as goddamn time and the whooshing blades of a Chinook hitting that hot LZ. "Sergeant?" The sound of his uniform being torn from his body, his blood flowing too freely.

"Sergeant?"

Quinn opened his eyes.

Lillie Virgil was shaking him awake. His boots swung to the ground and he was upright, taking in a big lungful of air.

"You OK?"

Quinn nodded.

Lillie handed him a foam cup of coffee. Quinn remembered he'd gone back to the County Barn and Boom's shop to sleep after the hospital. He hadn't heard his phone ring. It was still night, dark as hell outside, that wind and rain that seemed like it would never end.

"What time is it?" Quinn said, standing, lolling his neck from side to side.

"Five."

"Thought we were switching off at oh-eight-hundred."

"Something's come up."

"Shit," Quinn said. He walked to the bank of old industrial windows, his green truck sitting under a fluorescent light by the gas

320

tanks. Crews of county workers were already filling trucks with gravel and sand to patch eroded highways.

"Mary Alice got a call from Willie Tucker this morning," Lillie said. "You know Willie? He played tight end at Tibbehah when we were still in junior high. Went to Ole Miss and came back working for Senator Vardaman?"

Quinn shook his head.

"He came back last night and found the lights on in the senator's hunt lodge," Lillie said. "He saw a strange car parked outside and got up close enough to see two men, one black and one white, and a woman inside. The window around the back door had been busted out."

"You think it's our boys?" Quinn said.

"Could be," she said. "You want to pass this on to the Feds?"

"Maybe," he said. "He say anything about seeing Johnny Stagg?"

"Stagg showed up a few hours ago back at the Rebel," Lillie said. "Claims he escaped from the convicts and walked five miles to freedom."

"Hmm."

"No hostages."

"Let's take a look and see what we got," Quinn said. "Call Kenny, Art, and Dave.

Where's Ike? Is he on or off this week?"

"How's that coffee?"

"Tastes like shit."

"I bet," she said. "Just found it over in the corner by Boom's tools. Wasn't sure if it was motor oil at first."

"You're too good to me, Lillie."

"That's why you made me chief deputy," she said. "You need to go shake the dew off, or are you ready to ride?"

"Grab your weapons," he said. "We'll take my truck."

"You sure you're OK?"

"Why's that?" Quinn said.

Lillie hit the button on the bay doors, which rose up and exposed the big cracked asphalt lot and the bulldozers and backhoes and county supervisor toys. She pulled up the hood on her rain slicker and turned to Quinn. "You just kind of look like you're coming back from somewhere is all."

Esau stuffed some cans of Vienna sausages and sardines and fresh clothes into a camo backpack he'd found in a supply closet. Bones made eggs with deer sausage, and they ate at the kitchen table, watching the rain, feeling good about being out and free but not talking about it. Bones had a cigarette going in a saucer by his elbow.

"That eye looks rough," Bones said.

"I hoped that glass would work itself out," Esau said. "Got a few bits out, but son of a bitch won't open. When we get on ahead, I'll need to see a doctor. Tell 'em I got hurt on a construction job with no insurance."

"Then you're really fucked."

"I'll pay cash."

"If we got the cash."

Esau nodded as he broke apart the deer sausage with his fork and mixed it in with the scrambled eggs. He doused it all with a good helping of Tabasco, watching the rain hitting that rich man's lighted swimming pool, now knowing the son of a bitch was a U.S. senator, which made sense when you noticed all his photos and clippings about the man hanging everywhere but over the commode.

"You think Becky'll do right?" Bones said, sliding the plate away from him and picking up the cigarette.

Esau shrugged. He wore a nice Carhartt flannel he'd taken from the senator, a little snug with the sleeves rolled to his elbow. He continued to eat.

"Don't have much choice," Bones said.

"Nope."

"She either telling the truth or she ain't," Bones said. "Got to believe in someone."

323

"Only one I don't believe is Jamey Dixon."

Bones grinned, smoke scattering up in the ceiling fan. "What about Mr. Johnny Stagg?"

"You?"

"Hell, naw."

"Me, either," Esau said. "But I sure as shit believe he wants Dixon dead."

"And then he kill our ass."

Esau nodded. "Hands clean, everyone gone," he said. "And he keeps all that money. Yeah, I thought about that. But if he's got himself a small plane and a pilot, it's worth taking the chance. You know every road is blocked. If the old man makes a play, you and me gonna finish it."

"All about the women now," Bones said. "Next move decided by the goddamn women."

"It will work if Dixon's woman got any sense."

"You mind killing him?" Bones said. "We all pretty tight at the farm. I'm pissed but don't want to be the one turn out his lights. Something's gotta be bad about killing off a preacher. I don't know what kind of man he is or if I can trust him, but I think he's a man of God."

"I don't have a problem killing Jamey Dixon," Esau said. "Nobody forced him to keep that money. He can say what he wants, but he's a skillet-licking greedy mother-fucker like us all. We find his ass, I'll be the one turn out the lights. Trick is getting that money first. You think he may have spent it all?"

"On what? Bibles and hymnbooks?"

"Well, he ain't keeping it in coffee cans," Esau said. "And he didn't give it all to Stagg."

"That's what Stagg say."

"Makes sense to me," Esau said. "Becky never did show him that pond."

"If that happens," Bones said. "If he got it somewhere we can't get to and he can't get to fast, let's just get the fuck outta here, man. We outstayed our welcome in this county for a couple days by my account."

"Good place to be," Esau said, looking around all the marble and stainless steel. "Nicest place I ever been."

"You know I got that senator's underwear on right now," Bones said, grinning. "I think my momma be proud."

"Since we broke out, I've been meaning to ask you something."

"Shoot."

"When Dixon was praying for you and got you cleaning toilets and painting walls at the Spiritual Life Center, did you buy into it?" Esau said, putting down his fork. "Did you believe when he was preaching to us that Dixon was really somebody and that he'd been forgiven?"

"You know, I been thinkin' on that, too," Bones said. "Way I figured it out is that just 'cause a man is forgiven don't mean he won't fuck up again. Plenty of men ask for some forgiveness but go back to their old ways. I think when you shared that about the truck and all that money, it was just too much for Jamey Dixon to take. Like a drunk man staring at a whiskey bottle."

"I believed him," Esau said. "Reason I told him. I believed he had the hookup with Jesus. Now I know I was just bending over and taking it deep."

"We out, ain't we?" Bones said, throwing Esau his sack.

"Yes, sir."

"And free?"

"Not yet."

"Maybe Dixon was right," Bones said. "God got a plan for everyone."

"To shoot to kill until you get that money you stole?" Esau said, slipping on the backpack, checking the load on the .357 and reaching for the shotgun he took off Dixon's woman. "That it?"

Bones shrugged. "Maybe this ain't our story," he said. "Maybe this is Dixon's, and

326

we're here to set things straight."

"Hand of God?"

"Both of 'em," Bones said, and bumped fists with Esau.

Quinn had the deputies rally two miles from the hunt lodge, still wet and dark as hell. Quinn had on a slicker, same as Lillie, same as Kenny, Dave, Art, and Ike. Ike had just driven up in his sheriff's office truck, another Ford painted the same dark green as Quinn's. Only Ike's didn't have the winch and the big tires or the rack of KC lights that lit up the spot where they met. Lillie showed them all an aerial map she'd downloaded and covered in a Ziploc bag.

"I just got off the phone with Willie Tucker, and he told me the layout inside the lodge," Quinn said. "We'll enter at a rear door by a swimming pool. Mr. Tucker even told us where to get a key, so we move in quiet. This is just like what we drilled all summer and fall at the shoot house. No different. Art is our breech, I'll go first, and we pie up that space. It's a big space, a big open room for the senator's trophies and a bar and TV. What we need to worry about is eight doors opening from up above. The rooms all look down on the open space, and we'll make for fine targets. You'll need to be aware of not only the room but anything popping up from above."

The shoot house Quinn had constructed over the summer was considerably smaller, him trying to get the deputies ready for houses and trailers with a main room and a couple doors off center. It was pretty much just a barn with inside and outside walls made of railroad ties and filled with gravel, a tin roof, and a catwalk above to observe and critique. But the entry would be the same, his deputies all knew how to pie the room, carve up that space, and make sure it was all clear. If not, and if the convicts were there, Quinn had spoken to one and all of his deputies that hesitation was not an option.

"Remember, this isn't for show," Quinn said. "We hit that door and move as fast as tactically sound. You hear me? I don't want any of y'all to be in a rush to get shot. Move as fast as tactically sound."

There were mumbles of approval. A couple *yes, sir*s. Quinn would have felt better with a loud "Roger that, Sergeant," but that shit wasn't going to happen here. They headed back to their vehicles, driving within a quarter mile of the house. Quinn handed Ike the keys to his truck and told him to be on standby; he'd radio if the men tried to escape in a vehicle. Kenny would park his patrol car on the opposite ridge in case they ran in that direction.

Quinn, Lillie, Dave, and Art walked uphill all the way in their slickers and hats and carrying pistols and shotguns. Quinn smiled at the deputies as they moved, thunder shaking the low Mississippi hills. First light still a half hour away. All of it felt familiar and right marching in the muck in his boots.

"Am I crazy, or are you smiling?" Lillie said.

"I love it."

Rain poured down on her face and into her eyes while she repositioned her ball cap. "You let me know when the fun starts, OK?"

"You'll know," Quinn said.

"What if it's not them?"

"Then we would have scared the ever-living shit out of some squatters," Quinn said, marching on ahead and watching the big log house growing larger and closer, two yellow lights burning inside. "Right?"

31

Esau had gone ahead and gassed up a couple 4-wheelers, Kawasaki Brute Force 750s, the damn things looking as if they'd never been ridden. Esau was careful to check the oil, make sure the engine had actually been broken in, and started them up. Bones walked on in the tin shed that was clean as hell, with a polished concrete floor and rows of landscaping equipment, pole saws and chain saws and even a little backhoe. Esau wondering out loud if the senator ever used this stuff himself or just got people to clean up his shit.

"What the hell do you think?" Bones said.

"There's a fire road run south of here," Esau said. "I seen it on some maps in the man's study. It runs all the way down south till it dovetails with Highway 9. We get to 9 and pick up a new car down there. We ride out of here with only what we can carry. I don't give a shit about no souvenirs."

"If I could take that TV on my back, I would," Bones said. "But I hear what you sayin'. Sure like that Winchester special edition with the gold plating."

"I packed some food, shotgun shells, and bullets," Esau said. "He got about every kind of caliber in this shed. I'd fill up one of them backpacks before we head out. Ole Dixon won't take but the only bullet he's worth. But dealing with Stagg is going to mean some shooting. He'll probably bring that fat-ass police chief and some other good ole boys if he's smart."

Esau fitted on a ball cap that read O'TUCK FARM SUPPLY and tightened the backpack over his shoulders. He straddled the ATV and rode on out of the shed, the high-pitched whine of that fresh engine sounding good enough to ride clear on to California if they decided to head that way. Bones got on his and followed till they both slowed where a ravine ran down the hill with a narrow wooden bridge spanning into the fire road that would zigzag and trail south all the way to the state highway. Bones kept the engine running but told Esau he'd changed his mind. He wanted to carry that Winchester as a souvenir, saying it would come in handy when they finally would have it out with Stagg's boys. Esau nodded and

331

told him to hurry his ass up, heart beating, sweating a bit, excited to finish his business with Jamey Dixon as it all was supposed to be. He had a memory, a not too distant one, of Dixon preaching to the boys in Unit 27, hands raised to high heaven on the basketball court and telling them all to be grateful for every day God gave them. There were some snickers and laughs, just as the sun rose big and fat over the flat Delta land. A scattering of sparrows looping and swirling, tangled and bunched together in flight, Dixon's eyes closed talking about a life that was promised to all of them, a world anew with faith and strength and forgiveness. Death was all. He said everyone standing with him today on that court was given another chance. The laughter stopped. He said no man was fit to judge another. Forgiveness was a personal thing between you and the Lord.

The men listened. Esau listened. The sun rose just as promised.

Esau believed he could be forgiven for what he was about to do. He didn't just think it was necessary, staring down that zigzagging road that would lead him to Jericho, he knew it was damn well ordained.

Quinn, Lillie, Art, and Dave stood at the

back patio to the lodge, a pair of French doors looking into the wide-open den of the senator's personal hunt club. All the lights were on, as was the television, set to a morning show in Tupelo. With all the glass windows and the glass doors, there wasn't much chance to stay hidden. The best they could do is go ahead and bust inside before they had been spotted. Quinn had the key he'd found, just where Willie Tucker had told him, under a certain rock in a certain corner, and handed it on to Art Watts, who stood with his standard-issue Glock at the ready. Quinn waited behind him and Lillie and Dave in the respective order. Art turned the key and Quinn was inside, taking the center of the room, concentrating on nothing else, with his Beretta raised, finger on trigger, knowing from experience you don't set up to shoot when you find a target. You set up from the get-go. "One clear," Quinn said. "Two clear," Art said. "Three clear," Lillie said. "Four clear," Dave said.

They all walked as a unit through the house, the layout being unusual: since the back wall was made of glass, any son of a bitch could watch every move after entry. They repeated the entry into the kitchen and then mounted the steps in single file, no one touching the loud television explaining how to make meatballs from scratch with nothing but healthy and natural ingredients. About halfway up the stairs, Quinn knew it was just fine to use turkey sausage in the mix, some whole-wheat bread crumbs, and light olive oil. At the top of the landing, the team split. Quinn and Lillie took the rooms to the left, and Art and Dave took the rooms to the right.

They met in the middle. All was clear.

Quinn lowered his weapon. He was not breathing hard or tense. He could still to this day hear his RI telling him to slow the fuck down, breathe, and engage the brain. Don't get tunnel vision. See everything, slow down and relax in your own personal workspace. Quinn kept an eye on the back doors as they walked back down into the sprawling den. The meatballs apparently were delicious. The host of the show said she'd never eaten anything so good in her life and couldn't believe it was healthy, too. She said all she needed was a nice Chianti, and that really broke up the local cook and the host. They laughed until Quinn walked up to the big TV and turned it off.

"Let's check the grounds," Quinn said. "Make sure we're all clear. We got two outbuildings and some kind of pool house. Who the hell keeps a swimming pool at a

334

hunt cabin?"

"This isn't a hunting cabin," Lillie said. "This is a pussy palace."

"Where'd you learn to talk like that?" Quinn said as he followed her. Art and Dave already out back, checking on the sheds.

"You really think Vardaman comes up here to hunt?" Lillie said. "Stagg brings him in some of Memphis's youngest and finest tail."

Quinn shook his head, 12-gauge in hand, as he rounded the corner and heard the kitchen door slam. He looked to Lillie and then outside to see Art and Dave had disappeared, already into the big sheds. Quinn lifted the gun. Lillie moved quiet and fast to the kitchen door, standing to the side and nodding to Quinn that she was about to push it open.

Quinn kicked in the door, checked half of the room, Lillie behind him, sweeping the other. Room was empty. Refrigerator open. And the back door wide open, too. A blue-and-white gingham curtain in the door's window waving in the wind.

Somewhere close, Quinn heard the whine of ATVs as he reached for the radio to call Ike.

32

Esau turned the Kawasaki around just in time to see Bones running from the lodge and two sheriff's deputies walking from the shed. The men yelled to Bones, Bones hauling some serious ass with that goddamn gold rifle in hand. The wind whipped up some rain into Esau's eyes. He didn't wait a second to head on over that bridge, hoping Bones would come on but not being able to do a thing about it. His ATV rumbled up and over that footbridge and dug in hard and quick to the mud and stones, spewing up some dirt as he fishtailed and swung on into the tree line and onto the fire road, turning back just for a second to see Bones riding on behind him. He thought back to the time on the horses at Parchman, that feeling like ten years back. Bones looked a mite bit more comfortable with his legs straddled over an engine than a horse.

The trail was thick with mud and broken

in spots with runoff from the hill. Esau ran
it hard and fast, hunkered down with his
backpack strapped tight and rifle thrown
over his shoulder. He'd tucked his loaded
.357 into his belt ready and waiting for any
poor son of a bitch who decided to follow.
Back at the shed he'd only seen the two
ATVs, but there could have been more,
probably would be more, and he'd sure bet
the sheriff had brought his own up into the
hills.

There was lightning and thunder as the
wet branches whipped across his face. The
cool rain ran down over his bad eye, good
eye firmly on that narrow path that was
sometimes hard to follow, but they kept rolling on some ruts in the road that a truck
had made sometime in the last year and
looked to where the saplings and weeds
were no taller than your knee. The whine of
the ATVs filled the forest, turning and cutting, Esau's foot not touching the brake a
single time. He raced on down that hill,
thinking about Becky, hoping she would do
what she had said and go and follow through
with what needed to be done. She had
sworn to him, pulled his hand to her, up
under her shirt and her bra, to feel her heart
beating for him to know it was true. Esau
knew it hadn't been her heart that he'd

337

trusted, feeling that big ole titty in his hand and that familiar swelling between his legs, knowing he'd follow Becky into the depths of Hades itself. More branches swatted his face and his bad eye, though he ducked some. He turned at a sharp, muddy curve where the road got a bit steeper, touching that brake for the first time, looking back to Bones, who rode up beside him, breathing hard, smiling big ole crooked teeth, that golden rifle tucked into a camo backpack.

They both turned the ATVs to the empty road and looked down the fire road and the wide expanse of the valley. They could see Highway 9 and a few trailers down that way. A couple cars and trucks. Good pickings. But they'd need to move fast before word got out; everyone would know this road only led in one direction.

Thirty seconds later, Ike McCaslin drove up behind the hunt lodge and hopped out of Quinn's running F-250, asking which way those boys were headed. Quinn jumped in behind the wheel, Lillie following on the passenger side, as he pointed down the fire road, all the deputies understanding where it spilled out and the direction they should head. Quinn knocked the truck in four-wheel drive and headed in the direction of those 4-wheelers, coming to the bridge and straddling it, big tires running fine and smooth over the ravine and on to the curve.

"Couldn't resist it," Lillie said, buckling in, which was a true task with the jostling. "Could you?"

"Nope."

Branches swatted at the windshield and scraped the sides of the truck as it rolled up and over rocks and down into ruts, crushing fallen logs as Quinn cracked the window, listening but not hearing the motors. Another limb appeared in the windshield, and Quinn turned to the right, evading it, picking up the path again and turning down into the drop-off. The valley below, three contiguous farms, their early plantings as clear and defined as Highway 9. He hit the lights and the siren.

"Sheriff," Lillie said. "What happened to 'move as fast as tactically sound'?"

"Learned that in Ranger training."

"And this?"

"Being wild-ass crazy."

In all that jostling and bucking, Lillie actually nodded. "Roger that," Lillie said.

Esau and Bones had slowed, rolling back the throttle a bit before turning through the woods and toward that little group of trailers down by the highway. Rain was going full tilt now, making it harder to see the path. Bones was up by Esau's side, pointing an opposite way, showing where that road to the right petered out and the other path would take them down through a ravine and on into the valley. Esau nodded and gunned the Kawasaki, turning around just in time to see a big green Ford with a growling engine bust through the brush and woods, chewing up that narrow path and coming right at them with sirens and lights. With not much else a man could do, Esau headed down the new path, Bones right behind him, bucking up and nearly falling off the 4×4, hitting another stump and then coming up hard around a half-fallen tree. Esau wanted to reach for his pistol but didn't want to risk his ass falling off. Down on the other side of the ravine was a long, flat space that spread out treeless and open, a deer stand sitting right there at the edge of the forest.

Esau motored on down into the ravine, water coming up past his knees and up to the seat, but the Kawasaki revved up and then out up a sandy hill. He was not the first to ride these trails back here. Bones stopped at the edge, and Esau, turning back, told him to come on. Bones looked up at the top of the bed, squinting at Esau, almost like he couldn't believe he'd actually made it through the water. But Bones sat back into the seat and gunned the engine and came up on the other side, following the trail again. Those sirens were coming up quick toward them.

Quinn knew the road. He hadn't been on it since he was fourteen, but time didn't seem to matter. He was waiting for that big, wide creek bed to come up. It was the same creek bed he'd fallen into after it had frozen and Boom had to lift his ass out and build a fire and make sure his socks and coat were dry before they headed on out of the forest. When he saw the break in the woods, he slowed, just a little, and edged the Ford down the slope.

"I don't care for this," Lillie said, looking like she might be sick.

"It's the only way."

"I don't care for this at all." She put her hand to her mouth.

"Trust me."

"We're getting stuck."

"Nope."

"Yep."

Lillie nodded. The engine whined and tires spun, sinking them down into the ravine a little more, water coming up nearly past the big tires before Quinn knocked the truck in a low four and lifted out of the bed. The thin path on the other side gave his truck a decent place to grip, even if just on one side, as the nose of the truck lifted up and then over the hill, windshield wipers swiping away the dead leaves and pine needles and rain. Quinn turned on into the curve, seeing those two convicts running the stolen ATVs toward the final stretch of hills before things flattened out into country roads and farms and plenty of trailers and houses.

"Some truck," Lillie said.

"Second time Boom got me through that patch."

"Yep," Lillie said, craning her head, holding a rifle in her hand. "I can get a shot from here."

"Hold it."

"I can get a fucking shot from here."

Just as Quinn slowed, one of those boys opened up with a pistol, spiderwebbing the windshield dead center between him and Lillie. He pushed Lillie down far into her seat while he made himself smaller, Quinn following the road but backing off a little. The man on the rear ATV, the tall one they called Bones, aimed that pistol again, bullet whizzing off the hood.

Bones had done got those boys off their ass.
Esau turned back to the road, looking down
the slope, seeing they'd be coming off that
big hill really soon. Bones fired again, waiting for those deputies to start shooting back.
Esau leaned forward, tasting smoke and oil,
trying to duck the wind, and cranked that
son of a bitch hard, taking the turn fast and
reckless and loose. This was a hell of a
morning, rain in the face, police coming up
hard against him. Esau grinned and looked
back at Bones to give him a salute.

Bones raised the gun again and fired. Esau
turned in time to duck a big ole branch,
coming back around the bend to watch
Bones shoot again but not turn back around
in time. That branch plucked his black ass
off the ATV like some kind of magic trick,
the ATV still running and gunning while it
tumbled riderless off the path and down the
hill over and over into some saplings. Esau
just saw Bones for a moment, caught in the
crux of a branch like a man's thumb and
forefinger, hanging guilty as hell, legs kicking back and forth and dead-ass stuck.
Down in the valley ahead of them, Esau
could see the lights and hear the sirens from
the deputies' cars. Behind them, that big

green truck eating up the forest and tearing right for him.

Quinn had to turn the wheel hard to the right to miss the man hanging from the tree. As the truck recovered, the front end dug in hard to a ditch, lifting the back right wheel up out of the dirt, spinning as useless as the other. Lillie and Quinn jumped out at the same time, finding Bones Magee caught still and lifeless in the crook of an oak. Lillie didn't hesitate to try and pull him out, but he'd been snagged at the base of his skull and wouldn't move. Quinn got under the convict and lifted his legs. Esau Davis headed on down the hill on his ATV, down to where the rest of the Tibbehah sheriff's office would be waiting for him.

Quinn laid the man down in the dirt. His eyes were bloodshot and open, mouth busted, with his jaw knocked out of socket. Quinn tried for a pulse, listened for a breath, but the man was dead.

Lillie walked away with rifle in hand, training the scope down the hill. She put down the gun and shook her head, passing the weapon to Quinn, who searched the scope, seeing Esau ride through a clearing of trees at about three hundred meters. He lifted Lillie's .308 Browning to his shoulder.

"I can make it."

"I give you the gun, and you'll shoot," Quinn said, shaking his head.

"We have every right," she said.

"Too easy."

"You take the shot, then, Sheriff," she said. "That boy has nothing to lose."

He passed the gun to Lillie, knowing between the two of them she was a better shot, and she quickly lifted the gun, running the barrel to an open pasture where the ATV would appear. It would be a hell of a shot, about four football fields, but not too far for Lillie. She slowed her breathing, arms set in bronze, taking aim on the space, and without a word, squeezed the trigger. Even from that distance, Esau Davis left the seat of the ATV and toppled to the ground.

Across the greening farmland, corn sprouting immature and small in neat rows, walked his deputies. Art, Dave, and Ike moved side by side through the tilled earth, guns high and at the ready, with Davis sprawled in the dirt.

Quinn and Lillie walked down to join them.

Esau rolled, knowing he'd been shot in the fucking back. He lay there for a moment, thinking, *Well, shit, we gave it a hell of a run.*

But besides that sharp-ass pain in his side, he could breathe just fine. The sky was gray and flat but moving. Rain pinged down into his face, bringing him back. He turned his head to see those deputies coming, still a good bit away in a couple pastures. Some son of a bitch nearby had a dog. He heard that barking. Those men had fanned out, walking in a row of four. If he was gonna make a move, it needed to be fast and hard. Ain't no going back for Bones. Everything in the world was now between him and Becky. He moved his hand to make sure he still had the gun.

He could feel the backpack up against him.

He was maybe twenty, thirty feet from the tree line.

If those bastards wanted him, he was gonna make them work.

When he got to his feet and started to run, he felt like someone had stuck a fire poker into his side and started to twist it. He figured he might be able to get that bullet out with a hot knife himself like fucking Rambo. But first he needed to get gone up into those hills with as much distance between him and those deputies as he could.

He had a gun and supplies. His heart was good and his lungs were good, and if he could shut off that bleeding for a while and move, they'd have to make a hell of an effort to find him. Esau was a woodsman, always been a woodsman, and with every step into the green-ass woods he felt more at home.

There was shouting and then some more shots. He ran and ran, thinking about nothing but branches and cover and being invisible.

33

"Yes, sir, that's him," Johnny Stagg said, nodding down to the body of Bones Magee on a cool, stainless-steel slab. "That's the son of a bitch who took me by gunpoint and would've killed me if I hadn't escaped."

"How'd that happen, Johnny?" Quinn said, looking to Ophelia Bundren. Ophelia looked up over the doctor's mask, waiting to slide old Bones back in the cooler.

"They got to arguing and weren't paying attention," he said. "I just walked right out the door of Senator Vardaman's and on down the road."

"You walked the whole way?" Quinn said.

"Most of it."

"Thought you told Deputy Virgil you got picked up on Highway 45," Quinn said. "That's quite a walk from the Vardaman place."

"Don't I know it."

"What time did you break loose, Johnny?"

Stagg scratched his cheek and smiled at Quinn. He smiled over at Ophelia, who pulled down the mask from her face but kept on the latex gloves. She nodded to Quinn. Quinn nodded back, and she wheeled away the body.

"Where's the other one?" Johnny said, grinning like he was happy as hell, just ear-to-ear, wanting to hear the good news.

"Don't have the other one," Quinn said.

"That a fact," Stagg said, nodding some more, being dumb enough to place a hand on Quinn's shoulder. "I am a little surprised at that, son. Weren't you supposed to check in with them federal agents if you saw anything? I don't think it was our county's place to go in there and spook those ole boys."

"We were checking on the lodge," Quinn said. "Someone had broken in. We had taken precautions. Those men were already leaving the lodge, on the ATVs. With the time issues and the weather, we acted the best way we could."

"Quinn, I know this is all new to you," Stagg said, "but a country sheriff can't make decisions like that ahead of some federal agents. Them men gunned down two Marshals in the parking lot of the Booby Trap. There's jurisdictional things and laws you just ain't thinking of. This ain't the Ponderosa."

"Like I said, Johnny," Quinn said, "with the time and the weather and not knowing who was in that house, I made that call. That's my job."

Stagg shook his head sadly for the young man not quite tracking on his information. Ophelia walked back into the room in a sweatshirt and jeans and tennis shoes, hair pulled into a ponytail. Her big brown eyes switching from Quinn to Stagg, hands deep in the front pockets of her jeans.

"You mind removing your hand off my person, Johnny," Quinn said. "With my training, I sometimes react involuntarily. You don't want that."

Stagg removed his skeletal hand, still preacher-smiling and happy with himself. He nodded, taking it all in, looking down, as if he were capable of philosophical thought, not just a gesture he saw in the movies. "Did I hear you had a chance to take that shot on that other boy?"

Quinn stayed silent.

"I don't know your reason there," Stagg said, sticking a peppermint candy in his mouth and crunching away. "I just hope nobody else gets hurt based on your assessing that situation. See y'all later."

Stagg left the back room at the Bundren Funeral Home, door shutting hard and final behind him. Ophelia looked to Quinn, hands still in her pockets, and shrugged. "What was that all about?"

"He wanted both these jokers dead," Quinn said.

"They did kidnap him."

"He didn't walk ten miles in a half hour," Quinn said. "He's trying to cut out the middle man. You know he's connected with that armored car somehow."

"So who's he doing business with?" Ophelia said, walking back over to the worktable and putting away her tools.

"Jamey Dixon," Quinn said. "Who else? Your family was right, Ophelia."

Caddy walked outside the Tibbehah Regional Hospital for a smoke break. Caddy had tried to quit smoking and had been successful at it last year. But there were times when bad habits came back like old, familiar friends, and right now, she needed a pack of Marlboro Lights and some fresh air. Outside, there was a little worn area under a magnolia tree where visitors and mostly patients could smoke free and clear of the doctors. The soft ground was littered with cigarette butts, the sky above turning blacker than coal. An obese man in a hospital gown and in a wheelchair had taken to the edge of the little patch and smoked down a cigarette in ecstasy. He was missing a foot and a hand, unaware of Caddy, only watching the traffic on the slick, busted highway. Thunder threatened far off in the west. The clouds sped above like a deep black, churning river. Caddy wasn't cold but held her arms against herself, some kind of thick charge in the air.

"You got an extra?" asked a busty woman in a short jean skirt and white tank top. She was probably not much older than Caddy but had the tired, worn look of someone who'd hit a few rough patches. Her makeup was thick, her nails long and red.

Caddy nodded, handing her the pack and letting her shake loose her own. Besides the fat man in the wheelchair, she was alone with the woman. The man in the chair checked out and loving on his cigarette, the passing traffic drowning out their words. More thunder broke, closer now.

"You're Caddy Colson," the woman said.

Caddy nodded.

"How's Reverend Dixon?" the woman said then, taking a pull on that cigarette. "Everyone is real worried about him."

"Do I know you?"

The woman smiled, makeup caked at the edges of her smile. "Yeah," she said. "We do have some connections."

"Do you go to The River?" Caddy said, smiling and feeling confused. The cigarette burned warm in her fingers.

"No, ma'am," the woman said. "I hadn't been back to church since a wild man running an Assembly of God out of Aberdeen tried to get me to handle the snake in his britches."

Caddy tilted her head, finished the smoke, and ground it under her boot.

Those long, black clouds were moving even faster now, looking like ragged pieces of cloth, draped and flying past. The wind scattered Caddy's short hair, a little rain but not significant enough for it to matter.

"I like your hair," the woman said. "You sure can wear it."

"Thank you," Caddy said, studying the woman.

The fat man in the wheelchair turned back around, wheeling himself away from whatever he found fascinating on the roadside, and made his way back to the hospital. He nodded at the two women as he passed and said, "Damn, this don't look too good."

"I'm confused," Caddy said to the woman.

"I'm friends with Reverend Dixon," she

said. "Of course, I just always called him Jamey. I used to meet with him over at Parchman, and I helped him get settled when he got out. I was the woman who picked him up at the processing center and took him to Walmart to get a fresh change of clothes. He went into jail with nothing but six dollars and some change. Did you know he had that girl's blood on his jeans?"

"Funny," Caddy said. "He never mentioned you. What's your name?"

"Don't really matter," the woman said, slipping a neatly folded piece of paper into Caddy's hand and pressing it closed in her fingers. "All you need to know is to pass this along to Jamey. I was supposed to come to you as a woman with similar problems. But you and I know we're not gonna meet on any common ground. You got too much on your mind."

Caddy opened the piece of paper and saw a phone number written on it. She looked up into the woman's eyes.

"OK," the woman said, taking another cigarette. She'd yet to hand back the pack, something that hadn't been lost on Caddy. "Let's go ahead and show our goodies. All right? Esau and his buddy are pissed off as hell at your boyfriend. Esau is my man. You understand? He and Jamey had an under-

354

standing. I helped the good reverend get settled. I made sure he was fine and took him to meet Mr. Stagg, just like it had all been arranged."

"Why?"

"Hell," the woman said. "You know why. What you don't seem to know is that your man kept back a good portion of what he said he lost. That may not mean nothing to you, since you seem to really and truly found Jesus. But it means something to me and Esau and Mr. Bones, and if Jamey can walk upright and quit hiding behind the cross, then everything just gonna be fine."

"He didn't take any of that money," Caddy said. "He gave it to Stagg for his freedom."

"Says who?"

"Says me."

The woman shook her head, the smell of cheap drugstore perfume all over her. Her bright red nails looked like something that should be hanging on to a branch. "He got to you? Didn't he? That sandy hair and blue eyes and talk of this world and the next. Don't be so fucking stupid. That ole song goes something like this. Jamey Dixon agrees to meet up with Esau in the next hour or else I'm gonna strut my ass into the sheriff's office and lay down the whole story about making that deal with Johnny Stagg. All them walls will come down for Jamey, old man Stagg, and even that fat, pig-eyed piece of shit ex-governor and this whole hypocritical world. You'll be the one left at home on a rainy night smelling him on your cold pillow."

"Go away," Caddy said.

"Fine by me," the woman said, tossing the cigarettes back to Caddy and turning. Designs in silver thread had been sewn on her ass pockets.

"Tick fucking tock," she said, and walked into the parking lot.

Up and over that ridge, Esau walked till he couldn't walk no more. He was bleeding bad out of his side and needed time to drink some whiskey and eat. Out of the mist high on the hills, he walked into a clearing and found a little deer stand not much bigger than a child's play fort. There was a great deal of pain hauling his ass up a ladder into the structure and lying down on his side. He pulled the backpack away from him and searched for some of that Wild Turkey, drinking down a half-dozen good swallows.

He lay on his back, careful to get off his side, and stared up at the tin roof, rusty and torn. The rain dancing a good bit on it, the edges lifting up and back, up and back. He cocked his head forward a bit to drink down another quarter of the bottle. Amazing thing how whiskey could make the world seem like a better place even though it had turned to shit. He remembered hearing as a kid about those Confederate soldiers about to lose a limb and all they got was some whiskey and a prayer before that hacksaw moved in on them. He just hoped like hell he could boogie on down the road before the eye got to be even more of a mess. Becky had told him that morning that he looked real rough, but she'd love him one eye or not, kind of making a joke about him wearing an eye patch, just like a pirate, at whatever warm locale where they were headed.

Shit, right now it was like driving at night, when you can't see a damn thing except for ten feet ahead in the headlights. He drank down the whiskey, just a little golden sliver of it left at the bottom. He knew he should eat, but he didn't want to eat. The wind started kicking the hell out of the little house on stilts, Esau feeling like God himself had him in his hand. He leaned back and touched the side of flesh that had been shot into. He knew there had been muscles torn and lots of blood gone. He pulled back the cloth wrapped about his side, stained with the darkest shade of blood he'd ever seen.

He leaned back and closed his eyes. The roof shook a good bit until a whole goddamn section lifted off and flew away. A damn shitstorm poured inside the structure, and Esau crawled into the corner of the little house, placing the backpack up under his head, and closed his eyes. The wind moved so fast all the wood was creaking and moaning and rocking the son of a bitch back and forth. But if he crawled back out into the wilderness, where the hell would he go? This little place had probably taken on worse.

He closed his eyes. He'd rest up. Wait to hear from Becky.

The roof had been torn in half, half rust and half black-ass sky. The structure wobbled some more on the pilings, like a drunk on unsafe legs. Rain, rain, rain.

Under his head in the backpack, he heard his cell phone. Becky. He knew she'd find him, wondering if she'd heard about poor ole Bones's ass. He turned, cursing that damn wound, and opened the sack. He pulled out the phone and said, "OK, baby. It's OK, baby."

"Esau?"

"Who the hell's this?"

"You came to me."

"Dixon?"

"I'm sorry about Bones," he said. "I didn't want this to happen."

Esau worked himself up to his knees and then used a two-by-four ledge to stand, wind and rain shooting on into the house. It was tough as a son of a bitch to hear what Dixon had to say, and he screwed his ear down into the phone.

"I ain't got time to play," Esau said.

"You're the one who wants to meet," Jamey said. "You tell me where to go."

"I want what is fucking mine."

"I understand what you want."

"And you got it?" Esau said.

He didn't say a word for a long while. "I got it."

Esau nodded and reached for the last bit of whiskey. "All right, then. This how's it gonna go." But as he spoke and turned to look out of the open patch of roof, a border of blackness swept in from the west, reminding him of stories of frogs and locusts and creatures that would cover the sun and devour the earth. In his drunken mind, for that moment, Esau wondered if Dixon wasn't conjuring the whole thing or if the

359

Wild Turkey hadn't just busted
sel.

"Where?" the voice said on t
can't hear you. I can't hear not t

"I'm here," Esau said, yellin
goddamn you."

34

Mr. Jim's barbershop was just as Quinn had left it. Mr. Jim trimming some fella's hair while Luther Varner sat on the waiting bench thumbing through *Field & Stream.* The television atop the Coke machine should have been playing *The Price Is Right* or *Days of Our Lives,* the old men loving that stuff, but the local station had interrupted it all to run down the weather reports, bad night across Oklahoma and Arkansas, more bad weather for most of the mid-South. "They had two tornadoes touch down in Clarksdale, and I'm hearing about one over near Oxford," Mr. Jim said, working the snippers to trim away a few stray hairs from a man's bushy eyebrows. "What do you know, Sheriff?"

Quinn still wore his slicker and ball cap. He'd ducked into the barbershop just to see what the local news was reporting. He'd been checking the weather all morning after the events at dawn. "Sugar Ditch is a mess, and the Big Black is about to crest up off Cotton Road."

"Memphis says we're under a tornado warning," Luther said. "Figured if I'm gonna get killed, might as well be at Jim's barbershop. That way, when they find the body, I'll be all ready for the suit."

Quinn nodded, listening more to the news, watching a band of green and big spots of red rolling in from the west. The radar showing a thousand crosses on the screen for lightning strikes and talking about conditions being ripe with this cold front. Rain hit Main Street hard, falling diagonally, street signs twisting back and forth.

"Aren't you glad you went ahead and chased those fellas?" Mr. Jim said, not smiling, just easy talking, in his old brown shirt and comfortable shoes. "Just been getting worse all day. Y'all had any luck with that other convict?"

The tornado warning was for most of north Mississippi but went on to name every county, including Lee and Tibbehah. Quinn turned to Mr. Jim as he was lathering up the old man in his spinning chair. "Nope," Quinn said. "But it's not a good day for him to be roaming the woods unless he found some shelter. He's injured. When this shitstorm clears, we'll start beating the bushes."

"How's your truck?" Luther said.

"Hooked the winch to a big old oak," Quinn said. "Lifted her out of the ditch and set everything straight. I dropped the truck with Boom and I'm using his. I admit the front end is a bit out of alignment. Boom's trying to get the windshield replaced this morning, too."

"How bad is it in the Ditch?" Mr. Jim said, easing that razor off the man's neck and wiping it clean with a rag.

"Bad," Quinn said. "I got the ag building cleared for those who been flooded out. We got a school bus sent down there, but I'm headed to do some door knocking and try to reason with some of the more stubborn folks."

"It's shameful we got people living down there like that," Luther said. "Ain't no difference between that and some villages I saw on No Goi. People cook outdoors in pots, got clothes hanging out down off that nasty creek."

"And to think they got to pay rent for it, too," Mr. Jim said.

Luther shook his head, turning back to the television on the Coke machine. Quinn leaned against the wall. All the decorations in the place had been the same since he was five years old. The big bass, the trio of deer heads, Mr. Jim's state barber license, and a local newspaper clipping with a photo of himself and one of George Patton.

"You shoot that convict on the run?" Luther said.

"Nope," Quinn said. "Lillie."

"She's a hell of a shot."

"Coming from a Marine sniper, that's a real compliment."

"Boom still driving that little Ford?" Luther asked.

"Yep."

"That thing doesn't have four-wheel drive," he said.

"No, sir."

Luther nodded and looked behind Quinn at the street scene behind the glass. Everything outside started to turn black, as if night had fallen early. It was only three in the afternoon.

"Come on," Luther said, stretching out his long legs and pointy-toed cowboy boots. "I'll drive you. Ain't nobody wants to get stuck in this shit. Maybe I can help a bit, too."

Quinn nodded. The old man with the skull tattoos on his forearm reached for a hat that read DA NANG and hobbled toward him.

Rain beat against the barbershop picture glass, sweeping along Main, with all the cars and trucks driving slow with their hazards on.

"Something just don't feel right today," Mr. Jim said, pulling away the apron from his customer. "I think something real bad is about to happen."

"Shit, I just hope the cable don't go out," Luther said, tugging on his hat and following Quinn out into the elements. "Then we'll have to have some authentic conversation in this place and discuss our feelings."

Jason had stayed home from school on Monday on account of Caddy not really being sure how much his teachers would know about Jamey, not wanting to face them. The whole town knew about the service and the "Model Church" sermon, but she was pretty sure they were more aware of his attendance at the Booby Trap Shootout, as they had called it on the morning news. Much was made that Jamey had been one of the former governor's pardons, not a single one of those news dipshits taking the time to know Jamey had been kidnapped and was a victim, too. She blamed Quinn for that. He could have kept his name out of the mess.

When she walked into Jason's room where not five minutes ago he'd been curled up reading a book, now she found him on his knees, praying. She stood in the doorway listening, the light outside changing weird and dark, the only light in the room from a little cowboy lamp by his bed, making it seem oddly like bedtime. "Help us, Jesus. Help us, Jesus. Help us, Jesus."

Caddy came on in and got down on her knee beside him, seeing that he was crying. She used her shirtsleeve to dry his eyes and told him, "Don't worry about anything. Mr. Jamey is fine. Maybe we can go and see him for supper? He's just fine, baby."

She gave a reassuring smile but saw in Jason's face that he wasn't talking about Jamey. He clung to her neck and whispered, "Momma, I don't want to die."

Caddy laughed a little, an involuntary laugh of relief. She rubbed his back. "Oh, baby. Nobody is going to die. What are you hearing? Who has filled your head with all that stuff?"

He shook his head and wiped his nose on her shoulder. The thunder crashed again and shook the house hard, and he hung on tighter. She'd been so damn wrapped up in Jamey and that crazy woman and what they would do about Esau Davis that she hadn't even considered the storm and rain, wind beating the hell out of the house. "We're just fine. We got a nice room and a comfy bed with all your sleep friends. You want me to read to you?"

Jason nodded. A neat row of stuffed animals lined his pillows.

"Are you hungry?" she said. "I can make some cookies." But he didn't hear the last of it, Jason turning toward the window and the closed curtains, everything shaking and vibrating the old bungalow.

Both of them turned, Caddy running to the bedroom window and seeing what looked like a wall of soot and dirt a mile long swirling toward them. Far off, it didn't sound like a train. It sounded like a big, rolling beat of thunder with no beginning and no end.

She reached for Jason and pulled him up into her arms. The lights flashed on and off and then off. The room was black, still and quiet except for all the noise of that rushing, horrible sound just getting closer and filling her ears with tension and pressure. Jason was sobbing and screaming as they ran for the back of the house.

"Help us, Jesus," Caddy said. "Help us, Jesus."

Jason stopped screaming for a moment

and prayed along with her as they sought shelter.

"You blame 'em?" Mr. Varner said about a mile back from Sugar Ditch, where they'd spent the last hour trying to convince five families to leave their houses and come into town. Varner drove, Quinn in the passenger seat.

"Not especially," Quinn said. "Hard to leave everything."

"Reason I don't keep a lot," Mr. Varner said. "You?"

"What I can carry," Quinn said. "And some special books and guns. Old records and photos that belonged to Uncle Hamp. I prefer to travel light."

"Even when you ain't goin' nowhere," Varner said, nodding as he drove.

The men didn't speak for a few miles, everything dark as midnight, street signs twisting back and forth, traffic signals jangling from chains. Two of the families had agreed to leave; the other three politely declined help, worried about their stuff getting waterlogged or people coming back early — even though the Ditch had been closed off by the sheriff's office — and stealing their shit. Quinn left them ankle-deep in water, sandbagging their front doors and praying the rain would stop.

Quinn stared out the passenger-side window at the trailers and faded shotgun houses situated along what had been the old railroad line. A skin-and-bones dog ran across the street, tail between its legs. A haggard man in coveralls emerged from the transmission shop, mouth open. The American flag behind his fat body popping tight on the pole.

"Shit," Mr. Varner said, staring into his rearview. "That don't look too good."

Quinn stared out into the darkness, everything blocking out the sun. "Sir?"

"Look behind you, Sergeant," Varner said. "I think we got some incoming."

Quinn turned around to see a black swirling wall of debris and dust a half mile wide coming up the highway. In the passenger-side mirror, the twirl and force of the thing was enough to make Mr. Varner mash the accelerator, running flat out for downtown Jericho. The Dodge's hemi engine growled, RPMs redlined. Varner turned the wheel this way and that to get around downed trees and electric lines snapping like whips.

"You think we can outrun it?" Quinn said, holding on to the door.

"We sure as shit gonna try."

Quinn hit auto dial on his cell phone,

reaching out for his mother, the phone going straight to voice mail. Goddamn it. He
tried Caddy, the line busy. Behind them,
the long ribbon of blacktop was being
devoured by that cloud, electric poles that
ran along the highway broke off like match-
sticks, electric lines sparking bright red and
white in the wind and dust.

"Goddamn," Varner said.

"Sheriff's office," Quinn said. "Try and
make the sheriff's office."

"Then what?"

"Get inside," Quinn said. "Hide and pray."

All at once, Varner turned the truck's
wheels hard to the right, tires squealing,
blackness coming up on all the windows.
The back window in the pickup exploded
as the entire back end lifted off the ground,
and it felt for a moment like the truck would
flip end over end. A hard whirl of dust blew
from the east, opposite from the clouds,
blowing out Quinn's window, and then the
whole windshield spewed glass in their
faces. The tail of the pickup crashed to the
ground, and just as the men crawled onto
the floorboard, the whole truck started rolling and rolling, the thing slamming the
entire truck down hard on the passenger
side. Quinn's face burned as if touched by
fire, wind and mud like a sandblaster in his

ears and across his closed eyes. He was a million miles away, back in Iraq, Trashcanistan, the Cole Range in Georgia, the swamps in Florida, an RI screaming into his face telling him die, motherfucker, die. Fight it. Hate it. Get up. Dying is too fucking easy. Quinn's ears were filled with screams and tearing sheets of metal. His eardrums exploded. He tasted blood in his mouth.

35

There was a storm shelter in Betty Jo Mize's backyard, Miss Mize being the owner and operator of the town's newspaper who had never forgotten what had happened to Jericho back in '81 before Caddy had even been born. Caddy's house was on the opposite street from Miss Mize's, and she and Jason had to rush through a chain-link gate and run over a small stream, shoes sloshing into the water, till they got to the big open space at Miss Mize's house. Caddy knew she shouldn't but had to look behind her and see that black, massive, shapeless wall twirling and spinning, breaking with lightning and coming up on south Jericho now, blowing straight for them, the sound of it all something terrible mixed with the rain and the wind and the tornado siren. That siren just now coming on, not even giving people a proper goddamn warning. Jason was a big kid but felt light in her arms as

372

she ran over Miss Mize's tomato plants, all set in neat rows, and her large bottle tree shaking and shuddering in the wind. That sound of endless thunder filling her ears, more trees shattering and breaking and now what smelled like ozone and fresh-cut timber, and she was to the shelter steps, trying for the door and knocking like hell, screaming, "Open up, it's Caddy Goddamn Colson and Jason. We're about to die. Open the fucking door, Miss Mize. Please."

Her ears started to fill and the wrecking and crushing strength of the thing was on the city, shit flying everywhere. Limbs and shingles and plastic bags from the Dollar Store and the Pig. Glass breaking. "Open the door," Caddy said, yelling. "God, please open the door."

Jason's face was firmly buried in her shoulder, her clutching him tight, pressing herself against that steel door, knowing that Miss Mize was gone. As they were about to be sucked up into the air and nothingness, she wondered why God would create such a terrible monster. She prayed some more, making themselves small in that little scoop of earth by the door. "Please, God."

The door opened. A man's hand yanked them inside, door shutting hard and locking behind them. Miss Mize's son, Wade, and an elderly couple she'd never seen in her life huddled inside. No one spoke. Wade, who had never been at a loss for words, since he was the Jericho Chamber of Commerce president, had his eyes closed. The old couple held on to each other, the woman in a flowered housecoat and the man in sweat pants and a T-shirt for Pap's Catfish in Ackerman. She cuddled Jason and whispered lies into his ears about everything being just fine, just a little storm outside, and look at Miss Mize's neat little playhouse. The room was just a little cinderblock space in the ground, maybe five by five, with two-by-fours fashioned into benches on each side. On the wall, Miss Mize had hung a plaque for Outstanding Community Journalism 1989 in some sort of joke that would be funny and private to the wry old woman.

The thing was passing over them. Caddy held Jason. She prayed.

That thunder mixed in with what sounded like a giant jet engine being fed with sticks and wood and eating up everything that passed through its sharp blades. The low rumbling shook the entire shelter, and cinder blocks fell off the wall. One of them fell and broke on the old man's shoulder, but he didn't pay it any mind, holding his wife tight. Caddy had seen them before, knew them when she was a kid, and they weren't so old. Wade Mize didn't say shit, just stared at Caddy and smiled, Caddy not giving one single shit for a look that said to her, "We're fucked to hell." She'd take her chances on Jesus, not the Chamber. She rocked Jason back and forth, ground shaking, the jet engine from hell eating the town, thunder shaking the entire earth like the eight-headed beasts and the Four Horsemen of the Apocalypse and the final judgment on this world.

Dear Jesus. Dear Jesus. Protect us. Keep us safe. Protect this child. Our Lord, please have mercy and grace upon this child. You may suck me into the next world, but keep this boy safe. Door rattling and shaking. All the adults looked to one another, because this wasn't a human hand trying to get them, this was the beast seeking and ripping and tearing and destroying everything it touched. *Dear Jesus. Wise Jesus. Good Jesus. Jesus, please save our asses.*

"Momma?"

She had her eyes shut tight.

"Momma," Jason said. "What happened?"

Her ears wouldn't pop. She was breathing hard and sweating, with a heart jackhammering in her chest. "Where are we?"

375

"Miss Mize's playhouse," Caddy said. "Isn't it fun and neat?"

Wade looked down at his hands. He was thinking of his mother.

"It's gone," Wade said, Caddy just realizing all the noise and shaking had left them alone. The silence was so absolute it was electric.

"Where did it go?" Jason asked.

"It's gone, sweetheart," Caddy said, hugging Jason close and kissing his face. But her thoughts turning dark and worried, wondering about Jean, Quinn, and Jamey, and the whole damned town.

Wade took a breath, wiped his sweating face with a rag. Caddy only just noticing he wore a pair of blue jeans and no shirt or shoes. She'd never seen him in town without a coat and tie while he ran his downtown bank or the Chamber meetings. He patted Jason's head and gave a sad smile as he turned the lock and the door opened with a pop.

A strange, hot white light filled the room. "God help us," Wade said, and began to help them from the shelter.

"You all right?" Quinn said to Luther Varner, who'd been thrown into the back of the cab.

"The dirt people can't claim my ass yet."

"Can you help me out?" Quinn said. "Seat won't give."

Luther leaned through the seats of the sideways truck, finding purchase on the driver's-side window, blown out and ragged with glass. He reached into the upper frame and started kicking at the passenger seat until it broke free and Quinn could crawl out. Varner got his wiry old frame out first and then stood atop his truck and reached a hand down for Quinn. A fallen tree lay prone across where there used to be a windshield. "My Lord," Varner said. "You ever seen such a clusterfuck?"

Quinn jumped down off the truck and onto the torn-up asphalt, taking in Jericho in all directions. Trees lay uprooted, skinned like animals of their bark. Paper and tin and pieces of wood had been scattered all across the road, and littered a field that was once a pine forest but now had been wiped down to mud. Quinn tried his phone. All circuits were jammed or the towers were down. Either way, it was useless. He went back to the truck and crawled inside, searching for his radio. He called for dispatch. Nothing.

"We got to hump a mile to town," Varner said. "I'm sure your people and my people found some shelter. You remember the last one?"

"No, sir," Quinn said. "I was only one."

"Your daddy was there," Luther said. "Saved a bunch of folks."

Quinn shook his head.

"Better believe it; Jason Colson was a man."

They followed the trash-strewn road, the tornado siren still going from near the water tower. People emerged from some houses; other houses lay in heaps; some had just been cleaned from their concrete foundations. Quinn would be back and help them all, but he needed to find his family and Anna Lee. He needed to find Lillie and his deputies. Quinn moved as fast as he could, Varner not slacking one bit at his side, bringing back memories of the last fight he'd been in with the old man. The ex-Marine going back to his training on Parris Island, coming back to an operational mindset like a rubber band. Nothing familiar. Nothing stood. Everything was a mess, a pile of debris.

"You got to think of them being OK," Varner said. "You check on your people."

"What about you?"

"Well," the old man said. "My son is rightly in prison, and my wife is dead.

Smartest thing little Darl did was move to Nashville."

They stopped only twice before reaching the Town Square. A woman and her two children had been trapped inside a toppled minivan. They had all been scared to death but were fine; Varner used his combat knife to cut them from their seat belts. Another time, they stopped to find a young girl, maybe six or seven, a little older than Jason, asking for her momma.

The house behind him didn't even make sense, a trash pile caught in the path of that thing; nothing familiar stretched out to Quinn for miles. Varner grabbed the little girl and hoisted her onto his shoulders, keeping her there as they walked on to the sheriff's office, finding a section of the roof gone but most of it and the walls standing. Lillie Virgil stood outside with a group of people, some covered in blankets, all bruised and bloody, seeking some type of direction. Their eyes were wandering and glassy, the look of refugees he'd seen in the Afghan mountains, everything they'd known taken away in an instant. The mind not quite catching up with the eye.

Varner helped the little girl off his shoulders. She ran to a woman standing by Lillie and wrapped her small arms around her neck.

Quinn looked over the growing crowd to Lillie. Lillie just shook her head.

Quinn started running for home.

After the silence was the crying and the screaming and the folks walking out into what used to be a street and asking, "You seen my daddy?" or kids asking, "You seen my dog?" People were confused and turned-around as they stood, frozen, trying to make some kind of sense of what just happened and where to go next. No homes, no cars. No roads. People who had survived hugged a lot. Caddy saw many people dropping to their knees and praying to the clearing skies, the first time Caddy had seen the sun in a week. She walked with Jason in her arms back through the backyard, Wade going to find his mother at the newspaper and check on the bank. The old people just remained in that shelter, trying to get enough courage to see what the hell was left. Caddy wanted to see it, had to see it. She felt full of courage and wonder. If a tornado couldn't take out her and Jason, then there was more purpose to her life, more meaning, and God was indeed good. She kept on patting Jason's little legs and squeezing his feet as they passed over the creek and saw what had been a neighborhood since after the Second World War nothing but a landfill. Their little home was just gone, her white Honda had been flipped upside down, and water shot up in the air from what had been their bathroom. Caddy thanked God once again for her not being so almighty stupid as to try to ride this son of a bitch out in a bathtub. She kissed Jason's cheek. God was good. They had been spared.

She had come back to Jericho with nothing. She'd come back from this.

Everything else around her didn't make sense. The hundred-year-old oaks that had lined the quiet street and cooled during the summer were gone. You could smell the oak and the pine in the air. People screaming and shouting, some in pain and some in joy.

Down the street, or what had been a street but was now a river of clothes, busted wood, and garbage, she saw a man in a long white robe. There was a moment of foolishness, but her eyes cleared and she smiled, holding Jason up so he could see Jamey Dixon hobbling down the road in a hospital gown, scruffy and worn, silly in a pair of cowboy boots. His grin and open arms were everything.

She rushed to him, Jason clinging to her neck.

36

"You know I never much did like that damn kitchen table, anyway," Jean Colson said, hands shaking while she lit a menthol with a match. "I hated those old knotty pine cabinets, too."

Most of the Colson house remained. The open back porch, the kitchen, and a stretch of magnolias and pines did not. Quinn had his arm around his mother as they walked up the hill where he and Caddy played as kids. The old tree house still sat perched oddly alone in four pine trees that were skinned up pretty good but still there. Jean saw Quinn staring. "Maybe I could live in that tree house?"

"Sure."

"I ran down the hall to get in the linen closet, come to find the closet wasn't even there."

"Where'd you go?"

"Nowhere," she said. "Duck and cover in

the hallway. Like an atom bomb had landed."

"You see it?"

His mother shook her head, blew a stream of smoke upwind. Folks walked up and down Ithaca Road, most of it a mess but a lot of houses still standing. A ton of trees were down, most coming down right in the middle of people's houses. Quinn had been in touch with Lillie by radio, learning the supervisors had sent a team of bulldozers into downtown Jericho to clear the roads so emergency vehicles could get through. The deputies were going door-to-door looking for survivors, Quinn saying he'd join them as soon as he checked on his mother.

Quinn had come up on the house at the same time as Caddy and Jason. Jamey Dixon, looking like a true convict, limped up behind them, his long hair and beard wild and his ass exposed in the hospital gown he wore with cowboy boots.

Jason ran for Quinn, leaping three feet up and into his arms. He squeezed his neck tight, and Quinn told him that he loved him. Caddy walked up and hugged her brother. She cried for a moment but cleared her face as Jamey walked up and offered his hand to Quinn.

"You know, I got some pants inside,

Dixon. How about you put them on?"

Dixon nodded and walked up past Quinn and over the lawn and into the house, Quinn not moving an inch. Jason was smiling with all the excitement, telling Uncle Quinn all about the 'nado that about knocked the whole earth on its ass.

"Where'd that kid learn to talk like that?" Quinn said.

Caddy shrugged. They walked up to the steps to the house and sat.

"The Stevens house is half gone," she said. "Thank God they got a basement."

Quinn's blood quickened. "You see her? You sure they're all right?"

"Had to walk right by their house to get here," Caddy said, nodding. "It's a mess, Quinn. Lots of people got to be dead."

Quinn radioed in to Lillie again. They had two dead in a house right off from the old rail depot. She wasn't sure but thought it had been the Sayleses, man and woman in their seventies. When Quinn asked about an ID, Lillie said that would take some doing. The tornado had blown into Tibbehah right over Choctaw Lake and then cut up over the city and on up toward Carthage and the hills and out into Lee County, where things sounded just as bad.

"You gonna put Jamey back under arrest?"

Caddy said.

Quinn shook his head.

"We need the help," Caddy said.

"I just asked emergency management if we could get a gimpy leg preacher," Quinn said. "Must be my day."

"He wants to go back to The River," she said. "If it's still there, it can be a place for folks to get washed and fed. We need that right now."

Quinn nodded.

"Those men forced him with a gun," Caddy said. "He can help."

Quinn nodded again, Jean walking around the corner of her house, crying a bit, arms around Miss Davis, whose house next door had been split in two like a birthday cake. Caddy let Jason to the ground, the boy running for his grandmother with excitement, pointing to all the carnage and destruction. Caddy stayed seated on the stoop, not taking her eyes off Quinn. "We nearly died."

Quinn nodded.

"That means something."

"Sure."

Caddy ran her hand over her face and massaged her neck. "Just give him a chance," she said. "This town doesn't have much, but we need him today. Our ministry. His ministry. This is what we do."

"Hell, I gave him my pants, didn't I?"

Caddy looked at Quinn, shook her head, and then smiled. Just slightly. Quinn smiled back and ran, double-timing it all the way back to the sheriff's office, where they were already bringing in the dead.

"Afternoon, Mr. Stagg," Esau said, as soon as Johnny Stagg climbed into the driver's seat of his Cadillac and stuck the key into the ignition. Esau came up from the back-seat and told Stagg to just be cool and just drive. "Don't study on things too much."

"In case you hadn't fucking heard, son, we got ourselves an emergency situation."

"I saw the whole thing from the hills," Esau said. "That twister must've been a half mile across. Sky turned black as midnight. Saw sparks of the power lines, whole cars being picked up and tossed like they was toys. When it come up on Jericho, I was sure the whole town would be gone."

"It just might be," Stagg said. "So, you mind getting your ass out of my vehicle? I have official duties to perform and such."

"Start the car, old man, and drive," Esau said. "This don't mean nothin' to our business."

Stagg just sat there until Esau placed the gun behind his right ear. Stagg turned halfway, staring out at the truck stop parking lot and a mess of ambulances and police cars and fire trucks. A bunch of folks scattering off every few minutes. All of north Mississippi coming on up to Tibbehah County.

"My county doesn't have no water, no power," Stagg said, driving away from the Rebel Truck Stop. "Most of our county seat been wiped out. I got constituents with immediate needs."

"Same as me."

"Ain't same as you," Stagg said, turning onto the highway toward town. "All that business can wait, son. This is bigger."

"Says who?" Esau said. "You say that to the man who's running for his life with the hellhounds sniffing for his asshole? 'Hold on just a minute, partner. I'll get right back to you.' *Bullshit,* Mr. Stagg. My needs must be met. I ain't got nowhere to sleep, no money, and I need some medical attention and clothes. My eye swolled up like that fella Quasimodo."

"Take a number," Stagg said. "Do you know how many people died in this shitstorm?"

"No, sir," Esau said. "And don't much care, neither."

"Just what the hell do you want of me?"

"To let you know nothing has changed."

"You're soiling my car," Stagg said. "You smell like you been rolling in a cow field."

"Been living like an animal since your lawmen chased me into the woods this morning like I was a ten-point buck," Esau said. "Caught my best friend. So excuse me if I might have shit my britches."

"This Cadillac is brand-new."

"Get an air freshener," Esau said. "And turn down that side road."

"You gonna kill me?" Stagg said, peering up every few seconds into the rearview. "That it? You think I called the law on you? I told you we have a deal and we got a deal. I can't help that the hand of God reached down and tried to shake this county off the map."

"Pull over there."

"You kill me and you don't get nothin'," Stagg said. "Jamey Dixon is a liar. A false prophet who ran over his old girlfriend and then sat by the roadside to watch her body be pulverized into nothing. You throwin' in with a man like that?"

Stagg stopped the car on the highway. A fire truck raced by. A hundred yards down the highway, it stopped dead cold. A tall old pine fallen over the road. Some firefighters hopped out of the truck and took to the pine with a chain saw, the tree splitting in half, four men grabbing one end of the tree and pulling it out of the road. They drove off, and an ambulance followed with lights and sirens. More police cars. A couple state troopers.

"When?" Esau said.

"When for what?"

"When can you get me a lift out of here?"

"I'm reaching into my glove box, son, but there's a weapon there," Stagg said. "Going for it nice and easy, don't get jumpy. I just need to get some breath mints. The smell of everything is giving me a migraine."

"What kind of man needs a breath mint after his hometown is blown apart?"

"A man who needs a minute," Stagg said. He reached for a couple peppermints and offered one to Esau. Esau took it. Stagg crunched on his, eyes darting up to the rearview.

"I got five hundred dollars in my wallet," Stagg said. "I got a private shower in my office. It runs off a generator. You don't make a mess and I'll come back after I assess the situation in Jericho."

"This situation is that your little town is fucked to hell," Esau said. "The trumpet has been sounded. I seen it. Looks like what happens after a dog gets after your trash.

390

You better be thinking on the future, old man."

Stagg finished the breath mint, swallowed, and half turned back to Esau.

"You mind if I start up my vehicle and turn back to the truck stop?" Stagg said. "You can clean yourself and help yourself to my refrigerator. I got ice cream and whiskey. I'll find out about Dixon. And then you can finish it."

"Be easy for a man to get lost right about now."

"Yes, sir," Stagg said. "It would."

"You threatenin' me?" Esau said. "You want to do that, and I'll blow your goddamn head all over your dashboard and these nice, clean leather seats. Ain't no air freshener for that."

"Sit back, Mr. Davis," Stagg said, turning off the shoulder and heading away from the stopped fire truck and the downed tree. "Let me take the wheel for a bit and find out exactly what we got left."

37

Quinn could see where the tornado had crossed the Jericho Square, up from the southwest and slamming into the town diagonally. It ripped a good section of the storefronts, a copy shop, a Laundromat, the *Tibbehah Monitor*'s office clean off their foundations. Cars and trucks had been turned on their backs, brick walls had been busted through. The force of it had come on across Cotton Road, the county highway running over to 45, taking out the Hollywood Video, the Dollar General, and the roof of the Piggly Wiggly. To the east there was a broken and busted world; turn to the west and everything looked the same, the old movie theater, the Fillin' Station diner, and the Jericho General Store. Even the Veterans' monument stood straight and proud in the dead center of the Square. Junk and trash and busted pieces of Sheetrock littered the lawn, now surrounded with emergency vehicles. But some of the town had been spared, and there was a small miracle in that.

He and Lillie searched for survivors in a neighborhood right off the Square where Caddy's house had been, sending survivors back to the sheriff's office, where Quinn had helped set up a command center. Not an hour since the storm and the Salvation Army was already there, feeding and clothing people. They put out tables and chairs in front of their trailer, hot meals and coffee. All seven of his deputies were working traffic, while Quinn and Lillie worked with volunteers, searching for people who may have been trapped or for the dead. Memphis was sending down rescue dogs to sniff for cadavers.

The entire neighborhood was just gone. The little saltboxes had been built for GIs after the war, turning into slums during the seventies but recently becoming rediscovered by young families. Caddy had spent most of last year fixing and painting the house, planting flowers and a small garden. Quinn had helped screen in her back porch, where they'd spent hours talking things out. Caddy finding a lot of strength and pride in that old home.

"Piggly Wiggly is giving out water and

food," Lillie said, wiping dirt and sweat from her face. She wore a gray T-shirt with her uniform pants and combat boots, gun on her hip. "People rushing over there like it's Christmas Day. Free T-bone steaks and Coca-Cola."

The streets were not streets but heaps of Sheetrock, busted boards, and bricks. The old oaks that kept upright looked naked and obscene, as if they'd been whipped bare. Quinn had on his old Merrell boots and carried a flat-blade ax. There was quiet and stillness, dogs barking, sirens far off. Families gathering. They tried not to talk, but to listen for cries of pain or help. Quinn had worked three hours straight, his shirt soaked with sweat, bloody calluses on his hand from the ax handle. A gas crew had set up on Main Street, shutting off the entire system.

"I wouldn't light up a cigar just yet," Lillie said.

Quinn nodded, standing on top of what used to be a house, the rusted blue water tower still looming over town, reading JERICHO in faded, worn letters. Lillie took a call from Mary Alice.

"Found another one," Lillie said. "Old woman laid out in a field by the high school stadium. Mary Alice says she'd been impaled by a four-by-four."

"Anyone we know?"

"Don't think it's easy to tell," Lillie said. "They're going to need you back at the SO. Nobody could have survived in here. Better just wait for the dogs."

"I'd like to ride up to Carthage."

"Lee County and Lafayette County are going door-to-door," Lillie said. "Someone is going to have to talk to the press. Mary Alice says TV crews want permission to enter the Square. I think the town would rather see you on TV than Johnny Stagg's grinning pumpkin head."

"I'd rather search."

"We got six counties who've come to help," she said. "You can't direct it all from radio. And those boys from emergency management need a little input on the local terrain."

"What about you?"

"I want to check on Rose and your momma," Lillie said. "See how they're doing together."

"Caddy took Jason to the church with her," Quinn said. "I appreciate you giving Jean something to do and a place to stay. She needed that."

"You say it ripped off her kitchen?"

Quinn nodded. "But you know Jean," he

said. "She said she'd always hated that kitchen and wanted to remodel anyway."

He and Lillie walked down the trash-strewn street and destroyed neighborhood. Quinn held the ax loose in his bloodied hands. Volunteers from the local churches continued to dig into the piles, spraying all-clear symbols on vacant houses. So far, the county had accounted for six dead. A quarter of the downtown was just gone, the business district wiped clean.

On the hill off Main Street, Quinn searched for the Stevens home, seeing the old Victorian still standing but the right side splitting away from the center. A hundred-year-old shade oak had sliced away a solid portion. Quinn motioned for Lillie to walk on as he took a call from Mary Alice, directing Kenny and Art Watts over to the Piggly Wiggly for crowd control and to direct traffic.

Anna Lee stood on the hill, holding her child, speaking to a photographer who stepped back and framed her against what had been a town showpiece. Anna Lee wore jeans and boots, a cowboy shirt loose and flowing over a tank top. She looked proud and strong, resolved on the big hill, with the baby on her hip. Quinn wanted to run to her but slowed his pace to a jog.

The photographer, a big guy with gray hair and glasses from Oxford, left a card and moved on. Quinn stepped up to Anna Lee. He wanted to put his arms around her and hold her close and kiss her neck and cheek and take her with him. Wind pulled the hair into her face, and she pushed back a few strands, just staring at Quinn.

Quinn nodded. Never in his life had the town seemed so silent.

At the foot of the hill, a crew of local volunteers gathered around Lillie. Lillie sent them in the direction of the tornado, away from the old saltboxes and onto a grouping of larger, older houses that had been built not long after Reconstruction.

"Caddy said she saw you," Quinn said.

Anna Lee nodded.

"Can I help?"

Looking sad, she shook her head.

"Can I put my arm around you?"

She shook her head.

"This is hard."

Anna Lee nodded as if she might cry and turned back to the house. From over her shoulder, her daughter stared back at Quinn. In the west, the sun was starting to set. Just the thinnest edge of clouds, blood-red and black, streaked the horizon, shadowing the violence and wreckage.

As he got close to the Town Square, Quinn watched a young boy and his father raise an American flag off a toppled pole and lean it against a gazebo, where it caught the wind. Rescue workers and volunteers crowded the sheriff's office parking lot. Television news trucks and wreckers and power company workers sat waiting with engines and lights idling. The night was coming on quick, the sky purple-red behind the old Jericho water tower, flash bars strobing atop police cars and sheriff's department vehicles from as far away as Laurel.

Lillie saw Quinn and nodded. She held the door as he walked on into the SO, crowded as it had ever been. "Sheriff," she said. Maps covered the conference room table. Mary Alice and two other dispatchers fielded the radio and calls. Someone had started to brew coffee. A crew was on top of the building, hammering up new tin.

"God is good," Jamey Dixon said.

"How can you say that?" Caddy said. "At this moment? With what we've just seen?"

They stood next to the old barn, unwrapping hamburger buns and mixing sweet tea in five-gallon buckets. Jamey smiled and said, "Pretty easy."

A few hundred people had just shown up

at The River, unprepared and unaware but knowing something had to be done. Uncle Van, looking like a rat shaken loose from his tree, and some other men had started to pull out the picnic tables from the barn. Generators started whirring, long strands of the Christmas lights lit the mouth of the church and glowed out from the barn onto tall wooden poles where grills were lit, tablecloths were laid, and pitchers of water and tea were placed. After the storm, Jamey set out a feast, a celebration for everyone who came onto the old farm still hanging on to the earth.

They cooked out hot dogs and hamburgers and served sweet tea and Kool-Aid. Boxes and boxes of used clothes Jamey had gathered for a thrift store in town were thrown open and sorted at the church altar. Buckets were left by the front door for donations.

"God is at work in all our individual lives," Jamey said. "You see it here."

Caddy had moved into the barn and to a big table by the altar, folding and spreading out blue jeans and shirts and underwear and socks. Inside, you could take a hot shower and change and get a cot to sleep. She shook her head, overwhelmed with the sadness for her town and everything taken away. Caddy felt like she had a rock in her throat.

"Sorrow and joy are part of life," Jamey said. "Without one, the other isn't recognizable. We thank God for recognizing it all. We shouldn't ever take this day for granted. It's a gift. Everything is good and proper at the right time."

"I don't have a house."

"God will provide."

"Everything I own is gone," she said.

"God will provide," Jamey said.

Caddy looked out the big barn door to see Jason playing chase with some other kids, shadowed on the rolling hills by giant rounds of hay and an old tractor. Jamey stepped in and hugged her. She put her hand to her mouth and tried to steady herself.

"Be happy, Caddy," Jamey said. "We're here. We're alive. We now know the gift the Lord has given us. Without the storm, we are blind. Now we're prosperous."

She took her hand from her mouth and shook her head. "Preachers sure have a funny way of looking at the world."

"Everything is pointless, useless vanity. This is what is everlasting."

Jamey pulled her in tighter, and for a moment she rested her head on his shoulder. Donation buckets filled with cash and coin.

Elvis Presley sang "The Old Rugged Cross" as the air filled with electric light and the smells of meat on the grill. The color of the sky had gone from a deep blue and gray to the deepest shades of red and black, a soft, warm wind blowing over the dinner tables and on into the church.

"There will be times we will be down and out, but this is when we put our pain away," Jamey said. "Look to that sky and see the promise He made."

"You think that's why you came back?" she said.

Jamey nodded. He stepped in front of her, held her face in his hands and kissed her on the forehead.

"There will be a long time of mourning," Jamey said. "But we have to help these people mend. That's why we are here. This is providence, not fate."

"You know what I think?" Caddy asked. "I think we're finally free of your past. I think this is bigger than us all and we can finally be left hell enough alone."

"Everybody knows the material world is temporary," Jamey said. "God's love is everlasting. Don't look at this life apart from God. A sovereign God has given us everything for a reason and a purpose, and He takes it away for the same purpose. God is completely in control. He has a purpose for everything. Even storms."

"You do realize that only a crazy person could see beauty in today?" Caddy said.

Jamey smiled and nodded. *"God is our refuge and strength, an ever-present help in trouble. Therefore we will not fear, though the earth give way, and the mountains fall into the heart of the sea, though its waters roar and foam, and the mountains quake with their surging."*

"Faith ain't easy," she said.

"Easy as stepping off a cliff and hoping for a net."

Caddy nodded and went back to sorting and folding. A slight woman in a huge yellow T-shirt and bedroom slippers walked up to the table, toting a couple kids under five, a boy and a girl. Caddy sized them up and looked for a box to fill. The children stared blankly and did not speak as Caddy spoke to them. The slight woman held them close to her side, a hand over each, saying they had just seen their aunt carried away.

"She lay over them, pressing her body against them," the woman said. "The roof blew off, and she was sucked up into the sky."

The woman bent at the waist, shaking. Jamey got down on one knee and smiled at the children. "That's supreme sacrifice," Jamey said. "I know she must have loved both of you lots. That love you feel in your heart for her won't ever go away. You keep her there."

Jamey Dixon touched each of their small hands, their eyes finally meeting his as if just coming awake. Caddy kept folding, crying a bit but folding, as more boxes of clothes appeared from strangers and friends. Food was served and then ran out. More food appeared. So many people lay up under the big tin roof that tarps were brought in to expand the shelter. God was good.

38

Quinn and Boom drove Kenny out to see his daddy, after getting word that his mother had been missing since the tornado. Kenny's daddy, whose name was Ken Senior, lived in a little white cabin about five miles outside Yellow Leaf. He was a veteran, seeing too much action as a Huey pilot in Vietnam, picking up the dead and the wounded from hot LZs, and had spent most of the last twenty years sitting in a La-Z-Boy recliner, chain-smoking cigarettes and drinking cheap bourbon. He was a good man, round and bald like his son, who got out of the chair only for church and hunting season. His den was filled with the heads of a dozen trophy bucks. The bucks had held firm on the wall even though most of the house had been chewed up and spit out a hundred meters away.

"Why didn't y'all just get in the shelter?" Kenny said. "That's why we put one in."

Ken Senior shook his head, eyes red-rimmed with sadness, cigarette in hand and a gaping wound in his chest as large as a fist. He said some flying glass had caught him.

"You're going to die," Kenny said. "Come on."

"Not without her," he said. "I couldn't get in the shelter because she couldn't get there."

Quinn looked to Kenny, knowing that Kenny's mother had been bedridden since a car accident three years ago left her with bad knees and frequent migraines. Kenny took off his ball cap and turned and studied his parents' house as if it were the first time he noticed that half of it was gone.

"Quinn?"

He turned as Boom walked into the wreckage, that weird part, the chair and the three walls and the deer heads looking like some kind of theater prop. The sun was nearly down, red and bold all across the west like something out of a John Ford film. He nodded to Quinn and motioned with his head for him to come on away from Kenny and the old man, who kept up the arguing about going to the hospital.

"About a quarter mile to the north," Boom said. "Right in the middle of the cornfield."

"You sure?"

"It's an old woman," Boom said.

Quinn nodded and turned.

"Woman is nekkid," Boom said. "Bring some water, her face gonna have to get clean of the dirt to tell for sure."

Quinn motioned across the way for Kenny, who rushed out at attention in his usual unselfish way. "Sheriff?"

"Boom found something," Quinn said.

"Is it her?"

"I can take a look, Kenny," Quinn said. "I'll let you know."

Kenny shook his head, looking down at his boots. His father yelling from the remnants of his home, "If y'all know something, you boys better tell me. I ain't leaving here until I know. You fucking hear me?"

Kenny nodded more to Quinn than his father. "How far?"

"Boom says a quarter mile."

Kenny nodded and turned over his shoulder to his father, dropping his voice. "He ain't going to get help unless he knows. You think we can get that four-wheeler out of your truck? I can ride him on out."

"It's just a body," Quinn said. "We don't know for sure."

"What's Boom think?"

Quinn didn't say anything. Kenny nodded. Quinn went to his F-250, Boom already having repaired a lot of the damage before the storm hit, but the truck still showing lots of dents and scrapes from the chase in the woods that morning.

Quinn slid down the ramps and drove the ATV out of the truck bed. He left it idling, walking back with Kenny to his father, helping the old man out of his old recliner. They both held on to an arm, propping him up as he shuffled more than walked. Kenny got onto the 4-wheeler, and Quinn helped Ken Senior onto the back, the old man wrapping his arms around Kenny's waist.

Quinn started the truck and rode with Boom down the road scattered with broken limbs and fallen trees, zigzagging in and out until Boom pointed the way to the big open field. The field had been recently planted, small green corn plants dotting straight and true across the acreage, some pulled up in thick swirls of upchurned earth. Halfway across the plantings, there was a body. Boom had spotted it from the road.

Boom took his good hand and lifted a water jug to his mouth. He offered Quinn a drink, and the two crawled out, carrying the jug with them, walking across the cornfield in the last red light of day. The 4-wheeler came up behind them, running slow and solid by their sides as they walked, not overtaking them, Kenny still letting Quinn take the lead to the body.

The woman was old and portly. She lay contorted and twisted, naked but covered in mud and debris, her face coated in dry, blackened earth. Boom looked to the men, loosened the cap from the water jug, and began to pour.

The wail from the old man, still perched on back of the 4-wheeler, filled the little valley. The wail became deep sobbing, and Kenny held his father the way a father might hold his own child.

Quinn and Boom turned away, walking back across the field and toward the truck.

The men did not speak. The red-and-black twilight was turning to gray and full black. You could see the stars and a sliver of moon.

"That's a hell of a thing," Boom said.

"Yep."

"You make any sense why this stuff happens?"

"Nope."

Boom held on to a fence post with his only hand before jumping across a narrow ravine and over to the highway. "Yeah, me neither."

■ ■ ■ ■

Johnny Stagg had promised Esau a fucking doctor.

Instead he sent up some teenage girl with a goddamn sewing kit, telling him she'd done a full year of nursing at junior college before she said to hell with it and became a stripper.

"Baby, I got glass in my eye," he said. "I don't need no one to feel around my nut sack."

The girl said she was twenty-one and that her name was Sandi Jo and if he had a problem with her skills, he could go wait at the county hospital. "But I don't think they have power or lights, and you might have to wait maybe, I don't know, two weeks before seeing someone."

Esau nodded. Sandi Jo opened up her doctor's bag and pulled out a syringe and a vial, Esau thinking, *OK, this is how it goes; Stagg is going to shoot my ass full of dope or poison and drop my ass in some deep hole.* "No way, baby."

"You really want me to start digging in that eye with a set of tweezers and no pain management?" Sandi Jo, maybe a hundred pounds, no ass or tits, with black streaks in

409

her blond hair, just sort of shrugged. "Fine by me, Red."

"Don't call me Red."

"You the reddest man I ever saw," she said. "I bet you get burnt to a crisp, you down on the coast. That's where I was supposed to be this weekend until this shitstorm hit. Now Mr. Stagg says we all need to stay if we want to keep dancing. He said we can earn an assload of cash with all them emergency workers, Guard folks, and all. He's probably right. Mr. Stagg kind of reminds me of my grandpa."

"Shit," Esau said. "Go ahead and stick me."

"You sure?"

"Goddamn, I'm sure. Go ahead stick me."

The girl shot him in the closed eye, the damn eye feeling so swollen and puffy that it wasn't any pain. He gritted his teeth anyway, her turning a table lamp from Stagg's desk full on his face, trying to work that lid open.

"You are swelled tight."

"No shit."

"You swelled too tight and I won't be able to see that glass."

"Where you do your nurse training?"

"Northeast."

"Mmmhhm."

410

She let out a long breath and winced. "Damn, Red. That looks like shit. Your whole eye ain't nothing but blood. I got some antibiotics in my bag. I get most of my shit from a veterinarian who thinks I look just like Carrie Underwood."

"Who you work on?"

"Girls don't have no money," she said. "You know, lots of female kind of afflictions."

"Can you get it?"

Esau was not seeing shit right now but that hot, white light, thinking of getting this thing settled and then meeting up with Becky and then getting right with Jamey Dixon. Ain't no one expected the wrath of God to come down onto this godforsaken county and say hello, least of all Esau. Esau thought maybe some of this had to do with Dixon and that girl he'd killed and then him getting pardoned. If Dixon hadn't been trying to hot-jockey things, maybe Bones's poor, dumb black ass would still be alive. Johnny Stagg told him his neck had been broken on a tree limb, his body sent back to the Farm. The worst part of it was that Bones would be going back, buried in that no-luck field by the horse stables where they planted the convicts whose families didn't even want to acknowledge that you had a life.

"Got it," Sandi Jo said. "Got it."

Esau's good eye shifted off the light and saw a sliver of glass, maybe a half-inch long, dripping with blood from a set of tweezers. She picked up a big bottle of something and squirted it hard all over into his eye, bloody water dripping off his face and onto his hands and down his shirt and across Johnny Stagg's desk, the nameplate saying: JONATHAN T. STAGG, BOARD PRESIDENT.

Sandi Jo wiped up the mess with a roll of paper towels and handed him a wad. "Hold that against your eye," she said. "I'll get some gauze and tape, and you better not be taking it off for a couple weeks. Go see a doctor when you can. But not here, they got enough shit to deal with."

"How bad is town?"

"You ever been evicted from your place and come back and find the landlord threw all your shit out into the road where it gets messed by the rain and wind and dogs?"

"Damn right."

"That's the way our town looks right now," she said. "Hey, you want some Percocet? A nice old trucker just left me with the bottle."

"What did you do for him?"

"Danced five times to 'Achy Breaky Heart' sung by Miley Cyrus's daddy."

Esau stood up, feeling no pain but only the throbbing. The harsh light shone in the one eye, bringing on a hell of a headache. Sandi Jo walked over to him and placed some gauze on the eye and sealed it with some hospital tape. "Just what the hell happened to you?"

Esau took the bottle of Percocet from her and washed it down with some Turkey on Johnny Stagg's desk. "Everything, little girl."

39

Ophelia Bundren slid into the church pew behind Quinn and handed him a foam cup of coffee, lingering her arm over his shoulder. She patted him on the chest and asked him if he was doing all right.

"You're the one doing the packing and shipping."

"Not much shipping," Ophelia said. "Most will be buried right here."

They sat together in the quiet little chapel at the funeral home. The building seemed to have the only lights coming up off the Square in the early evening, two big propane generators softly chugging from the sally port. The chapel itself had paneled wood walls with a small stained-glass window up front of a white dove being let free and flying toward the yellow cross. Yellow tulips sat in a vase at the lectern.

"With Kenny's momma," Quinn said. "How many?"

"Nine."

Quinn nodded.

"Where were you when it hit?" Ophelia said, scooting from behind Quinn and coming up beside him, taking a seat, hands in her lap.

"With Mr. Varner, coming in from Sugar Ditch," he said. "We got the edge of it, knocked Mr. Varner's truck upside down."

"Is he OK?"

"He's mighty pissed about his truck."

"Everyone accounted for?"

"Yep." Quinn nodded. "Even my Uncle Van."

Ophelia smiled slightly, nodding. "My brother and I had gone up to Tupelo to drop off a client and saw it on the way back. I couldn't stop driving toward it. It was raining and we could see the funnel dropping from the clouds. I knew it had crossed the Big Black and was headed north, so we thought Jericho must be gone. We just parked the van up off the Trace and stood there. You know that spot where they have the Indian Mounds? Lots of folks had pulled off, just watching it spin and move with no purpose at all. I thought it might just wheel off and come for us. But you couldn't keep your eyes off it, the power and energy it had. Would it be strange if I said it had some grace to it?"

"Yes, it would."

"I heard about Caddy's house."

Quinn nodded. Ophelia rested her hand on his knee. Quinn drank some coffee. The generators whirring outside keeping the coolers nice and chilled for the dead.

"Can I get you something to eat?"

Quinn shook his head.

"You been to your farm yet?"

"Nope."

"What about Hondo?"

"That dog is so smart, he probably opened the shelter door himself."

Quinn placed his hand over Ophelia's and kept it there. She rested her head on his shoulder, her pale skin feeling cool and comfortable against his face.

"I better get back to the SO," Quinn said.

"Is Caddy with Dixon?"

"Yes."

"Helping to feed and clothe the masses?"

"Something like that."

"He'll make this event into something for himself," she said. "He'll find a way to turn a profit."

"Probably."

"At least he got shot in the leg," she said. "Only I wish it had been right in his ass."

Quinn patted Ophelia's hand and stood

from the pew. She stayed seated, looking at him with her small brown eyes and closed mouth, always seeming like she was holding back an important thought. She brushed back her bangs with the flat of her hand and said, "If you ride out to your farm, I'd like to go with you."

"I'll do fine."

"I don't think there is anything left."

"If nothing is left, there won't be much to clean up."

"You will come back for me?"

"Probably won't be till the morning."

"I'm not going anywhere," she said. "I want to be there for you, Quinn."

Quinn nodded and pulled on his ball cap, walking toward the ornate double doors. "Appreciate the coffee, Miss Bundren."

"What a fucking mess," said the trooper.

Stagg nodded. He was in the passenger seat of the trooper's car, surveying the damage around Jericho that night and across the highways where the twister had cut through like a giant lawn mower. County road crews used everything from chain saws to backhoes to get the highways clear, but half the county roads were still blocked. The electric co-op only had about ten percent up and running again, anyone with power

417

doing it by generator. But like Stagg had told the trooper, these were hardscrabble folks who weren't down-in-the-mouth about things. They'd hitch up their britches and get on to the rebuilding.

"Why?" the trooper said. "What's the point?"

"You ain't from here," Stagg said. "You don't get it."

"No, sir," the trooper said. "I'm not. But I am from a place just like it and hadn't gone back twice in twenty years."

He was an older, slim man, with silver hair cut within a quarter inch. He wore his uniform, hat resting neatly in the backseat of his black car, flashers going while they roamed the back highways and town streets, cutting around the Town Square choked with TV trucks from Tupelo, Jackson, and Memphis. Stagg licked his lips, checking the time, because he was all set to be interviewed for the ten o'clock news. They called the thing a live stand-up, where he would report on what he had heard from his constituents.

"You can drop me back at the Rebel," Stagg said. "That boy Davis is inside my office, probably drunk as a skunk and dry-humping one of my dancers' legs."

"I thought you'd locked him up."

"He ain't goin' nowhere," Stagg said. "Ain't nowhere to go. Besides, the convict has the idea that we are some kind of business partners."

"Why'd he come to you?"

Stagg grinned as they passed more emergency vehicles headed in the opposite direction, flashers lighting up the inside of the trooper's car. "I don't have the slightest idea."

"But you want him gone."

"Yes, sir," Stagg said. "I do."

"You got a tarp or something I can use?" asked the trooper, driving with the tips of his right fingers. "Sure as hell hate to make a mess in your office."

"Yes, sir," Stagg said. "That's very much appreciated."

"When?"

"Wait till I pull out and go into town to speak to them news folks," Stagg said. "You need any help?"

"Shit no."

"He's a big son of a bitch."

"You think I hadn't done this kind of thing before?"

Stagg grinned, everything smelling of freshly milled pine and rich spring earth all tilled and fertile. Jericho hadn't smelled so good in years. Almost like the city was about to start anew. "Your talents come highly recommended."

"Me and you both got us some good friends."

"Yes, sir." Stagg smiled, shielding his eyes a bit from the oncoming lights. Two trailers lay upended on the roadside, leaning against each other like Ritz cracker tins. "That we do."

Lillie called Quinn on the radio, cell phones not working since the storm, and told him to meet her at the hospital.

"What's the trouble?" he asked.

"If I told you, that would spoil the surprise."

Quinn shook his head and turned on the light bar of his truck, feeling lucky the Green Machine was back in commission after chasing the convicts and surveying the damage. If they ever got through the day and the whole mess, he'd be looking to award Boom whatever kind of citation befitting his service to the county. And then Boom could take it and mount it over his shitter at the County Barn.

The hospital was a mile north from Jericho up on Main Street once it became County Road 352, or as most folks knew it, Horse Barn Road. He bumped up and over the edge of a parking lot for what had been the old ammunition factory but now was the city baseball fields. Someone had decided to light up one of the fields with railroad flares burning as bright as the sun in the crisp spring night. Lillie just stood by her Cherokee with a bemused expression. Quinn got out of his truck and spotted Chief Leonard yelling at his three officers to get the fucking area clear 'cause they had shit to do.

Lillie shook her head and looked down at the ground.

Without a word, Quinn walked up to Leonard and asked what exactly he was trying to accomplish.

"Don't it look clear?" he said. "I'm setting up a landing zone to fly folks out to Jackson. What'd you think, I'm taking tickets for a movie show?"

"And whose idea was it to get railroad flares?"

"You got to light up the zone," Leonard said. "Damn. Thought you'd know that, since you always the one bragging about your time in the service."

"When?"

"When what?"

"When have you ever heard me talk about my time in the service?"

"Can we fucking get on with this thing?" Leonard said, wearing his blues and a ball cap that read CHIEF. "I got hurt folks need to be on their way."

"You're gonna have more if you try and use that ball field as an LZ," Quinn said. "You set up traffic cones that could be sucked up into the prop wash along with those hot flares that could ignite the liquid oxygen. You sure you thought this through, Leonard?"

"I got this," Leonard said, turning his back to Quinn. "You worry about the booger woods while I take on Jericho."

Quinn put a firm hand on his shoulder, Leonard spinning around, walleyed and red-faced, lip dripping with snuff juice.

"In times of emergency, county sheriff takes over all jurisdictions," Quinn said. "Now get those flares and those cones out of the field and move your vehicles back another hundred meters. You hear me?"

Leonard stood, face contorted, not much else to do but spit on the ground.

Quinn walked in a step, not an inch from Leonard's face, and Leonard blinked, choking a little bit on that Skoal when he saw something in Quinn's eye that let him know there was nothing to discuss.

Quinn stood there while Leonard moved

toward his officers, asking them why they had been so goddamn almighty stupid as to put out hot flares in a landing zone. "Clear that shit up. Right fucking now."

"Lucky to have men like him," Lillie said.

"Makes you proud."

"We got Bennett Dickey on this flight coming in," Lillie said. "You know Bennett? Has that custom cabinet shop."

"I know his wife," Quinn said. "She's secretary at Jason's school. Sells jams and jellies at the farmer's market."

"That's the one," Lillie said. "She thought her husband was dead when she found him, knocked out cold. A flap of skin from his forehead coming down and covering his eyes like a hood. Luke says there's some brain damage but can't see with the facilities he's got here."

"I'm glad Luke was here," Quinn said.

"Me and you both," Lillie said. "He's stand-up. He's got no requirement to be pitching in but was at the hospital maybe five minutes after the storm passed through. Front of his scrubs looks like he's been in a bloodbath. Didn't Anna Lee tell you?"

Quinn shook his head. He walked side by side with Lillie toward the hospital.

Off in the distance, Quinn heard the helicopter and looked south for the lights.

He pointed to the night sky.

"You sure?" Lillie said. "I don't hear it."

Quinn nodded, got in his truck, drove up onto the ball field, and turned on his headlights and KC rack. He got out of his truck, ordered the deputies and officers to stand back as the beating of the helicopter blades kicked up the dirt of the infield.

40

Mary Alice had set a battery-powered hunting lantern in Quinn's office, the generators working to keep the dispatch desk and a little light in the conference room going. He'd spent the last hour slicing up sections of the county for all the law enforcement and emergency heads who'd be working side by side with the local folks well into the night and the days to come. Quinn pulled the Beretta and the leather holster off his belt and set it on his desk next to a paper plate of purple-hulled peas and cornbread. It wasn't much, but it would keep him going. He took a bite and stared out the back window of the office, down into the parking lot jammed with cars and a darkened jail lockup luckily empty except for three drunks and a hold for Lafayette County on failure to pay child support.

Quinn sat on his desk and ate until the door opened and in walked Johnny Stagg.

Stagg had his hair swept back like an old-time preacher, hands in the pockets of a blue Windbreaker with the official seal of Tibbehah County. "My heart is aching, Sheriff."

Quinn put down the cold plate.

"I heard about Kenny's momma," he said. "Lord. How is the family doing? Ken Senior and all."

"Kenny is back on patrol."

Stagg shook his head in wonderment. "That boy has some sand."

"What is it, Johnny?"

Johnny smiled, bemused as hell, taking his hands from the Windbreaker pockets and showing Quinn his palms. "I heard you and Leonard really got into it over them helicopters landing."

"That's not true."

"Leonard said you threatened to whip his ass," Johnny said, nodding.

"Nope."

"Whether you like it or not, Quinn, in situations like this, we have to delegate some authority," Stagg said. "And in the city limits, Leonard is the police chief. We can't be having our county sheriff charging in like a bull and threatening to take a man's head off."

"You need to check out the law," Quinn

said. "In times of natural disasters, I'm in charge. And what Leonard told you was a lie. Whether I would have whipped his ass or not is beside the point. I told him he didn't know shit about setting up an LZ. He had spotlights aiming to blind the pilot and railroad flares that could have been sucked into the wash and caused a real mess. He also had too many cars and trucks crowding the zone and shit that was going to make it tough on the pilot."

"Let's just let Leonard run things in Jericho," Stagg said, smiling. "OK?"

"Nope."

"Nope?"

Quinn took the paper plate back and began to scrape up the peas and eat a bit of cornbread. You ate when you found yourself with a second of downtime. You slept if possible. You kept yourself running right, so you could hit it hard when the time called.

"Listen," Stagg said, hands back in his pockets, one coming back out with a breath mint. "We got more problems than just the storm. We still got ourselves a crazy-ass murdering convict running wild."

"Maybe he's dead or left the county."

Stagg shook his head, smile dropping, crunching on the mint. In the shadowed light from the lantern, Stagg's satyr features became more pronounced. The long pointed nose and chin, rounded goat eyes. Quinn half expected to see the tips of horns pointing from his slick, rockabilly hair.

"He ain't gone," Stagg said. "He busted into my office, forced an employee of mine to remove some glass from his eye. He dropped blood all over my desk and carpet, drank down some fine whiskey, and even used my commode."

Now Quinn smiled. "And why would he return to the Rebel, Johnny?"

"Looking for money," Stagg said. "Who the hell knows? But I just want you to know something. You have my full support in these turbulent times to use your own judgment if you run across this fella. If it come down to it and you need to make that call, you have my backing."

Quinn finished with the plate of peas and dropped it into the trash. He reached for his gun and set it back on his hip. He sat down on the edge of his desk, a couple feet from Stagg, crossing his arms and nodding. "Shoot to kill?"

"If it come to that."

"Appreciate that, Johnny," Quinn said. "Still can't figure out why he came to you."

"The Rebel ain't exactly a secret location," Stagg said. "He probably wanted to hijack some trucker and get gone."

"Maybe he did."

"No," Stagg said. "I think he's still around."

"And you want me to shoot him down."

"Man killed two U.S. Marshals," Stagg said. "Who's gonna be singing 'I'll Fly Away' for that son of a bitch?"

"And Leonard?"

Stagg sucked on his tooth, smelling of enough cheap cologne and breath mints to cover up something truly rotten inside. "Use your judgment," Stagg said. "Sometimes Leonard ain't what I call a thinker."

Quinn nodded and walked by Johnny to the door, standing in there, trying to facilitate Stagg moving on. Plenty of folks coming in and out the front door to the SO, the road outside filled with fire trucks, electric company bucket trucks, and big trucks filled with men and women with axes and crowbars, trailers loaded down with bulldozers and backhoes. The parking lot and on down the road lit up with red and blue flashing lights.

"Can we do anything for Kenny?" Stagg said, letting himself out and into all the chaos. "I'd be glad to round up a collection."

"Why don't you ask him?"

429

"He really go back on patrol?"

"It was his idea," Quinn said. "How he operates."

"Boy's got sand."

Stagg popped in another peppermint and walked out in the SO to shake hands and show his deep and sincere appreciation.

An old couple from Alabama who brought over a donation of fifty gallons of water, twenty cases of Coca-Cola, and two rounds of hoop cheese had given Jason a dollar bill. He'd been proud of it, carrying it soggy and crumpled for the last hour, until he thought on it for a while and said, "I don't need nothing, Momma."

"No, we don't," Caddy had said back. "You want to add it to the collection?"

Jamey took the dollar from Jason and kissed him on the top of his head before adding it to the coins and cash in a five-gallon Home Depot bucket. He'd been sitting with a black family of four who'd lost everything in the tornado. As Jason walked away, Jamey held hands with them and prayed.

"Where are we gonna live, Momma?"

"I'm not sure," Caddy said, getting down on one knee and hugging him. "Where would you like to live?"

"Disney World."

"Besides Disney World."

"With Uncle Quinn and Hondo."

"Besides there."

"Always with you," Jason said, proud of himself for giving away the dollar. "I just want to be with you, Momma."

She hugged him tighter and picked him up, carrying him outside the barn and down a short, worn path to a ragged trailer Jamey had rented along with the property. The trailer was white and blue, rusted at the edges, the official place where he was supposed to live had he not shacked up with Caddy. They had power in the old trailer, most of Tibbehah County not being able to see or flush the toilet, but somehow they'd gotten power in that tin box.

She and Jamey had set up a small office in the kitchen of the trailer and cleared off a bed and changed the sheets for Jason. He had not once asked about his Matchbox cars or stuffed animals or the train set he had collected, piece by piece, for good behavior reports each week at preschool. The boy was tired, yawning and following Caddy as if in a daze but unable to sleep. She put him down on the bed and told him she'd be right back. But he reached up and grabbed her by the neck, holding on even

431

tighter, not wanting to be apart for a second. So she carried him with her, Jason hanging around her neck, and took a seat at the kitchen table, where Jamey had set up a laptop, trying to get Wi-Fi through his cell phone, share the day's stories with his outreach, without luck.

Caddy absently hit the refresh button on the computer, wondering how she would ever get Jason to sleep seeing what he had seen, without her crawling in bed with him. And Jamey needed help. She needed to be with him, working with the church, sorting clothes, stacking food and water, keeping up with the donations, praying with the survivors.

The quiet in the trailer was strange, her ears still filled with the tornado and with big trucks and bulldozers scraping away half the town. It had seemed like a hallucination, standing there at the edge of Jericho Square and finding everything she'd known and expected to just be gone. She held on to Jason very tight and kissed his cheek. "Hold on a minute, baby."

"Why?"

"I got to tend to business."

The laptop refreshed to the homepage for The River, and with Jason on her lap, she got into the church's e-mail account, noting pages and pages of e-mail notifications that donations had been put into the church account via a PayPal button that they never thought anyone would use when they set up the site. Jason squirmed in her lap, wanting to go back to the barn to play tag with all those homeless kids, Caddy telling him to hold still for a moment as he rested his head on her shoulder.

Caddy logged in to the church's bank account where the donations had been made. She stared at the screen and then hit refresh as if thinking she was having eye trouble.

"Jamey?" she said, calling out through the open door. "Jamey?"

She helped Jason off her knees and pushed him along. "Go get Jamey and tell him to come quick. Oh, Lord. Tell him to come quick."

"What's wrong, Momma?"

"No, sir," Caddy said. "Nothing's wrong at all. It's just as Mr. Jamey told us it would be."

Caddy sat back down slowly in the aluminum dinette chair, hand over her mouth, seeing all those zeros and shaking her head in wonderment.

41

Quinn broke free at 0300, riding north with Ophelia up toward Providence and the old farm that had been in his mother's family for generations. Ophelia leaned against the big truck door, a light coat spread over her thin body, staring out into the darkness, most of the action around Jericho and off to the east, nothing out in the country and along the National Forest but darkness. They didn't talk much, Quinn knowing he may not find much, didn't expect to find much, but hoped at least he could come back to the office with Hondo. He loved that old house, but he loved the dog more.

"They think they can get the power back on at the Rebel Truck Stop and a couple of the gas stations."

"What about school?"

"It's going to be a while," Quinn said. "A lot of damage, walls of the cafeteria about caved in. Thank God they didn't. There were two hundred people inside."

"We didn't get anything," Ophelia said. "Not even at my mother's house. Not a tree, not a loose shingle."

"Count your blessings."

"What's your momma gonna do?"

"Some workers put a tarp over her kitchen," Quinn said. "But she insists on staying. She's got nothing out there but a little Honda generator and has to flush the toilet using a bucket of water. I tried to get her to come with me. But she's got neighbors and friends, and she's looking out for Lillie's daughter while Lillie works."

"Your mom is a good woman."

"Most positive woman I've known, and I can't figure out why."

"How old when your dad left?"

"Ten."

"You seen him since?"

"Once," Quinn said, concentrating on the yellow centerline. "I was sixteen and drove to Memphis where he was signing autographs at a Hollywood memorabilia show. It was at some Holiday Inn by Graceland, and he'd been advertised as 'The Man Who Made Burt Look Good.' "

"What did he say to you?"

"Nothing," Quinn said. "He signed his name on a picture of him and Burt Reynolds with that director, Hal Needham. Didn't even look up as I was standing there."

"And Caddy?"

"I don't know," he said. "I think he and Caddy corresponded for some time. I think he has a new family now. Tries to keep his past life separate. It broke Caddy's heart. She idolized him."

"Your father sounds like a real asshole."

"You said it."

They passed Varner's Quick Mart, oddly still and dark without the soft glow of night lights on by the coolers, and up past Hill Country Radiator Shop and Blake's Used Tires and a little old house where a family sometimes opened up a karaoke and steak restaurant. No lights in the trailers or the houses on into the curving of Highway 9 and past signs for Fate and Providence, the founders of the county obviously having some fun with the loggers and moonshiners who'd settled up into the hills. Most of the early folks had lived in tight families, little clans, and not much had changed, most folks not asking where you lived but who your people were.

Quinn turned onto his road, County Road 233, twisting along the scraggly pines planted to harvest and a big, wide-open piece of land that Johnny Stagg had recently clear-cut as a settlement on a debt with Quinn's Uncle Hamp. The empty, eroded hills looked like a moonscape.

"You miss the Army?"

"Sometimes."

"You ever wish you'd stayed?"

"I don't think I had much choice."

"Because of Johnny Stagg?"

"Nope," Quinn said. "Lots of things."

"Your family," Ophelia said. "You came back to look out after them?"

"Ten years is a long time," Quinn said. "The last six I never got home."

"What exactly did you do in the Army all that time?"

"Jumped out of planes and killed people."

Ophelia turned from the window and laughed. Quinn glanced at her, expressionless.

"Seriously?" she asked. "How'd that feel?"

Quinn had started to slow and turned over the small wooden bridge that crossed Sarter Creek, switching on his high beams and KC lights and shining up toward his home. A huge oak that had been planted as a shade tree maybe a hundred years ago lay sideways in front of the house. Quinn got out of the car, leaving on the lights, and walked up the stone path, finding everything intact. He turned the corner, Ophelia walking with him now, fitting herself into a short jacket, hands in her jeans.

Behind the house, the big Genco generator he'd installed before the winter hummed with a quiet efficiency. It was enough to run his freezer and refrigerator, lights in the back of his house, and the pump that worked his well. He and Ophelia made their way up to the front porch, Quinn opening the gate for her. She came up first, stepping on the big metal feed sign he'd set near the door. The creaking metal sound made her jump a little bit as if she'd seen a snake, and she turned in to Quinn. Quinn had been walking forward and caught her as she turned, wrapping an arm around her, smiling and pleased everything was pretty much the way he'd left it.

He turned, Ophelia still in his arms, and whistled and called for Hondo. Only a sharp wind answering back from the wooded acreage.

"He's OK."

Quinn nodded.

"What's that?" she said, pointing to the rusted sign for Purina feeds under their feet.

"Homemade security."

"You expect many people to sneak up on you?"

"You bet."

Ophelia shook her head, the porch darkened and silent, unable to see Quinn's truck over the huge tree lying on its side in the front yard. He turned and pulled his arm away, but Ophelia grabbed him by the wrist and tilted her chin upward and closed her eyes, kissing Quinn hard on the mouth.

She held it a good moment, letting her arms fall but reaching for Quinn's hand. She held him at length and studied him, biting her lip.

"Hello," Quinn said.

"Hello," she said. "God, it's been a hell of a goddamn day."

Quinn nodded.

"When I was a kid, I used to come out here with my grandfather and climb trees while my granddad and your uncle would sit on this porch and drink whiskey and smoke cigars."

"Planning the future of Tibbehah County."

"They did a pretty shitty job of it," she said.

Quinn nodded again. He whistled for Hondo, reaching for the keys in his pocket and unlocking the front door, leaving it wide open and airing out as they walked inside. Ophelia held his hand as they made their way through the space.

"Hardly any furniture," she said. "No pictures."

Quinn shrugged, looking for signs Hondo
had been inside.

"Quinn, I think this is the emptiest house
I've ever seen."

"Is that real money or pledged money?"
Jamey said, looking over Caddy's shoulder
in the trailer.

"It's already into the church's account."

"It must be on account of those news
people," Jamey said. "That interview with
Tupelo went out on CNN."

"Well, it's real."

"I just took the reporter around The
River," he said, shaking his head. "Showed
them the food and water we'd stockpiled
and where people could sleep, take a
shower, and get a hot meal. I showed them
how we were helping people who didn't
have any insurance, talking about how we
would help them get resettled. I didn't ask
for any money. I didn't say anything about
us needing money."

"But we do need money."

Jamey nodded, scruffy and tired, walking
with a bad limp. He had on a Haggard
T-shirt and faded jeans with no shoes.
"Good Lord."

"Yep."

"To say the word makes it not seem as special."

"A miracle?"

Jason turned from over Caddy's shoulder. Caddy had thought he was asleep. "What's a miracle?"

"We're going to help out a lot of folks," Caddy said. "It's going to happen."

Jamey smiled, but there was hesitation in his face as he stared back at the computer. Caddy couldn't quite place it, but it seemed as if he was trying to come to some kind of decision on something that didn't seem to be a question.

"What's the matter?"

"Nothing, baby."

"What's wrong with the money?"

"Nothing."

"Why won't you look at me?"

Jamey turned away from the screen and ran a hand over his exhausted and scruffy face. "I guess we all been broke so long that I'd grown comfortable with it. Having money and means makes me nervous, is all."

"As your commitment to helping people?"

"When you give to the needy, sound no trumpet before you, as the hypocrites do in the synagogues and in the streets, that they may be praised by others," he said. "I guess

441

I feel like a hypocrite."

"You didn't sound a trumpet."

"Cable TV news is the modern trumpet."

"Then we just get rid of it fast," Caddy said. "OK?"

Jamey turned again, face half hidden in shadow, with no smile and a short nod. Caddy walked into the back room and laid Jason onto the bed. His eyes were hooded with sleep, but he asked, "What if it comes back? Where do we go?"

"It's all over, sweet baby," she said. "Close your eyes."

Esau Davis mingled with all the twister survivors and helped himself to a plate of cold fried chicken big enough to reassemble the whole bird, and a big, fat portion of beans and potato salad, and walked back to the truck he stole. He had the radio on and a half bottle of Percocet and a nearly empty bottle of Turkey. He listened to a song by Miranda Lambert and thought of Becky, glad she was out of Mississippi and safe and waiting on him at a motel in Birmingham. She had wanted to double back and come for him when she found out about Bones. Damn if the woman didn't cry, making up stories about how Bones had been a good man and a handsome man and a friend who had showed nothing but love. Horseshit like that.

Esau upended the Turkey bottle and studied the backside of the old barn Dixon had turned into a church. A barn church made a lot more sense to him than a church in prison. How had he ever bought into Jamey's lies about redemption and change when the bastard couldn't even work a miracle on himself? Esau's face grew red with shame at the memory of Jamey laying his hands on his head and talking about being washed clean with the blood of the Lamb.

He drank some more, took another Percocet, and studied his bad eye in the rearview. He still was looking a hell of a lot like old Quasimodo. But half-drunk, he was looking better and better.

Twice he had spotted Dixon.

Once he had spotted Dixon's woman and her nigger kid.

He wondered how much of his money Dixon had used for all those piles of clothes and food and portable showers and shitters. He clenched his teeth, the radio playing a song as a tribute to the survivors of that terrible storm that had hit Jericho, Mississippi. Miranda again. "Safe."

Esau turned off the radio, searched into

the old GMC's glove compartment, and found some cheap gas station sunglasses. He had on a new black silk shirt, embroidered with roses on his shoulder like some Mexican pimp, and jeans so tight that his business looked bold and exposed. That crazy stripper nurse brought him fresh socks and a new pair of boots that creaked and squeaked when he walked. A pack of Marlboro Reds in his breast pocket and a loaded .357 on his hip.

"Fuck, yes."

He wasn't leaving this town, torn to shit like him, before getting what he had earned and what he had been promised. The Marshals, the police, and the FBI could fill him with more holes than Bonnie and Clyde, but his ass wasn't leaving till this got right. But to make that happen, he needed to push Dixon and make him want him to settle up, come to him. But Dixon didn't seem to give two shits about his own life, letting them turn him into a human piñata, being beaten and humiliated, pissing down his leg, and still keeping the secret of the deal safe with him. Had Mr. Stagg not shown Esau the light and the truth, he'd still be chasing his pecker in circles.

Get the money. Call Stagg. And then get gone.

Just like that.

He called Becky.

"You sound like shit," she said. "Just come on."

"You know I'll go out hard," he said. "You know I ain't scared of shit."

"That's the dumbest fucking thing I ever heard," she said. "Run. Save your ass. Let's go to Florida and eat crab claws and drink margaritas and screw till the sun comes up."

"You don't get it, do you?"

"Hell I don't get it," she said. "You think I enjoyed them guards listening to fucking sounds outside that couple's house we used? You don't think they used those security cameras to zoom in on my tits?"

"Why didn't you tell me Dixon kept some money back? Why? Why, goddamn it?"

" 'Cause I didn't fucking know, Esau."

"OK."

"Are we good?"

"Yes."

"Come on, Esau," she said. "It's over, baby. That money's gone, and if Dixon still got it, he spent it by now. Leave it alone. If it hadn't been for that tornado, you'd have every U.S. Marshal looking for the tallest tree in Mississippi."

"But they didn't," he said. "Ain't nobody seeing me, baby. Town is blown apart. It's just beautiful."

"Now you're talking like a crazy man," she said.

"Hell," he said. "Now you're finally listening."

"What are you gonna do?"

Esau was silent for a while, catching Dixon walking from that old trailer and heading back into the barn. He stared at the trailer where his woman and that kid had holed up. He saw rows and rows of red plastic containers filled with diesel to run those generators and stacks of hay bales by the open door of the barn.

"Esau? Hello? What the fuck?"

"Huh?"

"I said, do you even know what you're going to do?"

"Yep."

"What is it? Jamey is never going to get square with you. Not now, not after all that's happened in Jericho."

"No?" Esau said, licking his cracked lips and grinning. "Then maybe I'm gonna smoke his ass out."

42

Boom came into the sheriff's office at first light, dirty as hell, holding a gallon jug of water from his prosthetic hand and wiping his face with a clean towel.

"Woman was trapped in a pile of rubble," he said. "I don't know if she was more scared of dying in that mess or seeing my hook reach down for her."

"What'd she do?" Quinn said.

"Took the hook."

Hondo rested at the edge of Quinn's desk, full of water and biscuits after Quinn and Ophelia had found him snoozing in the barn with a couple calves. The dog rode all the way back into town in the truck bed, Quinn dropping Ophelia back at the funeral home while he continued on with search and rescue, patrolling the now-empty streets.

"Power?" Boom asked.

"Twenty percent online in the county," Quinn said. "City may not have power for three weeks."

"Any more dead folks?"

"Holding at nine," Quinn said.

"Kenny?"

"With his daddy," Quinn said. "I told him to get gone. We got most of the streets cleared; crews going to be searching through the mess for a while. He needs to rest, take care of his father."

"His old man ain't never been right in the head."

"Nope," Quinn said.

"You think it's possible for Ken Senior to get worse?"

Quinn shook his head. Boom took a swig from the gallon jug and took a heavy seat into the chair across from Quinn. A large topographic map of the county had been spread on the wall, pins and colored threads to track cleared houses, cleared roads, and the path of the tornado. Quinn had a fresh cup of coffee on his desk and a half-eaten sausage biscuit. The other half had gone to Hondo, who rolled over on his back in sleep, back leg twitching in some kind of dog dream.

"I'm going back to the barn," Boom said. "Two trucks broke down last night. Both of them waiting on me."

"You tired?" Quinn said.

"Nope," he said. "You?"

Quinn shook his head. Hondo startled himself awake and got to his feet, shaking his mottled black and gray coat, and trotted over to put his head into Quinn's lap. Quinn scratched his ears.

"Funny thing about PTSD," Boom said. "This is the first time my head's been right in a while."

"Yeah?"

"Feels like my ass is on high alert for a reason," Boom said. "Right."

Quinn nodded. "Feels comfortable, doesn't it?"

"Broke-down streets, houses all fucked up, and people walking around all bloody and crazy," Boom said, grinning. "Shit. This is where I live."

Quinn toasted him with his coffee mug, the sharp gold light coming through the blinds of his office window. Boom grinned and grabbed his jug and turned to the door, Mary Alice meeting him halfway, not pleased about something. "Sheriff?" she said. "I told him you didn't have time. But he is insisting."

"Who?"

"Jamey Dixon is at the desk," she said. "He said it's an emergency."

"I heard about that fire at The River,"

Quinn said. "They said it's under control."

"Dixon says it's not about the fire."

Boom raised his eyebrows and shook his head.

"Great," Quinn said.

"You really want to see that SOB?" Mary Alice said.

"Yep," Quinn said. "Why the hell not? Tell the preacher to come on in. It's not like we have other shit to do."

Esau Davis had crawled out of his truck two hours earlier and made his way to the back of that big wooden church and started soaking the shit out of the timbers with diesel. Nobody saw him as he worked or as he coolly flicked his cigarette down at where the fuel had puddled in the dirt. The fuel turned to flame, zipping up onto the barn and across the wood to bring on a crisp fire and black smoke. Esau didn't stick around to watch the show but just kept on walking with fascination toward that broke-ass trailer up on the hill, people now yelling and running for the barn. People calling for water, an extinguisher, telling all those folks inside sleeping and tired to please get the hell out. Y'all had a tornado, now here comes a fire. If Esau could pull off a flood later, he could guarantee he could fuck all

them up.

The door to the trailer was open, Jamey's woman standing on the concrete steps, hand over her mouth. Dixon ran fast for the barn, coming within ten feet of Esau without noticing him walking toward the trailer. The woman ducked back inside, the light on in the trailer, everything dark as hell. The grass and ground still wet and soggy from the storm, mud caking on Esau's new boots.

Esau turned back for a moment to see that fire spreading up into the loft, crackling and feeding on the wood, folks running from the back of the barn and around the side. Women and children screamed, some poor bastard with a garden hose trying to peter it out.

Esau was feeling no pain as he got to the stoop and peeked into the trailer, seeing the girl and the kid lying on the sofa. The woman held the child's head in her lap, stroking his hair, taking a moment to look up and register just who was that big red son of a bitch dressed like a Mex pimp at her door. She just sat there, smoothing the child's hair and face without a damn word to Esau. To the boy, she was saying everything was fine, Jamey was taking care of it. Everything was just fine. Just some smoke.

"Knock, knock."

"What do you want?" the woman said.

Esau smiled, pulling the .357 from his belt and motioning them outside. "Leverage," he said.

"How'd you know it was Davis that took them?" Quinn asked.

"Your Uncle Van saw him forcing them into an old truck," Jamey said. "He yelled and tried to stop them, but Esau sped off. I followed, couldn't find them. We called y'all but couldn't get through. Put that fire out ourselves, even though it took off the back of the church. I know you don't care much for me, Quinn, but I need help."

"Feds from Oxford are driving over this morning to keep hunting for Davis," Quinn said, grabbing the phone. "Even though they thought he'd left the state."

"He won't leave," Jamey said. "He thinks I owe him something."

"You want to explain your meaning?" Quinn was on his feet, coming around the desk.

"It was a misunderstanding and doesn't matter now," he said. "You missing the part about your sister and nephew being taken?"

Quinn tried to slow himself, his blood starting to heat and an all-too-familiar feeling rising up from his gut. "You missing the part where this shit happened because they were in your company? I'd whip you some more if you didn't look like you'd already been through the wringer twice. You walk in here with your gimpy leg and wanting me to take care of this mess without you explaining? Let me ask you again."

"I don't know."

"Why is Esau Davis on your ass? What did you do to him? I know this is about a hell of a lot more than him watching your ass at Parchman."

Dixon shook his head, dirty and unshaven, shoulders slumped, unable to face Quinn and look him in the eye. Quinn walked toward him and punched him hard in the thigh where he'd been shot, Dixon falling onto the floor and rolling there in pain, wide-eyed and openmouthed.

"How about we start this conversation again?" Quinn said. "Why did Esau Davis take my sister and Jason? And how am I gonna get them back?"

Dixon gritted his teeth, rolling on his back like a turtle but smiling, truly smiling with joy up at Quinn, and nodding. "Yes," he said. "That's what I want. That's what I came for. We are going to get them back. He'll call. He'll call me and tell me how to square it with him. Please. Help me. Just follow me and we can get them back. OK?"

Quinn moved back to the edge of his desk and sat down. He picked up his coffee and took a puff of the last bit of a cigar. Jamey's eyes had watered from the pain, his face flushed with blood, and he was grinding his teeth.

"Please," Dixon said. "We tell the Feds and Esau will kill them."

Quinn stood and reached down to yank Dixon to his feet, the man's bad leg nearly giving out, Dixon holding on to a file cabinet to steady himself. He grabbed Dixon by the neck and force-marched him out of the office and through the reception area, Mary Alice and the other dispatchers staring with open mouths, and out to the Big Green Machine, tossing him in the passenger side and slamming the door.

"Start talking," Quinn said as he cranked the engine and turned out onto the road.

"I told you."

"Start talking or I swear to Jesus I'll drag you behind this truck till you do."

"Let me explain how this situation is gonna go," said the convict Esau Davis, driving the truck at the proper speed limit, waving nicely to the cops parked about every quarter mile. "I don't want to hurt you or

454

the kid. This don't have nothing to do with you or with the boy. This is between me and Dixon, and I do sincerely apologize for involving you. I don't usually fuck with kids or women."

Caddy didn't speak. The smell of the man's body and breath was overwhelming in the truck cab. Jason sat in her lap, her arms tight around his body. He was still and quiet, not sure exactly what was going on. Davis wore sunglasses and spoke in a calm but slurred voice, a pistol resting between his knees.

"Just don't give me no trouble. Don't try to grab the wheel or yell to someone or make a scene. You know I can snatch your ass up pretty quick. Besides, folks here got a lot worse shit on their minds and won't be out looking for you."

"Jamey doesn't have your money."

"That's where you're wrong, sweet baby," Esau said. "He's the kind of man holding out on us all. You think that boy just love you and Jesus Christ? Lord."

"You just want to kill him," she said, hating to say it in front of Jason but saying it just the same.

"That's not true," Esau said. "I'm not in the wrong here. I ain't the one who took something that didn't belong to me, trying

455

to profit from another man's work."

"Y'all killed two men and robbed a bank truck?" Caddy said. "Something's wrong with your brain. I know what happens to some men in prison. They drink Drano and lie with other men."

"How about you just shut your mouth for a while," Esau said. "I ain't never hit a woman, but you don't want this little half-breed seeing my first."

"Anyone ever tell you that your breath smells like you've been licking a cat's ass all day?"

"Damn, you're a hellcat," he said. "Dixon must love that."

Caddy didn't speak for a couple miles, trying to figure out just where the convict was going. After he hit the county line and doubled back, she realized he was lost, trying to stall a bit, waiting for something to happen.

"Just what are you waiting for?"

"A phone call."

"From who?" Caddy said.

"Don't concern yourself with that, Hellcat," Davis said, reaching down to the floorboard and picking up a bottle of Wild Turkey. "All you got to do is sit tight and keep yours and the boy's mouths shut. Let me think on things."

He took a swig of the whiskey and looked down at a cell phone. Caddy kissed the top of Jason's head as he stared up and studied the odd man in the sunglasses driving the old truck. "Mister?" Jason said.

Caddy held him tighter and told him to hush. Davis glanced over at the boy. The convict kept driving, snorting as he turned down a county road that cut back over the Trace. "Huh?"

"Don't be mad at my Uncle Quinn," Jason said.

"What the hell's that boy talking about?" Davis said.

" 'Cause he gonna shoot you real bad and make you die."

Davis took a long swallow of whiskey, Adam's apple bobbing up and down, and watched the blacktop unfold in his headlights. Caddy smiled.

43

Quinn and Dixon drove, Dixon holding his cell phone tight, telling Quinn that Esau would call and work out the terms. But whatever happened, Dixon had to do this alone; Esau specified it.

"How'd he specify if you didn't even see him?" Quinn said, hitting the Square and going around it twice. The place torn all to hell, electric trucks setting up new poles, workers clearing off debris, Salvation Army serving food from a trailer where a check-cashing business used to be.

"He left a note," Dixon said, reaching into his jeans and handing it to Quinn. Quinn read it. It wasn't exactly eloquent. *Don't Bring Nobody Nor the Law or I Start Shooting.*

"You believe him?" Quinn said. "Would he kill them?"

"He's pretty pissed off right now."

Quinn finally broke off the Square and headed east on Cotton Road, a line from the front door of the Piggly Wiggly out to the street. More trailers for Emergency Management and the Red Cross and a mobile command center RV from Jackson. "Why'd they come here, Dixon?"

Jamey swallowed and nodded. Quinn switched his view from the roadside and the damage to Jamey Dixon's messed-up face with bruises and scratches, one leg of his Levi's cut off so he could wear pants over a thick bandage. Dixon was red-eyed and unshaven, long hair worn loose over his shoulders. He looked as if he hadn't slept in a while. Quinn hadn't, either.

"Esau thinks I got some money that's his."

"Do you?"

"No."

"A lie only adds to this shit sandwich you made."

Quinn got close to the highway while Dixon studied his cell like he was willing the son of a bitch to ring. Quinn doubled back on the highway, drumming the wheel. His blood was racing, mind working over every possibility of how this could work out, but he tried to stay even and cool. You bring emotions into it, and your enemy has you beat. He needed to figure what could work on the mind of Esau Davis right now.

"I don't have his money."

"From the truck robbery."

"Yes, sir," Dixon said, lapsing into prison mode, looking at Quinn not as a potential brother-in-law or parishioner but the guard. Quinn did not correct him.

"Who got the money?"

"Johnny Stagg."

Quinn slowed down, turning on his windshield wiper to cast off some dew. He grabbed the stub of a nice Fuente from his ashtray and punched the lighter.

"You're being pretty cool about this," Jamey said. "I kind of expected you to punch me in the throat."

"Still could happen," Quinn said. "But right now I need you to answer that phone and tell me where Esau wants you to meet him."

"I need you to take me to the bank," Dixon said. "I need to bring him something."

"You think a few hundred will appease him?"

"I got more than that," Dixon said. "It may be enough. We got a lot of donations and such, and I don't care what happens, as long as we get Caddy and Jason back."

"And you really don't believe he won't just drop your ass right there and then do something to Caddy and Jason? You thinking this through?"

Dixon was quiet. Quinn drove.

"I need to borrow a vehicle," Jamey said. "He's only expecting me."

"I'm driving us both in."

"You can't do that," Dixon said. "Didn't you read that note?"

"Looks like it was written by a third-grader," Quinn said, cracking the window, letting out the smoke. He had everything he needed in the truck, the Beretta 9, the Remington 12-gauge in his rack. He could wear the 9 in an abdomen holster; everybody expected you to conceal at your back.

"I love them," Jamey said. "I couldn't have known Bones and Esau would break free and come here. I would do anything in the world for Caddy. I want to marry her. We will get married. She will be all right. She and Jason."

"But you can't get clean of this," Quinn said. "I don't know and may never know what happened between you and Adelaide Bundren. But you opened wide the gates of hell when you shook Johnny Stagg's hand. If you do walk away from this, all of this, you better keep walking out of Jericho and Tibbehah. Understood?"

"I love them, Quinn," Jamey said. "They're my family."

461

Quinn shook his head, cigar burning down to a nub, body flushing from the nicotine and coffee and lack of sleep. "You're Caddy's boyfriend. I'm their family."

He looked over at that cell phone in Dixon's hand, waiting and willing it to ring.

It finally did.

For all his apologies, the convict Esau Davis was just a low-level toilet scrubber without the sense that God gave a goat. If she could get to a pistol or a shotgun or a hammer or a screwdriver, Caddy Colson would go all redneck on his ass and tear him a new asshole. That's the way she was feeling, sitting there in the front seat of his shitty old truck, muffler rattling loose and wild, while he took Kleenex to his bleeding eye and talked about old times with Jamey Dixon like he thought they could still be friends after all this shit went down.

"There was a time I felt love from him," Esau said.

Caddy stayed silent, letting him talk. How do you respond to a crazy red-haired bastard with a .357 on his knee talking about his friendship with Jesus Christ?

"But he turned on me," Esau said. "I never heard from him again."

Caddy couldn't stand it anymore, pulling

Jason closer into her chest, arms wrapping his little body. "You talking about Jamey or you talking about Jesus?"

"Both of 'em," Esau said. He was high as hell and drunk to boot, and Caddy figured if they sat there long enough at the edge of the old landing strip, not jack shit around, he'd just pass out and she and Jason could walk back to the highway.

Caddy scratched the top of her boy-short hair, to wake her up, keep her focused.

She thought of The River and the old barn and the people rushing to save it.

"Why'd you have to burn the barn?"

"Make Jamey think on things."

"He doesn't have your money," she said. "Johnny Stagg has your money."

"Stagg said Jamey was a liar and that he'd never even known about that car."

"Christ Almighty. It takes a true genius to take Johnny Stagg at his word."

"I ain't gonna kill you," Esau said.

"I know."

"I just had to take y'all to make him think on things, get some money. If I don't have money, they'll throw me back in Parchman. And this time, I ain't ever getting out. They got this one son of a bitch who busted out ten years ago, wound up in Indiana hunting deer and shit. He hadn't left lockdown since he come back."

"And with you killing three men, two of them lawmen," Caddy said, leaving it hanging right there in the air. Jason turned to her, snuggling tighter. Despite everything that was going on, the boy had nearly fallen asleep once they rode around in the truck awhile. She had not yelled or screamed. She'd remained calm and definite, Jason sure that Uncle Quinn would be coming for them soon.

She'd even pointed to all the pretty flowers and trees and cows. Jason loved cattle. But before he fell asleep, he'd made a point that Uncle Quinn had cattle and a cattle prod, although he just called it a shocker.

"I can't promise you about Jamey," Esau said. "As much as it pains me."

"Why does it pain you?"

"He saved me for a bit," Esau said. "We had this one old guard named Horace, who was working on killing me. Man was a sadist, licking his lips as he'd break me, working me without no water in the summer. Gave him some kind of pleasure that I didn't have heat stroke although my skin would fry up like bacon in the sunshine. This was before all them reforms and the new wardens and superintendents they got now. ACLU sued the whole prison system.

You read about that?"

Caddy shook her head.

"Jamey and I met at the infirmary," Esau said, staring over the steering wheel of the parked truck. Rusted Quonset huts and World War Two-era airplane hangars clustered near the ridgeline of woods. The morning light was gray and misty, the old tarmac running for hundreds and hundreds of yards reminding Caddy of when she used to come out here to raise hell with Quinn and Boom.

Esau was talking more. Caddy wasn't listening.

"Got me medical care and food, my arm treated, had me reassigned to the canteen," Esau said. "You know what that means?"

"You work at the canteen?"

"That's the best job a prisoner can get," he said. "Food, Coca-Cola, movies to rent. And then we started working at the Spiritual Life Center. I was a deacon, although really just a trusty. I had value and purpose. You know what it meant to have them things?"

Caddy swallowed. She held Jason tighter. The sun was rising full up from the east, burning off the mist in the tree line.

"I woulda done anything for that man," Esau said. "Why'd he have to go and fuck me in the ass?"

465

■ ■ ■ ■

Quinn met Lillie at the Dixie gas station where she'd parked her Jeep Cherokee by the fallen metal sign. A crew worked to secure the gas lines from the damaged pumps, Lillie seeming unconcerned as she spoke to the crew, calling in to dispatch from a handheld as she approached the driver's side of Quinn's truck. She leaned into the open window and spotted Dixon. "This the shit sandwich?" she asked.

"Part of it."

"What's the rest?"

Quinn told her.

"And so we're off the books?"

"Yep."

Dixon was smart enough to stay quiet, knowing he couldn't talk Quinn out of driving right into the meeting spot at that broke-ass airfield in the north county. "We could call in SWAT or use all the law enforcement we got on patrols right now," she said. "I imagine the Marshals are pretty intent on turning the lights off for this son of a bitch."

"I'd rather not have too many boots on the ground."

"Esau didn't want anyone but me," Dixon said.

Quinn shot Dixon a look to ensure he shut his mouth until he was finished speaking with Lillie.

"Do I need to explain?"

"That's an insult even in the asking," Lillie said, leaning back out of the window. She was chewing gum and back in her sheriff's office uniform, dark green with no hat, her brown, curly hair knotted in a ponytail and her Glock on her hip. "I ride with you?"

Quinn nodded.

"Let me get my rifle, Sheriff," Lillie said. "Just reset the scope."

44

"I'm sorry," Esau said.

"You said that already," said Caddy, tired of the bullshit, hoping he'd pass out soon. Jason stirred in her lap, asking why they'd parked there. She told him they were waiting on an airplane.

"That's right," Esau said. "How do you think I'm getting out?"

"How's it supposed to land?" she asked. "Last plane to land here was the *Memphis Belle.*"

"Mr. Stagg said he had a private plane that could land anywhere," Esau said, one good eye hooded and nearly closed like the mangled one. "Dixon better show."

"And what does Stagg get for his good deed?"

Esau snorted, smiled a bit. He settled into the driver's seat, watching the length of the broken landing field, weeds and small trees poking out of the cracks. Caddy knew the convict had definitely switched over to another wavelength if he believed he was ever gonna fly out of here.

"Where's the plane, Momma?"

"It's coming," Esau said.

"Just watch the sky, baby," she said, and turned back to Esau. "What did you tell Stagg you'd do?"

Esau put his sunglasses back on and folded his arms across his chest, gun resting butt-up obscenely between his legs. If he would just nod off, Caddy would grab it in a second and plug that son of a bitch. She did not want her child here. Jamey did not want him here. And God sure didn't want this. She would use what was given to her and take action. Caddy pointed to the gray sky and rising sun. "You hear it, baby? You see that plane?"

"Nope," Jason said, pointing. "But I see those men coming out of the woods."

Two men dressed in hunting camo and ball caps walked out from the trees close to the old Quonset huts. They both had a serious gait about them like they had already shot down a prize buck and just had to drag it back to camp. The man on the right looked vaguely familiar until he got close, and then Caddy was sure it was Leonard, the fat-ass police chief. The other was just as fat and no-necked, with eyes like BBs.

"You knew they were here," Caddy said, shaking her head. "That's why you haven't lifted your gun off your pecker."

"Hell," Esau said. "You think I trust Dixon to do what I say? Stagg's got three more of them boys in the woods."

"Please don't do this," Jamey said, begging Quinn. "Just let me be the one walking in. I got money. I got as much as the bank would let me. Twenty thousand dollars. Esau isn't gonna turn that down. Not now. Not after all that happened."

Quinn stayed quiet as he turned right off County Road 337 and down a rutted dirt road past an old settler's cabin, wisteria growing wild and making all the trees purple, early light cutting across the rough-hewn timbers cut a century and a half ago.

"Pretty," Lillie said.

"Oldest place in the county."

"What about that cabin in Dogtown, near the place that sells worms and crickets?"

"Nope," he said. "This one here is before the war. One of the only places they didn't burn."

Quinn drove a mile down the road and came to a cattle guard with a lot of notices about how trespassing would be prosecuted to the fullest extent of the law. He swung open the gate, got back into the cab of his F-250, and headed on down another long rutted road; this road was so rutted and busted that Lillie had to grip onto Quinn's headrest until the road smoothed out into a big clearing of trees with a ridge running up to the north and east. He stopped the truck, got out, and helped Lillie from the backseat with her sniper rifle. She disappeared into the trees and thick, old-growth woods, tall as a cathedral, some of the last uncleared land he could recall.

Quinn drove on toward the big open fields where the Air Force had built a test range back in the forties. There were still some signs of the old hangars where he and Boom used to blow shit up and smoke dope before Quinn got tired of acting that way. The broken path opened up at the edge of the dirt road and became broken squares of concrete. A brown GMC truck waited for them in the center, not shit around them but the half-bowl of the valley and a hard wind sweeping through after the storm.

Quinn let down his window. "We get out of the truck at the same time," he said. "But I do the talking."

"Do I bring the money?"

"Yes."

"What was that you handed Lillie?"

"A flash-bang."

"What's that for?"

"To split Esau's mind."

"Let me walk alone."

"Nope."

"He can be reasoned with," Jamey said. "He's a good man in his heart. He feels used and betrayed, and I understand why."

"Appreciate the sermon, preacher," Quinn said, getting within two hundred meters of Esau's truck, one-fifty, one hundred, and slowing down.

Esau was out of the vehicle, walking with two men with rifles and marching toward the truck, a .357 outstretched in his right hand. Jamey tensed, pressing back into the seat. Quinn calmly kept driving forward. "He's gonna shoot you," Jamey said. "He's gonna shoot you."

"I'm not worried about Esau," Quinn said.

"Who's with him?" Jamey said.

Quinn slowed and stopped. He knocked his truck into park, opening the door and raising his empty hands. Esau kept moving toward him, Quinn now knowing he'd have to deal with Leonard's dumb ass and that moron who worked as his assistant chief. He couldn't recall his name.

Caddy and Jason stayed in the truck.

Quinn silently willed Caddy to grab Jason and go to the floorboard until this business was all done. Quinn tried to stare at her, give her a nod, but it was too far, and there was a hard, dull glare across the windshield.

He felt, rather than saw, Jamey walking at his side.

He got within five meters of Esau and his buddies and tossed over two thick, brown Piggly Wiggly grocery bags at his feet. Esau didn't move, keeping the gun on Quinn, never on Jamey, Quinn's hands still raised as Esau squatted and looked at the cash.

"How much?"

"Twenty thousand."

Esau spit.

"I can get more."

"Ain't no time."

Quinn kept a distance from Jamey, who stood to his right, facing the huts. His most immediate threat would come from Leonard and then his fat-ass police officer. Quinn now recalled that his name was Joe Ed Burney. Burney had once been expelled from high school after being caught hiding naked under the football bleachers during cheerleading practice.

"I want you to know, I didn't lie," Jamey said. "This money comes from good people trying to help everyone in this county. I

473

don't have your money, never wanted it. Take this and just go."

Quinn stood calm and relaxed, hands still in the air, thinking about but not looking toward where Lillie would set up her shot. She'd see it was Leonard and Joe Ed, too, and that wouldn't stop her getting to work in the least. She'd pick up Esau first, Quinn could draw on Leonard, and then a second shot could take out Joe Ed, who apparently had never been fast with his hands, the reason he'd been caught all those years ago.

Leonard told Quinn to turn around. Leonard walked over to him and patted down his legs and his back, just as Leonard would be inclined to do. "Drive away, Quinn," Leonard said.

Quinn shook his head.

"You can take your whore sister and the nigger kid," he said. "But you leave Dixon."

Quinn didn't move. He took a breath, feeling the wind on his face, trying again to get to Caddy. He stared at her, and she seemed to get some kind of sense about her, pulling Jason down with her onto the floorboard of the truck. Quinn looked away from the ridgeline and placed a hand on Dixon's elbow. "Come on."

The rifles centered on Quinn. Esau squatted on his haunches like a primitive man, thumbing through the money in the Piggly Wiggly bags. He looked up from where he sat and nodded up to Leonard and Joe Ed. "It's good. It's good."

Quinn kept pushing Dixon forward, around the men on the busted tarmac and to the truck with Caddy and Jason. He'd drive that old truck out, get as free and clear of these sons of bitches as possible, and then settle the thing with Leonard and Stagg. A long time coming.

Quinn stared down the bead of Leonard's rifle and pushed Jamey forward. As they brushed past Joe Ed and Leonard, the fat chief turned red and purple in the face, telling them both, "I swear to God, I'll shoot both y'all in the fucking back. I swear to you, Quinn. I'll shoot you down right now."

"I'll stay," Dixon said. "Get 'em out of here."

"He won't shoot," Quinn said. "He's just a worthless turd. Come on."

"Get Caddy and Jason and get gone," Dixon said, and shook loose of Quinn's hard grip on his elbow. He walked toward Esau, squatting down with the convict on the tarmac, telling him he was sorry how this all happened. He placed his hand on Esau's, Esau's shirt blowing up in the wind, his expression confused and pained. "I love you, brother."

Toward the north, there was a glint off glass, way too far for Lillie to run. Quinn yelled, too late, "Get down, Jamey. Get down."

Dixon's head exploded in front of him, misting Esau's face with blood. Quinn had already hit the ground when Leonard fired his weapon where Quinn used to be. Quinn had pulled his gun from the appendix holster and shot Leonard twice in the head and turned toward Joe Ed. But Joe Ed had already dropped from another far-off rifle crack, this one farther south on the ridgeline. Lillie.

Esau dropped the .357 and picked up the grocery sacks, running for his truck with Caddy and Jason still cowering inside. He got about five meters before he fell to his knees as the northern rifle sounded, the big round hitting him square in the chest. The sack of cash falling with him, tumbling open, paper money catching on a hard gust of wind and spreading all across the valley like a ticker-tape parade.

Quinn was on the ground, crawling forward, weapon in his right hand, to that old brown GMC and his family. Two more rifle shots from Lillie's position.

The unknown sniper on the hill kept fir-
ing at Quinn.

45

Quinn made it up under the old truck. If he yelled, he could talk to Caddy through the floorboard.

"Are the keys in the ignition?"

"Nope."

"Is the steering column busted?"

"He took the keys."

"Shit."

Quinn said "shit" more to himself than Caddy, telling her to keep down and stay down. "Where's Jamey?" she asked. "Was he shot? Is he OK?"

"Stay down," Quinn said. "You stay on top of Jason and protect him no matter what you hear. You understand?"

Esau Davis lay facedown in the mud about fifteen meters away. From under the old truck, Quinn could hear Caddy's low, mournful cries. He tried to shut them out, looking back at fifteen meters away — which may as well have been a hundred —

at Esau's dead body, red hair lifting up and blowing in the sharp wind.

More money caught in the wind and swirled and spread across the open field.

A silver truck spewed gravel by the Quonset huts and sped off down a fire road.

Quinn knew it wasn't the sniper, figuring it for who was left of Leonard's men. Lillie and the sniper still traded shots at each other.

Quinn took a breath and crawled from under the truck, running for Esau's body.

He reached for the dead man's legs and pulled him back as fast as he could. More bullets pinged around him, and one hit Esau in the gut as Quinn dropped the body and scrambled back under the truck. He reached out under the driver's-side door and searched his pants pockets. A couple bullets hit the dead man and busted out glass from the truck.

Jason was crying now. Quinn could hear Caddy trying to calm him down.

"I got the keys," Quinn said. "Is the truck locked?"

"It's open."

"I'm going to crawl in on the passenger side, and lay crossways on the seat," Quinn said. "Which window was shot out?"

"The back."

"Hold Jason tight," Quinn said. "When the shooting starts again, I want you to throw open that door and I'll get inside. You got that, sis?"

"He's dead," Caddy said. "Isn't he?"

"Think of Jason and hold tight," Quinn said. "You ready with that door?"

The shooting started up again and Caddy yelled "go," and Quinn crawled on his back, kicking off for traction on Esau Davis's body and off the weedy concrete, and scrambling out sideways, rolling free from the truck and jumping up into the cab. A rifle shot took out the rearview mirror as he slammed the door shut.

The cab was quiet, and he could hear Caddy and Jason breathing down in the broad space of the floorboard. Quinn lay on his back on the bench seat, which was covered in material like an old Indian blanket. He slipped the key in the ignition, winked at Jason, and said, "Ain't this fun, buddy?"

Jason rubbed his nose and nodded.

"Stay down," Quinn said. "And I'll let you drive us home."

He cranked the truck. The engine wouldn't turn over.

He cranked it again, revving it, the alternator trying to bring to life a weak battery,

Quinn turning it and turning it and knowing if he didn't quit the son of a bitch would flood. The front window exploded, the man shooting through the cab now from the rear, glass falling down on them, just as the engine sparked and caught. Quinn slid as far down into the seat as possible and yanked the shifter into drive, heading straight down the broken and worn tarmac, Caddy and Jason bumping up and down, Quinn not being able to see shit but feeling his way, the truck rolling hard over something or somebody. Quinn didn't give a damn as long as they moved forward. He felt for the spot where he'd parked his own truck, raising up just a bit over the wheel to catch a glimpse, turning hard to the right to avoid smashing into it, and kept on rolling. The shooting continued.

Quinn drove, raising his head up more as they hit the edge of the tarmac.

Caddy held Jason in the floorboard. She was crying harder now, knowing for certain nobody was left behind.

"Did you kill that red man?" Jason said, crawling up into the seat, keeping low like Caddy had told them. Quinn drove as fast as the old truck would move out and away to the dirt road and then stopped hard where the woods started.

481

"Why'd you stop?" Caddy said, getting up into the seat beside Quinn. The wind broke through the open space of the windowless cab. There was glass in Jason's hair and blood on Caddy's face. "Why are you stopping?"

Quinn opened the driver's-side door and brushed away all the glass with the flat of his hand. Caddy rocked Jason and kissed the top of Jason's head.

"I'm sorry," Quinn said. "I'm truly sorry."

"He loved us."

Quinn wasn't sure what to say.

"He was true and real."

"I know."

"Who?" Jason said, looking up at his mother. "Did Uncle Quinn kill that bad man?"

Lillie emerged from the woods with her rifle, out of breath, her face shining with sweat. Without a word, she tossed the rifle in the backseat and crawled in after it. Quinn got back behind the wheel and they hightailed it up and away from the old airfield. "Jesus, who was that?"

"That wasn't an amateur," Quinn said.

"Hell no, it wasn't."

"And now they're gone?" Quinn said.

"Sniper quit working as soon as you knocked that truck in gear," Lillie said. "I

482

was worried for a second that this piece of shit wasn't going to turn over."

More glass broke free of the windshield frame as they jostled over the gravel road and then turned toward the main highway. Lillie reached her hand from the backseat and touched Caddy's shoulder.

Caddy dropped her head into her hand and started to cry hard.

Wind and leaves rushed through the open car as they fishtailed onto the main highway. Quinn pulled Jason into his lap and pretended to let him steer the truck.

Lillie was on her handheld radio, calling in to Mary Alice for all available to meet them at the roadside. "Four dead," Lillie said. "And we got a shooter loose in the hills. We need guns and some dogs."

Johnny Stagg pulled his maroon El Dorado off to the southbound shoulder of Highway 45 and took a leak. He walked back to his car, burned down a cigarette, and looked up ten minutes later to see a man dressed in black come out of the woods with a long black gear box that he carried by a handle.

The man got into Stagg's car and shut the door. Stagg took one final puff off the cigarette and tossed it from his window as he drove off the shoulder and followed the

18-wheelers moving on down to Meridian and Mobile.

"It's a mess."

"Are they dead?" Stagg asked.

"They're dead, but so are your boys, too."

"Son of a bitch."

"Dixon brought the sheriff with him," the trooper said. "And he had a sniper up in the hills. You should have studied the situation a little bit more. How'd Dixon connect with the fucking sheriff?"

"He was fucking the sheriff's sister."

"Been good to know."

"Is the sheriff dead, too?"

"Nope."

"Who'd he kill?"

"I don't know who killed who," the trooper said. "I took down Dixon and Davis just like we had agreed."

"And they killed how many?"

"Two."

"What about the three other boys?"

"When the shooting started, they hauled ass," the trooper said. "If I were you, I'd be looking into hiring some more quality folks, Mr. Stagg."

"Son of a bitch," Stagg said. "Did they see you?"

The trooper didn't answer him, Stagg knowing the question was dumb right as it came out of his mouth. But then he started thinking about Leonard and whoever had walked with him being dead, too, and caught in some kind of situation with Quinn and the sheriff's office. That whole mess ain't gonna look good to anyone, no matter how you try and explain it.

Stagg took the exit for the Rebel Truck Stop. That old neon mudflap girl kicking her legs up and down, welcoming and servicing all those who would be coming down to save the soul of Jericho, Mississippi.

Stagg slowed and lit another cigarette. "I got me an idea," he said.

But the trooper had already opened the door and was walking across the lot to his black patrol car. He slid the case in the trunk and walked around the driver's side, peeling out of the parking lot with the sirens and the light bar flashing.

Headed to some kind of emergency.

"This doesn't look good, Lil."

It was midnight. They sat across from each other in Quinn's office, a dull light coming from the lamp on her desk.

"I told those agents they could go fuck themselves."

"Probably doesn't forward our cause,"

Quinn said.

"They think we fired on Leonard and Joe Ed's dumb ass to protect Jamey Dixon?"

"They called into question who shot Dixon and Esau," Quinn said. "They saw all those hundred-dollar bills scattered all over the place and think maybe we started shooting to keep the spoils of two convicts."

"That's pretty sorry."

"It is."

"What'd they say about Stagg helping Dixon with his pardon?"

Quinn scratched his cheek. "They wrote it down. You?"

"They asked me how a woman got to be so good with a gun."

"What did you tell them?"

"I let them know I was captain of the Ole Miss rifle team and would challenge them on the range. Any time. Any day."

"It ain't easy being the good guys."

"They're going to talk to Mary Alice," Lillie said. "She'll try to cover for us, but there's nothing on dispatch showing what we were doing."

"I explained all this."

"And they still don't believe there was a sniper?"

Quinn shook his head. "All that money and those dead people are thickening their skulls. They got to wait for the state lab to run a test on your rifle and try to match it to the bullet that killed Jamey and Davis. Then they'll still try to prove it was connected to us."

"You know this puts us head to head with Stagg," Lillie said. "This working-separate-in-the-same-world shit is done."

Quinn nodded. "It's a mess," he said. "All of it."

"I feel for Caddy," Lillie said. "God."

"Yep."

"Where is she?"

"They took Jamey's body to the Bundrens'."

"God."

"Where else could they go?"

"And did the Bundrens accept it?"

Quinn nodded. "Ophelia tried to console Caddy," Quinn said. "Caddy is as busted up as I've ever seen her. She and Ophelia talked. About what, I don't know."

"I can't believe the Bundrens allowed it."

"What's left to discuss?"

"All I know is that I don't have time to be asked a bunch of stupid-ass questions about why I shot two of the most worthless, evil men in this county," Lillie said. "Did you know Joe Ed Burney was so God-Almighty stupid he once got his dick stuck in an intake valve of a Jacuzzi? You think I'm mourning their loss?"

"And they tried to shoot me."

Lillie grinned and turned toward the door. She shrugged. "You really blame 'em?"

Quinn stood up and reached for his hat. "Where you going?"

"We got the lights back on some streets," Quinn said. "More houses to be cleared."

"When have you slept?"

"Hell," Quinn said. "I can't sleep."

"Me, either," Lillie said. "But today sure made me miss my daughter."

"Go."

46

"I guess the entire town is waiting for me to turn to shit," Caddy said. "Again."

"That's an awful thing to say," Jean said.

"But true."

"Yes," Jean said, blowing cigarette smoke away from Caddy. "I guess it is true. But I know you won't."

"I wish you'd explain it to me."

They sat together on their normal bench, watching Jason at the playground on Choctaw Lake. Everything at the lake was the same, and on the days and weeks following the tornado, they'd come there almost every afternoon. Caddy thought it strange how you could get ten miles from town and it was as if nothing had ever happened, the grounds along the lake still dotted in old oaks with branches filtering the gold afternoon light.

There had been so many funerals in town. Nearly one a day. The skinned-up trees that remained were filled with black ribbons. Out on the lake, she could fucking breathe.

"If I said Jamey Dixon didn't change you, that you were coming for a change all along, what would you say?"

"I'd say that's a bunch of crap, that Jamey did change me. Not his guidance or him being a man, but he gave me a stronger sense of faith and purpose. I'm not about to start building a shrine or wearing a hair shirt, but God, Momma, I loved that man."

"I know."

"And it's not like you and Daddy," she said. "He's gone. I think that's what rips the shit out of me. I won't see him on this earth. I haven't made sense of it all yet. I've heard from so many people telling me this was all God's plan for me. If that's the case, why couldn't He have done it without all the shooting?"

"Maybe it's a test."

"Jamey gave up his life to protect me," she said. "But I don't believe it was God's will. My God isn't that cold."

"I love you, baby."

"I'll get through it."

"I know."

"I hate it," Caddy said, taking the cigarette from her mother's fingers and taking a puff. "But I can do it."

"I know."

Jason crawled onto the balance beam, trying to cross over the sand trap, keeping his arms wide like an airplane, the chains holding up the log rocking and wiggling, the little boy smiling but unsure if he should take another step. Caddy waved him forward with a big forced smile that hurt her mouth.

"So now I plan on running a ministry out of a half-burned barn with no minister, no music, but a decent bit of money if we can ever find where it's been scattered?"

"Wasn't that sweet for that Mills boy to bring in two hundred like that?"

"I think he kept a thousand."

"You don't know that."

Caddy shrugged, took a puff of the Kool, and handed it back to her mother. "What's Quinn say about us moving to the farm?"

"He's the one who asked us," Jean said. "He wants us all out there."

"Might bust up his sex life a bit."

"Caddy."

"You do know?"

"Yes."

"But won't say it."

"It's all over."

"I don't believe that," Caddy said. "I don't think things are ever over for Anna Lee and Quinn. It's a sex thing."

491

"Lord."

Caddy shrugged.

"And now Luke is the town hero, and people don't know what to make of Quinn," Caddy said. "Will they really put him and Lillie on trial?"

"Looks that way."

"He should have never come back here," Caddy said. "I don't understand it. We love to build up our idols and then just rip them down."

She took back the extra-long cigarette, feeling herself choke back those black, horrid thoughts, seeing how it must have been for Jamey to be beaten and broken down and still come back for her and Jason, not stopping till a bullet from a coward up in the hills laid him down into the earth. She shuddered in the warm wind.

"Don't think on it," Jean said. "Just let your mind rest a bit."

"I'm too young to have a cold bed, Momma."

Quinn took the nights, Lillie back on the days.

Jericho had a bandage on it. Homes with blue tarps for roofs, whole neighborhoods now neat and tidy trash heaps with cleared streets and lights shining on empty blacktop roads. The Town Square was pin neat; the buildings that had been broken apart were as if they never existed, swept clean to the foundation, a five-foot wooden fence covering the spaces from the sidewalks.

There were funerals. There were town meetings. There was a lot of finger-pointing and whispers. Johnny Stagg told the local newspapers he was shocked that one lawman could so callously gun down another. Rumors cropped up again about Lillie's possible sexual orientation, as if that were the root of the matter.

Quinn drove the nights, thermos filled with black coffee and shotgun loaded in the rack of the Green Machine. He took Hondo with him, patrolling the roads, the county returning to the Mayberry of domestic violence, drug use, child endangerment, and roadhouse brawls. Quinn liked it better that way. He was tired of seeing the town walk around half awake and shell-shocked. At least the violence felt real again.

As the summer heat replaced the thunderstorms and the cool evenings, the blacktop baking even after the sun went down, Quinn often would find himself driving by Anna Lee's place, seeing the old Victorian coming to shape again, the bedroom and kitchen adjoining the rest of the old house, windows

493

being installed, roofers adding cover day by day. Sometimes there was a light on in the kitchen, and there was Luke at the table across from Anna Lee, their baby daughter between them in a high chair. Sometimes it looked like they were happy.

Early in the mornings, there'd also be light on at the Bundren Funeral Home — serving Jericho since 1956 — and Quinn would park his truck and walk inside, taking a seat and helping himself to fresh coffee that was always on. And Ophelia would emerge from the back room, Quinn never bothering her while she worked, and she'd join him and they'd laugh and talk for a while out under the portico by the hearse. A weird feeling of them being awake while the whole town was still.

Quinn didn't care to talk about the federal charges against him and Lillie. But he'd talk to Ophelia if she asked.

"It's going to be a long fight."

"How could they believe Stagg?" she asked.

"When I was out at that airfield, there was a lot of equipment out there," Quinn said. "Looked to me like Stagg was trying to reopen the field. He's greasing things statewide."

"This is a hell of a convenient county."

494

"And with me gone."

"You won't be gone."

"Even if charges are dropped, I run for reelection in the fall," Quinn said. "Stagg's making his play."

"And you'll beat him," Ophelia said. "There's more good here than you think. The way people pulled together after the storm? Everyone in this town reached out to help folks. I see it here. That's the gift. I see everything at its worst. I saw Caddy. I saw what she went through losing Jamey."

"You called him Jamey."

"I worked on him," Ophelia said. "Did you know that?"

Quinn shook his head.

"I had to put him back together, working from photographs, not memory," she said. "He became something else."

"But he still killed your sister."

"I don't know," Ophelia said, sighing. "Sometimes I don't think he did, either."

Ophelia walked Quinn out to his truck. The temperature was up in the eighties even after midnight. She had on a thin white cotton T-shirt and faded jeans, her hair pulled back in a ponytail to work on dead folks.

"You got a full house now," she said.

Quinn opened his truck door. "I do."

"What are you going to do with your nights when you and Lillie switch back?"

Quinn rested his hand against the door frame of the truck, the funeral home's neon sign buzzing in the hot summer night. He shook his head. "Have any ideas?"

Ophelia smiled. "Several."

ACKNOWLEDGMENTS

The author gratefully acknowledges the following people for their help during the writing of this novel: the Lafayette County Sheriff's Office, Sheriff Buddy East, Deputy Art Watts, and Deputy Dave Cullison; Jay Johnson, former USMC recon team leader; Grace Fisher and Superintendent Ernest Lee, Mississippi Department of Corrections; and Kristina Goetz, *Memphis Commercial Appeal,* for her singular narrative of the Smithfield, Miss., tornado.

ABOUT THE AUTHOR

Ace Atkins is the author of fourteen novels, including *New York Times* bestsellers Robert B. Parker's *Wonderland* and *Lullaby*. He was nominated for an Edgar Award for Best Novel in 2012 for *The Ranger*, the first book in his Quinn Colson series, which also includes *The Lost Ones* and *The Broken Places*. Atkins, whom the bestselling author Michael Connelly has called "one of the best crime writers working today," lives on a farm outside Oxford, Mississippi.

The employees of Thorndike Press hope you have enjoyed this Large Print book. All our Thorndike, Wheeler, and Kennebec Large Print titles are designed for easy reading, and all our books are made to last. Other Thorndike Press Large Print books are available at your library, through selected bookstores, or directly from us.

For information about titles, please call:
  (800) 223-1244

or visit our Web site at:
  http://gale.cengage.com/thorndike

To share your comments, please write:
  Publisher
  Thorndike Press
  10 Water St., Suite 310
  Waterville, ME 04901